DIVAH

Also by Susannah Appelbaum

DIVAH

SUSANNAH APPELBAUM

Sky Pony Press
NEW YORK

Sky Pony Press books may be purchased in bulk at special discounts for sales promotion, corporate gifts, fund-raising, or educational purposes. Special editions can also be created to specifications. For details, contact the Special Sales Department, Sky Pony Press, 307 West 36th Street, 11th Floor, New York, NY 10018 or info@skyhorsepublishing.com.

Sky Pony® is a registered trademark of Skyhorse Publishing, Inc.®, a Delaware corporation.

Visit our website at www.skyponypress.com.

10 9 8 7 6 5 4 3 2 1

Library of Congress Cataloging-in-Publication Data is available on file.

Print ISBN: 978-1-63450-674-8
Ebook ISBN: 978-1-63450-675-5

Cover design by Georgia Morrissey
Cover image credit Arcangel
Interior design by Joshua Barnaby

Printed in the United States of America

Angels walk this earth, and sometimes you're lucky enough to meet one. This book is dedicated to a favorite of mine, Susan Willson.

DIVAH

divah—(n) (singular) (archaic Persian) a revengeful demon, bent on domination and destruction. Indefinitely female, and more precocious than devhils, their male counterparts.

See also: deva, daeva, and more popularly today, diva

If you want to discover demons, take sifted ashes and sprinkle them around your bed, and in the morning you will see something like the footprints of a cock. If you want to see them, take the afterbirth of a black she-cat, the firstborn of a firstborn, roast it in the fire and grind it to powder, and then put some in your eye, and you will see them.

—The Talmud

Hôtel Ritz
Place Vendôme
Paris, France
Suite Impériale

My dearest, darling Marie,

The image of you on our last day together shall forever
haunt me. You were not at your best that morning in Paris,
were you, my naughty one? But then, it must have been so
very hard—the peasant uprising and all that. That whole
"Reign of Terror" thing was really a drag.

The vulgar crowd, they were despicable. The things
they called you, their own queen!

The executioner, his leather corset and galling chest hair.

You, your dress the color of a thundercloud.

What was it they said, as they led you to the
guillotine, my sweet?

"Démon! Démon!" the scourge shouted.

I cried for both of us, I did. My tears mixed with the
stench of mortals and your blood.

They were selling souvenirs.
I bought a lock of your silver hair.
I keep it with me at all times, awaiting your return.

Your loving angel,
    L.

Ritz Paris

Hôtel Ritz
Place Vendôme
Paris, France
Suite Impériale

Marie,

I am a disgrace.
   I am ruined. Fallen. They have taken my wings and cast
me aside.
   And for what crime? I ask.
   For love. For the love of you, my pet. Consorting with
demons!
   But it was worth it. Ours is a love unbreakable.

Yours in eternity,
   L. B.

Hôtel Ritz
Place Vendôme
Paris, France
Suite Impériale

My dearest,

When, O when will we be together again?
    I grow impatient. The days drag so. Time, for all eternity,
stretches out ahead of me.
    I have taken to my rooms, which I keep dark and
shuttered.
    I leave at night, and then only to visit your unmarked
grave.

Dismally,
    L.

Ritz Paris

Hôtel Ritz
Place Vendôme
Paris, France
Suite Impériale

My beloved Marie,

My darling—wonderful news!
    They have given me one last chance! I shall no longer
be disgraced.
    I am to earn back my wings. All will be forgiven!
    I merely must save one young soul—a girl, they say.
Of special provenance.
    How hard could that be?

    LLRB

PS: I shall decamp. Paris no longer suits me—
too many memories.

Hotel Carlyle
76th and Madison
New York, New York
Tower Suite

My Marie,

I am so excited!

Today my charge was born. The day was very much like that one in October 1793, on which you lost your head. The air was chill and everywhere was an overwhelming feeling of inevitability.

I think you would very much like this child, on whom they have bestowed the somewhat unfortunate name of Itzy. She is small, but not at all sickly—the advances in medicine today would astound you!

I must go. I am eager to get to work. A new lease on eternal life!

Missing you,
   L.

Hotel Carlyle
76th and Madison
New York, New York
Tower Suite

Marie,

I do apologize for my lapse in correspondence. There is really no excuse. Yes, a love like ours deserves my full attention.

It's just . . . I am distracted. Itzy is proving to be a handful.

At times, when my thinking is clouded, I worry they have set me up with an impossible task. I do so fear I will not succeed. When I am at my weakest, I long for you.

Adolescent girls! A crasser breed of human I have never encountered. The child is so completely reckless—so very uninterested in her own eternal welfare—it is as though she were born damned.

I know, I know. That is not possible—this is, of course, your domain.

Yours,
    L.

The Carlyle

Hotel Carlyle
76th and Madison
New York, New York
Tower Suite

Mme Antoinette,

I have had a Visitor, and I fear the news is of the worst sort.

My darling, I am to cease all correspondence with you. They call it a Conflict of Interest.

I am torn in two. I fear not having you will doom me to a life of mediocrity. But having you—that will doom me entirely.

I must go. There is knocking at my door.

I am returning to you your lock of hair. I implore you to answer this kindness with one of your own. My feather—the one you plucked from my wings at Versailles. I eagerly await its return.

I fear we will not meet again.

The Carlyle

Hotel Carlyle
76th and Madison
New York, New York
Tower Suite

M.A.—

How very, very distressing, your last letter!
    I implore you to reconsider.
    If you have any decency—any at all—do not come. I beg of you!
    How cruel—after all these years—to finally have
orchestrated your return. It can be no coincidence. I can
only assume your intentions are upon the girl—and on this
point, I will not waiver.
    She is mine, this one, if I am to return to grace.
    Mine.
    And you shall not have her.

    L.B.

PS: If you have any decency at all, return my feather
forthwith. I beseech you.

PART I

THE NEW REIGN OF TERROR

1998

1

Looking back on it, the day was like any other, the day before the demons came.

The sun rose, and the sun set. The clouds pushed their way across the sky.

Itzy Nash was traveling by train that day, and as the Hudson River sped by, she pressed her face to the train's window. The wide river was a deep ribbon of a bruise; above, bloated thunderheads sagged beneath their weight, nearly touching the water. Her camera sat in her lap, cradled between her two slightly damp hands, and she raised it and took a picture.

The car was unusually empty, and between the silence and the train's steady progress, Itzy felt her eyes grow heavy. The only other occupant, as far as she could see, was a man in the far corner, down the aisle by the sliding doors. She could just see the top of the man's head—balding, stringy hair combed over a shiny circle of skin. She took a picture of this, as well.

Itzy was traveling to the city—New York City—to stay with her aging Aunt Maude—her father's idea of a fine summer break. But her father's sister was old and mean, an appalling combination in anyone. She was also incredibly rich, which magnified her meanness and bestowed an unfortunate entitlement to all her opinions.

Aunt Maude did not like children. The affliction of childhood, in Aunt Maude's view, continued until one was safely in their middle age. It was Aunt Maude who had advised her father to put Itzy up for adoption when Itzy's mother had first disappeared—claiming, unsuccessfully, it was best for the infant. When he refused, she disavowed any future dealings with the child, speaking to her only when it was unavoidable and then directing her gaze at some vague point over Itzy's head. At seventeen, Aunt Maude still placed Itzy at the children's table at family events. Her father begged her to endure these embarrassments with grace, muttering something about Aunt Maude's contributions to polite society. And now, a long summer in polite society lurked ahead. Itzy Nash was doomed from the start.

Itzy's eyes finally closed as an inevitable rain ran thick rivulets down the window.

In her sleep, she was on a train—remarkably similar to the one she had boarded that very morning. The sky outside loomed just as threateningly, her old duffel bag was at her feet. Only the occupant of the corner seat was different—the man had undergone a startling transformation and was, for all intents and purposes, no longer a man. He was bigger, for one. A hunchback bulged depressingly from between his shoulders and he had more hair than Itzy remembered. His breath appeared labored as he struggled to his feet. Rising finally with the aid of his armrest, he turned, and it was here that Itzy saw his eyes. Eyes like these, she hoped, could only appear in a dream. They burned with something eternal and dark— and entirely *ruined*. The creature shuffled toward her, twisting on a broken ankle. He drew closer, and Itzy saw there was something in his hand. In a delicate gesture, almost an afterthought, he tossed it lightly at her as he passed, and it seemed to flutter around like a dying bird. It settled feebly on the seat beside her as the car filled with the stench of burnt hair.

Itzy's stomach flailed, and she felt herself falling—and, to her great relief, she jerked herself awake.

The rain poured down. A streak of lightning lit the purple sky.

The man was gone.

Beside her in the empty seat sat at small card. The thing was wrinkled and dirty and showed evidence of being greatly handled. It was the kind of card she had seen before, littered on the subway containing some plea or other for money, some fortune or blessing scrawled across its face. She peered closer at the card. The script was old-fashioned, the letters mismatched and uneven. It said:

The End of Days Is Nigh

Holding the card in one hand and her camera in the other, Itzy's train pulled in to Grand Central.

No one was on the platform to greet her.

2

The remarkable vaulted ceiling of the station stretched out over her as she made her way to the center kiosk. Immense arched windows opened onto the morning, beams of hazy light angling down upon the polished floor. Commuters passed briskly, wearing their uniforms of dark coats and determined glares. At the information booth, Itzy paused.

The card was still in her hand, although she had stowed her Leica in its case and buried it within her bag. Carefully, she placed her bag on the floor between her legs. She thought of her dream and shivered. *In dreams begin responsibilities*, she remembered hearing somewhere, and now this phrase filled her mind.

High above, the blue-green ceiling was dazzling. Stars arched across its cavernous span, golden constellations twinkling. Itzy craned her neck, fascinated.

A voice spoke softly beside her. "It's backward, you know."

Itzy jumped. Beside her was a young man, perhaps only a few years older than she. He wore dark, expensive clothing and carried a folded umbrella. Itzy took an involuntary step away.

"What's backward?" she asked suspiciously. She crossed her arms, waiting. His face was like a very old painting; his flesh seemed radiant. He was startlingly attractive.

The young man gestured. "The heavens."

Itzy looked up again, despite herself. She saw the golden outline of Orion, the hunter. His club was ready, aloft and deadly. All seemed to be in order.

"The heavens are backward?"

"They were painted in reverse—the mirror image."

"Oh. Whoops."

She stole another look at her companion, and this time she found herself wondering if indeed she had been right about his age. Upon closer inspection, he seemed older. Or, rather, ageless.

"Actually, it was intentional," he offered.

"Really?"

"There are rules, you see."

"Rules? What sort of rules?"

"It was painted by a friend of mine, an artist named Paul Helleu. He knew that one must be very careful when depicting the heavens. Perfection, you see, is seen as an insult."

Itzy scowled. The famed ceilings of Grand Central Terminal were painted long ago. She narrowed her eyes at this person and his preposterous story.

"Miss Nash," he said. "Would you like to know another rule?"

A chill ran up her spine. "How did you know my—" She stopped, looked suddenly around.

Her companion reached out, pointing to the strange card she still held. She examined it again—the awful dream returning to her quite easily. The card had fared poorly in her possession; the scrawl was faded, now illegible, and some of the ink had smudged on her palm. The paper appeared burned at the edges. She frowned, looking back at him.

The stranger was now holding her bag.

"Hey—"

"Miss Nash," he said. "Never place your bag upon the floor. A demon will crawl inside."

"Yeah, right." But Itzy now remembered something from the train: curiously, when she stowed her camera, she had found her bag unzipped. She was certain she had not left it open.

3

Still holding her bag, the young man took off.

Itzy hurried after him as he headed toward the station's Vanderbilt exit. He seemed to move effortlessly, parting the sea of commuters, while behind him, flocks of people closed in and around, an army of overcoats and briefcases. Determined, she put her head down and charged after him. Harried-looking New Yorkers shouldered their way by her, jostling her curtly, blocking her view.

Running now, up the long marble steps, she finally caught up with him.

"What do you think you're doing?" Itzy grabbed for her bag, ripping it out of his hands. She looked around with the thought of finding a policeman. "How do you know my name?"

The stranger looked at her quizzically, a smile finally etching its way across his elegant features. His eyes were amber-colored, with flecks like small insects trapped in them. His teeth were startlingly white, luminous, and his dark curls were rumpled in a way that called to mind a sleepless night. He was the kind of good-looking that made Itzy's insides flutter as though she'd had too much caffeine.

"I beg your pardon, Miss Nash. I was under the impression you were expecting me."

"Have we met before?" Itzy forced herself to scowl.

"I am Luc," he said quietly. "I've been sent to look after you."

He reached for her bag again as Itzy flushed a deep shade of scarlet.

Outside, the streets were glossed from the earlier rain. Although the weather had cleared, Luc paused and opened his wide umbrella.

"Just here," he indicated a waiting black car. Itzy recognized it as one favored by Aunt Maude.

"Wait," she said, reaching into her duffel bag and finding the metallic case. She removed her beloved camera, a gift from her father, and handed the duffel to the waiting driver. The man, wearing a dark uniform and visored cap, placed Itzy's meager belongings into the trunk, and Itzy saw that one of his eyes was clouded over, blind.

Luc turned from the car, his hand on the door. As he did, his umbrella was lifted by a sudden wind gust. Through the viewfinder, while Itzy quickly turned the focus ring and adjusted the aperture, she saw something extraordinary. Before the wind died and Luc had recovered his umbrella, his feet left the earth. For a moment, it was as if he were as light as air. This was the same moment she depressed the camera's shutter button and it made a pleasurable *click*.

4

The city's noises died away as the driver pulled out onto the small side street. Luc had folded his umbrella and stowed it at his feet. The car traveled quietly, shifting lanes now and then, and soon they were on Madison Avenue. The driver seemed unimpeded by his blind eye.

The town car's interior was black and luxurious, as were the shops and storefronts they passed. The Upper East Side, Itzy knew, was where people like her aunt lived—a neighborhood, Aunt Maude said, that had "good bones." Some people lived in enormous town houses and employed a large staff. And others, like Aunt Maude, lived in fancy hotels, with even more staff.

"How was your train ride?" Luc asked. His gaze seemed to pierce her.

"Fine," Itzy shrugged, but the image of that creature, its slavering face and burning eyes, returned to her.

At Sixty-Second, they stopped for traffic. Itzy gazed out her window at an impressive corner building. This shop was different from the others in that it was a single story—albeit a very tall one. Atop its square marble facade was a solarium of sorts, a glass chamber. And atop that was a carved stone figure of a horse, rearing up spectacularly.

On the street, a figure stood in the opening of the building's large glass door beneath a sign.

"What is Hermès?" Itzy asked Luc.

"*A bringer of dreams, a watcher by night, a thief at the gates,*" Luc quoted.

This answer was so very much like one her father would have given, Itzy was momentarily taken aback. He was a professor of obscure French history and was often cryptic and unforthcoming. Itzy turned to look at the shop again, but the figure in the doorway was gone.

"I see."

Raising her camera and adjusting the focus ring, she took a picture of the building and the rearing horse.

"Hermes is the god of thieves and of persuasion," Luc explained. "He carries the souls of the dead to Hades. But most of all, Hermes is the guide to the Underworld."

"Actually, I meant that store." Itzy pointed, but Luc was silent.

Something was thumping loudly in the trunk.

The car glided into place before the Carlyle hotel, on Seventy-Sixth Street. Itzy stared down at her old torn Levi's and black trenchcoat. A uniformed doorman opened the car's door, and the trunk was emptied of Itzy's luggage. She stood on the inlaid walkway beneath the Carlyle's black and gold awnings and breathed the rarefied air.

"This way, Miss Nash," a valet spoke after conferring with the driver. He ushered her through the revolving golden doors while her duffel bag was whisked away elsewhere.

Itzy entered the hotel lobby. A great chandelier hung above her, glittering like cats' eyes in the dark. Ahead, Itzy saw the dining room, and, off to the left, the elevators. The black polished marble of the lobby's floor caught her eye, as did a man standing upon it. He wore a dark morning coat and immaculate white gloves.

"Miss Nash, I am Mr. Wold. The concierge," he announced crisply. "Welcome to the Carlyle."

"Thank you." Itzy found herself smiling broadly. The gesture was not returned.

"I trust you found your way, then, easily enough?" the concierge asked.

"Oh yes. Someone met me at the station."

Wold looked at her blankly. Itzy looked around for the young man and his umbrella, but Luc had not followed her inside.

"Miss Nash, your aunt has left something for you. This way, if you please." He gestured with a gloved hand to a golden door, tucked into the wall beside the entry.

Itzy nodded and followed Wold to a small, elegant room decorated with antiques and old Persian rugs—the concierge's private office. Wold indicated she was to sit on a spindle-legged chair.

"Your Aunt Maude sends her apologies."

"Apologies?" Itzy asked. That seemed highly out of character.

"Yes. And this letter."

The concierge brandished a cream-colored envelope with the Carlyle's insignia upon it. It became apparent that he expected Itzy to read it.

Itzy,
I am away and unreachable for an indeterminate amount of time. As you are a child, I have taken the precaution of securing a governess for you. Upon her arrival, please mind her in Every Way,

as you would me. She will keep me abreast of
your studies, so see to them satisfactorily. As
this is a fine and exclusive hotel—not a theme
park—you are to keep to your room at all times.
Never forget your behavior at the Carlyle is
a direct reflection upon the Nash name, and
therefore upon me. Remember, Gratitude is the
only appropriate emotion for a child of your
circumstances.

Your aunt,
Maude

"A governess?" Itzy's jaw dropped.
"A tutor," Wold explained.
"But I'm seventeen! I'm too old for a governess!"
Wold suddenly looked extremely nervous.

5

Back in the lobby, Itzy remembered something.

"Wold? Can you tell me where I can get 35mm film developed around here?"

Wold seemed relieved at the prospect of dispensing information, a concierge's one calling in life. "I believe there is still a place that will do that on Lexington, Miss Nash. Obscura & Co. Would you like the address?"

"No, thank you. I can manage."

Itzy surveyed the room before her. Richly dressed people were moving about quietly, coming and going from the elevators and the front desk. Wold's station appeared to be in the far corner of the lobby, where a discreet window was perched, small letters announcing CONCIERGE below. To the left, in a tidy vestibule, the gentry awaited their elevators amid the opulence of fresh-cut flowers and overstuffed chairs. A small hearth twinkled between two large and dreary paintings. The famed Bemelmans Bar lay past the elevators, up a narrow set of stairs and around the corner.

Itzy watched a birdlike older woman in dangerous-looking shoes march over to the front desk. She dragged a small dog behind her. The dog strained uselessly against the leash, its manicured nails skidding along the high gloss of the marble floor. The dog turned, panting, its black eyes falling on Itzy. Itzy stared back. A low, throaty growl emerged from the back of the creature's throat.

Behind Itzy, a small commotion broke out. A gust of fresh air swept in through the front doors, and a parade of bellhops pushed by, obscuring her view. With them came a sea of packages stacked on polished brass carts. The uniformed men, each with their gilt epaulettes and tilted little hats, wheeled by Itzy with great flourish and converged upon the gleaming black floor. A creaking tower of elegant boxes and shopping bags merged in the lobby's center, and for a moment the bellhops stood around uneasily. When they finally parted, Itzy was left staring at a younger version of the dog owner, a girl about her own age.

Itzy stared, despite herself. The girl was a different species. She was tall and her hair was strikingly blonde, and it fell over her shoulders and down her back. Her skin was smooth and flawless, her lips painted a bright red. A string of pearls wrapped itself tightly around her long neck.

"Pippa, darling!" The older woman yanked the small dog behind her.

"Mother!" They exchanged a series of air-kisses. The bejeweled dog's leash was now on Pippa's wrist, and with each gesture the dog was being yanked about like a puppet, its front feet leaving the floor. Itzy watched, fascinated. The animal bared its small, sharp teeth at her.

Itzy's eyes strayed to the vast array of purchases Pippa had made. It seemed impossible that one person could have bought so much before lunch.

And then her stomach sank.

There, at the very bottom of it all, Itzy saw her scuffed and threadbare duffel.

In a panic, Itzy turned to Wold, but he was gone.

She eyed her old bag, debating. Who needed clothes, anyway? She had her camera, after all. But the long summer stretched out before her with one pair of Levi's, and she thought better of it. Itzy walked over.

"Um, excuse me?" Itzy said in a small voice. She pointed to her flattened bag on the cart beside her. The pair hadn't heard her, but the dog approached the bag and sniffed. It began a confused growling.

Itzy cleared her throat. "There's been some sort of mistake—"

The dog let out a sharp yelp, followed by a terrified whimper. The girl finally turned.

"What is it, Paris?" Pippa asked her dog. She scooped up the animal, which did little to comfort it. Paris strained, kicking its hind legs, trying to return to the duffel.

Pippa's eyes finally found Itzy, and she glared at her. "Pick on someone your own size."

"I—"

The words died in Itzy's throat, for the animal now emptied its bladder in a wide stream upon Pippa's fine clothing. A damp blotch spread across her silk shirt. Pippa screeched, releasing the dog into the growing puddle on the marble floor, where it barked furiously at the bag.

"Mother!" Pippa wailed, hauling the dog back, streaks of wet radiating from its paws. The dog strained against the lead, and its little black eyes bulged.

The older woman turned to Itzy, her face oddly frozen in place.

Itzy felt herself flush as a cold silence descended upon the luxury hotel.

"M-my bag is mixed in with your stuff."

A pitiful whine escaped the dog's throat, but soon died.

Pippa's cool blue eyes narrowed. They took in Itzy's tattered Levi's and vintage coat. She raised a perfectly groomed brow. "Mother, find Mr. Wold and tell him a *vagrant* has managed to wander in, and she's trying to steal my bag."

People were looking.

"Hey, *I'm* not the one stealing a bag here," Itzy said. She tried to pull her bag free, but Paris was ready. Scrabbling its stubby nails for purchase on the slick black marble, the creature charged Itzy, sinking its teeth into her ankle.

Itzy felt the row of sharp teeth puncture her skin and looked down. Paris stared up at her vacantly, its green eyes narrowed to slits. She saw its tiny pointed teeth and heard a low throaty growl as it jerked its neck, digging deeper into her ankle. Burning pain ripped through skin and muscle. Suddenly lightheaded, she had the unusual sensation of falling a great distance. Then she kicked the creature away. The tiny dog sailed back to Pippa through the air in a high arc and landed with a sharp yelp on the stone floor.

"Paris!" Pippa gasped, bending down. The dog was eerily still. "Paris! Help! Mr. Wold—someone! The vagrant's killed my dog!"

6

Itzy yanked with all her strength and retrieved her duffel bag. A cascade of packages tumbled down after it, landing in the puddle. French silk lay in limp piles. Something shattered as it hit the floor, and the air smelled suddenly of perished flowers.

Wold appeared by the mother's side.

"Mrs. Brill, what seems to be the problem?" the concierge asked.

"Who *is* this child?" Mrs. Brill asked, pointing a long painted nail at Itzy.

Wold cast a sharp look at her and stiffened.

"Maude Nash's niece," he allowed. A look passed between the two.

"Maude Nash?" Mrs. Brill leaned in, regarding Itzy with a new interest.

"Indeed," he replied.

Itzy scowled.

"Miss Nash is visiting for the summer," Wold continued. A porter appeared at his side, and Wold whispered to him. The man scampered off.

"Mommy? My *dog*?" Pippa whined.

"It *bit* me," Itzy said sullenly. "I hope it has all its shots."

Paris was twitching its front legs pitifully, and Pippa tearfully clasped it to her damp chest.

"That thing's possessed," Itzy grumbled, and a shocked silence spread throughout the lobby.

It was then, in the quiet, that Itzy heard the tapping. Methodical, it originated from somewhere across the room—the stabbing of something sharp against the marble floor. As it grew nearer, the crowd parted. Itzy was left staring at a peculiar man. He was balding, stringy hair combed over a shiny circle of skin. He carried a sharp cane at his side.

"Ah, Dr. Jenkins," Wold exclaimed. "Thank you for coming so quickly. There has been an *unfortunate* incident."

Dr. Jenkins's eyes met Itzy's and she felt a rush of terror.

"Let me see the patient," he said.

Itzy took a step backward. There was something utterly dreadful about the man, something ruinous. He was the man from the train, from her dream. Pippa had pushed Paris into the doctor's arms, but the doctor's eyes lingered on Itzy. Finally, he handed his cane to Wold and reached to examine the dog.

"You better have a good lawyer," Pippa hissed at her. "You'll need it."

7

Aunt Maude's suite was on the eighteenth floor. Itzy waited beside the bellman who was carrying her old duffel bag in front of the bank of elevators. She tried to not look at her bag, how old and scuffed it was. She tried to pretend it wasn't hers at all and stepped away from it, turning to look with feigned interest at the pair of gloomy paintings dominating the small vestibule. Both were extremely dark, with age perhaps. One depicted a pair of bored-looking cherubs, and the other a still life with fruit. She snapped a photo. The fire in the hearth crackled, spitting embers at her.

Wold was huddled with the Brills across the lobby, and when Itzy stole a glance at them, the doctor was staring at her intently. She looked away quickly.

A polite chime announced the elevator, and Itzy boarded along with the bellman holding her bag.

"Eighteen, please." Itzy looked at the elevator boy in his beige uniform. He was young—a slight fuzz of a mustache shadowed his upper lip. His skin was the color of toffee.

The numbered panel blinked as they ascended in silence.

"Eighteen, Miss Nash," he said as the elevator alighted and the door opened.

"Thank you," she mumbled.

"Call me Johnny."

"Thank you, Johnny." Itzy smiled.

She followed the bellman to the right and around as the carpeted hallway veered off at a corner, past an unmarked door. The door was forlorn, different from the others in the hotel. It was old, of inlayed wood, and scuffed here and there with deep gouges. It had a worn mat—also unusual—which was piled high with several days' worth of newspapers.

"Who lives there?" Itzy asked the bellman.

"No one," he said.

But from somewhere far inside, a distant piano was playing.

When they arrived at her aunt's door, Itzy realized her ankle was throbbing. The bellman unlocked Suite 1804 with a brass key, and Itzy entered a small anteroom with an elegant side table and a gilt mirror. The door to the coatroom was slightly ajar, and Itzy could see a long row of her aunt's furs.

"Where would you like this?" the bellman asked, indicating the offending duffel.

Itzy sighed. The bag was her father's, and she suddenly felt a stab of anger at him for simply owning such a thing.

"I'll take it," she said, reaching for it.

The bag seemed heavier than she remembered. The bellman nodded, handing her the brass key before leaving.

A swinging door separated the suite from the anteroom, and Itzy pushed it open.

It was a room full of shadows.

She felt for the light switch, her anxiety mounting. The dark made her uneasy, a small remnant of her childhood that shamed her. Her hands ran along the molding and she took one nervous step in.

Aunt Maude's apartments were large and rambling, and Itzy had never been permitted to explore them entirely. Her eyes were adjusting, though, and soon she saw thick drapes that lined the tall windows, and through them small slivers of daylight the color of dust cut through the gloom. A silence settled over her—the walls of the hotel were old and thick. Here was the living room, she knew, its tall ceilings and patterned toile couches. Off to the east was the dining room, and ahead stretched an arched hallway lined with her aunt's priceless art.

A table held an antique lamp, but the switch on the cord produced nothing.

She threw open the nearest velvet curtain and stared out at the narrow wrought-iron balcony. At one point, a small but pretty garden had been permitted to grow, but it was brown and dying. Beyond that lay Fifth Avenue and the park, and, finally, the west side of Manhattan.

Itzy inspected the living room. A fireplace dominated one wall, but Itzy knew it was merely for show. Her aunt would never allow something as cheery as a fire to glow in a hearth. A wheeled cart sat before the nearest couch, a white tablecloth draped over it. A tiered silver tray held a selection of petit four pastries, and a tea service was off to one side. A basket of plump scones and croissants sat beside a selection of miniature jams and honey. A gleaming dome covered a plate, beside which was an untouched napkin.

As Itzy neared the room service cart, she suddenly realized her own hunger. She had eaten cereal when the sun came up, alone, before catching the train, but nothing since. She grabbed a croissant and bit into it quickly, but it was stale and hard, and she spat it out into her hand.

Looking closer now, she saw the cart had been sitting in her aunt's living room for some time. A veil of dust had settled on the drinking glasses and the silver dome.

She ran her finger along the dome's dulled surface and reached to lift it.

On what was once a half grapefruit was a tight ball of writhing insects. Disturbed, they fell apart, scattering about the white linen. Slamming the cover back on the plate, Itzy groaned. They were earwigs, she noticed with disgust. They scuttled along, their rear pincers dragging behind them or raised in the air angrily.

Stomping on as many as she could, she watched helplessly as the rest made their escape into the shadows beneath the toile couches or in the cracks of the base-boards.

8

The Blue Bedroom was to be Itzy's, Wold had informed her in his office. It had been the servant's quarters at one time, he stressed, as though talking to a child. Itzy would know it, he continued, by its color.

"And what color would that be?" Itzy asked innocently. The annoyed look on his face was reward enough.

The Blue Bedroom was down the far hall—a smaller, twistier version of the main hall, devoid of precious art. She passed the kitchen on her way, noting its gloominess. Her bedroom was done up in powder blue wallpaper, with a thin and meager-looking blue blanket over the iron frame of the bed. Above the flimsy pillow was an embroidery, a family tree. It was the only thing on the wall, and Itzy examined it closer.

It appeared to be the Nash family tree, if the banner was to be believed. Many branches twisted out from the gnarled main trunk, and upon the leaves were the names of her various ancestors. There was a noticeable bald patch beside her father's name, and Itzy's name was nowhere to be found. In an artistic flourish, the embroiderer had sewn depictions of Adam and Eve at the tree's base and a serpent between them. The serpent wore a human head, its face twisted and bloated.

Eyeing the serpent warily, Itzy put her bag down upon the floor.

Her room had a window, but after parting the curtains, Itzy saw that it let out onto a brick air shaft. She shut them again.

She brushed away a few earwigs on her pillow and lay down on her bed. It creaked in protest.

The rest of the day stretched out before her, and she wondered what further surprises it held. She thought of Pippa and Mrs. Brill, her mind idly turning to Pippa's threat. Could she call down to room service for a lawyer? She thought of Luc, the boy with deep amber eyes. And then, in the way your mind circles those thoughts that you try hard not to think, she thought of her father. And wondered why he had left her behind.

Lifting the hem of her jeans, she inspected her ankle. A small row of puncture wounds laced her Achilles tendon. She would wash in the bathroom.

She began to unpack her bag. She hadn't brought much—she didn't own much—and her clothes fit easily into the plain chest of drawers in the room. The closet was filled with more of her aunt's fur coats and a few steamer trunks and offered little room for anything else. She stacked her few toiletries on top of the dresser, beside a small hand mirror. She inspected her reflection quickly; the mirror was quite ornate, and heavy—probably silver. There was a patina of age beneath its glass. Itzy could see her hazel eyes, and her hair the color of molasses, but everything was clouded with a gray bloom. *Angels' breath*, she remembered it being called.

As she pulled out the last of her things, she saw something black skittering in the deep shadows of her bag. Gasping, she jumped back. Luc's warning returned to her. *Never place your bag upon the floor. A demon will crawl inside.*

Plucking up her courage, she grabbed her Leica and crept back, camera at the ready. She slowly peered down into the bag's depths, adjusting the viewfinder. After her eyes grew accustomed to the bag's dim interior, she gave it a soft nudge with her shoe.

Nothing.

She tried the other side, where the black thing had gone.

Still nothing.

With an audible sigh of relief, Itzy relaxed and stood. She wiped her hands on her jeans and blew a lock of stray hair from her face.

Then she saw it.

A black, shadow-like creature emerged from her old duffel bag and raced for the small closet. As it fled, it made a horrid clacking sound.

A rat, she thought. *There was a rat in my bag. I'm in the city, and there are rats in the city.* Itzy snapped a picture. *Big ones too.*

Picking up the duffel bag, Itzy threw it into the closet and slammed the door. She leaned against it, breathing hard. It took her a long time to realize somewhere in the suite a jarring phone was ringing.

"Hello?" Itzy said, lifting the old-fashioned beige phone to her ear. On its base a series of lights twinkled, various call buttons.

Itzy thought she heard something—something scratchy, as if the call were coming from far, far away.

"Hello?" she tried again.

The scratching noise continued. Itzy thought she heard a whisper on top of it. She slammed the phone down. Picking it up again, she stabbed the room service button.

"Room service," a kind, matronly voice answered.

"Hi. This is Suite 180—"

"Yes, good afternoon, Miss Nash. What can I get you?" said the calming, melodious voice.

"Um. Well, nothing. There's a cart here, though, that was overlooked. It's been here for some time. Can you send someone up?"

"Immediately. And I apologize for the disturbance."

"Er—that's okay. Thanks."

"You're welcome, Miss Nash."

Itzy hung up the phone thoughtfully, and almost instantly it started its loud jangling again. Ignoring it, she slung her camera bag over her shoulder and walked to the door.

9

A small parchment had been pushed beneath the suite's front door, and Itzy bent to retrieve it. It had been ripped from a book and had been folded hastily, erratically, many times over.

Itzy opened it.

Ava Quant's
OBSERVATIONS
Historical and theological, upon the NATURE and NUMBER of the OPERATIONS of

divahS.

Accompanied with Accounts of A brief treatise on the Grievous Molestations that have Annoyed the country, with several remarkable CURIOSITIES therein occurring, and some CONJECTURES on the GREAT EVENTS likely to Befall.

I. Ava, how do you RECOGNIZE a *divah*?

A. A divah is a demon—a she-devil, a powerful force of wickedness from the Underworld, one you ignore at your own peril. Divahs are quick, ruthless, and nothing can match their feverish desires. You don't stand a chance.

B. The identification of a divah is very, very difficult. Demons are not the coarse, crimson, pitchforked creatures of medieval paintings— in their dangerous, parasitic form they are indistinguishable from you or me. They walk the city streets, their diabolical origins invisible to all but a select few. They are served by various servants and spies, each more hideous than the next, who cultivate them through their early— and vulnerable—larval stages.

C. Demons augment their eyes so they do not glitter. This makes locating a demon more difficult. There are spectacles that reverse this. Hermès makes a fine pair.

D. Divahs possess a hearty aversion to the language of the French.

II. But, Ava, what do divahs WANT?

A. That's easy. Your soul.

B. Demons—all eternal beings as well—do not have a soul of their own. This is a constant source of annoyance for them. They will take possession of yours, if you're not careful.

III. But aren't demons the stuff of HEAVEN and HELL?

A. Yes! And the Upper East Side.

B. Theirs is a murky realm, as they are very much opportunists. The more dangerous ones are apt to be found in the worlds of fashion or film—although there's plenty to attract a divah to something as unlikely as politics. Demons are excellent mimics, and oftentimes can speak in tongues.

IV. What GETS RID of a *divah*?
A. This is quite difficult, as divahs are persistent and relentless.
B. An exorcisme gets rid of a divah.
   1. A good trick: throw an extra "e" at the end of a word. Instant French! This will come in handy on your demon-hunting adventures.
   2. Exorcismes are so misunderstood. Whatever you do, avoid conducting one in Latin; divahs simply can't get enough of that dead language. Pepper your exorcisme with a little French, et voila.

V. Ava Quant, what exactly IS an *exorcisme*?
A. Relentless French talk.
B. And water. Evian is the weapon of choice, but any imported French water will do. Douse the subject thoroughly. (It burns like acid.)
C. If necessary, follow this with the guillotine.
   1. Vive la France!

VI. A GUILLOTINE? Where do I get one?
A. See me.

Itzy read the pamphlet twice before dismissing it. It had the feel of some sort of crazed proclamation, something that should be pasted to a medieval church door. And it surely wasn't *the* Ava Quant—that old actress was most certainly dead by now. The real Ava Quant, star of the silver screen, had famously given up acting and renounced public life. There was rumor, Itzy remembered, of a nervous breakdown, of inner demons. Then, she was simply never heard from again.

This Ava Quant, Itzy frowned at the parchment, was apparently a lunatic.

10

Itzy slung her camera bag over her shoulder and checked the pocket of her coat for her key, a habit she had in place from home. Her father's hours at the university were unpredictable, and he always seemed to be on call for some research project or moderating some lecture. She no longer thought a lot about her mother, and when she did she wasn't entirely sure if the memories were her own.

The hotel's hall was as silent as a tomb, the muted oriental runner thick beneath her feet. Stealing a quick glance at the lonesome unmarked door, Itzy noticed the pile of newspapers was gone. She paused, listening, but there was no piano, no sound at all. Quietly she tried the knob, but it wouldn't budge. Still, a chill crept up her spine, and she blinked back a sudden rush of adrenaline. Someone was watching her.

Hurrying around the corner, Itzy stabbed at the elevator's buttons. The hall was empty except for a lavish vase of flowers, which perfumed the entire landing. Lush Audubon birds were frozen in gilt frames upon the walls. Her stomach dropped as she thought she heard a soft click—as though a door were opening—and she jabbed the illuminated call button once more.

Itzy thought of the rat-creature in her bag, the noise it made as it skittered across the floor.

Sometimes, at home and mostly at night, Itzy would get panicky, and these attacks were unpredictable and unpleasant. She would be overwhelmed with a cold fear, and if unchecked, her heart would race and she could barely catch her breath.

She squeezed her eyes shut and tried to calm her breathing—but this simply made her hearing more acute. Were those *footsteps* she heard down the hall? Her hand found her metallic camera case, and she flipped open the clasps, grabbing the Leica from its snug, padded interior. Instantly she felt better.

"Miss Nash?"

Itzy had not heard the elevator arrive.

She opened her eyes and tried to smile.

"Everything okay? You look a bit pale."

"Yes, fine, Johnny. Thank you. I was—never mind. Call me Itzy, by the way."

After stealing a look over her shoulder, she stepped into the elevator.

"Exploring?" he asked, indicating the camera she gripped with white fingers.

"How did you know?" She flushed, putting the Leica away.

"You look like a tourist." He smiled.

"Better that than a vagrant," she said. She thought of Pippa, her perfectly manicured appearance, and hoped she wouldn't be lurking in the lobby. Itzy contemplated her camera bag. "Do I really look like a tourist?" That was not a good look for anyone in the gilded zip code of 10021.

"No. But if you want, when I'm off later, I'd be happy to show you around."

"That would be great!" she smiled. "I mean—sure." Itzy stole another look at Johnny. His hair was dark, and his lashes were long. The little cap upon his head was oddly endearing.

"If you really want to see something," he whispered, "I'll show you the basement."

"The basement?"

Johnny smiled. His cap was slightly askew, his eyes a deep dark brown.

"There's a maze of tunnels down there, and no one knows them like me. I'll give you the insider's tour of the Carlyle," he said proudly.

The elevator reached the lobby, and Itzy had already stepped out into the small vestibule when he called her name. She turned.

"Bring your camera." He winked.

Itzy walked to the front desk, grateful the lobby was quiet.

The clerk looked right through her.

"Any mail or messages for me? 1804," Itzy asked. Her father had promised to write from Paris.

"Nothing." The woman smiled blankly.

"Can you mail this, please?" Itzy slid a cream-colored envelope over the smooth surface.

The clerk snatched up the letter to her father, and the counter was once again empty and spotless.

Outside, the weather had turned colder, unseasonable for late June. Itzy pulled her black coat around her tighter and flipped her sunglasses down over her eyes. Wold had said the photography store was on Lexington. She headed off, guessing at the direction, not wishing to appear like a tourist.

11

Obscura & Co. was not easy to find. Nor did it appear to be open.

Lexington Avenue was a smaller avenue than Madison, and far less grand. The photography store was incredibly run-down, sandwiched between a dated-looking high-rise and a cobbler with a flashing neon sign in the outline of a man's shoe. Metal grates were pulled down over the small, filthy windows, and access to the door was through a dreary recess that smelled not unlike a toilet. Undeterred, Itzy braved the entry, avoiding an oily puddle as she did. The door was wooden, and the shade was pulled down, a sign marked CLOSED dangling on the other side of the dirty glass.

Itzy knocked anyway.

On tiptoe, she peered through the window and saw a glass-topped counter, its contents blurred but promising. She knocked again.

Behind her, Itzy felt the warm sunlight vanish and she stiffened. She was suddenly aware of her Leica, the warnings she'd received from her father about carrying her valuables out in the open in New York. She turned, hoping to appear casual. A silhouette blocked the passage. She scrutinized it.

"We have to stop meeting this way," she said finally, hands on her hips.

Luc folded his umbrella and stepped into the dingy entry.

"Sightseeing?" Luc asked, a slight smile on his lips. "Or just a little breaking and entering?"

"Actually, if you must know, I was hoping to get some supplies—and have a roll of film developed." She gestured to the sign. "But they're closed."

Luc walked nearer, and Itzy stepped back to let him by. She breathed in his smell—indescribable, like cherished leather-bound books. Luc reached for the battered front doorknob.

"Now who's breaking and entering?" she asked.

His hand closed on the wooden knob, and he twisted it, his eyes never leaving hers. As the door opened inward—easily—a small bell chimed.

"Itzy," he explained, "nothing is as it seems."

Luc had almost disappeared into the shadows of the store before Itzy had recovered herself enough to follow.

12

Somehow the interior of Obscura & Co. was bigger and brighter than it appeared from the shop's exterior. Music drifted down from unseen speakers, a low, rhythmic techno beat. Shelves held tools for measuring light and dark and equipment for capturing it—some completely foreign and arcane. Itzy was enthralled. This was a store to rival none other—it alone was worth the trip to her aunt's. She walked the aisles in a daze.

She heard them before she saw them—speaking in soft tones, an occasional burst of laughter. She rounded the corner and came upon a table littered with coffee cups. Young people were gathered around the mess, gossiping and exchanging news beside a large lightbox scattered with various photographs marked liberally with a red grease pencil. They were her age, maybe slightly older. But this was hard for Itzy to tell, for she found everything about them—their clothes, their hair, their makeup, worn not only by the girl but also by one of the boys—so hip, so incredibly cool, so foreign, that she nearly backed up the way she came.

At the sight of Itzy, all conversation ceased.

"Don't mind me," Itzy said.

The music pulsed, quickening in the silence.

The girl was nearest, and she turned to look at Itzy. Her eyes were gray like mist, and her hair was long and black. Around the table, the three boys blinked, looking at Itzy with undisguised interest.

"Itzy!" Luc's voice came from behind her, and for a moment Itzy saw a different look on the girl's face as she gazed in Luc's direction. This look told Itzy more than she wanted to know.

Luc was at the counter, talking to an older man. Their low tones stopped as Itzy walked over, casting one last glance at the table.

The old man turned to Itzy, an amused look on his face. "This the one?" the proprietor asked Luc, who nodded.

"Itzy," Luc said. "This is Maurice."

The man had been wearing a pair of magnifying glasses, which he now unhooked from his ears, sighing. He squinted at Itzy, appraising her.

"I'd say you have your hands full," he finally pronounced. To Itzy, he said, "Luc tells me you like to take pictures."

Itzy nodded.

The old man's face was weary and lined. His eyes were a startling copper. Itzy resisted the impulse to photograph him.

"I'd like to have this developed, please." Itzy retrieved a roll of film from the pocket of her trench coat. "It's T-MAX," she added, clacking it down on the counter.

His gnarled hands picked up the small yellow canister. On his fourth finger was a black circle of ink. A tattoo of a ring, in the deepest of blacks.

"Processing?"

"Standard."

"Prints?"

"A contact sheet is fine."

Maurice paused, squinting.

"What's that you got there?" He nodded at Itzy's camera.

Itzy placed her Leica on the counter for him to inspect.
He turned the camera over in his hands, cocking the arm
and peering through the viewfinder. "An M6. Zeiss lens.
This is no toy." The old man looked at her. "Not many
people shoot in black-and-white these days."

"Is there any other way?"

"What did you say your name was?"

"Itzy."

"Itzy. What kind of name is Itzy?"

"What kind of name is Maurice?"

"French." Maurice smiled. "Itzy, what kind of photography do you do?"

"Portraits, mostly. Candids. I really like Mary Ellen
Mark," she said shyly.

"Well, that's some weapon you got there, Itzy. Hope
you know how to use it."

"I do."

"Film has a habit of exposing reality." He shrugged,
returning the camera. "Be careful what you wish for."

The old man placed the roll in an envelope.

"Anything else I can get you?"

"Actually, yes. I need a really fast film. For shooting in
the dark. Have any 3200?"

"What sort of dark are we talking?"

"A basement."

"What sort of portraits are you doing in a basement?"

Itzy found herself flushing a deep scarlet. "It's good to
be prepared," she said.

"Try this. It's IR. Infrared. I bet you'll have all sorts of
fun with it." Maurice placed a roll on the counter and slid
it toward her. "A dying art form." He peered into her eyes.
"Consider yourself warned."

13

"How do you know that man?" Itzy asked Luc as they walked beneath his umbrella along East Eighty-Fourth.

"Maurice?" Luc asked.

"Maurice."

"The war," Luc said vaguely.

"War?" Itzy stopped walking. "What war?"

"It was a while ago."

"It must have been," Itzy said. "That man's ancient."

Out of the corner of her eye, Itzy saw Luc smile. She was pleased.

"Some people say there's really only one war, Itzy."

Itzy could think of many, including some that were not yet finished, and she said so.

"They are all the same war, fought again and again. The battle between good and evil."

"Oh," she said. Luc had a point.

Luc appeared to be listening to something, his head cocked. He frowned and grabbed Itzy's hand. The rain was coming down in earnest.

"Time to go," he urged.

Itzy liked the feel of his hand in hers. "What's the hurry?" she asked. "A little rain won't hurt you."

She could hear something now, clearly through the downpour: the sharp metallic tang of horse hooves against the cobbles. Luc heard it, too, coming closer. She thought she saw a teetering carriage at the intersection, turning the corner slowly, navigating on an unsteady wheel.

"It's just a hansom cab, Luc. On its way to the park. Even I know that—"

Luc appeared to be debating something, casting a sharp glance back in the direction of the photography shop. His features hardened. He was apprehensive.

The carriage had drawn nearer and appeared to be in a dreadful state. The lone horse was dead tired, and its head hung near the ground. It dragged its feet chillingly against the street, and its breathing was labored—its ribs protruding prominently upon its sides. Of the driver, Itzy saw nothing, and she craned her neck, morbidly fascinated.

Luc cupped her chin with his hand. "Whatever you do, do not look," Luc instructed her. His tone was firm, but gentle.

Before she could ask why, Luc had maneuvered himself so his back was to the oncoming coach, blocking Itzy from further view. He lowered his umbrella, another barrier. The horse and carriage were close enough now that Itzy could feel its rumbling beneath her feet. She heard the appalling breathing of the sick animal. The creaking of the faulty wheel sent a chill down her neck. It drew closer, slowly, until in one final groan, the carriage shuddered to a stop beside them.

Luc then did something entirely unexpected.

He pulled Itzy to him and kissed her.

14

It was a long kiss, and without very much to compare it to, Itzy felt like she had better enjoy every moment of it—who knew when such a kiss would come around again? She felt herself rising onto tiptoe and kissing him back. She felt weightless and overwhelmed with his scent again— the fragrance now of polished wood, starched linen, sunlit rooms. Luc's lips were softer than she had expected, and his arms wrapped around her protectively. All thoughts of the loathsome carriage had left her.

And just as suddenly, it was over—Itzy found her two feet cruelly back on the ground. She felt strangely heavy. Luc's amber-flecked eyes were upon her, searching her expression for something, some unnamable thing, and then, without a look over his shoulder, he grabbed her hand and pulled her down Eighty-Fourth Street, back to the Carlyle.

Itzy had recovered herself sufficiently at Seventy-Seventh Street and stopped, turning to Luc.

"What was that for?" she asked.

"What was what?" he asked innocently.

"That kiss," she said softly.

His stare penetrated her. "Your own good," he said finally.

Itzy looked at him closely—his tangle of dark brown hair worn to one side, his strange syrupy eyes, bright as sunshine. Again she noticed that his face held light, an aura almost. He was breathtaking.

"Take a picture. It'll last longer," he said without any trace of irony.

"I would." Itzy flushed. "But I only have the IR on me—and that sort of film I need to load in the dark."

Luc shifted his weight back and forth. He looked suddenly tired.

"Ah, yes. The basement."

"And tunnels," said Itzy.

"Tunnels? You don't say."

"Yes, many tunnels. Or so Johnny promised."

"Johnny, the elevator boy?"

"The one and only. In fact, I'm meeting him this way." Itzy indicated Seventy-Seventh Street. "The staff entrance."

"I'll walk you."

Itzy smiled.

"It's just a basement, Luc. What could be so bad down there?"

15

The staff door toward the end of Seventy-Seventh Street was discreet, unmarked. Itzy looked around. The street was quieter than the Carlyle's Seventy-Sixth, with none of the hotel's purring limousines and costumed doormen, the flurry of guests arriving and departing. *Like the dark side of the moon*, Itzy thought.

The awning to a high-rise apartment building jutted out over the sidewalk, and she stopped beneath it to wait out the rain.

"Johnny's late." Luc smirked.

"I'm a big girl. I can wait by myself," Itzy said. When Luc did not respond, she added, "Don't worry. I won't flag down any hansom cabs."

Luc spun furiously around to her, and she instantly regretted her words. But just as quickly, his anger vanished, defeat creeping in. He looked over his shoulder.

"Itzy, that was no hansom cab. If you see one again, promise me you'll never, ever get in."

"I promise," she said. She wanted to take it back—she preferred his anger to defeat any day. She preferred kissing him to all else.

"There are others. Far, far worse. And I can't protect you from them all."

"Other carriages?"

A doorman was positioned beside a pair of thick glass doors behind them. Luc glared at him.

"Servants. Spies," he said. "But it's too late, of course. She is already here. I can smell her."

"Who, Luc?"

Luc was suddenly close again, his body looming over hers. He looked down fiercely. The doorman nervously retreated into the small foyer of the building, talking to someone on a handheld radio.

"The Divah is known by many names," he whispered, his golden eyes squeezed shut. "But I knew her last as *la Reine.*"

"*La Reine?*" Itzy repeated. The word felt foolish on her tongue.

He opened his eyes—he looked feverish. She preferred them shut. "*La Reine des Démons,*" he whispered.

"The Demon Queen?"

Itzy stared up at Luc's face uncertainly. She turned, looking for the doorman, but Luc was upon her, grasping her shoulders. "How is your French, Itzy? Better dust off those textbooks and polish it up."

"You're crazy." Itzy tried to laugh, but her voice sounded distant, scratchy.

He let out a stream of expletives in antiquated French. She recognized few words.

"That carriage before—that was but a taste of what's to come. They are amassing—drawn to her like moths to a flame. They come, slithering out from their lairs to worship at her feet. Burnt offerings. Incantations." Luc leaned in, whispering in her ear. "She will be weakened from her journey, and she must be nourished. But once she has regained her former power, she will be unstoppable. Do you hear me?"

From his breast pocket, he brandished a crumpled and burned card. She recognized it at once, and all questions died on her lips.

The End of Days Is Nigh

Itzy nodded her head in a daze. His eyes flooded with relief and he carefully curled a lock of her dark hair behind her ear.

"But—" she mumbled. A thousand questions raced through her brain.

"Best get going." He nodded at her camera. "Tomorrow there will be little time for exploring."

16

"There you are," Johnny said, rounding the corner.

"Ah—here comes the young Hermes now." Luc smiled cruelly.

Hermes is the guide to the Underworld, Luc's words in the car came back to her. *He carries the souls of the dead to Hades.*

She turned to Johnny. He had changed from his uniform and looked younger, even cuter.

"Hey—you look like you saw a ghost! And I haven't even begun my tour yet," he said.

Itzy was suddenly shivering, hugging herself to keep warm.

"I'm sorry I'm late. Dinner hour at the asylum." Johnny laughed at Itzy's expression. "We're in VIP mode," he explained. "Someone's got them all worked up."

"Who's the VIP?" Itzy asked. With some annoyance, she found her teeth chattering.

"No idea. They're all the same in the end. Rich and crazy." He looked pointedly at Luc. "Evening, Mr. Beauvais."

"You two know each other?" Itzy asked, looking between them.

"Here—take my coat." Johnny unbuttoned his jean jacket and draped it over Itzy's wet shoulders. It was warm from his body, and Itzy was grateful. "Were you waiting long?"

"Long enough." Luc scowled. "Never keep a lady waiting."

"Or let her stand shivering in the rain." Johnny eyed Luc's overcoat.

"No worries," Itzy said quickly.

"I'll take it from here." Johnny grinned. He turned to Itzy. "Got your camera?"

Itzy nodded, indicating the bag on her shoulder. Luc was eyeing Johnny fiercely. Itzy turned to him.

"Mr. Beauvais." Itzy's eyes twinkled at the formality. "It's been a pleasure."

Luc's gaze met hers, his eyes staring deep inside her. Her stomach flipped over as she remembered the kiss. Luc leaned into her then, his eyes smoldering, and she held her breath. His mouth found her ear.

"Like moths to a flame, Itzy," he said. "Like moths to a flame."

He turned and walked away, a dark figure along Seventy-Seventh Street.

"You ready?" Johnny asked.

She looked once more for Luc, but he was gone. "Ready," she said. Johnny took her hand and walked over to the doorman.

"Hi, Stan." Johnny smiled, and the doorman nodded at Itzy.

"Wait—" Itzy asked as they entered the apartment building's lobby. "Through here? This isn't the Carlyle."

"Never fear!" he said, leading them past the small entry and a low set of locked mailboxes.

They stopped beside a metal door marked NO ACCESS.

"Ever heard of Marilyn Monroe?" Johnny asked. He took a ring of keys from his pocket and flipped through them. Nervous, Itzy looked over her shoulder for Stan, but he had reclaimed his perch on the sidewalk, whistling.

"Of course," Itzy replied, annoyed.

"I've got keys to all sorts of places." He grinned. Johnny found the right key and opened the old metal door. It was warped, and it scraped against the floor tiles. Beyond, Itzy saw a few wooden stairs leading down—and then darkness. It smelled like oil and damp. Itzy's stomach sunk.

"Welcome to Marilyn's tunnels."

Johnny flipped on the light switch and the stairs emerged from the shadows.

He skipped down a few steps and turned, holding out his hand. Itzy did not move.

"You're not afraid, are you? I've got a flashlight." He clicked it on, holding it beneath his chin ghoulishly.

"Cute."

"Flattery will get you everywhere." Johnny smiled.

"Why are these called Marilyn's tunnels?"

"Why indeed?" Johnny replied.

Itzy tried to peer around the boy, but the remainder of the stairs fell away into a thick blackness.

"Aw, come on. Don't make me ruin the surprise."

Itzy eyed him skeptically.

"All right. They're called Marilyn's tunnels because it's how she used to sneak into the Carlyle. To see JFK."

Itzy nodded. Swallowing her mounting nervousness, she followed the elevator boy down the creaky steps.

17

"Everyone wondered how she did it—how the most famous woman in the world could rendezvous with the president of the United States in secret. Well, here's your answer."

They had passed though an unremarkable boiler room and from there through a small passage. They stood now in a tiny room, the low ceilings damp and bulging overhead. There was a mildewed tabletop set upon bulky legs, the remnants of someone's workstation spread out as though their owner had left in a hurry. Rusty vices were clamped to the table's edge and blocks of wood held scattered old-fashioned hand tools and cut nails. Off to one side, Itzy could see a set of bricked-up stairs, evidence of an old passageway. The place was draped in cobwebs.

"Glamorous. I see how it's been hard to keep this a secret."

Itzy watched, unimpressed, as Johnny grabbed a side of the old table. "A little help?" he grunted.

The table was surprisingly heavy, the wood bloated with decades of damp and slick with mildew. It would have been impossible to move by herself, and the pair scraped it across the floor, upending much of its contents. They set it against the far wall.

"*This* is how she did it." Johnny gestured.

Beneath the table was a trapdoor made of rough wood about four feet across. A handle made of thick rope was tied in an intricate knot. Itzy bent to look at it.

"That, my dear," he said, "is called the demon hitch."

"The knot?" Itzy asked.

Johnny nodded.

"What do you know about demons?" Itzy asked sharply.

"Not a thing." Johnny smiled widely. "But I do know knots. My father was a sailor."

"I've got to load my film." Itzy looked around the small room. The lightbulb had a rusted metal pull cord. "Can you turn that off? I need to do it in complete dark."

Johnny raised a flirtatious eyebrow, but Itzy ignored him. "It's really fast film—for shooting in the basement without a flash. The silver crystals on the emulsion are extremely sensitive. Don't worry, Johnny—I can load this thing in seconds. I practice with my eyes shut all the time."

"Hey, I'm not afraid of the dark." He winked, reaching for the cord.

Itzy still slept with the lights on, and as the room plunged into blackness, she felt her heart pound. Squeezing her eyes shut against it, she imagined herself, as she always did, in her most favorite place: the gardens of her father's small cottage in Brittany. It was her father's retreat, the place where he'd go when researching or writing a book. It was where he had first given her the Leica—to keep her busy, and out of his hair—and she had spent all the daylight hours outside learning to use it. The sunlight there had a particular quality to it, a paleness that she could recall even here—in the dank workshop—perfectly. It was her trick for surviving the dark.

Eyes shut, she unfastened the camera's baseplate and put it into a pocket of the borrowed jean jacket. She had done this hundreds of times. Now the camera's backside opened easily, and she pulled a few exposures out of the film cartridge, dropping it into the camera's well. Sliding it along with her thumb, she felt the film catching in the camera's take-up chamber, and she tensed the advance lever to feel it take. Retrieving the baseplate, she hooked it on, and, after advancing a few exposures, was done.

"Okay—" she gasped.

The light clicked on again.

"All set." Itzy smiled shakily.

But Johnny wasn't looking at her. He was looking at her camera bag by her feet.

"Why, Itzy Nash!" He smiled, one corner of his mouth upturned in mock seriousness. "Hasn't anyone ever told you never to leave your bag on the floor?"

"Yes, you'd be surprised." She snatched up the bag. "I thought you didn't know anything about demons, Johnny." She thought of the Blue Room, of the click-clacking of the horrid creature she'd seen.

Might be a little late for that piece of advice.

18

Johnny pulled the demon hitch and the door slid open. Itzy took a picture of the intricate knot.

"Certain cultures believe having your picture taken will steal your soul," Johnny said.

"Yeah? Where did you say you were from?"

"I didn't."

They stood side by side, looking down the yawning hole.

"What's that smell?" Itzy asked.

"Fire and brimstone," Johnny said. He reached down and pulled on a rope ladder secured to the damp wall with a pair of rusted bolts. He soon disappeared down into the darkness. He paused, turned on his flashlight, and called up to her. "Come on—it's strong enough for both of us. Besides, if you fall, I'll be here to catch you."

Itzy gulped a lungful of air and reached down for the rope ladder. She tried to imagine Marilyn Monroe maneuvering down this dark passage. Steadying herself on the top rung, she let her foot drop into the shadows.

Johnny was waiting for her at the bottom, where the final few rungs were missing. When he could reach, he guided her over the treacherous drop and then helped her to the floor. Itzy noticed his hands around her waist were strong.

They were in some sort of bricked-up storeroom, dust-covered and forgotten. The floor was uneven, and Itzy found herself slipping on rocks underfoot. Ahead, a door was outlined in a blue-white fluorescent light.

"The coal room," Johnny whispered. "From back when they used to heat with it."

Itzy nodded.

From somewhere nearby, a small avalanche of derelict coal rumbled, eventually settling at her feet.

Johnny trained his flashlight on the coal-stained brick to one side.

"Look." He nudged her.

A pair of matching letters had been blacked on the wall with coal. They were written with a confident hand, curves and loops and graceful arcs. The beam of light framed them in amber. Itzy stared.

"Is that—?"

Johnny nodded, a twinkle in his eye. "I told you these were her tunnels. Some say she never really left them."

He clicked off his flashlight and the letters vanished. "You ready?" he asked. "Stay by me—they branch out and can get confusing."

"Wait." Itzy raised the camera and took a picture of where she last saw Marilyn Monroe's initials, now burned in to her mind's eye. "Okay."

Johnny cracked the door and a dagger of light lay at their feet. He listened for a moment and then nodded.

"All clear," he said.

All clear of what? Itzy wondered, looking over her shoulder.

They emerged into a shaft-like tunnel, also brick, but studded with florescent lights along the domed ceiling.

"The Carlyle was built in 1929, by one Moses Ginsberg, just before the stock market crash." Johnny turned to her. His face was smeared with coal dust, and she laughed. "And he spared no expense."

"Was Mr. Ginsberg aware of these tunnels?" Itzy asked.

"It's unclear." Johnny considered. "But no more interruptions of the tour, Miss Nash, or we will be here all night."

Itzy zipped her lips closed with her fingers.

"You see, Mr. Ginsberg—or Moe, as I call him—disappeared shortly after the hotel opened—at the exact time the banks foreclosed upon him. Now and then over the years there would be sightings of him, even sometimes as a guest in the hotel, but no one really knew for sure what happened to the man. The Carlyle flourished without him, however, and the hotel ledgers will show you an impressive guest roster—filled with kings and queens, aristocrats, and Hollywood stars. Over half of the apartments are residences, rather than rentals—no matter how important you are, if you are renting a room, you are still merely a 'transient.'

"Perhaps because of the exclusive clientele, or perhaps due to the missing Mr. Ginsberg, the hotel developed a reputation for secrecy. Strange goings-on occur and are handled internally. The *New York Times* calls the Carlyle the Palace of Secrets. There have been some big celebrity scandals here—and no one was ever the wiser. The Carlyle is the perfect place to hide something."

They had been creeping along the main tunnel when Johnny paused.

"A palace with buried secrets," he said meaningfully.

19

They had reached a crossroads of sorts, and the tunnel wandered off in various directions, all more or less threatening. Itzy shivered. Johnny's thin coat and her jeans were covered in coal dust.

"It's this way." Johnny pointed down a twisting passage to the right. "Or . . . is it this way?" He put a finger on his chin, pondering.

"Very funny."

"Which way do *you* think it is, Miss Nash?" Johnny asked.

"I told you to call me Itzy," she said. "And I wouldn't dare presume to know more than you—O expert guide."

"May I then commend you on your own expertise?"

"In what?"

"Why, on your expert taste in *guides*. If I do say so myself."

Itzy smiled. "Say, O guide, do you know anything about that unmarked room near my aunt's suite?"

"Unmarked room?" Johnny asked, turning to her.

"Yeah. Someone lives in there—and I think they're watching me."

"Now you're creeping *me* out. There are no unmarked rooms in the hotel, Miss Nash. What would Moe say?" He turned, gesturing grandly. "This way, *mademoiselle*." Johnny took the third tunnel, the one that burrowed down in a winding spiral, the mortar missing here and there and the joints of the bricks dripping with murky water. "Keep up. Those who lag behind get eaten."

"Say, how many other girls have you tried to frighten . . . I mean . . . given this tour to?" Itzy asked, as she crept along the slick brickface.

"None that lived to tell about it." Johnny turned, pointing the light down at their feet. He squeezed her hand in the dark. "Why, is it working? Are you scared?"

Itzy tried to sound otherwise. "Me? Not yet. Besides, nothing's more scary than Pippa and Mrs. Brill."

"You might have a point." He laughed.

There was a gap in the bricks here, a small jagged hole evident in the middle of the wall.

"Through there?" Itzy hoped she didn't sound as nervous as she felt. Whatever lay on the other side was hot, and the air was musty, and she heard the unnerving sound of water dripping around her. A deep, distant rumble pierced with an occasional mechanical clank. "What is it?"

"The dungeons," Johnny said solemnly.

They squeezed themselves through, and Itzy was hit with a blast of heat that made her eyes water. Squinting, she saw a long, low hall open up before them, the ceiling a maze of pipeworks and valves. Caged bare bulbs perforated the darkness at even distances, but did nothing to illuminate the far walls. These stretched on in either direction for what seemed far more than a city block. It was the innerworkings of the hotel, if not the entire city, she thought. She took several photographs. The noise was louder, too, and the heat had grown more intense. Talking was impossible. Somewhere ahead was the origin of the awful clanging.

"This is where they put people who can't pay their bills," he shouted, indicating one of the bricked-up recesses. "The king of Prussia stayed here for years—until a distant relative paid his debts." He signed for her to follow him, and, casting one last look at the dark opening behind her, Itzy did.

The pipeworks chamber was low—low enough that the pair could not stand. The stone walls were perforated with bricked-off passages, and where the bricks were missing, darkness spilled out. A few must have led somewhere, for the air they exhaled was damp and chill, and while the heat of the room was unbearable, Itzy found no comfort in the cold winds from those parts better forgotten.

She looked up. Strange stains coagulated along the pipes' undersides, beyond which was pitch blackness. Rats, cockroaches—anything could be hiding up there.

Johnny was already far ahead, and Itzy struggled to catch up, crawling under the low-hanging junction through an oily puddle. This was beginning to feel like less of a good idea than it had under the awning on Seventy-Seventh Street. What a strange afternoon—Luc's unlikely appearance at the photography store, and that gruesome horse and carriage afterward.

And the kiss.

Itzy somehow couldn't forget that kiss. If she closed her eyes, she could still feel it—effervescent—like little bubbles on her lips. And his smell. If it were a perfume, she'd sleep drenched in it.

The End of Days. Itzy thought of Luc brandishing that strange card from the train. What was it that had him so worried?

The Divah, she thought. *Luc's Demon Queen would surely feel right at home in the Palace of Secrets.*

"Hurry up! You don't want to wake whatever lurks in these old passages."

Itzy startled. Johnny was right in front of her, grinning.

"I thought the king of Prussia checked out," she said, looking over his shoulder. Something was moving on ahead, weaving in and out of the shadows. "Isn't that Pippa's dog?" Itzy pointed.

20

"Where?" Johnny spun around.

"Just there—see?" Itzy pointed again, but it was no use. The thing had moved off into the darkness.

"I don't see anything. You sure it wasn't a rat?"

"Only if the Carlyle's rats wear jeweled collars," Itzy said. "It was Paris—I'm sure. What's it doing down here?" Itzy felt a sudden rush of nervousness. "Where Paris is, Pippa can't be far."

"Pippa, down here?" Johnny snorted. "When Hell freezes over."

"It's only a matter of time before they notice the dog missing—and send out the search party."

"Better make a move then." He held out his hand, head cocked.

Itzy peered into the shadows. There was no sign of the animal, nothing at all. Johnny squeezed her hand encouragingly and she followed behind him. Soon they came to a small dented grating that had been unscrewed and lay propped before them.

Johnny went through silently and turned to help Itzy. They emerged from the dark pipeworks into a room of white. The walls and floors were industrial tile, circular drains scattered about the floor. A blast of steam hissed at them. Itzy's eyes ached in the brightness, but soon she could make out enormous steel washing machines, industrial dryers, and presses.

"Over there." Johnny pointed. "Beside the laundry chute."

Itzy saw a boxy door.

"The cargo lift. It's how they move the mountains of laundry around the hotel. That's how Marilyn did it—from there, it was smooth sailing up to the Presidential Suite. They say no one knew these tunnels like Marilyn."

A door opened and Itzy and Johnny crouched down behind a rolling canvas cart filled with towels. A burst of laughter filled the room like confetti—and was gone.

"This way," Johnny mouthed.

They ran the last bit—opening the far door onto a room filled with the staff's lockers. Johnny skidded to a halt and turned, pushing a tuft of hair from his face. Itzy liked the gleam in his eyes.

"Well?" he said, his cheeks flushed from the run.

"Well, what?" Itzy laughed.

"Welcome to the Carlyle."

"Why, thank you. It was a most interesting adventure."

"We're not done yet, Miss Nash."

"We're not?"

"I saved the best for last."

"Did you?"

"Are you hungry?"

"Actually, yes. Famished!"

"The kitchens are right there. Come—" Johnny froze.

"What is it?" Itzy asked. And then she heard it—tight, clipped tones. A familiar voice. It was the concierge, Wold.

"Quick!" Johnny turned, panic sweeping across his features.

Itzy looked around the room. There was a small, tidy desk that held a telephone and pad of paper; a chair was pushed underneath. Beyond, Itzy could just see a white-washed door, but it was closed and there was no time.

Johnny swung his locker open.

"In there?" Itzy was appalled. It was small. It was dark.

"I'll lose my job," Johnny pleaded.

The sound of the concierge's voice was louder now. The sharp click of his polished shoes rounded the corner. Itzy jammed herself into the locker just in time. The metal door clanged shut.

Itzy squeezed her eyes shut and tried to concentrate on her breathing. The muffled tones of Wold and Johnny sounded far away.

Itzy didn't like the dark because the dark took things.

The dark took her mother, all those years ago.

They had been at the cottage for the summer, her parents' retreat. There had been guests, Itzy remembered, but she was young—three or four. After a large, boisterous dinner, Itzy had fallen asleep in her mother's lap by the great stone hearth. Later, Anaïs must have moved her to the small couch, for she was tucked in up to her chin under a heavy, scratchy blanket. One of the guests had lingered, and their lilting conversation punctuated her sleep. Her parents were eager for the man to go, but he kept pouring himself more wine.

The next thing she knew, it was later, much later—and pitch black. The fire had burned itself out. At first, Itzy was disoriented, waking alone in the cold living room. Where was her mother? She listened. The cottage was old, very old, and its wood floors held gaps wide enough to lose a marble. Itzy heard the familiar creaking of the floor in the kitchen, but there was something else. A shuffling sound, as though someone were walking on a lame leg. A footfall, and a heavy dragging. A pause. The room smelled strange, bitter and burned.

Anaïs was there suddenly, but Itzy sensed that something was wrong. There was an old wooden ash bin to one side of the large hearth that was used to store matches and firewood. Itzy's mother pulled it out, and—kissing her once—closed her inside. Itzy did not cry out, because she felt something searching for her. Snarling, sniffing. Dragging itself upon the old floors, burrowing in the ashes of the hearth.

Time passed, and Itzy slept.

It was the last time she'd slept in the dark.

21

"Coast is clear," Johnny's face filled the slash of light as the locker door opened.

Itzy scowled, blinded. She had balled up Johnny's uniform jacket she had found hanging and used it as a pillow against the locker's partition.

"I see you made yourself comfortable," he joked. He held his hand to her and helped her from the opening. "That was weird. Wold doesn't come sniffing around here normally— this VIP has him really on edge. Let me make it up to you."

"If it's all the same to you, I think I'll end the tour here," Itzy said. She noticed her hands were shaking.

"You can't!" Johnny looked genuinely upset. "I've saved the best for last."

"Johnny, I'm tired. Maybe some other time."

"You gotta eat, don't you?" he begged.

"I guess."

"Then come. No more surprises." He crossed the room to the small door behind the desk and opened it, gesturing grandly. A set of stairs curved up to a short landing, and then turned, angling back on itself.

Itzy shrugged, curious. The stairs were narrow, but lit from above, and Itzy heard the tinkling of a piano in the distance.

"Go on," Johnny smiled.

Itzy listened. A snare drum rasped and she heard the low buzz of polite conversation. A sprinkling of applause, and then silence.

She mounted the steps.

The room was small and stacked with crates, but someone had cleared the center and a picnic of sorts awaited. As Itzy looked around, the music started up again, this time louder. A woman began singing, soft and low.

"Where are we?" she asked.

"Bemelmans Bar!" Johnny grinned. "Well, as close as I can get you. This is the stockroom. You like jazz?"

Itzy nodded as he pushed past her and stood in front of the makeshift table, set with the Carlyle's familiar china. He pulled out a crate draped in a tablecloth.

"Best seat in the house," he gestured.

"You did this?" Itzy asked, amazed.

"With a little help from the guys in the kitchen," Johnny nodded.

"You went through all this trouble for me?"

"Don't you like it?" Johnny asked.

"It's lovely," she said, and he beamed.

Itzy sat, and he pushed her crate in closer to the table. He leaned over and reached for the silver dome that hid her plate, and Itzy suddenly remembered the earwigs.

"Ta-da!"

Itzy peered at her plate tentatively, but it held a towering club sandwich. Little delicate pots of mayonnaise and mustard were off to one side, an impossibly small pickle glistened in the low light.

"I'm impressed," Itzy said.

"We aim to please," Johnny smiled, sitting down opposite her. Leaning forward, he lit a small votive candle, and its flames danced behind the glass.

They ate in silence, both quite hungry, serenaded by the jazz quartet in the next room.

The female singer launched into something soft and slow, and Itzy listened to her gravelly voice.

"So how do you know Luc?" Itzy hoped her voice was casual.

"Mr. Beauvais?" Johnny shrugged. "He's a big tipper."

"Luc stays at the hotel?" Itzy asked, surprised.

"Luc *lives* at the hotel. He's a resident. Tower Suite." He popped a french fry into his mouth. "How do *you* know him?" Johnny asked, eyes intent.

"He picked me up at the station." Itzy shrugged. *And then he kissed me.* "How about I take your picture now?" Itzy asked, changing the subject.

"Aw, you don't want to do that." Johnny flashed a genuine smile. "Have you seen Bemelmans yet?"

Itzy shook her head. "You know, you don't strike me as much of a jazz fanatic," Itzy decided.

"Itzy, nothing is as it seems."

"So I've heard."

"The bar's covered in murals. Painted by Ludwig Bemelmans. The guy had a thing for bunnies. It's really something."

"Bunnies?"

"Yup. The entire place—the walls, the lampshades—you name it. Covered in bunnies. Bunnies picnicking, bunnies ice-skating, bunnies frolicking in Central Park."

"I'm not really a bunny person." Itzy shrugged.

"Right. I forgot. Not much of an animal lover."

Itzy raised an eyebrow. "What do you mean?"

"Picking on poor little Paris like that." He smiled.

Itzy considered this. "That dog had it in for me from the minute it stepped into the lobby."

"That thing's got a brain the size of a pea."

Itzy nodded, but wasn't sure. The dog had seemed terrified of her duffel bag.

"So, you're here for the summer?"

"Yes." Itzy rolled her eyes. "My aunt pulled a vanishing act—sent a governess. Can you believe it? I'm seventeen!"

"Weird about your aunt."

"What do you mean?"

"No one ever saw her leave."

22

"Sit tight—there's just one thing missing." Johnny stood, brushing himself off. They were both streaked with coal dust.

"What do you mean?"

"It's not a meal without dessert."

"No—I mean, what do you mean no one saw Aunt Maude leave?"

"Oh." He shrugged. "Usually she's got us running around in circles with all those steamer trunks of hers. Guess this time she's finally traveling light."

A round of polite applause rose from the bar, and the band settled into another number.

"Back in a jiff." He touched his forehead in a mock-salute.

Itzy smiled, but she was distracted. Her ankle throbbed, and she stretched, wincing. The music had grown discordant, jarring, in the way that some jazz could. A trumpet screeched. Itzy stood—the music put her on edge.

She had seen her aunt's steamer trunks stacked in the closet of the Blue Room, she remembered, before slamming the door on that thing from her bag.

She checked her camera thoughtfully. She only had a couple shots left. Idly, she tensed the advance lever with her thumb; she could feel the film tightening from the pressure as she did. *A dying art*, Maurice had said. *Consider yourself warned.*

Looking up from the Leica, Itzy froze. The light from the stairs framed the stockroom door in a warm amber hue. In it was a tiny silhouette of a dog, its long shadow stretching out, writhing on the floor like a snake. Silently, Itzy took a picture.

"Paris!" Itzy called in her best Pippa voice.

The little dog cocked its head.

"That's right—come on," Itzy coaxed, but as she stepped forward on her sore ankle, pain radiated up her leg.

"Ow!" she gasped.

In a flash, Paris shot off into the dark, and, swearing under her breath, Itzy found herself following.

At the bottom of the narrow stairs, Itzy skidded to a halt. Off in the direction of the kitchens, Itzy heard Johnny, joking in familiar tones with a few of the staff. But Paris had disappeared through the door to the laundry.

Itzy threw open the door and blinked in the bright room. Several women in white uniforms were stationed by the industrial steam presses, and they stopped their work to look at Itzy.

"Did you see a dog?" Itzy asked, but they stared at her blankly. "*Perro?*" she asked in her grade-school Spanish. One of the women nodded and pointed, and Itzy dashed off again. "*Gracias,*" she shouted over her shoulder.

At the end of the tiled room, Itzy stared at the entrance to the pipeworks. The grating was still open, the air smelled like rot.

"Stupid dog," Itzy swore.

The pipeworks were no less intimidating on the second viewing, and Itzy tried not to look at the dark recesses set in the brick walls. The heat was stifling.

"Paris," she called weakly, and then when there was no answer, again, louder.

Sighing, she steeled herself and crawled forward on all fours.

Itzy called for the dog several more times but it soon felt futile—Johnny would be wondering where she'd gone. She angled herself around so she was staring back at the grating—a small rectangle of light. She had come farther than she thought.

Something scampered along the pipes above her head and Itzy cringed. Whatever it was had upset years of filth, which drifted down upon her. Squinting, Itzy began crawling back when she heard a familiar barking.

Itzy scrambled forward toward the barking, but then heard a muffled thud.

"Paris?" she whispered, eyes wide.

The silence was followed by a sickly wet crunching.

Itzy's mind reeled. She was suddenly acutely aware of the dark. *Forget Paris,* she thought. She never should have come after that ridiculous dog. She crept forward, panting. She focused on the distant grate, afraid to blink, hitting her head more than once on the low-hanging pipes, white stars drifting in front of her eyes. Still, she never looked away from the small rectangle of light, hurrying her pace with each second as it loomed larger.

And then, simply, it was gone.

Something had stepped in front of the grate—something big. Something—judging from the crisp outline of matted hair and thick, disfigured legs—completely terrifying.

Somehow, Itzy managed to keep her head. With shaking hands, she felt desperately for her camera and took a picture. It was only when she felt something warm close around her ankle that she started screaming.

23

Itzy kicked with all her might and rolled, arms wrapped protectively around her camera. She crawled the rest of the way until she met a wall and sat, crouched against it, trying to catch her breath. She realized she was in one of the recesses, and, peering around the corner, she could again see the rectangle of light from the grate.

Whatever she had seen was gone. But where?

Panic rose in her throat and she felt lightheaded. Steadying herself against the damp wall, she fought to control her mounting terror. She pictured the sunlight at the cottage in Brittany, its pale yellow. She saw, in crisp Technicolor, the detail of her father's garden, the warm hearth of the living room, the smell of ashes. She heard the sound of the lone guest who had stayed late into the night after that last, final dinner.

Itzy felt around blindly.

Her hand fell on something small, furry, and lifeless. She recoiled—it couldn't be Paris, she told herself. It was too cold. Too stiff.

Searching the other way, Itzy crawled farther into the recess, using the brickface as a guide. But her stomach sank as the wall soon met with another, and she realized she had reached a dead end. The recess was merely a few feet deep, but at least she could stand. Desperately, she felt along this new wall, fingernails digging into the mortar, pulling, scratching, searching for any opening.

Something was carved here; she was sure of it. Words in stone, like a grave. Blindly, she ran her hands over them. They weren't words; they were letters, she realized. A matching pair.

Relief poured over her. Marilyn had been here. These were her tunnels, after all.

A narrow opening let off onto some wooden stairs, leading up. But as she felt her way along them—crawling in desperation on her hands and knees—she heard something from below. A shuffling sound, as if someone were walking on a lame leg—a footfall and a heavy dragging. A pause.

The same noises she had heard as a child in the ash bin.

24

It took several moments for Itzy to realize she was above-ground, for although there was a window, it was dark out. The headlight of a car traced its way across the ceiling. She was in a small room, sparsely decorated, with a lone cot. A black satchel was the only other thing in the bedroom, the kind favored by medical men. It was on the floor.

She leaned against a tall and narrow door of thickly painted wood. Her heartbeat rattled in her head and she shut her eyes, catching her breath. With shaking fingers, she slid the flimsy latch, locking the door. She put her ear to the door, listening.

She had heard that noise before, that terrible dragging, the corrupt footfalls. The stench of rotten eggs filled her nose, and with it the panic returned.

Another car's lights passed by, this one slower, and Itzy followed the beam of light along the ceiling and down the far wall. Strange, burned markings were traced there, black symbols against the old paint. The smell was of acrid powders: flint and sulfur. A small metal table held peculiar tools, menacing scalpels, a few rusted clamps. A roll of yellowed gauze.

A wave of revulsion passed over Itzy.

There was another door across the room, and she rushed for it. Throwing it open, she staggered into the next room, upsetting a small table, which crashed to the floor. A bulky beige hotel phone came crashing down, too, smashing on the floor with a hollow metal tang. Rows of square buttons flashed sedately along the phone's face. The impact had knocked the earpiece loose, and it hung like a ghoulish eyeball from a ganglion of colored wires.

"Evening, Dr. Jenkins, what can I do for you?" the earpiece said.

Itzy looked around the room. She was obviously in a medical office of some sort. Framed certificates were clustered on the wall. A rich oriental carpet lay upon the floor. Beside her was a glass-front cabinet containing rows and rows of gleaming ampoules. The light caught them in just such a way that they twinkled attractively. She tried the cabinet door, but it was locked.

"Dr. Jenkins?" the voice called hollowly from the broken phone.

Itzy knew that voice.

It was the concierge's.

Itzy took one last look around Dr. Jenkin's office. There was a door to the street, she could see—and another more familiar one. This let her out into the black polished marble and gleaming gilt of the Carlyle's ground floor, a hallway with other offices—all closed and locked at the late hour.

Music from Bemelmans washed over her. Itzy jumped at the sound of a woman's laughter, but when a woman appeared from around the corner, giddy, she stopped short at the sight of Itzy, backing away in fear.

Itzy looked down at herself. Her Leica was in one piece, but her clothes and hands were streaked in dirt and grime, and something dark and oily was splattered on her jeans. *I must make quite a picture.*

She slumped down, leaving a trail of grime on the pristine wall. When a familiar voice spoke beside her, she was too tired to care.

"Miss Nash. I see you have been enjoying your stay," Wold said.

Wold accompanied her the rest of the way to the elevators and ushered her onto the first one.

"Eighteen," he told the elevator operator, an older man in an ill-fitting version of Johnny's uniform, hunched with age.

Itzy turned, facing the concierge. She straightened her shoulders.

"Miss Nash," his voice held none of the reprimand she was expecting. "May I suggest a nice hot bath? And some sleep." He looked at her intently. "Who knows what tomorrow brings."

25

The flowers on the eighteenth floor had been refreshed, the bouquet changed for something bright purple and thorny. Itzy stared at the flowers for a moment and reached out and broke one off. It was nice to hold something living, of the earth, after being underground. She held it to her nose as she rounded the corner.

The hallway stretched out, affording her a perfect view of her aunt's suite at the far end. Itzy walked halfway and stopped. The door to 1804 was slightly ajar.

Itzy's fatigue vanished and adrenaline coursed through her body again. Her mouth went dry.

She had locked the door; of this she was certain. Maybe it was housekeeping—didn't maids come and go in hotel rooms at all hours?

She took a tentative step forward.

But maids—housekeeping in general—came with carts, did they not? Carts with linens and soaps, shower caps and terry robes. Little packages of nice-smelling things. There was no telltale cart in the hall. And her aunt's door opened only into darkness.

Itzy paused, torn. She dreaded facing Wold again. But which was worse? What new terror awaited her in her Aunt Maude's home?

Itzy didn't have to wait for an answer, as—with horror—she saw the dark-suited figure of Dr. Jenkins emerge from the suite and turn to lock the door. He removed something from his breast pocket and hung it on the doorknob. Beneath the Carlyle insignia were the words:

DO NOT DISTURB

In panic, Itzy pressed herself against the wall. Any moment he would turn and see her. She had no time to run.

Something hard was at her back, she noticed. A knob. The unmarked door.

Out of the frying pan, into the fire, she thought. Desperate, she turned and wrenched the doorknob. With a soft click, it opened inward.

26

This suite faced west, like Aunt Maude's living room, but that was where the similarities ended. The room was wide and bright and dominated by a large white grand piano. In fact, everything was white, and standing before it all, hands on her hips, was a woman unlike any other Itzy could remember seeing—and yet, this wasn't entirely so. Her face was strangely familiar.

"Well, if it isn't our intrepid explorer," the woman said in a smoke-stained voice. Someone had been playing the piano, but the music abruptly ceased.

Itzy stared at the woman in amazement. In the way of many aging rock stars, she was all sinew and veins. Her face was lined, yet somehow ageless. Her eyes were sharp, and her hair was cut into a blunt bob and dyed candy-apple red. Her thin arms were weighted down in a heavy array of bangles, which clinked as she moved. She wore a pair of leather pants, but what drew Itzy's eye was the scarf around her neck. It was silk, and patterned, and tied in an ornate knot—a demon hitch.

The woman smiled.

"You're never too old to wear leather," she said, gesturing, a sparkle in her eye.

Itzy liked her immediately. "Wow—you're that movie star, Ava Quant, aren't you? You're supposed to be dead!"

"They haven't killed me yet," the star scoffed. Ava crossed the room to Itzy. "Here, let me take a look at you. Underneath that layer of dirt, you're the spitting image of your father!"

"You know my father?" Itzy's jaw dropped.

"Of course I do. Jack Nash, scholar, obscure French history. *Everyone* knows your father."

Itzy allowed herself to be led into the room. A figure rose from the piano bench.

"Luc," Ava said. "I do believe she's brought you a flower."

Itzy looked at her fist where she still grasped the purple thistle from the hallway. Her cheeks were fiery ovals.

"Oh, don't mind me." Ava smiled, prying the flower from Itzy's grasp and threading it through Luc's lapel. "When you get to be this old, you call it as you see it."

Ava stepped away, leaving Luc staring at Itzy.

Itzy's head spun, but not unpleasantly, and she felt weak at the knees. His amber eyes searched hers. Vaguely, she was aware of Ava's voice on the phone behind her.

"Room service?" the movie star said. "Send me tea for three—yes, three. I have visitors, believe it or not. Oh—and a cabbage. Yes, a cabbage. You know, big and round—about the size of a head."

27

"Okay, kid. Show us what you got." Ava leaned back on her sleek, white sofa and crossed her legs.

Itzy looked at Luc, confused, but Luc was inspecting his shoes intently.

"What do you mean?" Itzy asked.

Ava smiled encouragingly, waiting. Itzy shifted her weight from her sore ankle. A frown appeared upon the star's face.

"*C'est une blague, n'est-ce pas?*" Ava turned to Luc, who had now turned his attention to his nails. "She *is* the scholar's daughter, is she not?" Her tone was cautious.

Luc nodded.

"And she is your *charge*, yes?"

Luc nodded again, smaller.

"Did you teach her nothing?"

A silence hung over the room.

"I was forbidden," he finally said.

"What?" Ava stood suddenly, a clatter of bangles jangling on her wrist. Itzy was surprised at how quickly the woman moved. Luc and Ava were soon conferring across the room, and Itzy could make out the movie star's angry tones. "You knew of this and did nothing?"

Luc towered over Ava, his words too low for Itzy to grasp, but his face was tormented.

"All these years, Maude was right! She warned me, but I didn't believe it." Ava cast a quick, withering glance at Itzy. "Just look at her. The poor thing looks meeker than a dormouse."

Itzy felt a stab of anger, and she clenched her fists.

"There are certain *expectations*, Luc. She was supposed to be trained."

"Excuse me—Miss Quant?" Itzy narrowed her eyes. "Luc? Hello? Could somebody tell me how you know my *father*?"

Itzy realized she had been shouting.

Ava turned, and Luc stormed over to the window. The star sighed, the anger vanishing. "I studied with him," Ava said simply.

Itzy sank onto the sleek white couch.

"You what?"

"At the Institute."

"What Institute?"

"The Hermès Institute."

"I see." She thought of the shop on Madison Avenue, the rearing horse on top.

"It seems we have a little catching up to do, Itzy—but you're tired. I can see it's been a long day."

It *had* been a long day—the morning, her train ride, Grand Central—it seemed a lifetime ago.

"I'm not leaving until you tell me." Itzy glared.

Ava sighed, shooting Luc one last sharp look, and sat beside Itzy on the couch.

"The Institute is old—ancient, in fact. An ancient alliance of *exorcistes*, of scholars. We are demon hunters. Your father is the director."

"Isn't my father in Paris?" Itzy squeaked, suddenly unsure of anything.

"Yes, dear." Ava patted her knee. "The Institute is based there, although there are outposts everywhere in all the best neighborhoods, posing as fine luxury-goods shops."

"He's there teaching?" Itzy asked.

"Call it *research*."

"What sort of research?"

Ava looked at Luc, who was watching, his expression inscrutable.

"He's looking for the Gates to Hell, Itzy," Luc said. "Their last location was in Paris in 1789, around the time of the Reign of Terror, and there's reason to believe they will rise up there again."

"The Gates of Hell?" Itzy repeated. Her father was a professor of obscure French history, not a crusader to the Underworld.

"The demons are coming," Ava said simply.

Itzy thought of the pipeworks again, the dragging sound of the creature's footfalls.

"I think they're already here," she said.

28

"The last time the Gates appeared, Itzy, Marie Antoinette was queen of France." Luc had joined Itzy and Ava on the couch.

"That was over two hundred years ago," Itzy said.

"A blink of an eye for eternal beings." Ava smiled at Luc. "That was a particularly difficult time for the Institute—the chaos of the French Revolution, the peasant revolt. People got carried away. We lost control." Ava's eyes narrowed. "There were riots in the streets every night, demons and innocents torn from their beds. Blood lust. It was lawless. No one can say for sure how many demons were banished during the Terror. We are at a bit of a disadvantage, you see. Most of our records—dating back to ancient times—were lost in the uprising." Ava grew thoughtful, her voice low. "Still, she almost succeeded."

"She?" Itzy repeated.

"Marie," Ava said, blinking.

"Marie Antoinette?"

"Really, my dear. Haven't you been listening to me at all?"

"Of course," Itzy stammered. "I just—" She paused. Inexplicably, a rhyme her father taught her as a child ran through her head.

Keep the demons from your stair
  —find her lair, find her lair.
Keep the demons from your bed
  —off with her head, off with her head.
Keep the demons from your soul
  —heads will roll, heads will roll.

"She raised the Gates to Hell, but we succeeded in stopping her before they were opened," Ava said.

"Are you saying Marie Antoinette was a demon?" Itzy asked quietly.

"Not just any demon, my dear."

Itzy looked at Luc, who finally returned her stare. His amber eyes made her stomach feel funny.

"The Divah," Itzy said, her voice flat.

"*Touché.*" Ava stood, walking to an orderly shelf. "She was beheaded just in time. Demons are not the coarse, horned and beaked creatures of medieval paintings, Itzy. No, they appear, for all intents and purposes, very much like you and me." She returned with a large book, full of glossy, richly colored prints. "Oh, there were simpler times, I assure you, when a demon was a demon and there was no guesswork involved identifying one. But these days their faces are smooth, youthful, perfected by surgeons."

"But the thing I saw in the basement—" Itzy said.

"Things from Hell are corrupt—rusted, broken, or defiled. But not everything from Hell is a demon, Itzy. And not all demons are queens."

Ava placed the heavy book on Itzy's lap, and Itzy examined it. The book was open to a portrait. She recognized it immediately. She knew this painting—she had seen it on her father's wall beside his desk, where he had torn it from a catalog. Marie Antoinette stared back at her from the opened book, her porcelain skin smooth and supple, her hair piled high upon her head in a wig of lavish blonde curls, her waist impossibly thin. Her cheeks flushed, her lips scarlet. A dimpled chin. She leaned on an ermine fur upon a cushion, a frilled ribbon tied around her neck.

"Do you see?" Ava asked, waiting.

Itzy peered closer at the reproduction.

"Her eyes, child. You can tell a demon by its eyes."

Itzy stared again. Indeed, the queen's eyes shone with an inner light—a humanizing twinkle, both bemused and coy. Even from the page, they held her gaze.

"Relax. It's like looking at the surface of a still pond—and then shift your perspective to beneath the surface. Look deep into the water, to the bottom. To the rocky depths. You'll get it. It will come, in time. A fever helps."

Itzy did as she was told. The surface of Marie's eyes were glassine, and Itzy stared at them. She let her eyes relax, and soon she was aware of only the weight of the book on her lap and the likeness of the last queen of France upon it. What Itzy had first mistaken for a touch of humor now seemed to be an expression of haughty arrogance. Relaxing further, she saw that beneath this was a vast, eternal depth—small windows, she thought, into another world—not a winning place, she realized, but a place of torment. These were eyes of the wicked, the devious—not at all human. They were dark, congealed pits. Itzy felt her stomach clench. Marie Antoinette's eyes were like those of a beast.

The book slid from Itzy's lap.

"You will know a divah by her eyes." Ava nodded, satisfied. "But don't worry. The males are easier. Devhils carry pitchforks. Later, when you're up for it, we will discuss the entire diabolical menagerie." Ava ticked off a few on her fingers. "The sympathies—some of those you are aquainted with, such as earwigs. There are spectres, servants and spies, fiends, imps, acolytes, conjurers, fanaticks. The fanaticks are some of my favorites."

"And the woodwose," Luc said bitterly.

"Yes, of course. And the woodwose." Ava looked at him with pity.

"But Marie Antoinette is long dead!" Itzy heard herself say.

"The arch-demon that inhabited her can never die," Ava said. "And she has unfinished business. Marie Antoinette was interrupted by the guillotine. Now, the Divah's back to finish what she started. And, Itzy, she's coming to the Carlyle."

A discreet knock sounded from the door. Itzy jumped.

"Ah!" Ava spun on her heel. "I do believe it's teatime."

A white-uniformed waiter rolled a room service cart over to the far wall, beside the balcony door. On it was a silver tea service, a tiered platter of scones, finger sandwiches, and a familiar domed plate cover. Ava waited for the man to leave before continuing.

"You'd be surprised how many celebrities are drawn to the work of demon hunting. I was recruited at the height of my career. Demons are drawn to fame, you see, so it's helpful for demon hunters to be famous."

"Marilyn Monroe!" Itzy gasped. She thought of the tunnels, Marilyn's reassuring monogram.

"While some critics have questioned Marilyn's acting talent, there can be no dispute about her demon-hunting abilities." Ava peered into the teapot, approvingly. "Marilyn was one of our brightest stars. In the end, though, those demons got her." She held up a delicate teacup. "Sugar?"

Itzy shook her head, wide-eyed.

"Who—who else is a scholar? A demon hunter?"

"In time, you will meet the few of us who remain. Many, like Marilyn, died in the line of duty. Even during the Old Reign of Terror, the demons far outnumbered us. And then we were at the height of our powers."

"Is everyone famous?" Itzy blurted.

Ava smiled. "We are all famous in our own way, Itzy. Even you."

"Me?"

"You're known the world over! At least, in our circles. The daughter of Jack and Anaïs Nash. Such high hopes we have for you. You're to follow in your father's footsteps."

Itzy took a sip of her tea and cradled the steaming cup in both hands. She thought of her father in Paris.

"Is my father in danger?" she asked quietly. "What will happen when the Gates open?"

"Hell, and all its coagulated souls, will have free passage here upon this mortal sphere. It is unthinkable. Your father's job is to prevent this from happening. He is an expert scholar and well prepared."

"But the demon carriage . . . the thing in the basement."

"There are always demons on the earth, causing mischief. Low-grade infestations, keeping scholars busy. How do they get here? They escape from Hell, or are called by incantations and allies through human error or bad judgment. Much in the way angels walk the earth, so too do demons—stretching back to the beginning of time. Angels, demons, and, yes, humans, are wrapped in an eternal embrace. The Divah has very powerful spies and allies in place already. But she still has not succeeded in opening the Gates of Hell. That, Itzy, must never happen."

"Why not?"

Ava blinked. Finally she said, "Well, Itzy. Then we are doomed."

"If the Gates are in Paris, why is the Divah coming here?"

"*Oui.*" Ava turned to Luc. "Seems our friend, Luc, invited her."

29

"What do you mean, Luc *invited* her?" Itzy asked, wide-eyed.

"That painting?" Ava said, pointing to the book on the floor. "The one of Marie Antoinette you just so successfully examined?"

Itzy nodded.

"Luc painted it."

"I'm sorry?" Itzy scoffed. "What?"

"Tell her," Ava commanded.

"I painted it," Luc said simply.

"You painted Marie Antoinette's portrait?"

"Many times over. I was her—um—favorite artist."

"Just how *old* are you?" Itzy demanded. She thought of his comment in Grand Central about his friend who painted the ceiling. At the time, it had seemed preposterous.

Luc shrugged. "It's complicated."

"So she's back from Hell for more?" Itzy asked, turning to Ava.

"Something like that."

Ava looked between the two of them and cleared her throat.

"The Divah has been known by many names throughout history. Many you would recognize from your history books. Many more, while thoroughly evil, have left no scholars behind to write of them and are lost to history. *Divah* is

the ancient Persian word for 'demon,' you see. Before she
was Marie Antoinette, the Divah inhabited the body of a
young nun in the fifteenth century who brought about the
Spanish Inquisition—a deadly witch hunt created by her
lies. We've charted her earlier incarnations, and each time
she appears, the world is ruin and ash. She is banished, she
regains her strength, and through the help of her servants
and acolytes, she returns in a different form for more."

They were finishing their tea, and Itzy was picking
halfheartedly at an apricot scone.

"What are you afraid of, Itzy—really afraid of?" Ava's
eyes narrowed.

Itzy thought of the creature in the basement, of that
last evening with her mother. There was only one thing.

"The dark," she whispered.

"Best stay away from it then."

Ava's bangles jangled as she walked briskly to the
room service cart. She lifted the gleaming dome from the
center. Beneath was a large cabbage on a silver platter, a
weak, anemic green.

"Your deepest, darkest fears are where your demons
lie in wait." Ava continued. "And demons have powerful
arsenals. They have the gift of foresight; they can speak
in tongues. They are great mimics and master manipu-
lators—they can and will say anything to get what they
want. They will hurl your innermost fears and secret vices
in your face. Demons kill, and demons possess. They'll
even summon the dead to their aid."

Ava lifted the cabbage and measured its weight in her
hand thoughtfully. "We hunters are *exorcistes*. We have in
our arsenal one sure thing: the *exorcisme*—a messy, unreliable discipline subject to the idiosyncrasies and failures

of each scholar. But there's another, newer way to stop a demon in its tracks."

Ava walked to the balcony and threw open the door. A night wind caught her vivid red hair, sending it whipping around her face like a flame.

"Come," Ava commanded.

Luc held out his hand to Itzy, and she joined him on the terrace, her heart rattling in her chest.

The balcony was unlit, but Itzy saw all she needed by the city's glow. Across the park, massive apartment buildings rose up against the slate sky like gravestones. Ava placed the head of cabbage on a worn wooden shelf, part of a much larger apparatus. It fit perfectly into a crescent-shaped lunette in the center. She lowered a similar worm-eaten board, locking the cabbage in place.

"With the Divah's return comes the New Reign of Terror." She shouted against the noise of the turnwheel. A honed blade gleamed in the low light, jerking upward with each rotation, clanking noisily. "It will put the Old Reign to shame."

Luc watched impassively, but Itzy felt his grip on her hand tighten.

"Wow—where do you get one of those?" Itzy asked.

The blade had reached its apex, and Ava steadied herself, staring up at the massive guillotine. She turned to Itzy and Luc, her eyes wild. "As Marie Antoinette was led shackled onto the wooden scaffolding before all of Paris, she stood before the jeering crowd, her hair as wild as her eyes were calm. Her last words were a promise. '*Je reviendrai*,'" she said.

I'll be back, Itzy thought.

"Don't blink," Ava warned.

And in an instant, it was over. In a straw basket at Itzy's feet lay the severed cabbage, neatly sliced in two. When she bent down to retrieve it, she noticed the basket was stained with something dark and rust-colored.

"The demon's head is cleaved from its host, dispatching the fiend back to the Underworld. The invention of the guillotine was a turning point in the hunt for demons. Our salvation."

"Not very practical, is it?" Itzy whispered to Luc.

"The blade that killed Marie Antoinette that day in the Place de Grève has never been found," Ava said. "All of Paris shook, it was said, as the demon was sent back to Hell. It rained ash and bone dust for thirteen days."

Looking up at Luc, Itzy saw a tear in the corner of his eye.

30

Itzy removed the DO NOT DISTURB sign from her aunt's doorknob, shouldering her Leica.

"Thanks, but I've got it from here," she said, turning to Luc.

"If it's all the same to you, I'd rather see you safely inside," Luc answered.

"I saw him leave, Luc," Itzy sighed. She regretted telling him and Ava about the doctor now. She was dead tired and her ankle ached.

Itzy stared up at him, annoyed. Luc stared back at her.

"Oh, all right then," she snapped. She took the key from her pocket and unlocked the door—holding it open in a grand gesture for him to pass.

"The doctor is not to be trusted," Luc said.

"No kidding," Itzy mumbled.

"Whew—mind if I open a window?"

"Be my guest."

Itzy followed him into the living room and frowned.

"Flies," he said, waving his hand in front of his eyes.

Itzy looked around. Flies were circling sluggishly in the center of the room. A few were large, like horseflies, angry and chaotic. Luc threw open the balcony doors, dispelling them.

"Where are they coming from?" Itzy asked, but Luc had disappeared down the hall toward her aunt's rooms.

Itzy wandered after him along the hall. It was crowded with art and lit from above. A framed black-and-white photograph caught her eye. It was a candid photo of a younger Aunt Maude sitting at an outdoor table in a sun-drenched garden. The photographer had apparently inter-rupted Maude's breakfast, which sat half-eaten on a plate before her, but instead of wearing her habitual mask of irritation, her aunt was laughing—staring brazenly into the camera—her reading glasses askew atop her head. This, however, was the least startling thing about the pho-tograph. For the garden, Itzy recognized, was her parents' garden in Brittany. And sitting beside her aunt, fingers sticky with jam, was a child.

Itzy wracked her brain for a memory of that day, but there was none.

"Let me take a look at that ankle," Luc called, his voice reaching her from the master bath. Itzy tore herself away from the image of herself as a young girl.

"How did you know about my ankle?" Itzy asked.

Luc leaned against a marble-topped sink, dark bottles of iodine and ointments arranged beside him from the medicine cabinet.

"The whole hotel knows about your ankle, Itzy," he said, a slight smirk evident at the corner of his mouth.

She sat beside him on a plush pouf of a stool and allowed her ankle to be examined. She watched his exquisite face as he gently lifted up her leg, resting it on his thigh. As he pulled her faded jeans up, Itzy cringed. The dull, pulsing pain grew sharper as he pressed his fingers upon it. Looking up at her sharply, he appeared about to scold her, but seeing the look of pain upon her face, he softened.

"Okay?" he asked.

She nodded, looking away.

"This might sting a bit."

"Is that what they told Marie Antoinette?"

Luc looked at her sharply.

"Sorry. Seems like a sore spot of yours. What did Ava mean when she said you invited the queen to the Carlyle?"

Luc was silent.

Vaguely, she heard a bottle open, the rip of a bandage. As Luc busied himself tending to the dog bite, her eyes wandered over the contents of her aunt's bathroom. Bottles of perfume and cotton swabs were lined up along a glass shelf; an old newspaper was yellowing on a nearby counter. Her body tensed as a searing pain shot up her leg, and she bit her cheek to keep from crying out.

She thought of the photograph in the hall, her aunt's buoyant expression. The way her glasses sat askew upon her head, a moment of uncharacteristic abandon. Her father needed reading glasses, too. In fact, he never went anywhere without them.

Itzy's eyes returned to the counter.

There, on top of the old paper, were her aunt's reading glasses.

31

The phone was ringing again, its jarring bell insistent in the living room.

"Aren't you going to get that?" Luc asked.

Itzy dragged her eyes from the reading glasses and looked at him, distracted.

"The phone. It could be important," he urged.

Itzy frowned. "It keeps doing that. I think it's broken. When I answer, there's nothing—just static," she said.

"It could be your father."

Luc was right. Itzy jumped to her feet, but her knee buckled from a sharp pain in her ankle. "I'm all right," she said before Luc could ask. Still, she was grateful when he offered a shoulder, wrapping his arm around her waist, and she hopped like this to the bathroom's extension. As she reached for the phone, she hesitated.

"Hello?" she whispered. She listened for a moment. She shut her eyes—it sounded like wind from across the world.

"It's for you." She held the phone out to Luc.

"For me?" he asked, surprised.

Itzy pushed the phone at him, and he slowly raised it to his ear. Itzy waited—they were standing very close, and his other arm was still wrapped around her, supporting her weight. She felt herself trembling. This close, Luc's features were flawless. Breathless, she watched his lovely eyes as a vague frown flitted across his features. A few stray flies circled overhead.

"No one's there—" he said.

"It's your conscience calling," Itzy explained.

"My *conscience?*"

"Yeah. It says it's time you start telling me what's going on around here."

Itzy took the phone from him, replacing it in the cradle.

They stared at each other, close, and her stomach flipped over.

"I don't have a conscience," he whispered.

"Just as I thought," Itzy replied.

"You don't understand," he said. An adorable crinkle appeared on his brow.

"Try me."

Luc was thoughtful. "I don't have a conscience, Itzy, because a conscience is something intrinsically human."

"What are you saying—you're not human?"

Luc held her glare, unblinking. His lips pouted and his cheekbones cut out at angles. But his eyes—the image of her own self reflected back in the golden spheres. Itzy suddenly felt light-headed. Her eyes strayed to the window, where she noticed many more flies were wandering between the glass panes, trapped.

"You're a demon, too?" she whispered.

A tragic look passed over Luc's face. "Itzy, I am no demon."

They were so close she could feel his breath.

Not demon, not human. Where does that leave us?

She held her breath, willing him to kiss her again.

The moment did not come. The phone had commenced its jarring ringing again.

"Let's get you to bed," Luc said, ignoring the phone this time.

Without waiting for an answer, he carried her, cradled in his arms, down the hall to the Blue Room.

"We'll talk about this tomorrow," he whispered, covering her gently with the thin wool blanket. He leaned down over her, concerned, brushing a lock of hair from her cheek.

"I never thanked you for that flower," he whispered in her ear. It was a miracle she could hear it over the thudding of her heart.

Far off, the elevator clanged, the vents rumbled. Luc sat on the edge of her bed with his hand in hers until she fell asleep.

When she awoke a few hours later, he was gone.

32

What had woken her? She struggled to remember. Perhaps it was a dream. She had the vague impression of something slipping away from her, something important. Alone, Itzy was staring at the powder blue ceiling, a phrase running through her head.

The End of Days is nigh.

She tried to fall asleep again, but the memory of the hairy creature from the basement kept returning to her. That, and the awful noises now coming from her closet.

At first, she thought it was her imagination, her utter exhaustion. Her ears strained to hear it again: a faint scratching from somewhere deep inside the closet— erratic, feverish. At times it seemed muffled, to disappear altogether, only to return with new vigor, closer. At the door.

She sat up, putting her feet on the floor, ignoring the closet.

She would get some milk—that would help her sleep. When she was little, this was exactly what her father would do for her. As she headed for the door, the strange scratching from the closet grew more desperate, but she did not look back.

My father went to Paris to find the Gates of Hell, she thought. *No wonder he didn't take me.*

In the small kitchen, she looked for a glass, but, strangely, none could be found. Each cabinet she opened was filled with one thing: cans—all bloated and dented. A hoard of putrid food.

She opened the refrigerator but instantly thought better of it. Obviously, her aunt had not cleaned it out before leaving. Still, a bottle of milk caught her eye, and she leaned in, reaching for it. This was a mistake, she saw. The stench was appalling. The bottle indeed once contained milk, but now was host to a curdled mass of writhing maggots. Black flies dotted the mixture, drowning in the foul liquid.

Itzy struggled not to gag, replacing the entire thing upon the shelf and slamming the refrigerator door.

The phone was ringing again, and a flash of hot anger coursed through her.

She raced into the living room and was relieved to see Luc had left the lights on for her. She picked up the receiver and slammed it down again, waiting. In the satisfying silence that followed, Itzy had an idea. She picked up the phone again, stabbing one of the illuminated buttons.

"Room service?" she asked.

"Good evening, Miss Nash," came the melodious voice.

"I'd like some warm milk, please. With a little vanilla, if you have it."

"Very good. Will that be all, Miss Nash?"

Itzy paused, thinking of the interrupted picnic with Johnny in the stockroom. "Actually, no. I'd like some dessert."

"A wonderful idea. What would you like?"

Itzy narrowed her eyes. "One of everything." She waited, wondering if this would be met with any disagreement.

"Excellent, Miss Nash. Will that be all?"

"No—there's something else." She looked around the living room. "I need something for these flies." She held her breath. Surely this was pushing her luck.

"Most certainly, Miss Nash," the voice said. "I have just the thing."

33

Itzy sat on her hands on a toile couch. The delicate fabric was patterned with a detail of huntsmen in a forest. One carried a torch, she saw—another a two-sided ax. She peered at it closer. Two children were running, eyes wide with terror.

She moved to a wooden straight-back chair.

The flies here had quieted, congregating in the corners and the walls. Occasionally a disagreement would break out, and they would buzz in tight, angry knots, but Itzy noticed a watchful calm would soon settle upon them, as though they were waiting for something.

"That's right," she said to the buzzing flies. "I ordered you up something special."

The doorbell rang, and Itzy jumped to her feet, and winced as pain shot through her ankle. She hobbled to the small foyer and threw open the door to the suite.

A lone figure stood before her, the crook of his cane draped over his forearm, a black satchel at his side.

"Good evening, Miss Nash," Dr. Jenkins said, a thin smile curling his lips up at the corners.

Itzy scanned the empty hall behind him desperately. The doctor reached out his arm, holding the door.

"Might I come in?" he asked.

Itzy stared at the doctor, dismayed.

"I'd like to take a look at your ankle," he continued. "I believe you have injured it."

She recognized his medical bag as the one from his office, and her stomach lurched.

"I didn't *injure* it," Itzy clarified. "I was *bitten*."

"Best take care of these things before they fester. Why, I've seen infections get the better of even the healthiest of persons—and once the rot sets in, well, there's really no choice other than to lose the limb. Gangrene is serious business. Of course—that was in the war. Things are rarely that drastic these days, wouldn't you say?" He paused, assessing Itzy. He cleared his throat. "I jest, Miss Nash. You've gone completely pale."

"Oh." Itzy attempted a laugh but it sounded thin, contrived. "I'm fine, doctor," Itzy said. "I took care of it myself, earlier. It feels much better."

"Miss Nash, I really *must* insist." Dr. Jenkins fixed Itzy with a look. "Surely your Aunt Maude instructed you to respect your betters here at the Carlyle?"

She moved aside for the doctor, who, after one curt nod, entered the foyer. He found the stand in the corner and placed his cane in it with a practiced gesture and then his bag upon the side table. He made a showing of unbuttoning his coat and opening the cloakroom. The task of hanging his coat was performed only after a full examination of the various furs hanging limply from the rod, as well as an inspection of the overhead shelf, which—as far as Itzy could see—contained only a selection of hatboxes. He lingered over one fur in particular, a showy fox, its long guard hair like an exotic caterpillar, its russet-colored pelts draping fully to the floor. The collar was trimmed with fox heads, and their black glassine eyes stared at Itzy.

She cleared her throat. "If you don't mind, I'd like to get this over with. I've had a long day."

"So I've gathered." Holding his bag, he pushed past her with a pronounced limp, entering the living room.

Itzy opened her mouth to apologize for the flies, but the doctor had vanished down the small hall toward the servants' quarters. She followed quickly.

She found him in the kitchen, peering into the cabinets, muttering to himself, scrutinizing the array of spoiled food. "Yes, yes," he said, tapping his fingers on the counter thoughtfully. He spun around, a feverish look of excitement on his shiny face, and a wisp of hair freed itself from the confines of his otherwise bald scalp. He continued down the hall to the Blue Room. There, he stopped short, sniffing.

"Is there something wrong?" she asked, sniffing too.

"Wrong?" His eyes gleamed. "Wrong? Hardly! No, child. Something is terribly, awfully, truly *right*." The doctor had been creeping toward the closet, and reaching it, he put an ear to the door.

Itzy eyed the closet nervously. The flies were thicker in her room, she noticed. She watched as one emerged from the crack of the doorframe. It wandered around in a disoriented circle, preening its wings, and then flew to join the others.

The doctor was listening intently now through his stethoscope, eyes closed.

"Dr. Jenkins, there's something in my closet, isn't there?"

A shiver overtook the man, and he tore himself away from the door. His eyes were bright, and when they found Itzy's, they appeared to see right through her.

"Doctor?"

Remembering the satchel in his hand, he looked at Itzy. "Right. Let's have a look at that leg." He patted the thin mattress with pudgy fingers, indicating Itzy should sit.

Beads of sweat dotted his brow as she did what was she was told. He opened his medical bag and rifled through it. She could hear the doctor's ragged breath as he bent over her, muttering occasionally to himself. She saw his head, the shiny circular patch of skin on his bald scalp, and she was reminded of the train—the lone passenger in her car. In his bag were more glittery ampoules and a long stainless steel syringe.

"Does this hurt?" he asked, prodding her ankle roughly.

She shook her head.

"How about this?"

Itzy bit her lip. His grip on her leg was fierce. From the closet, the scraping had begun again, low and insidious, but the noises—if he heard them at all—were ignored.

Turning his attention to his medical bag, he produced a metal hammer with a darkened rubber tip, and he tapped her knee. Her leg responded, reflexes firing. Her leg jerked. Itzy never had liked this feeling at her annual doctor's visits—body parts moving without her intention, a jittery loss of control—and she liked it even less now in the hands of Dr. Jenkins. Finally, he moved on to another tool. This one was vicious, rusty, and brandished for her inspection. He leaned in and, opening his liver-colored lips, a rush of fetid hot air poured out.

"A piece of advice," Dr. Jenkins said, his voice like a grave digger. "Be careful of the company you keep, your foolish explorations. The hotel can be a dangerous place for the uninitiated."

She thought of his bleak chambers, his small cot—the sinister scrawl upon the wall.

He knows I was in his office.

Itzy nodded, wide-eyed.

"You are to keep to your room at all times," he said, fingering his rusty scalpel. "We wouldn't want you getting *hurt*."

The little hairs on the back of her neck rose.

Dr. Jenkins straightened, his tone once again professional.

"Well then. I'm glad we had this little chat." He glanced offhandedly at her leg. "Everything seems to be healing nicely. Would you like something to help you sleep?" he asked, snapping closed his medical bag.

Itzy shook her head. She didn't trust herself to speak.

The doctor had examined the wrong ankle.

34

Itzy was changing into a pair of sweats and a fresh T-shirt when again the doorbell rang. Startled, this time she made sure to peek out the peephole. The fish-eye lens showed a small army of men in white coats waiting on the other side of the door.

She had forgotten about room service.

The bounty was brought in on three carts, which the waiters rolled efficiently into position by the toile couches. There was a bill, which Itzy signed with flourish, and when the staff had left, she turned to examine the carts.

The first cart held whole entire cakes—a towering chocolate buttercream, a wispy coconut bombe, and thin elegant tortes. Silver filigreed plates were stacked with delicate cookies and chocolate truffles. Next, a pot of whipped cream was dusted with cocoa, and coupes of ice cream sat in silver tubs of shaved ice beside steaming carafes of chocolate and caramel. Pillowy meringues floated in a thin, yellow custard within an enormous crystal punch-bowl, and Itzy poked at one.

On the last cart, Itzy found a pitcher of steaming milk beside a small silver dome. There were delicate teacups, and Itzy used one to pour herself some of the hot milk. She breathed in the steam, cradling the cup in her hands. It smelled of vanilla—and of home. She took a sip, and then another, and grabbed a sugar cookie from the platter. There were saucers, too—not at all like home—and Itzy placed the teacup and the cookie on one. She wandered over to the crystal punchbowl again, peering in. The white meringues bobbed like dead guppies. A fly was now swimming in it dispiritedly.

There was something faintly funny-tasting about the milk, and she put it down, as well as the half-eaten cookie. Returning to the gleaming dome, she lifted it.

On a silver tray was something small and cylindrical. At first she thought it was a single roll of film, for it was nearly the same size, but the scarlet print on its side told her it was something else. VENUS FLYTRAP, read the label. Flypaper. A small note on thick cardstock caught her eye.

Compliments of the Carlyle

She grabbed the roll of flypaper and returned to her bedroom.The flies circled lazily beneath the light.

Itzy approached the closet tentatively. The iron bed frame was too heavy to move. Working quickly, she pushed her chest of drawers across the room, leaving rough gouges on the lacquered parquet floor. She angled it against the door, leaning on it when she was done. No one was opening that closet.

Pulling out the bottom drawer, Itzy climbed on top of the dresser and produced the flypaper from her pocket. She found the taped closure of the roll, and slowly unrolled the sticky paper. It was a deep brown and slicked with viscous glue, glue that stretched in long stringy tendrils. The pull tab doubled as a thumbtack, and with effort she pressed the pointy end into the hard old wood.

Jumping down, she examined her handiwork.

The paper dangled in a limp spiral. Already several flies were attached, buzzing angrily. Theirs was not a happy fate, Itzy saw.

She crawled beneath the thin blue blanket, and with the lights burning, she fell instantly into a deep, dark sleep.

Quite a bit later, a bell tolled. This did not immediately strike Itzy as odd, because on the grounds of her father's university there was an old church whose chimes rang regularly. She listened. People were shouting. The window in the Blue Room no longer let out onto an air shaft, but rather, a vast open courtyard. It was thronged with people. The courtyard ended at the banks of a river, brown and turgid, but the city continued on long after, spirals of smoke rising from far off chimneys.

She struggled to sit up but her head felt wooden, and her ankle throbbed.

People were gathering, summoned by the bells.

An executioner stood beside a hulking guillotine in the center of the square. The blade gleamed, searing her vision.

"I sssssaid I'd be back," a soft voice whispered beside Itzy's bed.

Itzy turned—ghost-streaks of light followed her gaze, echoing the outline of the window. She felt dizzy and unbearably hot.

Somehow an enormous serpent stood before her. It was the serpent from the embroidery above her bed, and as so, its scales were made of iridescent threads. Its body was irregular, thickened from a meal, bulbous. It wore a human head, its face twisted and bloated.

"I am unssssstoppable," the creature gloated.

Itzy turned from the serpent, back to the square.

Itzy squinted at the executioner. He strutted about the scaffold. His body was barrel-shaped and he wore a black leather mask.

The bells ceased, and Itzy awoke in a cold sweat.

Her ankle was swollen twice its size, and she had a terrible thirst. She winced as she hobbled to the small bathroom across the hall. She ran the water in the porcelain sink for some time but it refused to get cold. She wrinkled her nose at the smell, like rotten eggs. She gulped it down anyway, finally, and with it several aspirin from an old bottle.

She looked down at her foot, not daring to check the bandages. She would ask Luc to look later. Something glittered in her reflection and she peered into the mirror, frowning. She parted the hair near her forehead. Overnight, several of her long brown hairs had turned silvery white. She half-heartedly plucked at a few before giving up.

Staggering back to her bed, the fever dream came rushing back at her. The serpent, the execution.

She stopped, staring at the far wall.

Her chest of drawers had been moved. The door to the closet stood open.

35

The governess was sitting among the pillows on the toile-covered couches. Her face had a shine to it, like a newly laid egg. Her hair was mousy, and her face was plain, bordering on ugly. Her jaw was set in the way of one unused to compromise. In her arms she clutched a lone, sturdy bag made from peeling paprika-colored leather that was charred in several places. The room, too, had a burned smell to it, Itzy noticed. The woman appeared to be wearing one of her aunt's furs—the fox she had seen the doctor admire—and had it wrapped tightly around her thin form, although the heat in the room was blazing. A rusted can sat beside her upon a Carlyle napkin, the metal of the lid a jagged wreck, a bent silver fork protruding at an odd angle.

"Hello?" Itzy said, surprised. "Are you my governess?"

"And who else would I be?" the woman replied, cross. She had a faint, unplaceable accent.

"I—uh—"

"Don't just stand there with that mouth of yours hanging open—something's liable to crawl in. Turn around, child. Let me inspect you. Ah—good, good. A bit scrawny—is this the fashion these days? I suppose you'll have to do." The woman sat at an odd angle, propped up by cushions. Itzy noticed a mouthful of unfortunate teeth.

"Now, make yourself useful and get the door. Something's making quite a racket in the hall."

"How did you get in here?" Itzy asked the woman. Her head pounded, she still felt feverish.

"Same as everyone else. Through the door." The governess sniffed.

Itzy peered at the woman closer. There was flypaper in her hair.

"Which door?" she frowned.

Itzy limped through the small foyer. She hardly recognized herself in the reflection of the gilt mirror. She had dark circles beneath her eyes and her hair desperately needed a wash. She peered through the peephole, but there was nothing.

Listening, Itzy thought she heard a hoarse yelp, followed by a labored dragging of nails.

She opened the door slowly and looked down at the source of the decrepit shuffling.

"Paris?" she gasped.

The tiny dog ignored Itzy and made its way past her slowly on a broken hip.

Itzy followed it into the living room where Paris attempted to jump on the governess's lap, but its ravaged hind legs crumpled beneath him.

"Oh, Mopsie!" the woman said, scooping up the broken animal. One of its back paws had been gnawed on. "How I missed you, little cabbage."

Itzy looked at Paris, incredulously. Something thick and yellow dripped from its eye.

36

Down the hallway, Itzy jabbed at the elevator button. When the doors finally opened, Itzy nearly collided with a passenger disembarking.

"Mrs. Brill?" Itzy gaped, before remembering her manners.

Mrs. Brill was carrying an unwieldy bouquet and her eyes were bright.

"Is it true?" she asked upon seeing Itzy, her face straining to achieve some sort of expression.

"Is what true?" Itzy frowned, making way for the woman and her bouquet.

Mrs. Brill didn't respond, but merely continued on her way, rounding the corner in the direction of 1804.

Itzy boarded the elevator thoughtfully.

"Lobby, please," she said.

An unfamiliar, unfriendly man wore the uniform today.

"Where's Johnny?" she asked him.

The man shrugged, not meeting her eye, and stopped the elevator at fourteen to let on a young, well-dressed couple. The remainder of the ride was completed in silence, Itzy's mind darkly contemplating the errand she had been given—to find Dr. Jenkins.

"Get me my servant," her new governess had ordered. "We are not amused."

"Your . . . *servant?*"

"Indeed. That doctor fellow. I had hoped for something better than *this.*" With Paris on her lap, the woman stared at her with those dark eyes while the dog cocked its head, showing its teeth.

Any further protests had died in Itzy's throat.

Dr. Jenkins's offices were on the other side of Bemelmans Bar, Itzy remembered, where the Carlyle had a row of tiny offices. But she simply couldn't bring herself to go. Itzy thought of the small, crooked cot in his back room, the strange symbols and unspeakable stairs that led below. Her governess would just have to summon him herself.

The front desk was unmanned when Itzy arrived, hoping for some word from her father. The staff was gathered in a tight knot conferring with Wold, their backs to her. Itzy looked at the concierge. His face was red, and his eyes shined, lit from above.

Her own head felt hot; the lights from the chandelier were burning her retinas. She surely had a fever. Itzy wondered when the aspirin would start working.

There was a commotion behind the desk as Wold's gathering dispersed, and several of the uniformed staff scurried to the elevator behind the concierge. Itzy watched as Wold boarded the elevator, his gloved finger working the floor buttons himself. He patted his hair into place and yanked at the flower in his lapel, setting it straight. As the doors slid closed, he was still issuing orders to his personnel.

Itzy watched as the remaining desk staff fanned out. Her eyes came to rest on the Carlyle Restaurant, off the lobby. Itzy had never paid the restaurant any mind—it had always seemed empty, and today was no different. A towering vase of flowers dwarfed the sole occupied table.

It was the young couple from the elevator, Itzy saw, having breakfast. They were seated in a plush banquette, quite close. The man leaned across the table to touch the woman's cheek and whispered something that made her laugh—a bright splash of gold flashed from her neck as she threw her head back.

A table in the corner caught Itzy's eye. The restaurant was not as empty as she had thought.

Itzy had been thinking about Luc just now, as she watched the couple from the elevator. And there he was. He was not alone.

Once, when she was younger, Itzy spent a day at a museum with her class. Bored, she had wandered on ahead and, rounding a corner, she saw an older girl with her mother. Itzy often looked at girls with their mothers with a certain curiosity, and she did so then. Only, this girl was so completely striking, so breathtaking, that she didn't quite know what to do with her eyes. Itzy watched like a deer in the headlights, frozen, until the girl and her mother had passed.

Pippa Brill was like that.

Itzy watched now, unable to look away, as Luc's arm reached out across the white tablecloth to take hold of Pippa's hand at the Carlyle Restaurant.

Finally, with her face burning, Itzy turned on her heel and made for the revolving doors.

37

Outside, the overcast day scalded her feverish eyes and tears streamed down her face. She wiped them away angrily with the back of her hand.

It was stifling out, but she hardly cared. The humidity pressed down upon her head and the air smelled of gasoline, of burning things. Sleek black town cars idled softly against the spotless curb. She walked, head down, staring at the sidewalk through bleary eyes. When she did raise her head, people leered at her—deviant, hungry looks in their eyes. In the sky, carrion birds were circling on unseen vortices—wide wings in search of prey.

She saw the neighboring neon cobbler's sign before she saw Maurice's shop, and, hurrying now, she rushed upon the doorway to Obscura & Co. Itzy ignored the CLOSED sign and entered, the door triggering a far-off bell.

Maurice was waiting behind the counter, paging through an open catalog. Soft French pop music drifted from the speakers. Beside him on the countertop was a flat wax-coated envelope and, without looking up, he pushed it toward her.

"Photography, of course, is an exercise in opposites," he said, lifting his head.

Itzy paused, catching her breath.

"Black and white. Light and dark. It is no accident that film shoots in the negative, and only through developing is the positive revealed. It requires great skill to navigate such extremes, to mold them into something of worth. I say *worth*—for it is not always a thing of beauty we create, now is it? A photograph can be brutal. What's the one thing a photograph always reveals, Itzy?"

Itzy shook her head, dumbstruck.

"A photograph always reveals the *truth*."

Itzy reached for the envelope.

"Oh," Maurice added casually. "It helps that the silver crystals on the film's emulsion are particularly good at picking up the supernatural."

He reached into the counter below him and plunked a small black object down on the glass.

"Don't say I never gave you anything." He smiled.

Itzy looked. It was a cylindrical object meant for looking through. Small white letters around its rim spelled out LOUPE.

"Do you have anything for me?" Maurice asked.

Itzy looked momentarily confused, but then she reached into her pocket, remembering. She pulled out her roll of film from the basement.

"How did you find the IR?"

"That remains to be seen." She smiled. "Maurice, what war did you know Luc from?"

Maurice studied Itzy, and she felt her face go scarlet. "It was a long time ago, Itzy. Luc disgraced himself, sadly. You are his last hope, you know."

"*I'm* his last hope?" Itzy scoffed. The image of his hand on Pippa's was burned into her memory.

"Luc lost something very, very rare. And very, very powerful. He is devastated, but not as devastated as we all shall be if it's not returned. And time is running out." Maurice pushed the roll of film into a small envelope.

"So. Shall I put a rush on this?" he asked, holding it up.

"Seems so." Itzy suddenly felt very tired.

The table by the lightbox was empty today, but the paper coffee cups spoke of a recent gathering.

She slid the contact sheet out from its casing and examined the print, flicking the toggle switch on the lightbox. The film had been cut into several segments and exposed to a timed beam of light, its images revealed on the paper to exact scale. Numbers, sprocket holes, and other manufacturing details ran along the edges. There was a slight tang to the paper's smell; the processing chemicals reminded her of home.

"How did Luc disgrace himself?" Itzy asked peeking up at Maurice.

"That is Luc's story to tell, isn't it?"

Itzy looked down at the contact sheet again, placing it on the light. The first few images were of home, Itzy saw. She had taken several photographs of her house, as an exposure test—but also to remember it by. An unexpected pang of homesickness hit her. There was one of her father looking harried the day he left for the airport.

A few were from the Blue Room, and Itzy recoiled at the blurred image of the dark, skittering creature as it ran to her closet. It was shadowy and it seemed to defy light, but Itzy saw that this was no rat; it had giant pincers protruding from its abdomen.

Her eyes then wandered to an image of Luc. It was outside Grand Central, the day she had met him. She held the loupe up to her eye and peered through the magnifying lens.

The wind had just stolen his umbrella, and he was reaching for it. Faint crescents rose from his sides. They were thin and uneven, but unmistakable. She traced them with a fingernail.

They were wings.

38

The walk back to the Carlyle was uneventful. She was half-expecting the horse and cruel carriage, so she walked quickly and kept her head down. She charged through the lobby in much the same way, hoping desperately to make it back to her aunt's suite and examine the photographs further without seeing Luc or Pippa.

"Miss Nash?" the desk clerk called politely as Itzy jumped. "I beg your pardon. There's a package here for you."

Itzy smiled wanly and walked over. She thanked the clerk and stared down at the package. It was thin and wide and wrapped in plain brown paper. Her name was written on the front in careful scrawl. She tore it open.

Inside was a burnt-orange box with an excess of brown ribbon, small embossed brown lettering spelling out the word HERMÈS. The box was filled with starched tissue, closed with an elegant oval sticker, which, when Itzy peeled it away, revealed a vibrant silk scarf. There was a note, and she read it eagerly.

Itzy,
Make sure to tie it properly. The correct presentation concentrates the demon-fighting power of the scarf in a tight mace-like knot.
  Yours in arms,
    Ava

Itzy unfolded the scarf carefully. It was the most beautiful thing anyone had ever given her.

Several papers drifted down to the floor, freed from its folds. More reading material from Ava. When Itzy bent down to retrieve the scattered papers, she felt the nail of a long, thin finger jab her on the shoulder.

Itzy straightened. The air smelled of perfume.

"Back to bite the other ankle?" she asked, turning.

Pippa had been crying, Itzy realized, and she quashed a momentary pang of sympathy.

"Paris is missing." Pippa sniffed as her eyes filled with water. Long streaks of her perfect skin peeked though a layer of makeup—trails of earlier tears.

"Last I looked, Paris was still in France," Itzy managed, before sighing. "I'm sorry—but it's a dumb name for a dog," she muttered.

Itzy looked at the girl. She was a mess. Her eyes were swollen and her nose was red. "What do you mean *missing?*" Itzy asked carefully.

"Missing. As in *gone*. I haven't seen her since yesterday."

"Right about the time she was digging her pointy little teeth into my ankle, you mean?"

Pippa sagged again. "I was hoping—I don't know. Luc said I should ask you."

This was a stunning piece of news, and Itzy tried hard not to betray her surprise.

39

"You look awful," Pippa said, blinking, and finally fixing her eyes on Itzy as though seeing her for the first time.

"You're one to talk," Itzy shot back. Her hand fluttered to her forehead. "Actually, I don't feel so good."

"I'll call the doctor—"

"No!" Itzy's voice echoed throughout the lobby. Pippa looked startled. "I mean, no, thank you. I just need some rest."

"I'll walk you to the elevator."

Itzy looked at her suspiciously.

"Come on, it's the least I could do. I promise—I won't bite."

Itzy smiled despite herself.

At the elevator bank, the girls were quiet.

"Nice scarf," Pippa offered.

"Thanks," Itzy said. "It was a gift."

"A timeless accessory."

"Something like that."

The scarf was a large square, and it ran through her fingers like water. The corners were rolled and hand-stitched—a thing of beauty. Ava had chosen one with gold and rich deep reds. The border was an intricately forged chain of gold, with a pair of beautiful wings in the center—their scarlet and gilt feathers heavy and luxurious, so detailed they might drift off the fabric and float to the floor.

"In Paris, at the Hermès shop on the Rue du Faubourg Saint-Honoré, they do this fabulous thing," Pippa said. "Have you been?"

Itzy shook her head.

"The glass countertop snakes around the whole showroom, and in it are nothing but scarves. Hundreds upon thousands of scarves. When you ask to see one, the shop clerk—like a magician—will shake it out at you in such a way that the silk billows and floats slowly before your face, settling down on the countertop on a puff of air. And then it's whisked away for another one. The room is near silent— just shimmering colors, the sounds of silk sliding through practiced fingers. It's just you, and color, and waves and waves of silk floating on clouds of air. Rather perfect."

And all that concentrated demon-fighting power in one place.

The elevators were taking longer than usual, and Itzy was growing impatient. She remembered Wold earlier; his crisp demeanor had abandoned him as he had rushed across the polished floor. "This VIP will be the death of Wold," she said aloud. "The entire hotel seems on edge. I hope they just hurry up and arrive."

"Mother says she already has."

"Really?" Itzy was surprised. "Who is it?"

"Some royal." Pippa shrugged. "A shadow queen, I'm told. Deposed—in exile. Waiting to regain her throne."

In the elevator, Itzy watched as Pippa fished out a tube from her purse and applied scarlet lipstick to her lips in two perfect swipes. "I think I know where you can find your dog," Itzy blurted. "But it's not pretty."

"How bad can it be?" Pippa asked her reflection.

Itzy opened the door to 1804 with Pippa behind her. "Are you sure you want to see this?"

Pippa nodded, jaw set in a determined line.

The girls entered her aunt's small foyer and were instantly hit with a blast of dry heat.

"What's that *smell?*" Pippa asked, appalled.

Warily, Itzy pushed open the door to the living room.

It was a hive of activity. The toile couches had been rearranged to make room for a long table that took up one entire wall. On the table, Itzy saw, were the flowers from Mrs. Brill, as well as many other bouquets—most still in their clear cellophane wrap. Everything was wilting in the heat. Every available surface was piled with offerings—boxes of bonbons, pyramids of marzipan fruit—a feast for the flies. In the corner, a large harp had been introduced, and a young woman plucked at it idly.

"You say she's your *governess?*" Pippa whispered.

Itzy shrugged. "My aunt's idea."

"What's that in her hair—a *crown?*"

"Flypaper."

The governess sat in the middle of everything on a high-backed chair, exchanging words with Dr. Jenkins in low tones. Atop her hair was the spent coil of the Venus Flytrap. Even from the door, Itzy could see it was covered in flies. She wore the fox fur still, and at her feet was a plump woman, busily attending to the governess's feet, filing her heels brusquely with a large paddle.

Itzy nudged Pippa in the ribs, mouth set in a grim line. In the governess's lap sat the dog.

"*Paris!*" Pippa gasped.

"She calls it Mopsie," Itzy said dully.

The dog shifted, turning its head in their direction. One of its ears was missing, a ragged black hole. A thin string of saliva hung from its mouth.

"I think, Pippa, it might be time for a new dog," Itzy whispered, squeezing her hand.

"Poor *chou-chou*," Pippa said, blinking back tears. "What *happened* to her?"

"Come on. My room's this way."

The pair darted down the small hall.

"We can try to rescue her—if you want," Itzy said.

Pippa swallowed. "There's, er, something dead in her eyes."

Things from Hell are broken, corrupt, and defiled.

"I don't really think that's Paris anymore, if you know what I mean," Itzy finally said. The girls sat numbly on Itzy's iron bed together. "I think something funny's going on at this hotel," Itzy confessed.

"I think you're right." Pippa nodded gloomily. "Mother's been strange. Stranger than usual. Course it's hard to tell with all the plastic surgery she's gotten." Pippa turned to Itzy with her eyes wide and face frozen with a blank expression. Itzy giggled. "She and the doctor are inseparable. If he gives her any more Botox, she won't be able to blink."

"Dr. Jenkins is a plastic surgeon?" Itzy thought of the doctor's office, the shining ampoules in the glass cabinet.

"What else? Itzy, this *is* the Upper East Side. Mother even wanted to name the dog Botox, but I put my foot down."

"In hindsight, I see why you settled on Paris."

Itzy did her own imitation of Mrs. Brill and the two fell over laughing.

Itzy took a deep breath. "Pippa, can I ask you something?"

"Ask away."

"This morning I saw you with Luc. At the restaurant."

Pippa nodded. Birds—pigeons most likely—cooed in the air shaft out the lone window.

"Are you—do you . . . like him?" Itzy blurted.

"Luc?" Pippa laughed, throwing back her head. "No! Itzy." Pippa looked at her, shaking her head. "Hardly!" Pippa smiled. "Ever since you got here, all he talks about is you."

"Oh." Itzy's ankle throbbed, and she was savaged with a wave of chills, but for once she didn't care.

40

"You should drink something," Pippa advised Itzy. "At least let me get you some water. Never underestimate the power of hydration."

"I'm not thirsty," Itzy said. "And the water tastes funny."

"We could send up for some. Or I might have something—" She rummaged in her calfskin purse. "Here. Take mine. You have to drink—you're sick." Pippa opened a bottle of water and, not finding a glass, handed over the entire thing.

"Thanks," Itzy smiled weakly. "Shouldn't I be worried it's poisoned?"

Pippa smiled and took a sip out of the bottle of Evian.

"There. Our fates are sealed. Now. You must let me call the doctor in for that ankle."

Itzy sat bolt upright, a look of panic overtaking her flushed face.

"No—Pippa! You can't. Not him. Something's just not right with that man."

"Yeah. It is criminal what he charges for a consultation." Pippa leaned across and put her hand on Itzy forehead. "You're burning up."

"Actually, I'm freezing." A wave of chills swept over Itzy, and she shivered.

"What can I do? I feel responsible. It was my dog that bit you, after all."

She tossed the pamphlet from Ava's Hermès delivery at Pippa. "You can start by reading this," Itzy said.

Pippa opened it.

Ava Quant's
OBSERVATIONS
Historical and theological, upon the NATURE and NUMBER of the OPERATIONS of

divahS.

Accompanied with Accounts of A brief treatise on the Grievous Molestations that have Annoyed the country, with several remarkable CURIOSITIES therein occurring, and some CONJECTURES on the GREAT EVENTS likely to Befall.

I.   Ava, what do divahs EAT?
A.   They avoid carbs.
B.   Actually, they eat only putrid food. But *Clostridium botulinum*, the botulism toxin, is their preferred diet.

II. And how do they get their food?
A.   Dented cans.
B.   Rotting meat.
C.   Or the readily available and highly popular anti-wrinkle subdermal injection, Botox.

Botox, by far, is the meal of choice for the demon set.

III. What exactly is BOTOX?
A. A deadly neurotoxin. Botox is a trademarked brand name. People pay money to have it injected into their faces. It is particularly enjoyed around the eyes. This bacterium, the *Clostridium botulinum*, is irresistible to divahs.
B. Note: This can be a problem for the non-demons who have participated in this boutique surgery procedure, for it makes their flesh irresistible to divahs. This is perhaps yet another explanation for the concentration of demons on the Upper East Side.
C. DO NOT attempt to approach a divah if you've had Botox work performed in the past eight months.

Itzy consented to another round of aspirin and she swallowed them down with Pippa's bottle of Evian. Pippa had rummaged in the small servant's bathroom and found a few water-stained Band-Aids and a dubious bottle of iodine. She insisted on removing Itzy's sock.

Itzy lay back on the thin mattress. The blue coverlet felt coarse and scratchy, and the aspirin felt lodged deep in her throat.

Pippa began slowly unwinding the gauze that Luc had dressed the wound in, taking care to handle Itzy's ankle delicately. Even so, the slightest pressure sent waves of searing pain up her leg.

"Stay still! Believe it or not, I do this all the time for my mother, post-op. Her various nips and tucks, you know.

I'm a regular Nurse Nightingale. The tummy tuck was the worst. It got infected and stank to high heaven." She had removed the last of Luc's dressing. "Here, it might be easier if you hang your leg over the side of the bed. I'm almost done. Mother's got this great big stash of pills—perhaps I should get you something—except with Mother you never know what you're getting. Oh." Pippa dropped the leg and pulled her hands back to her chest, looking at Itzy's ankle with undisguised horror. "Oh no—"

41

The room was spinning as people peered down upon her sickbed. Strange faces—eager, glinting eyes. Unknown cloaked figures, darkened features—the one light on the ceiling cast them in dark shadows. The smell of incense—burning, pungent herbs—was in the air.

The horde parted suddenly, and against the dull ceiling a single figure appeared, bending down. Itzy tried hard to focus but her eyes were so tired, the room so hot.

The governess crouched over her. Flypaper dangled from her ear.

She appeared to be sniffing at her, a look of immense disapproval on her face. She held Paris in her arms, one of the dog's legs swaying uselessly. She straightened, turning.

"Jenkins, attend at once."

The room grew dim, and Itzy struggled to stay conscious. The doctor stepped forward, his bag open at the foot of her iron bed. His cane gleamed, catching the light from above. The end was pointed and barbed.

"Your Highness." The doctor nodded. From his medical bag, he produced a shiny syringe and loaded it with an amber-colored liquid, tapping the side to clear an air bubble. He held it up to the light, inspecting the dose. A bead of moisture gleamed at the needle's tip.

Itzy struggled to sit up, but unseen hands held her down. Her mouth tasted like bile—her throat raw and sore. Her eyes found Pippa's frightened face where she cowered against the wall.

"Pippa," Itzy called. Pippa's eyes darted nervously around the room. *"Pippa, please—get Luc."*

The fiendish gathering parted then, and a figure emerged. The crowd gave him wide berth—his twisted wings, Itzy could see, brushed against their dark cloaks.

42

The scene was one of grainy film, flickering light. At times, when she opened her heavy eyes, her room was too bright, overexposed. At others, murky dark. All the while Luc was there, by her side, sitting on an old straight-backed chair, holding vigil by her bedside.

Others came and went, but it was only Luc she saw. She refused the water brought for her unless Luc held the glass to her parched lips. Her skin was hot and dry, her ankle far away—someone else's ankle.

Once, she awoke as the filtered light from the air shaft played against Luc's features. His face, soft, radiant—utterly beautiful.

For the most part, she slept.

He would talk to her. He would tell her stories. She would wake and he would still be talking, as he would be when she drifted off again. She listened, somehow. It seemed vital, his voice familiar.

His voice.

She had heard his voice before.

He had been there before—by her bedside—in childhood illnesses. But that was not all. Luc had been the lingering guest at that last fateful dinner party in Brittany. He had talked, late into the night, refusing to go, pouring more wine. Her mother had laid Itzy down on that scratchy blanket by the fire, and, as the embers died out one by one, she had slept to the sound of his voice. Luc had been there, the night the awful creature had come searching for her by the ash bin.

PART II

LUC'S STORY

Oh Fiery One,

You have charmed me, I am ssure!
    Distracted me, I am certung!
    Toppled my lonlinez, distracted my reveriess.
    Do not again vhissper of a love born of
oppositess. SShh! Zat is your youth showink, my dove.
    Do you vhish to know vhat it vas zat flashed
zrough my mynd vhen first I saw you?
    Zey do not make zem any better zan zis.
    I shall have zem embroider zose words on a
silken hankercheef to remynd me of you.

I cannot resist you.

Your Muse,
    M.

My Lamb,

Resisst me not.
  I see zee otherss, how zey look at you.
  I zee your Host does not of me approve. Tell zem zey are silly boyz, born of too much Prudence and Temperance. Zere is so little to be zaid of such qualitiess, no?
  Be notorious!

Your Queen,
  M.

You came, my Sveet.

I vaited at your atelier, vondering. Thinking all zee vhile perhaps you changed your mynd.

Your fine and gentle hands, your eye for light and dark. Zee smells of linen and oilz are now and foreve zee smellz of you, my angel. When I pose for you, it is as if nothink exist in all of time eternal but zee two of us, separated only by your canvass. My love. My artisst. Vhat a gift you give, to be your muse!

Zis tiny beating heart vithin zis temporary body.

I dedicate it all to you.

Vithout you, I am lost.

Tomorrow?
Bazin of Apollo?

BRING NO ONE.

M.

o not blame me my pet.

It had to be done.

It iz, after all, only a faether. Vhat a big deal ou are makink, you and your Host, and your threatss f varring. Var! How tediouss!

I do keep it bezide me, and watch zee air play on its vondrous plumeage, and zink of Our last dance ogether.

It zmells of you.

God and Demonz alike all had consortss. Do not ok back! I vant only to steal your thoughtss of omorrow, and make time lie.

am unssssstoppable.

Vhere vill you be, for my ultimate humiliation? Zis vain Guillotin and hiss abominable invention. As if zeese cell wallss could hold zee likes of me.

Your silence speakz loudly.

Zis will not be zee end of us, never fear.

I love you, my Luc, vith a burning fiery love zat can never be extinguished. Ve are immortalss, you and I.

Can you not see?

I vill look for you amongst the broken and zee damned. And I vill find you.

And zen, as evermore, ve shall let our love vash over us like zee hot dry windss of Hell.

43

Paris, 1771

I met her in la Grande Galerie—the famed Hall of Mirrors—at Versailles. Marie Antoinette was all of sixteen, or so she appeared. Even amidst the crowded hall, she was the undisputed beauty—her alabaster skin, her eyes of blue, a faint flush upon her cheeks.

The room stretched out in all its glory, golden mirror after golden mirror, and as she giggled, turning to me, one thousand thousand of her reflections beheld me. Her ladies-in-waiting tittered, each a beauty in their own right, whispering, while Marie Antoinette and I locked eyes.

She smiled and exhaled on a mirror, leaving behind a small bloom of fog.

"Angels' breath," she said, tracing a heart in it before it faded.

Maurice was there—he knew her for what she was.

"She is trouble, that one. Stay away from her," he said, grabbing my elbow. "Look—" He pointed to a pretty woman in courtly attire. "That one fancies you. And that one with the fan. You can have your pick of anyone here, Luc! Anyone but *her*."

I ignored his warning.

I saw her next the following week; I knew her habit of walking in the gardens.

When she saw me, she smiled. It was bewitching.

She ran ahead playfully, and I followed. Her gown billowed out behind her like some sort of confection, her little dog chasing her heels. She wore a small hat pinned to one side of her beautiful head, atop her bright curls. She walked as if on wings.

It was spring, and the grass of Versailles was a sea of emeralds. We sat together in the shade of an ancient tree beside the fountain of Apollo's Basin. I threw a stick, and her dog, Mops, chased it into the reflecting pool, and she laughed, clapping her hands together in delight. Mops returned, drenched, and she laughed further as the small pug shook himself vigorously, drenching me in turn. She turned her pale blue eyes to me, smiling. Hers was that rare beauty, the kind that derails you, that possesses you, the kind that is painful to behold.

Here was something new, I thought.

O, Itzy! I should have known, for an angel not much is new.

I kept a studio atop a carriage house near Montmartre, and I painted her. She would sit for hours, staring into my eyes, and I into hers. My brush swept across the canvas in tones of shimmering pearl, lush peach, sky blue. The light—it was impossible to describe. It was different then, younger, brighter. It gathered around Marie Antoinette in shimmering waves. When she moved, it chased her. And when she departed my studio, it was as though the sun had set.

There, in my atelier, we were finally alone. At court, she was trailed by hangers-on, courtiers, servants, jewelers. But she could sneak away and did, alone. I would shoo away my manservant and bar the doors.

We would talk. She would tell me of the various gossip of the day and I would listen, entranced by even the dullest of tales. She would pose, surrounded by canvases in her own likeness, mirroring back her face. They lay everywhere, propped against the wall, discarded in the corners, stacked willy-nilly, as if we were again in her Hall of Mirrors, meeting for the first time.

A fever burned in me to paint her face, and I did. Over and over and over again.

I painted at night by candle.

I painted sleepless and staggering, trying desperately to capture that elusive spark in her eyes—as if she were forever laughing at me from someplace deep inside. I painted like one consumed, like one possessed. I painted her beautiful, shimmering face by memory alone, trying desperately to fill the loneliness in me.

For here, Itzy, is the truth.

Angels—demons, too—are not whole. What we lack are souls. O, the irony! Humans—unbeknownst to them—are intrinsically whole, having both a body and eternal soul. How we envy you, your perfectness, your *completeness*.

And what we have in place of a soul is an aching desire to be whole, an all-consuming feeling of loneliness—as if some fundamental part of me was torn away at birth and forever, *forever*, denied.

How we curse your ignorance.

That last good day, it is etched forever in my mind. We spent the afternoon together in the gardens of Versailles. The Basin of Apollo, its twinkling fountains.

Her hands ran through my hair, my wings. She had gold dust on her lips. She whispered other things in the dappled shade. She drew close, her handmaidens giggled.

Somehow it happened.

My beloved Marie plucked a feather from my wing.

The *pain*—the pain was new and terrible. The color drained from the exquisite gardens all around me as I gazed up in confusion to where she stood towering over me; the sky behind her was bleak with roiling clouds. Gone was the glory of Versailles, and in its place some forlorn moor, some wasteland of despair. I saw Marie Antoinette then, as she really was—as Maurice did.

The Divah was horrible to behold, her eyes—no longer blue—were dark eternal pits; her alabaster skin, where it was not charred and peeling, clung to her form. Her dress was the moldering cloth of the tomb. Her hair, once a thing of beauty, was a soiled, rotting wig, and insects crawled in and out, nesting in its dreary curls. From her spine sprouted terrible things—wings, yes, but in what world could such wings be used? They were covered in scales and taut, veined skin. My stomach recoiled as they unfolded. Her handmaidens had become gaudy, awful things—aged streetwalkers on shriveled legs. They cackled and blew me kisses from their putrid, toothless mouths.

Her dog—that cursed hellhound Mops—turned on me, teeth bared, blocking my way. My wings—they shriveled and lay at my sides, tattered and broken.

Marie brandished my feather, laughing. It was long, the plume soft and billowing. Her eyes locked with mine and she licked the tip of the quill, sharpening it with her jagged teeth.

"Wicked angel," she taunted me. "Naughty, wicked angel."

I was now powerless against her. With my feather in hand, I was hers.

Eternally.

44

His name was Nicolas Jacques Pelletier, my darling Itzy, and he was about to die. A rowdy crowd had gathered to watch his demise at the Place de Grève, in Paris, that April day. Taut clouds stretched across the sky like scar tissue.

"This is to be your salvation, Luc," Maurice grunted. For months, Maurice had been distant, secretive. Now, his eyes were bright, his wings tensed and ready.

We wandered the crowd as they grew restless. In the center, a large stage had been erected, and upon it something new—something never before seen. A novelty of French innovation. It towered over the restless crowd and had been painted scarlet, the color of blood. Its blade was polished, and in it I saw the crowd reflected back upon itself in miniature, as if all the world had suddenly come to exist in its honed slant.

Vendors sold curiosities, hastily printed cards with heads torn from bodies, lead charms, roasted pigeons.

We took our places amongst the enthusiasts who had gathered up front. An old woman next to me had brought thread and needle, and she busied herself making a lace collar, while the executioner lurked upon the scaffolding in the shadows of the strange, new apparatus.

"They'll not like this. You watch." Maurice turned to me, grimacing.

"Why?"

"Too clean. Too quick."

I nodded.

"They need to see pain," Maurice continued, scanning the buildings on the edge of the square. "Their insides need to come out for them to feel satisfied."

The executioner, a gargantuan man named Charles Henri Sanson, dallied—allowing the crowd to grow restless and bloodthirsty. He was a showman at heart. He had tested the machine on corpses from a lunatic asylum for weeks. He had perfected it.

Finally, the thief was assisted onto the scaffolding.

Nicolas Pelletier glanced up at the guillotine but once. Instead, his eyes scanned the crowd and found mine. The crowd heckled and jeered. Sanson asked the prisoner for any last words, but Pelletier had none. His eyes bore into me.

The prisoner did not struggle as he was made to lay upon the bascule, his neck fitted into the lunette, his hands bound in leather. The crowd grew still. Something startled a flock of crows and they exploded, squawking, flapping from one rooftop to another. Their grumbling was the only sound to be heard.

My neighbor had ceased her lace-making, and her gnarled hands were tensed in anticipation. Monsieur Sanson paraded from one side of the stage to the other, arriving again at the guillotine. The moment, he knew, was his.

The executioner released the lever upon the tall upright, and the blade fell, rattling as it went. All of Paris leaned forward, holding its collective breath, while a slight gust of wind caught the shock of white hair upon the prisoner's scalp. The anemic sun chose then to part the overcast sky, illuminating the diagonal blade as it flew down, lending a heavenly component to the killing spectacle.

The machine was well oiled, the blade sharp and polished, and it made short work of the condemned thief. It passed through skin, flesh, and bone with but a small sound, and then the severed head of Pelletier landed in a woven basket with a muffled thud.

Silence followed.

Some confused grumbling from the crowd.

"That's it?" someone shouted.

"Where are his agonized cries—mad ravings in the face of torture?" another demanded.

Sanson held Pelletier by the hair, parading him across the stage. A cluster of angry earwigs fell from the head.

A few ladies rushed forward to dip their handkerchiefs in the blood, waving them about dutifully, but the blood was dark, thick, and black—and only served to bring about more confused mutterings. As Sanson neared, my lace-maker leaned forward, and from her toothless mouth she shouted something loud and bawdy, then with one of her gnarled hands, she slapped the ashen face of Pelletier.

The executioner could never have been prepared for what came next.

Unlike his corpses from the Bicêtre Hospital who had been long dead, the head of Pelletier *blinked* when the hag's hand struck his cheek. His pupils focused, alert—and his eyes gleamed. They scanned the crowd hungrily—searching, glowering. They alighted upon mine, and his gray lips mouthed a hideous curse and then grew slack.

"*Démon!*" Maurice cried, turning to me.

The crowd was now a roiling, angry mass. Someone shouted, "Stoke the pyre! He must *burn*."

Then, from the rooftops came Gaston.

"Crows saw you," Maurice scowled. "You're losing your touch."

Beside me the old lady became René.

René and Gaston flanked Maurice stiffly, prepared for the worst.

"This thing—Luc," he turned to me, "this guillotine. It is your salvation."

I looked at it again. They were removing Pelletier's headless body on a gurney quickly as the crowd surged forward to storm the stage.

"I hardly see—"

When I turned back, my angels were gone.

The crowd was furious. They had come for a show, and this had not satisfied. Sanson, for his troubles, received a stone aside the head and, clutching a bleeding temple, he marched toward the stage shouting for the coward who threw it. Rotten eggs, a lady's corset, and a stiff dead cat sailed through the air alongside several old and worn boots. As I pushed recklessly, making for the edge of the square, something hit my shoulder. I turned.

The head of Nicolas Pelletier lay at my feet.

I grabbed it, wrapping it inside my cloak, and I ran.

I ran, Itzy, because I could not fly, for I was already a prisoner then. My wings were shrunken, atrophied things—useless on my back.

Maurice had warned me.

No good will come from consorting with demons.

45

Nicolas Jacques Pelletier's beard had been trimmed by the same stroke that removed his head, so I held him by his thinning white hair as I trudged across Paris. Rain had set in, and we were soaked. The dregs of chamber pots mingled with horse manure and became a river of sludge that ran through the streets. Near the cemetery, the ditches held worse things. I stepped over a foul pool beneath the entrance of the cemetery of les Innocents. A femur bone floated in the murk.

"Cassedents!" I cried.

The grave digger appeared finally, lumbering along at the speed of one employed by the dead.

"Give this a proper burial," I said, slapping the head down upon a sepulcher. It made a muffled thud.

Cassedents looked at Nicolas and then at me. He was shirtless and wrapped in an old, stained shroud below his waist.

"Where's the rest of him?" he grunted.

I found some coins of the king's mint and tossed them down beside the head. Pelletier stared at the silver with cloudy eyes—more money than the thief likely saw in his lifetime.

"Right here," I said.

"Full up," Cassedents shrugged. He scratched a lousy armpit.

"Surely you have room for one head. A small one at that," I gestured.

He showed me a stack of bodies behind him. By the looks of them, they had been waiting for some time. "We're closed. By order of la reine."

I took a moment to look around the crowded cemetery. Graves stood open and in them men toiled, rainwater up to their waists, gathering bones, some still dangling flesh.

"The queen?" I asked sharply.

"Plagues, wars, famine—the dead come. We're outnumbered by them. They never cease; the cemeteries of Paris are overflowing. Stacked ten high in the pits, they are, and still they come. 'Cassedents,' they say, 'just one more body.' 'Cassedents, surely this little one will not burden you. A babe! *Une petite*. An innocent for les Innocents.' But I'm no *magicien*. The babes? I have a broom closet that I throw them in. Everyone else I let rot, you see, before I stuff them in the ground. They're smaller then; they take up less room. Men are but grave soil."

"Where are they taking them?" I gestured to the workers.

"Who knows? Who cares? So long as they're taking them, I say."

"This is the queen's work?"

He nodded. "She's calling the dead."

I was silent for some time, until the sound of Cassedents's wheezing grew intolerable.

"So you refuse me, grave digger?"

Cassedents looked at me then. "What use have I of your silver? What would you have me buy?" He pointed with a soiled finger where the men were working. "I have everything I need. That's mine. The queen promised it to me."

"Yours?" I stared at a rectangular pool of filthy water.

"My grave. I'm saving that one for me."

46

I headed to an old funeral carriage, black curtains drawn, parked at the cemetery gates. The interior was stacked with bones, and the driver eyed me suspiciously.

"Where are you bound with such a load?" I asked.

"The Roman quarries. They're emptying all the churches of their dead and taking them there."

"For what purpose?"

The driver looked around nervously. "A massive crypt, some say. Catacombs."

Oh, I knew the catacombs. As it happened, I was headed there myself.

"Might we ride with you?" I raised Nicolas's head up for his inspection.

The driver hesitated. I tossed him a coin.

"If you don't mind riding up front," he said, biting the silver with a chipped tooth.

I rode with Nicolas's head on my lap, swaying over the rutted street. We traveled south in silence. The few people we passed averted their eyes or crossed themselves nervously. Nicolas stared off ahead into the growing darkness.

The driver pulled a cork from a dented flask and offered it to me. I took it happily, the bitter taste of wormwood stinging my throat.

"A friend of yours?" the man asked, indicating Nicolas with his square chin.

I held Nicolas up and looked at him.

"Never knew him."

The driver cast me a sideways glance.

"That the thief they put down today?"

I nodded.

"Nothing spoils a good execution quicker than a painless death."

"Perhaps," I said, throwing back more of the man's swill. "But this was no man."

"No?"

"This was a demon."

"You don't say. Mind?" The driver passed me the reins and grabbed the head. "Can't say I've seen me a demon ever before. How can you tell?"

"Oh, you can't. Not now, at least. Whatever possessed the man left soon after the guillotine did its swift work."

"Now that's news. Thought nothing could rid us of them diabolical fiends." He leaned in, whispering conspiratorially. "They should use it on that demon queen of ours. She's paving her underground palace with bones."

"You're not the first to think that today, my friend."

The driver returned his attention to the road, and I reclaimed Nicolas. His skin was putty-colored, and his mouth, in death, was pulled back as though tasting something bitter. I tipped the flask back, letting the pungent liquor burn my throat, and then I tipped some into the poor head's mouth.

"This one's for you, Nicolas," I said, holding him up. The absinthe, tinged green, dripped from his severed gullet.

"Can't hold his liquor," the driver chuckled.

I smiled and settled into the ride. Darkness had come in thick, and few lights burned inside the buildings we passed. A mangy dog kept pace with us, keeping to the shadows. *He smells the bones*, I thought.

"They don't want you at les Innocents, Nicolas," I said, contemplating the thief's glazed eyes. "Perhaps, then, I should afford you a royal burial? How would that suit you? I was thinking Saint-Denis," I mused. "Cemetery of kings."

The driver spoke, tongue loosened by his spirits.

"Kings—*bah*. We have all the kings and queens we can handle. An Austrian demoness sits on the throne! She reviles the language of French, our native tongue. She disturbs the dead in their sacred slumber, gathering them like firewood for the flames. Evil spirits amass inside her palace walls for midnight balls where all manner of things happen, evil things. They march beneath the banner of the Underworld throughout their empty chambers, throwing children from high towers, while outside the city gates there is no food to be found. We are under siege, my lord. When will we see better days?"

Better days, indeed.

"I'd be careful of what you say," I said wearily. "Lest you end up like *le pauvre* Nicolas, here."

I eyed the night sky. The moon was veiled with a shroud. My wings burned with an eternal itch, an itch that might never be appeased. I was damaged goods, Itzy. My only consolation was no man could see them.

When the driver next spoke, his voice was hoarse, and he spoke urgently, in hardly a whisper lest he wake the dead.

"I hear the queen's got some angel held hostage in that glittery palace of hers. It's where she gets her evil power from. Word is, he helps her build her demon empire. It's End of Days when angels and demons share an unholy embrace, I tell you. Fallen angels are the devil's playthings. Soon enough they'll be making demon spawn."

I handed the flask back. I had suddenly lost my taste for absinthe.

"Perhaps the poor wretch was tricked—thought he was truly in *love* with Her Highness? Perhaps this sorry creature finds himself *always* inconveniently falling in love, always trying to do the *right* thing and *never* succeeding? And now, because of bad taste in women, this angel faces utter ruin? Did you ever think of that, driver?"

The driver, slowing the carriage, raised an eyebrow.

"Or perhaps the poor wretch is merely biding his time," I backtracked.

That brought about a sharp burst of laughter from the driver. "Well then, *monsieur*, what's he waiting for?"

47

The mangy dog had drifted nearer to the funeral carriage and was keeping pace with the horses. A gust of wind picked up, throwing the dank scent of the gutters in our faces. The road turned sharply and we took the corner quickly, and I was thrown against the driver, nearly losing Nicolas. When we straightened out, the dog was still there, tongue lolling with the effort of exertion. He was close enough to touch.

Suddenly, there was the clatter of heels upon the carriage roof behind us. I turned, peering into the darkness. Maurice stood there, his windswept wings stretching out behind him, as dark as night, his gray eyes missing nothing.

I turned to the driver, who was muttering under his breath, intent on the road.

"Good of you to join us," I said as another angel landed, rattling the coach. "And Laurent. What a surprise."

"Slumming, lover boy?" came Laurent's voice, sharp and haughty.

"You do what you can when you don't have wings," I sighed.

"How the mighty have fallen," he sneered. He tossed his own wings—spectacular golden things, arched high over his shoulders and falling far below his waist in jagged, thorny feathers. Laurent was statuesque, carved beautiful but cruel.

I eyed the driver, who was oblivious. And then I turned to the mangy dog.

"Gaston," I said. "Out with you."

The dog became Gaston, soaring easily over the backs of the workhorses, wings like a falcon's, a coppery brown to match his skin. His crooked smile was a welcome sight.

"All we're missing is René," I said. "What could possibly be keeping him? He's never late for a party."

"Who says I'm late?" the head of Nicolas Jacques Pelletier spoke from my lap. "Got any more of that absinthe?"

The carriage soon halted. Beside us were rows of similar coaches, creaking with the weight of the dead. Hunched figures were tasked with unloading them into three-wheeled carts that formed a line snaking through the barren plot. I thanked the driver and jumped down with Nicolas, the angels falling in behind me.

We walked the length of the path of bones to the broken stone archway marking the quarry's entrance. I stood, Nicolas hanging from my hand from a tangle of white hair. Above us, in desperate scrawl, was a sign.

Les Portes d'Enfer

Hell's Gate, it read.

"Perhaps we *are* too late," said the head.

48

These new catacombs of Paris were no Hell, Itzy, although they came close.

We descended a dark and tremulous spiral stair into the earth, and from there entered a long low hall, which here and there was perforated with yawning tunnels marked by iron bars. These ancient Roman tunnels undermined all of Paris, I knew. They were uncharted, unmapped—they weakened all of the city with their gaps and sinkholes.

The air was chill and damp. Laurent held his staff aloft, and a bluish white light lit our way, casting slithering shadows of our forms upon the walls. I was drawn to the flickering shadow of my wings, their hideousness somehow magnified. Maurice saw my stricken face.

"You must not despair," he said. "There is hope ahead."

"Why, is my stolen feather here?" I asked grimly.

Maurice set his jaw, his stout wings bristling, and we walked on in silence. Soon, another portal awaited us. Here, a short and hasty scrawl could be seen, and René—having abandoned the head of Pelletier—leaned in, whispering to me.

"Overkill, *non?*"

Laurent waved his staff slowly over the scrawl.

"*Arrête! C'est ici—l'Empire de la Mort*," he read, contempt in each word.

The low-slung door swung slowly open, and I was forced to take several steps back. We had left Gaston to guard the entrance, so there were four of us to watch as a dark figure swept through the doorway.

"Welcome to the catacombs, my lords," the man said, a smile playing at the corners of his lips. He was tall and graceful; a long green waistcoat about his thin form was closed with silver-tipped antler staghorns. "The Empire of the Dead is a silent one. I've heard no voices from the graves, my friends. The dead do not speak tonight."

"Perhaps not to you, Professor." I brandished the head. "But Nicolas here has been quite chatty this evening."

"May I?" The man stepped forward eagerly. Taking the head, he examined it at once. "Ah, *oui. C'est parfait!* The finest of incisions, the sharpest of razors. And the most painless of deaths."

"Surely the loss of one's head arrives with some discomfort?" I asked.

"I assure you, my machine"—the man stood tall—"is swift justice."

"That seems to be the people of Paris's main complaint with it," Maurice noted, waving the comment away. "Professor Guillotin," he grumbled. "Pain or no, it makes no difference to our errand. Let us talk privately," he said. "The thresholds have ears."

We entered what seemed to be an enormous amphitheater, following the professor's lead. Laurent's staff grew brighter, but still did not pierce the ceiling's gloom. All around us were worn seats made of gray, crumbling stone as far as the eye could see, receding into the darkness. *Gravestones*, I realized. Urns, small statues, and carved cemetery sentinels stood as fixtures, breaking up the monotony of the defiled tombstones. It was only then that I realized what these slabs rested upon. They were built upon bones—more bones than I'd ever seen in one place before, orderly stacks of yellowed long bones, blemished with rot, skulls piled one on top of the next, empty eyes gazing out at us. The room was a gruesome theater of death, and at its center was Professor Guillotin's familiar machine, gleaming, new and virginal. Like its sister, it was painted scarlet.

The scholar was turning Nicolas over in his hands eagerly.

"I searched in vain for this head after my demonstration in the *Place* today. I have made it my passion to study it. How did you come upon this?"

"A good left hook," Maurice said.

"I see." He looked doubtful. "Monsieur Pelletier was a classic example of severe, entrenched possession. *Possession-by-inches*, it is known by us at the Hermès Institute. Such a possession happens in increments, over time. It is unclear why this occurs; it is as if the demon were toying with its prey, the way a spider does a fly. Or perhaps, the subject has hidden abilities at his disposal—abilities to somehow reject the demonic possession. Fascinating—from a scholarly point of view. But beyond the help of any *exorcisme*."

"All that from a head," Laurent sneered. "You're quite a salesman."

"Forgive me for being a skeptic, Professor, but possession-by-inches is incredibly rare," Maurice said.

"So you see why we wanted to study him."

"Make an *example* of him, you mean," Laurent said.

"The bedevilment is normally identified and arrested. But should it be allowed to continue, it is impossible to cure, which is why my guillotine—"

"Impossible?" I interrupted.

"*Impossible*. No one has survived such possessions," the professor insisted, holding up Nicolas as though to offer proof. "There is a point of no return, after which the possession proves too much for the victim, who is unusually and cruelly aware of the possession. This differs, in my experience, from the more traditional possession, where the body is more of a shell for the occupying force. Possession-by-inches is like being eaten alive, *messieurs*. In the end, they have been occupied for too long; the demon is too entrenched. It is *toujours fatal*."

"The signs?" I pressed.

Laurent exhaled loudly, clearly exasperated.

"They vary according to the origin and power of the demon," said the professor. "A common sign seems to be the odd graying of the hair. I've seen subjects' tresses turn pure white overnight." Again Nicolas was waved about. "Insects and their larva are somehow used as the conduit, and these sympathies prepare the body for possession, an unknown process—perhaps through a bite or wound, or entry through a bodily orifice such as the ear. The insect we call the earwig seems to pre-accompany any possession I've studied. Once the ear canal is breached, the earwig nests and multiplies in direct proportion to the demon's own rising, inch by inch. It is somehow symbiotic. In essence, the presence of an earwig marks a demon as nearby. This possession-by-inches is said to burn; the skin prickles with fever and is hot to the touch. The possessed are plagued with a confounding smell, a phantom one, like brimstone, or the River Seine. Memory loss and impulse control have been reported. I suppose, in the end, death comes along a welcome guest."

Guillotin assumed a look of modesty. "Until now, there has been little in our arsenal."

Laurent yawned. "Talk is cheap, gentlemen. Show us this machine we're buying."

"Yes," Maurice urged. "If what you say is true, your machine will win us the war, Professor Guillotin. History will celebrate your name."

"You are too kind." The Professor bowed. "I am but your servant." Around his neck he wore a colored silk cravat, I noticed. With flourish, he turned to stand beside the guillotine and began a practiced pitch.

"Gentlemen, France is filthy with demons. They walk among us; they eat our food; they wear our clothes; they marry our daughters. They steal all that is good from this green earth and leave nothing but wasteland and ash. But no longer. My lords, may I present—Lady Razor." He snapped his fingers sharply. From the shadows emerged a slight, nervous-looking apprentice, to whom he now tossed the head of Nicolas Jacques Pelletier.

"I'll take that," I said sharply. I had grown quite fond of him.

"Beheading has been around for time immemorial," the scholar was saying as he busied himself at the hulking contraption. His eyes were ablaze with a kind of fever. "But it is old-fashioned and clumsy, and the results are, shall we say, less than guaranteed. Headsmen are a thing of the past, my lords. Nor are they trained to fight off the demon if something should go wrong—as we all know it does." He looked at us intently. "Mine is a machine for mass demon extinction."

"If only things were so black and white," I lamented.

A lumbering cart of pale cadavers was produced, wheeled into place by the young assistant. A man who had been well fed in life was atop the quivering pile, and it was he who was rolled quite indelicately upon the gurney. As he was strapped in, Professor Guillotin busied himself with the uprights and the crossbar, inspecting the blade. The lunette was lowered in place, securing his neck.

"We've seen this already, good doctor," I called, pointing to Nicolas beside me. "Surely we can skip the theatrics."

"No—" Laurent said. "I want to see."

"Come to think of it," I said, turning to him. "Where were you today?"

Laurent cast me a dark look and did not answer.

"Hope she was worth it," René said.

"She was." Laurent smiled a thin, self-satisfied smile.

"You missed the execution because you had a *date*?" I cried.

"A cute little piece—a noble's daughter. I've got her wrapped around my finger."

Professor Guillotin, eyes bright, turned from his invention to face us. "My lords," he said. "Behold! My guillotine can cut through the neck in but a blink of an eye—through thew and sinew, gristle and bone. It is a thing of beauty."

The inventor released the *déclic,* and the blade fell with a loud rumble, severing the corpse's head neatly with a metallic tang. The head rolled along the floor, gathering stone dust, until it arrived at the feet of René.

"Why do humans always confuse the beautiful and the deadly?" René winked at me.

"That man was long dead. He speaks of it being swift and painless, but I have yet to see it *kill*. Maurice—if it is our salvation, should not we see what it can truly do?"

"We did. Today."

Laurent narrowed his eyes. "I will not commit until I see for myself. Five hundred livres of gold are at stake."

"A drop in your bucket," I muttered.

"*My* bucket, indeed. *My* spoils. I'll remind you I never asked to be thrown in with you misfits."

"Well here you are all the same," Maurice growled.

"Why not take it up with the Convocation? They were so accommodating the last time we were summoned." René's eyes sparkled.

Laurent fell silent.

"Bring in the demon," the scholar said to his apprentice, eyes sparkling with a strange excitement.

We looked at each other.

"You have procured a live subject?" Maurice asked.

"See for yourselves, my lords."

49

The apprentice was leading her in. She came willingly, Itzy, and she was secured at only one wrist with a silken scarf. She was young and plump, her skin like alabaster. In her other arm was a tiny babe, naked but for a swaddle of muslin and silk. The child blinked at the severe light from Laurent's staff.

"Surely not?" René said, appalled.

"Look closely," Guillotin instructed. "They are made docile by the silken Hermès cords that bind them. Such hand-stitched cravats and scarves are the signature of scholars for this very reason. Perhaps someday we will have a modern factory devoted to the production of said silks, but alas—they are as *chers* as they are colorful."

The young mother smiled shyly at me, blinking.

"She likes you!" Laurent's laugh was sharp.

"They *all* like him," René groused. "It's that pretty face of his."

"I see no glint," I cried. "This is a foul game you play, doctor."

"You have lost you powers, Luc," Laurent sneered. "She is a demon—plain as day. Is she not, Maurice?"

Maurice circled her, and the baby reached out for him with a pudgy hand, gurgling.

"There's one certain way to tell," Laurent continued, coyly. "Off with her head. If she doesn't spit or hiss, you were right, Luc."

"What must it be like to be an angel disgusted with humanity?" I cried. Then, turning to Maurice, "He speaks nonsense! We know them by their eyes. Dark, eternal pits. Like those of a beast."

Laurent turned on me. "Just like your beloved *Marie Antoinette*'s eyes?"

It was all I could do to hold myself back, and, seeing this, Laurent smiled cruelly.

The professor cleared his throat. "Yes, as a rule their eyes don't reflect light. But within the blackness, there is a glint, at times. A fire. Come closer," he urged Maurice. "She won't bite."

René and I exchanged looks, but Maurice had slipped in closer.

"That's right. You must move about the head to see it. The eyes flare, ignite even, flame like dry kindling. The term, my lords, is *coruscate*. A quiver. A flash. But by then, often, it is too late."

"If it is a demon, the disguise is good. The babe as well?" Maurice asked Guillotin.

"I assure you. The two. The Hermès Institute captured them yesternight."

"Surely today's demonstration"—again I waggled Nicolas's heavy head for all to see—"was sufficient? Must we reduce ourselves to such baser instincts as those of men—as the bloodthirsty crowd today?"

"As it happens, I like blood," Laurent stared at me coldly. "A little bloodletting before a feast of souls. *N'est-ce pas?*"

I charged Laurent then, without thought or reason, but he stayed me with one flick of his wrist. Defeated, I slumped to the floor, staring at Maurice, my head ringing from the blow.

"Feast of souls?" Professor Guillotin repeated uncertainly.

"We are all outlaws here, *monsieur*," Maurice snapped. "We play for high stakes. Eternal stakes."

"Still—you are angels."

"There is nothing pious about angels," Maurice growled. "Pious is a word created by man."

"If not pious, then what be you?" he asked. "Certainly you are no demons, for they are your sworn enemy. Is this not war?"

"We are soldiers," Laurent stated coldly. "Warriors. But we answer to no one. And we do all that is necessary to win."

"Professor," I said, standing shakily. "Open your eyes. Be it angel or demon, you will end your days with one of us. We are all just soul stealers."

"Well," said René. "We *are* prettier."

"I will not be a party to this." I pushed past him, cradling Nicolas.

"You're such a bleeding heart," Laurent sneered.

"Would that I had one."

50

Gaston was leaning against the stone archway where we had left him, picking at his teeth with a wooden splinter. He smiled at me when he saw me emerge, staggering into the yard.

"Is it everything they say?" He stretched, his wide, angular wings unfolded, articulating along bony joints that ran along the top side. Midway, at the joint, a sleek talon jutted from the neat feathers, a long and lethal claw. Gaston's wings were smaller than mine had been; flecked with shiny copper, they were wide and silent, made for speed.

"Yes," I said dully.

"Well, that's something."

"Is it, Gaston?"

"You'll have your wings again—isn't that what this is about?"

It's about desperation, I thought bitterly. *It's about downfall.* But most of all, Itzy, it's about the ravages of love.

I looked around the boneyard. Torches marked the entry to the catacombs, but shadows drifted at our feet, and I could just make out the few remaining funeral carriages. Above us was the sign for Hell's Gate.

"I wonder. Do you think she'll let this all go so easily?"

"She'll have no choice without a head."

I found the driver where I left him, his chin propped against his chest, flask in hand.

I cleared my throat loudly. He awoke with a start, grunting in protest.

"Couldn't bear to part with your friend?" he said upon seeing Nicolas.

"That is no final resting place," I said of the catacombs. "It is no place of rest at all."

The driver shook out his reins. "Eternal rest is hard to come by," he said.

The stair creaked as I mounted the carriage to recover my seat. "Take me to Père Lachaise." It was a rambling old cemetery, and my favorite. I threw another silver coin at him, and as it arced through the air, his eyes followed it greedily. But as I watched, a deep shiver overtook him and the coin clattered to the floor, unclaimed.

"I cannot," he said, his voice suddenly a low baritone.

"There." I tossed another coin at him. "If you drive your carriage like you drive a bargain, we'll be there in no time."

I peered into the gloom expectantly, but the driver had not stirred. When he turned his face to me, I saw his eyes. They flashed in the low light like a beast's.

I stepped down and looked over my shoulder for Gaston, but there was nothing but the night.

"On second thought—" I said casually.

"*You. Are. Summoned,*" the man said in a voice from the grave.

It was folly to run, for there was no escaping her servants and spies. I turned, my dead wings burning on my back, and I sprinted with all my might.

Run, Itzy, when you cannot fly.

51

The world spun by in a dark blur, the teetering slums and tiny alleys a grim smudge to either side of me. The road was a ruin, rutted with wagon wheels, muddy from the rain. It wound its way haphazardly through this part of Paris, never straight for long. A small market was being erected in the passage ahead, stalls of canvas and tent poles, sleepy merchants piling turnips and hard disks of cheese. Someone from a floor above was emptying a bucket, and its foul contents rained down on the roof of a fruit vendor, nearly splattering his wares. He shouted something with a raised fist, but his complaints were answered with another shower of filth.

I dared glance behind me and rejoiced that there was no sight of the carriage or its driver. Slowing my pace to a stroll, I slung Nicolas over my shoulder by his hair. Before me, a young woman in an apron emerged from a narrow bakery. Seeing me, she blushed.

She was flushed with her work with the ovens and covered in flour. I smiled in return, stopping entirely.

"*Bonjour!*" I smiled. "*Comment ça va?*" I angled closer, Nicolas in the crook of my elbow, leaning against the doorframe casually.

We talked in low tones, punctuated with occasional bursts of her laughter.

It pains me, Itzy, to recount to you what happened next. She was regaling me with some tale, now lost to my memory. Her face sparkled, her cheeks flushed—when a change over-took her complexion. She stared at something just over my shoulder, and her round face turned from confusion to fear.

A great rending filled the air.

"*Mon Dieu!*" she whimpered.

The ground trembled beneath me. Suddenly, the sleepy market had come alive; the vendors were scurrying about their wagons and their stalls, a wheel of cheese loping idly, *boules* of bread scattering into the dirt beneath their feet and disappear-ing into a growing smudge of darkness in their midst.

A vast hole was opening in the center of the market.

As I watched, the very earth buckled, and a yawning black orifice tore the small square apart, swallowing any-thing and everything that had stood there but an instant before. The street was gone, the market gone, and several teetering homes all toppled into the hungry abyss. The entire market square had vanished beneath the earth in a giant, deafening gurgle. There followed a moment of utter silence, where it appeared as if the sodden earth had finished its ugly business. The world was still. For that instant, I dared hope.

It was a small sound at first—a slippery *plink*. A soft *whoosh*. A quickening symphony of further gurgles. Chunks of the earth—of Paris—were slipping away rapidly into the sinkhole's mouth as the dark hole grew. The soil, soaked from the unceasing rains, would not hold—the world itself was slipping away. I watched as a chunk of roadway sloughed off into the growing pit, a cart and a tethered horse fell next, and I heard the shrieking of the beast. Tenements crumbled as if made of matchsticks, soiled lace curtains fluttering in the open windows as they tumbled into the void.

I looked for the young baker-girl, but she had vanished from the doorway—the doorway *itself* was gone.

When I turned my head back, the creeping hole had reached my boots.

All that remained of the market was the fruit vendor and his soiled tent, clinging with desperation to the crumbling wall behind him. He huddled beside his pile of apples— polished like garnets. The gaping black sinkhole had gobbled up all before him.

"Hold on! *Attendez!*" I called. I looked about desperately. He was so close—if only I could fly. I darted along the jagged edge of the sinkhole, each step, the very ground beneath my feet falling away, my boots squelching in the Paris muck.

The vendor's grip on the wall was failing—he floundered desperately, his hands grabbing a crooked iron hook that once secured a shutter. One by one, his polished apples tumbled into the gaping hole. I skidded to a halt—the tip of my boot jutting out over nothing but air. Steadying myself, I held out my hand, leaning out over the divide.

"Here, *monsieur!*" I called. "Grab my hand!"

He shook his head helplessly, frozen.

"Do it—or you will fall!" I commanded.

A terrible tremor shook the ground, and I fell back, watching as the entire wall to which he clung gave way. Down he went with the last of his apples. Down amidst the rubble and debris, the darkness. As he fell, his head lashed back, searching me out. He opened his mouth— his last words.

"*You. Are. Summoned,*" the vendor said to me, deep and guttural, and then he was gone.

A dank breath of moist air engulfed me. I stood there, on the precipice, staring into the bowels of Hell.

No. Not Hell, I realized, as I watched him fall. This was not Hell, Itzy. This was the catacombs. Hell was feverishly hot, I knew, and this was cool—cold even.

Looking into the sinkhole, I could just make out the tunnels of the old quarry that wormed their way beneath the city streets—beneath all of Paris. Everywhere there were bones. The ancient tunnels of the catacombs were undermining the street, the very ground the buildings stood on was swallowing them whole. A city built on shifting bones.

I looked up from the pit. The crooked slums of this section of Paris had blotted out the sky, but where once there were buildings, now there was nothing but open air. Wisps of clouds floated by, like fingers of the grim reaper. It was a beautiful sight, Itzy. There are no clouds in Hell.

From the head, still clutched in my hand, came a voice from the grave.

"*You. Are. Summoned*," Nicolas spoke, dangling from my hand. I raised him up so he was level with my face.

"*Et tu?*" I asked.

"*You. Are—*"

"I know, I know. I am summoned." My shoulders sagged. "When?"

"The dead can speak, and they can dance. July fourteenth. The Shadowsill Ball," said the head.

This was it, I realized. July fourteenth. This was when she meant to do it.

"*You—*" He began his message again.

"I'll be there," I said, as if I had a choice. I tossed Nicolas into the sinkhole in disgust.

52

I stumbled blindly through the winding streets as dawn gave way to morning. As I neared the city's center, the crowded apartments were replaced by more stately homes, the tiny *rues* widened into boulevards, but still the stench of the city stung my nostrils. The Seine was the worst, by far, as I crossed it at the Île de la Cité, and my stomach recoiled as raw sewage and slaughterhouse filth floated beneath me.

At the end of the small rickety bridge, I was jostled by a wild mob—farmers, perhaps, judging by their scythes and pitchforks—rushing by with riotous shouts. Further along, as I neared the Cathedral of Notre Dame, I saw a pair of bodies hanging from lampposts, still twitching. At their feet a ghastly word, scrawled in something thick and red.

DÉMON

I shaded my eyes, staring up at them. One was still alive, the rope having been carelessly flung about his neck to include an arm. These were no demons, I saw—just unfortunates.

The demon was lurking in the shadows of the hanging men. I saw it then, a tiny thing against the backdrop of Notre Dame. The hellhound. Her Majesty's small dog.

"*Bonjour*, Mops," I called pleasantly, removing my knife from my cloak. It had been a gift from Marie Antoinette —the handle was carved from bone, inlaid with rubies. The dog growled, baring its teeth. "A glorious day, wouldn't you agree? *Formidable*."

The dog's hackles were raised and it began a dangerous-sounding snarl. I brandished the dagger. "Just a knife here, you see, Mops? No tricks."

I sawed roughly through the hemp rope.

"Seems these poor fellows have been mistaken for your kind. *Et bien*. Who can blame them? The city is filthy with demons, wouldn't you agree?"

I returned my attention to the rope. The blade from Marie was a pretty thing, but duller than dirt. When the hanged men finally fell, I forgot the hellhound.

I recognized the survivor of the lynch mob. He was a priest named Foune.

53

The smell of your cathedrals, Itzy, I have always loved
them. The rank, dense scents of hope and misery, wax and
burned herbs. The stones are polished by the worn knees
of the devout, permeated with the human condition. Sadly,
that is all there is—such smells, and ponderous silence.
Whatever purpose built these vast halls is lost on my kind.
I am more at home in hotels, Itzy. We angels are solitary
creatures, not adept at life upon this mortal sphere. The
convenience of room service cannot be overstated.

I carried the priest carefully in my arms as I wandered
the checkered stone floor of the nave, the clacking of my
heels echoing off the vaulted ceiling. Notre Dame was
deserted at this hour of the morning, and stone statues
gazed down at me, saints and kings.

I laid Foune down on the high altar gently, beneath one
of the famed rose windows. The poor man was pale, his skin
mottled about his neck where the rope had been tightened.

"Foune," I called gently, and his eyes fluttered open,
once, twice, and then remained closed.

Birds—doves or larks I guessed—roosted on the upper
halls and were flying softly from one balustrade to the next,
their wings rustling. I heard one land behind me.

"Luc," someone said.

I knew that voice. My throat went dry.

"Anaïs."

54

I knew your mother as one knows a movie star—that is, intimately, and not at all. She was untouchable always, and rarely earthbound—until she had you, Itzy. There are consequences, you see, for lying with man—just as there are for consorting with demons. Still, it was your mother they turned to when things got rough. Your mother was a fixer, a member of the cavalry. She appeared when mistakes were made. Her job in the realm of angels was to make things right, to prevent war at all costs. Her presence could only mean one thing: someone had messed up badly. And, Itzy, that someone was me.

Your mother was not alone that day in the Cathedral of Notre Dame. Two more winged creatures sailed down from high atop the choir, circled, and alighted on the floor.

"Sabine. Colette." I nodded at them. "Always a pleasure."

Their faces were chiseled like the statues above them as they flanked Anaïs. A brightness emanated from them, a cold light like that of Laurent's staff. Their wings, great arched things, swept up from their shoulders and brushed the floor.

Your mother was wearing tailored silk atop tight riding pants and tall black boots from the Hermès Institute. Sabine held a leather riding crop in her hand, and Colette a coiled whip.

"You're looking well, ladies. The pinnacle of cutting-edge fashion. Speaking of cutting-edge, I saw your friend Guillotin today," I said to Anaïs. "Remind me, what is it that you like about *men*?"

"Remind me, what is it you like about *demons*?" your mother asked.

I noticed a slight smile on Sabine's icy features.

"Well, for a start, they don't answer questions with other questions." I shielded my eyes. "Turn it down a notch," I complained to the ladies. "You're hurting my eyes."

"Where are you staying?" I turned to Anaïs. "I hear the Basilla Athénée is good this time of year."

"Too many devhils." She wrinkled her nose.

"I can inquire for you at the Saint Honoré, if you'd like," I said politely.

"I have made my own arrangements," she said.

I shrugged.

"What happened here?" Anaïs indicated Foune.

"A priest—they thought he was a demon."

"Things are getting out of hand, Luc."

"Maurice has a plan."

"Yesterday's news, Luc."

"She means to open the *Gates*, Anaïs."

"Now we're talking. How far along is she?"

I hesitated.

"Luc," your mother said impatiently. "Do you recall the three things the Divah needs to open the Gates to Hell?"

"First the Divah needs a body, to be incarnate."

"Check."

"Right," I sighed. "I suppose she has one—the whole Queen-of-France thing."

"And?" your mother prompted. "The second thing?" I cringed as a note of frustration crept into her voice.

I frowned. "Um. An angel's feather," I hemmed.

"What's that?" She cupped her hand to her ear.

"She has my feather," I said meekly. I tried to ignore Sabine and Colette as they glowered at me.

"So now she has an all-powerful talisman to use for her feverish desires. Very careless of you, Luc."

I looked at my shoe.

"And, Luc, what's the final thing the Divah needs to open the Gates of Hell, releasing the legions of damned upon the earth, leaving nothing but torment and suffering in their wake?"

My eyes darted around the cathedral, searching for the nearest exit. They fell, in the end, on Foune and the altar.

"She needs a sacrifice!" I whispered. "To unlock the passage between the realms and imbue her with everlasting power."

"*Très bien*. Does she have one? An innocent to sacrifice before the Gates?"

"No?" I asked, hopefully. "Surely that's impossible, Anaïs! The innocent has to come willingly, and an angel must *bring* her to sacrifice. Clearly that will set her back some in her diabolical plans." I looked desperately around. "Those rules were put in place to make it impossible for such a sacrifice. *For what angel would do such a thing?*"

But I was suddenly unsure. "She *is* planning a Shadowsill Ball. . . ."

The threesome exchanged a knowing look. Sabine flicked her riding crop dangerously against her thigh.

The priest was groaning again, rolling about slightly as though he meant to sit up. I looked at him nervously.

"You found him strung up, you said?" Anaïs asked.

"Yes, some rioters had just passed."

"You should have let him hang." Anaïs was suddenly by my side, peering down at Foune.

"What say you—?" I was appalled.

"You know the man?"

"I do! I come to play the organ here from time to time."

"Your vision's clouded. She has charmed you. You're too long in the human world without wings. Now, your emotions shroud your eyes and make you take dangerous risks—risks that lost you your feather, that brought about your fall from grace. That might very well bring about the End of Days."

Your mother produced a flask from her belt and tossed the water upon the man. He writhed in agony, hissing. Colette and Sabine, like spider-angels, stepped forward and bound him in silk.

"How can you ever hope to succeed if you can't recognize your own enemy before you?" Anaïs accused.

"I recognize quite well the only one who matters." I shrugged. "She wears a crown." I gave Foune a withering look. He had gone quite docile again in the Hermès binds.

"So. What did you say brings you to town again, ladies?" I asked weakly.

"I'm here to clean up your mess, Luc." Your mother sighed. "I'll be at the Vieille Etoile."

"La Vieille Etoile?" I said. "Let the good times roll."

55

La Vieille Etoile was an exclusive hotel on the Left Bank, within walking distance of Notre Dame. It also happened to be *my* hotel. Angels, by definition, do not like to share. *Especially* lodging—quickly things can descend into a disagreeable competition for the finer things in life. Who has the better suite? Who has the proprietor's favor? Who gets the choicest meat from the spit, the warmest bricks to heat their beds?

I rushed home.

My stomach sank as I saw my things, my trunks and valises, the detritus of centuries of fine living, packed and stowed beneath the stairs. Quite quickly, it became evident that my suite had been given over to your mother—to Anaïs—and her entourage.

Madame Dupris offered me the only thing she had left, a small room off the games room—noisy and exposed. I banged my head on the transom as I entered the low-hung door.

"What of Charles?" I asked about my manservant. He had been a good butler, discreet, and many had said, quite handsome.

"I can offer you Roland." Madame Dupris sniffed.

"Anaïs has taken my manservant, too?" I asked. Your mother always had a weakness for handsome men.

Roland proved to be quite feeble and blind. He shuffled into the small chamber with a silver tray. By the time I retrieved my brandy, half had been spilled on the floor.

"Help me with my cloak," I ordered, but the old man could not seem to find the clasp, and my ruined wings became uncomfortably tied up in the tailoring. "Never mind. Leave me be," I said. "On second thought—can you have something sent up to the Suite Royal—my old rooms? A bottle of champagne for our new resident angel. Something good—that frolicking drunkard of a monk Pérignon is said to make something of decent quality."

I studied the disorder of my small room. There were bags on chairs, chests and trunks scattered haphazardly beside the hearth.

"And when you return, you can begin the tired business of shaking the demons out of my things."

56

Anaïs had said she was in town to clean up my mess, but I awoke the next morning with a mind to do so myself. Things had gone far enough, I now saw. A war was brewing—I could smell it in the rank air. Not a revolution, Itzy, but a *holy war*—between Heaven and Hell. A war of dread secrets, fallen angels, Satan's spawn. And Anaïs had all but said I was the cause of it.

So I left la Vieille Etoile early, with Roland asleep, snoring in an upright chair.

I walked quickly to the Pont Neuf, ignoring the beggars and street urchins as best I could. Not long into my errand, I spied him—his dark fur had grown in patchy and one eye appeared to be clouded over—but there was no mistaking Her Majesty's hellhound. He fell in with me silently.

"Mops," I said. "Looking good."

The streets were brewing some new threat of late, with the peasants hungry—starved by the queen—unsavory vendors were popping up selling edibles, things gleaned from the gates of tanneries and the glue factories.

"Here we are, Mops," I said, upon arriving at my destination. "You can save me a lot of trouble by telling me where she keeps my feather." The dog merely sauntered on ahead, its claws clicking on the cobbles.

"What's that? Divah got your tongue?" I called.

I stared up at les Gobelins. It was a fortress of stone, iron bars across slits of windows and walls as thick as a three horses wide. It was perched beside a small river, the Bièvre, a foul thing, which served various tanneries and slaughterhouses as it wound its way north to the Seine. Today, ominously, a bloated corpse was stuck up in the reeds, bobbing idly.

I straightened my shoulders, felt the pang of my ruined wings, and walked to the vast portal and banged the immense iron knocker. From somewhere far away, I heard the sound of footsteps advancing in no great hurry. Mops stood intent on the door, the creature's entire being locked on the entrance, its four short legs planted firmly on the ground.

"Last chance to save the world," I whispered to the beast. "Soon this will all be reduced to embers, Mops. Pyres of the dead. A wasteland. All for what?" I asked.

All for a feather, I answered when the dog did not.

"Monsieur Luc." The door opened, and I was greeted by one of the Divah's favored devhils. The man was lanky and bald, and stringy hair stretched across his pink shiny scalp, revealing a shiny patch of skin.

"*Docteur*." I bowed at Her Majesty's doctor.

"Well, if it isn't the tortured artist."

We inspected each other for some time. The doctor's eyes held no mirth in them at all.

"Her Majesty is expecting me," I offered. "If you could be so good as to show me to her, I would be most obliged."

The doctor sniffed, and, turning, he walked back though the substantial entry and into the courtyard. Les Gobelins was his residence, a family stronghold of centuries of mischief. The place was filthy with the years of soil from boots and cinders from the bellows. I spied Mops in the corner beside the guardhouse lifting a leg and urinating. By the smell, he was quite familiar with that corner.

"I love what you've done with the place," I called.

The interior of the palace was no cleaner. I stepped over the remnants of moldering food, spills from careless servants, and dead cinders and overflowing piles of ash by the hearths. Mildewed tapestries hung from the wall, their colors faded to muted browns and rusts.

Marie Antoinette sat by one such hearth in a room at the top of a tower. The hellhound ran to her on his stunted legs and she scooped him up into her lap.

"Mopsy-popsey," she said, allowing the dog to lick her face.

"My queen." I bowed low and extravagantly.

Her eyes turned to me, twinkling. Her small, pert mouth prickled at one corner, and I was reminded of that infamous day in the Hall of Mirrors, the day I first spied Her Majesty, when the world was still golden and my life had grace.

A row of courtiers lined the grim walls, in various flouncey fashions of the day. They tittered and whispered behind their bejeweled hands, and I was reminded how the peasants were currently butchering aristocrats in the street.

"Thank you for seeing me, Your Majesty."

"Of course. I always have time for the poor and downtrodden." From an ornate box beside her, Marie Antoinette selected a miniature outfit that bore a remarkable resemblance to her own.

"I see, yes, thank you. I suppose I am both of those things." I cleared my throat. "On that note. I was wondering, my love—there is still that small issue between us."

She held her dog, sliding the dress over its pug face, and wrenching the legs though the armholes. She admired her work. A little frown creased her alabaster brow.

"I've been so alone, Luc."

"Surely not, Your Majesty!" I protested, indicating her entourage.

She held up the small dog, inspecting it. Its body was slack, its eyes wide and pathetic. I shot Mops a look: *You had your chance.*

A maid entered, head bowed, intent on a heavy silver tray upon which were a pair of golden chalices and a pitcher.

"I miss you. I miss *us.*"

"With the utmost respect, Your Highness, there never really was an 'us'—"

The room, already cast in shadows, darkened further.

Careful, Luc. The Divah leaned forward, her eyes glinting.

We began our conversation now in earnest, as the room grew even dimmer. While the courtly ladies and the servant girls were still present, they were not privy to this discussion. Gazing upon us, our mouths seemed to issue syrupy pleasantries, a happy, clever reunion between two companions: an artist and his muse. Bright amusement pierced our laughter. Their room was not roiling stormclouds, and indeed, no such atmospheric change could they perceive.

But to me, Itzy, the room was now black at pitch, a few dripping tallows illuminating the Divah on her throne.

How dare you abandon me. Her eyes bore into mine. *Ours was a love born of brimstone. I will not be made a fool of. I will not suffer to be alone again.*

I was deceived, I said.

Deceived? A bitter laugh escaped her lips. *"We are meant for each other, a union of opposites. Something new!"*

Were these not your words to me? You wandered the streets in a delirium of love; you shouted my name in rapture; you painted my likeness at every turn—

Your likeness? Ha! Is it not but a body you've stolen? A shell? Is it not ultimately artifice and lies? I saw your true likeness, Madame, *at Apollo's Basin, that last day. Your true likeness bears none of this rouge and powder. It was decay, moldering flesh on bare bone. You tricked me, yes, and more the fool am I.*

All love affairs begin in artifice, Luc. A coquettish smile, a tilt of the head. A carefully chosen gown. It is a dance. Are you so ignorant of love? If there is anything I am guilty of, it is of trying to please you with this body. Do you not like it anymore? I will get another.

No! I gasped in horror.

Then come to me, my darkest angel. Come to me and be my love.

I live amongst the broken and the damned now. They welcome me.

That is my domain. And once the Gates are open, we will rule together over them. You will be my king and I your queen. It is everything I've promised.

Hot fetid wind blew now between us, whipping her vast skirts about like a sail, her lace petticoats rearing.

I am but a wretched shadow. You have made it so.

No, Luc, she said. *You have made it so. But I will not give up on us. Remember, we've got all the time in the world.*

I waited, the wind flapping my coattails, dark things soaring in the shadows.

I am unssssstoppable.

And in an instant, the room was returned to its normal squalor. "—as I was saying, I do so wish for you to continue painting me." She was laughing pertly at me, mid-sentence, posing sweetly.

My gut recoiled, and I struggled to maintain my composure.

"I have given up painting."

"A pity."

A golden wine was poured but the queen made no move to drink.

"Surely my services are of no further use to you, Your Majesty. All that remains is the small matter of my—*er*—feather."

Marie Antoinette exchanged a look with the doctor and reached for the goblet.

"You wish to leave my service?"

"I had thought—"

"The last person who wished to leave my service is floating in the river outside the strong door." She sipped her wine. "But," she said, considering her words, "are you devoted to me, as your queen?"

I swallowed.

"Tell me, Luc."

I felt myself raise my head and meet her eyes. I knew their pale blueness to be but artifice—like the rouge upon her lovely cheeks and the powdered wig upon her head. But all the same, my heart softened.

"I—I am, my queen."

"Of course you are. Luc?"

"Yes?"

"You must *show* me your devotion."

"Show you, my queen?"

"Yes. You must prove your affection. Earn my favor."

I glanced around nervously. "May I?" I stalled, indicating the waiting goblet of wine. I threw back the entire cup. My insides snaked with fire.

"As I was saying, my beautiful, handsome angel." She smiled sweetly. "You must not simply speak of your devotion, you must *demonstrate* it."

"What would you have me *do*, Your Highness?"

"Just one last thing, and I will return to you your feather."

The wine was making me feel faint. "My feather for what, dare I ask?"

The doctor coughed.

"It's really nothing. The very embodiment of simplicity. I need you to procure a night bride for me, for my Shadowsill Ball."

"An *innocent*?" I asked, horrified.

"Why, yes. I can hardly do so myself."

57

I stumbled from the stone ramp, away from the horrors of les Gobelins, and flung myself upon the rail beside the small river, throwing up the wretched amber wine. The corpse had righted itself and was now gazing skyward with its bloated, blue face. I eyed it miserably.

"What have I done?" I cried. "I set out to right my wrongs, but somehow have made it worse—much worse! A little mistake of falling for the wrong girl might end life as we know it. My love is humanity's downfall."

"Never make a deal with a demon," the corpse spoke, its flaccid mouth spilling a large quantity of murky river water from between its gums. "They're notoriously unreliable."

I sighed. "So true."

I watched the body bob and sway as a little wave licked the shore.

"Anaïs is in town," I confided.

Suddenly René was beside me. "Really? Did she mention me?" he asked eagerly.

"She had other things on her mind."

"*Oo la la*, Anaïs. What a fox!"

"She's out of your league," I replied. "Anyway, she prefers men. And the last thing you want is for her to pay a visit to you. It means trouble. She is here to clean up my mess. Which—by the looks of things—has now gotten much, much worse."

"What now?" Maurice flew down from a rampart.

"Careful," René said. "Someone might mistake you for a gargoyle."

Maurice ignored this and stood before me, arms crossed over his wide chest. His small, stout wings bristled.

"I went to her, thinking I'd simply ask for my feather back," I said miserably.

Gaston crawled out from the small, deep moat before the portal, joining us.

"I see. Prevail upon her decency. Good plan," Gaston said.

"I'm out of plans. It was worth a try."

"And now where are we?" Maurice asked. "What new abomination would she have you perform?"

"Just one—and then I'm free."

"Really?"

"What did she say?"

"Not much. A trifle, really. I am to procure her an innocent for sacrifice."

The host was silent.

I had not seen Laurent arrive; he had been perched quietly upon a lamppost.

"An innocent, you say?" Laurent drawled in the low menacing way of his. "If it will end this nonsense once and for all, I might have just the one."

58

It was with mounting horror, Itzy, that I heard Laurent's plan. His proposal was so horrific, so utterly mad, that for a moment I was left speechless.

"Even you are not capable of this!" I finally shouted, turning on him.

"I thought you'd be a little more grateful. Show some respect."

"It's horrific! You're offering up a human soul as if it were a wheel of cheese."

"A tasty one, too. Come to think of it, I've been keeping her for just such an occasion."

I turned to Maurice, who was brooding. "Tell him. Tell him this is out of the question. Tell him it's conduct unbecoming—and we will be *punished*."

Maurice rubbed his chin, his forehead pinched into a frown.

Laurent was smiling, his eyes cold. "What is one girl in the scheme of things, Luc? One small girl versus *war*? Do I need to remind you of the last war? We are still licking our wounds—slumming, seemingly, around Paris."

For once I must agree with Laurent, Itzy. He speaks the truth about the Fallen. Like it or not, we are bound together. We are fugitives, the tattered remnants of a resistance to a war long ago. That's all that binds us. That, and the black brands upon our fingers.

"You cannot be considering this!" I cried to Maurice. And to Laurent, "You love this girl—do you not? Only a beast could offer up another in such a way."

"You speak of love, Luc?" Laurent's wings bristled, their ivory-colored jagged ends rising up like hackles, the golden talons flashing dangerously. "We are here, in this mess, *because* of love. It is this thing called *love* that rains down destruction upon the heads of all. *Your* love, Luc. Pure, selfish, blind love. Murderous love." He spat. "And here is your reward for loving so. You shall see firsthand the consequences. Maybe this will teach you a lesson."

"I was tricked," I despaired.

"You love too easily," Laurent said, and then he was gone.

He was right, of course, Itzy. I have always loved too easily. And now—now some innocent would pay for my mistakes.

René was, for once, silent. Gaston was poking at the corpse with a stick. I looked at Maurice, miserably, and waited. He was thinking, weighing my options, pacing back and forth in a rutted ditch beside the stone castle.

Finally, he stopped. His eyes grabbed mine.

"What price for a soul?" he asked quietly.

"That price is too high."

"We shall see."

"If you give her an innocent, Maurice, she will use it to unlock the Gates. She will have everything she needs," René protested.

"No. I think not." Maurice drew himself up. "Tell the queen you will deliver to her what she demands. René, Gaston—back to my hotel. There is work to do."

59

Shadowsill—n. 1) The very edge of a shadow, between light and dark. 2) The straddling of two worlds: typically childhood and adulthood. A vague, confusing place. 3) A demon ball.

The day of July 14, 1789, dawned sooner than I could imagine, Itzy. The clouds were a heaving wet mattress in the sky.

A deep dread had taken up residence in my gut, and it was all I could do to keep from weeping. Roland was little comfort to me that day; he was even more bumbling, as if both of his hands had been exchanged for hams as he slept.

The Shadowsill was to be a masquerade ball, as the queen was amused by petty disguise. I, however, could not bear the thought of mirth, and after several botched attempts to attire me in my great cloak, I dismissed Roland and set off on a long walk.

In the courtyard, Anaïs cornered me. She was, as usual, impeccably dressed, even at this early hour.

"Luc." She nodded amiably. "Why so glum?"

"Anaïs," I greeted her. "Where have you been? I was wondering if the Vielle Etoile had displeased you—you've been so scarce."

"Oh, you know. Keeping busy. Where are you off to?"

"A walk. I thought it might clear my head."

"Quite. Just—Luc?"

"Yes?"

"Best stay away from the Bastille today."

"The prison?" I asked. It was an old, hulking thing I had no particular desire to see in a grim part of town.

"Yes." She smiled.

"Anaïs? Dare I ask why?"

"You might. And I might then tell you that it is an awful place, a terrible place, the place where Marie Antoinette sends those who displease her—in particular, scholars and hunters."

My eyes grew wide.

"And today, I mean to free them." She smiled and bowed slightly. I watched her as she walked away, her feet somehow never quite touching the ground. "See you at the party, Luc, *mon cher*," she called. "It should be a blast!"

60

The ghostly tolling of the cathedral's bells marked the beginning of the ball and summoned all those who would be guests to its doors. The deep, resonant chime echoed eerily off the Seine, along boulevards and twisting streets alike, impossible to ignore. Those who heard it shivered and clutched their children to them tightly.

Even Roland seemed affected by the insistent clanging, for his eyes shifted about my room nervously as he muttered strange curses to himself.

"Those bells!" he exclaimed. "They got no business ringing them! Why, they call the darkness out, they do. Those bells were forged in the bowels of the earth and nothing living should be made to hear them sound."

"Help me with my cloak, old man," I ordered. "Do you have my mask?"

The better part of a quarter of an hour was spent finding it, a small silken oval with holes for my eyes, the color of midnight to match my cloak. Once ready, I stared moodily into the hearth, unwilling to leave. I watched as the glowing embers went from orange to brown and burned to ash. Still the bells tolled, and still I lingered.

"Should not you go, sire?" Roland asked nervously.

I kicked the last of the dying embers with my boot and sighed.

"*Merci*, Roland," I said. "Do not wait up."

In the courtyard, I glanced about halfheartedly for Anaïs, but the yard was empty, save for a feral cat.

"Gaston?" I called, but the cat merely hissed, spitting at me before vanishing into the shadows.

I made my way as always from my fine hotel, pausing to inspect the empty streets. It was sundown, and the dwindling colors of the day were being chased by shadows. Up Rue Saint-Jacques I went, the large gate of the Petit Pont bridge looming ahead. The guards waved me by, and I proceeded over the span, my heels clacking hollowly on the wooden slats, the tarred pilings driven deep into the earth beneath the Seine. Several boats—many of them flying the queen's banners—were moored against the far side of the quay, on the Île de la Cité. The Seine looked like a pauper's mirror, reflecting back the glimmering exterior of Notre Dame.

I felt the bells more than I heard them now, and I found myself falling into step with their rhythm. I was not alone, I noticed. Figures approached the cathedral from all sides, some on foot, some in ornate coaches, all drawn to the same dark destination. An army of valets tended the arriving guests, their horses and liveries led off in a slow parade of finery, and the next arrival was announced.

The cathedral looked magnificent.

All three immense portals were thrown open and a golden light poured out onto the street. Inside, dark figures moved about. The pews had been moved aside and the entire checkered floor cleared for the ball. Above this, an ornate wrought-iron chandelier was installed with ten thousand flickering candles. Music echoed off the vaulted ceilings, harps were strummed, drums were struck, and a choir sung. Notre Dame. Our Lady. Notre Damned.

I shivered.

A ring of ash encircled the entire cathedral. I stepped over the ribbon of cinders sprinkled before the doors, and I was in.

I was now in her realm.

61

A girl-child greeted me, handing me an orchid for my lapel, and I secured it, without much thought, while surveying the crowd. Dancing had begun and the mood was merry, but I shared none of it. I looked around for Maurice, but if he was there, I did not see him.

I saw Laurent, however.

He leaned casually against a stone column, his face a playful mask. He had powdered his wings for the occasion, and they glittered in the candlelight. A girl was with him, with long strawberry blonde hair and an extravagant red velvet cape. He was teasing her, trying to peer behind her ornate eyewear. She tittered in delight and flushed as he touched her cheek.

Our eyes locked and he winked wickedly.

My stomach recoiled and I turned away.

It was a gathering of rare creatures. The queen's ladies-in-waiting were costumed as nuns, their rouged cheeks like polished apples beneath their flying headdresses. One flitted by, laughing coquettishly, trailed by a train of fools and admirers. "Luc!" she called, her voice husky and breathless. "Luc! Save a dance for me!"

A large clan of woodwose—wild demon-men from deep in the forest, savages covered in thick, curly hair, and dragging lumpen clubs behind them—prowled the periphery, sniffing for food and poking at things suspiciously. Ghostly, transparent beings with plaited hair, clothed in fashions long gone, drifted along the aisles upon scented boughs of laurel. They whispered in reedy voices and glided seamlessly though the statuary. Fairy lords, pale and arrogant, kept to themselves, boredom evident beneath their masks. The diabolical menagerie was out in full, alongside clothed bears, fallen angels, and a tall, elegantly dressed man with a jackal head. And of course, everywhere, demons.

I slunk down an empty corridor, preferring my own company.

I was beside a quiet little chapel, an unadorned statue of a hapless saint. The natural light was all but gone, and the stained-glass windows were shades of gray. The party continued without me, and I leaned against the cool stone to contemplate my future. Shame draped me like a cloak. As the party raged around me, I was wracked with *une crise de la foi*, a crisis of faith.

Itzy, for eternity, the life of an angel—the life of service, really—is uninterrupted in its monotony. We are not whole, those of us with wings. We yearn for a soul. Perhaps because I am closer to the human realm, I want it even more. I have been wandering for an eternity trying to fill an emptiness inside.

I tried to fill that void with art. With love. And now with despair.

I watched, from the obscurity of the small enclave as Laurent whirled the girl about the cathedral's floor. They made a lovely couple. How easy his manner—I envied him. What I lacked, I realized achingly, was *ambition*.

All of humanity was teetering on my selfishness, just as Laurent had said.

I staggered from my reverie, back toward the dark festivities.

No one would sink on my watch.

I stepped out from the gloom onto the golden light of the checkered floor. Masked dancers closed in around me. Laurent was whirling the girl about with a sickening grace, his feet a blur upon the floor. Other dancers, hundreds upon hundreds, filled the shadows, but for me, nothing else existed. Once, twice maybe, Laurent saw me, and he stared haughtily.

An insistent tap rained down upon my shoulder, and I turned, exasperated.

A young woman looked up at me, her chestnut hair coiled neatly into an intricate arrangement, her bosom heaving.

"What be it?" I nearly shouted.

"A dance?" she asked, taken aback.

I laughed then, my own voice sounding hollow in my ears.

"Child—away with you."

"*Child*? I am older than you," she smiled. "A dance, Luc. I *insist*."

I looked her over again, and she leaned in, whispering. "Get on your dance shoes, Luc, and stop your moping. This is a party, after all."

"René?" I asked, suspiciously.

"Maurice," she corrected, suddenly prudish.

"Oh—you don't say!" I smiled, stepping away to enjoy the view. "Nice rack."

The young maiden suddenly flushed an angry scarlet.

"Put your hands on my shoulders and start your two-step. *Now.*"

I did as Maurice asked. I set us off onto the dance floor.

"I've had an epiphany, Maurice," I confided.

"Agathe," she hissed.

"Agathe. Nice name—a bit difficult on the tongue."

"Silence it then."

"Agathe, I've had an epiphany. What I lack is ambition."

We whirled by Laurent, and to my delight I noticed him stumble.

"It's what makes you charming, your lack of ambition," Maurice-Agathe said.

"I don't want to be charming. It's my charming nature that got us here."

"No—it's your bad taste in women."

"*Touché.*"

We spun around, and suddenly I was overcome with the elegance, the *permanence* of this human structure, this Cathedral de Notre Dame. *Our Lady.* Not much could take it down. With a few improvements, it would make a charming hotel.

"Do not worry," Maurice said. "I have it all under control. Laurent's girl will be saved when René inhabits her."

"What?" I asked sharply.

"We won't let it go. The sacrifice. It is all arranged."

"Oh, is it?" I asked, whirling him around with undue force. A lock of the maiden's hair came undone.

"Easy," he scolded, patting it into place.

"Easy, nothing," I replied. "Nothing about this is easy."

62

As midnight neared, more and more people filled the vast cathedral, shadowy figures, dark things. The music soon took on a twisted, manic quality and the dancers adapted, dancing feverishly. I studied the span of flushed and feverish faces gloomily.

"This is ridiculous," I said to Agathe. "Outside the peasants are revolting. A *revolution* has begun. And inside—" I spun her about from one arm to the other. "Inside, we dance."

"Who knew you were so good on your feet?" Maurice grinned. "Who needs wings?"

"Where is René?" I snapped.

"He'll be here."

"Are you sure he's up to the task? He does tend toward distraction. Seems like an awfully big responsibility you've given him, to inhabit Laurent's innocent."

"René, unreliable? I hadn't noticed."

An audible gasp came from somewhere beside me. Maurice pulled away from me suddenly, falling over himself into a curtsy, and was gone. The crowd had given way and I stood, momentarily confused. Before me, the dancers parted, and it seemed to me the lights grew dim.

"Luc," the queen said. "So good of you to come."

She was ravishing, but I knew better.

Her scarlet dress was exquisite, trailing out behind her. About her pale shoulders was a silvery shawl as thin as a spider's web. But her mask bore my closest inspection. It was a golden oval, atop of which sat a fine net of spun gold and fiery opals that covered her hair. From one side floated a showy feather, light as air. My feather.

"Your Majesty," I bowed. "Might I have this dance?"

Her eyes glittered as I approached, bowing again.

Like my feather, she floated over to greet me. How could something so foul glide as she did across the floor, her skirts shimmering out behind her? We danced—or flew—across the cathedral's mezzanine.

"I admire your hat," I whispered. "But it might look better on me."

"I admire the girl," she said in return. I tightened my grip on her waist but she merely smiled. "Your friend Laurent did well to bring her."

"Perhaps you should have chosen him as your consort," I replied.

"He *is* a better dancer," she acknowledged, smiling.

We moved together in silence, dancing our way past a gathering of woodwose, their hides greasy and matted, the odor of musk nearly palpable.

My stomach tightened. "You promised me my feather," I reminded her, indicating her mask.

"Once I have opened the Gates, I will give you wings of flesh, of skin, of scales."

"*Merci*, but I'm partial to mine."

"I will be happy to never hear or speak the language of French again. Like razors on my tongue."

"The French seem to like it. They're rising up right now, as we speak."

"Let them," she laughed gaily. "The dead are rising, too."

She pulled away and clapped her hands. The music ceased.

The wild woodwose with their bulbous clubs cleared the floor of any last stragglers. High above, a bell rang, a deep resonant clanging, slow and booming. I could feel it in my very core. *Those bells were forged in the bowels of the earth and nothing living should be made to hear them sound.*

From the darkened halls of the cathedral, they came. The dead stepped forward from the shadows. Some were newly dead; they bore an expression of confusion and shambled forward on stiffened legs. And there were those whose eternal sleep had been interrupted much later— shreds of their burial shrouds clinging to them. And then the bones—yellowed and gnawed on by mice—they clattered forward to their queen.

I recognized a few—the street vendor. The pretty baker-girl. Cassedents was there—one gray eye hanging from its socket, a rusty spade in his blackened hand. The man toiled his entire life only to find no rest in the end, no grave. There were hundreds, thousands even, standing before us, all realizing the same thing. Eternal rest is hard to find.

Midnight had arrived, and still the bell tolled. With each gong, sand and mortar sifted down on us until the very stone walls of the cathedral were shaking. Finally, one last specter of the dead appeared, rolling onto the floor, landing softly against my boot.

Nicolas.

"René?" I asked hesitantly, but the head was silent, staring up at me with sunken eyes.

I looked up at the great vaulted ceiling of the transept. The walls were shaking now, visibly, and I wondered if she meant to take them down upon us all. Many guests were holding their ears, standing around dumbly. The great chandelier, with its thousands of tallow candles, was swaying. Hot wax was sloshing from the lit tapers and falling like searing rain on the guests below.

Agathe appeared beside me and on tiptoe leaned up to whisper to me.

"René is delayed," she growled.

"*Delayed*?" I hissed back.

"So, too, is Gaston."

"Laurent's not delayed," I pointed out. "Laurent is right here, true to his word. Look—he brings her out. He means to present the girl to the Divah! An angel bringing an innocent to sacrifice!"

Indeed, the young maiden with strawberry blonde hair was being led onto the floor before the queen.

"Where are they?" I demanded.

"At the Bastille. Things are slightly out of hand, I hear."

"Things are heating up *here*, Maurice. Things are about to get scorching."

"*I* will do it then," Maurice assured me.

I looked at him sideways. "*You* will inhabit the girl? Forgive me, but it is not your area of expertise."

He smoothed his dress and fluffed his hair. "I managed this one all right. Took me most of the afternoon. Peasant stock, *mon ami*. Thick skin, hearty souls."

"It has to be done quickly," I hissed over the bells. "The Gates want an offering, and they won't wait."

"Shh. Wait and see. Have faith, my friend."

"Faith? That is a word of those who are destined to die."

63

The chandelier was swinging, raining down hot wax, but the maiden did not seem to feel it. It glazed the dancers like porcelain dolls. Her face was beatific, an inner rapture shone upon her features. Laurent removed her red cloak, slipping it easily from her shoulders and allowing it to fall—a puddle of velvet on the floor. Beneath, the girl wore a dress of bejeweled silvery cloth, so thin and rich it was nearly weightless.

Marie Antoinette stood in the very center of the cathedral, beside the choir, watching Laurent and the girl. The doctor was by her side.

"What hole did he crawl out of?" Maurice whispered.

"Pick one," I shrugged, pointing.

The enormous bells were rattling the very foundation of the ancient church. A crack had appeared in the stoneblock wall, its angry zigzag like a madman's stairway, and a red glow oozed from the void. The walls shook; the floor under our feet was suddenly insubstantial, as if it might open up beneath us and swallow us whole. The candles above surged to an impossible brightness, and, as we looked around desperately, they flickered, dimmed, and then—taking the cursed bells with them—were gone.

"What bestial horror has she saved for us tonight?" Maurice cursed.

A strange silence followed. The eerie yellow glow of the torches at the front portal were all that remained—and then, with one final *pop*, they too were extinguished. The vast space descended into pitch black.

But there was no relief in the darkness.

We soon spied many pairs of red, glowing embers. *The candles?* I thought, absurdly. The dull red of the embers grew brighter, taking on a fiery, vivid orange—glinting, reflecting. These were not candle tapers, I realized. I gazed at one in confusion, and it blinked. *These were eyes of the damned.*

Something brushed the back of my wings, and I felt cold terror for the first time in many, many years. I found myself wishing yet again I had never spotted Marie in the Galerie—that I had never held her hot, dry hand. It was a pathetic wish, a momentary wish, and although I was destined to wish it forever, it would soon disappear in the chaos of the room.

I invited demons among us that day, Itzy. They haven't left us since.

Notre Dame filled with a low, inhuman growl, and the unearthly howl overtook everything. We covered our ears with our hands, eyes wide. Raspy, indistinct words threaded beneath the insidious noise, pleading in desperate tones—the cry of the damned. They spoke an old language, the language of burials, of decay.

The floor rippled. It buckled and swayed. The worn black and white tiles went flying through the air like flapjacks. A charnel stench filled the air, sulfur thick and pungent. The huge *pierres* of the underfloor heaved as something vast, something evil, pushed up from beneath them. Where a moment ago we had been dancing, making merry, now rose from the wasteland of the nether-world a hideous vision.

Death's door.

A desolate, Gothic archway pushed up savagely through the checkered floor like an enormous, jagged fang, sending broken rock and earth scattershot across the room. A roiling cloud of stone dust and ash filled the air, settling down on the Shadowsill guests. The heat from Hell blazed upon us, like hot breath from fetid bellows. The few woodwose that dared approach burst into flame, their shrieks echoing through the long halls.

Agathe whistled low and throaty. "*Merde!*"

Foul, protruding spikes dotted the Gates of Hell. The doors bulged, studded with rusted iron nails, but held. Deep below the Cathedral of Notre Dame, the stewing cauldron of souls began to stir.

64

You do not have to know your French history, Itzy, to know that the storming of the Bastille that day on July 14, 1789, meant the end of the demon infestation of France. Your mother had orchestrated it well. The peasants rose up and revolted, releasing the imprisoned beleaguered scholars from jail. They roamed the streets and took back what was theirs, beneath banners of Hermès silk, with flagons of pure French water. With help from the Institute, no demon would be safe. They would be flushed out, each and every one of them, from the smallest chimney pot to the largest gilt castle.

But your mother's work was not done. From the Bastille, Anaïs and the freed chasseurs made for the Cathedral of Notre Dame. They arrived in a rush of wind, of cool untainted air. And cold blue light.

In the gloom of the cathedral, the vast, circular rose window began to shine, its colors drenching us in reds and blues. I could find no sign of the Divah or her doctor. The colors played upon the floors, through the sifting dust that hung heavy in the air. We, who had but a moment before been lost in night as black as pitch, were suddenly released from the awful spell—waking as though from a nightmare to Christmas morning. Hell looked, if not a thing of beauty, then like its ugly stepsister, its cracked and withered rock and studded portals decked out gaudily from the colors of the stained glass. The rose window glowed as if the very sun were rising behind it. We shaded our eyes, and it grew brighter still.

Laurent had found us and stood beside me and Agathe, and we stared up at the unearthly glow.

"It's not a party," he said, "until someone calls the cavalry."

The implosion was terrible to behold. The enormous circular window was blown inward as if on the breath of a giant. The force of it knocked us backward, jerking my neck like a rag doll and catching my arms up in my cloak. Beside me, Agathe swooned and fell, as lead and colored glass from the famed rose window of Notre Dame shot through the air.

As the wondrous colors vanished, so did the sound. In the aftermath of the explosion, I heard nothing. Laurent was mouthing something—gesturing to the balcony above us—but my attention was drawn to the Gates. As I looked in vain for the queen, glass began hitting the floor. Emeralds, sapphires, and rubies rained down upon us.

"Gate-crashers!" someone shouted, as finally my hearing thrummed alive.

Through the gaping hole of the stained-glass window they came, the first wave, led by Anaïs. I spotted René and Gaston—exuberant looks upon their shining faces, staffs glowing impossibly bright in their hands. There were hundreds of them, followers of Anaïs and unknown to me. Arrows rained down, streaking silver through the air. From the towers came Sabine and Colette, and they fell upon the queen's guards and the shrieking harpies that were her ladies-in-waiting.

"Maurice?" I bleated at the buxom girl. "Agathe?"

The unconscious girl was surprisingly heavy, and I propped her sagging body in the corner, against a pillar. Her head lolled, and when I righted it, it merely drooped once more to the other side. I nestled her flailing arm in her lap.

"Stay out of trouble," I advised.

Her face was flushed, and she sighed blissfully in her swoon. The demon possessions always want closure, Itzy. The angelic ones never want it to end.

From somewhere behind us, I heard the sound of splintering wood, as the ancient door in the Lady Chapel was wrenched open in the far apse. Professor Guillotin and his liberated chasseurs were storming in through the rear entrance, brandishing torches. He looked different from the last I saw him in the catacombs—stronger, more alive. His hair had loosened from its severe style, and it hung free and wild in his face. Here was a man with a purpose, Itzy, and his purpose was killing.

"*Vive la France!*" he shouted, and his cry was echoed by his followers as they poured into the cathedral.

I spun around, turning desperately toward Hell's Gates, its jagged arches shimmered with heat. I could just make out Laurent's girl—she stood unsteadily, swaying, while the battle raged around her. To my horror, she inched forward, one toe at a time, toward the bloated and ravaged doors. The crowd closed in and she was lost to me.

Before me, a wildman fell, an arrow in his neck. His club clattered to the floor, and I grabbed the knotted wood handle. As I stumbled forward into the chaos of battle, the club glowed an icy blue. Everywhere, rats were scrabbling across the floor, like children running to their mother, as the angels attacked from above.

I moved stealthfully, darting behind upturned pews and crypts until I caught a glimpse of the queen. She stood beside the Gates now, in their monstrous shadows. She turned and found my eyes. They glowed with an orange fire, a devilish rapture. My pitch-black feather fluttered behind her ear.

Luc, does this please you? Her voice was harsh inside my head. *I only ever wanted to make you happy.*

As I neared the entrance to Hell, I felt a terrible, yawning terror. The doors rose horribly in a pile of rubble from the church's center, stabbing the heights of the transept. The thick stench of sulfur was intolerable. Laurent's girl stood mutely, mesmerized, a fine bead of perspiration across her lip. The heat was unbearable.

"Maurice?" I grabbed her by the shoulders, shaking her. Her eyes were glazed and looked right through me. I let go in disgust.

"Maurice!" I bellowed into the air, throwing my head back, receiving a mouthful of ash. "Maurice! You were supposed to occupy the girl! To save her!" I spun around hopelessly. The vaulted stone ceilings were achingly high. Angels circled, their wings cupping the air.

The soles of my feet were burning and blistering. I unclasped my cloak, throwing it over the girl in a vain attempt to shelter her from the searing heat. I bent, scooping her up in my arms, but she twisted and flailed.

"You will die!" I shouted at her.

"Do you see it?" she said, her eyes bright. "Is it not beautiful?"

"*No—ce n'est pas beau,*" I gasped.

Hell is real, Itzy. And the corrupt, congealed souls within are anything but beautiful.

Over the din, in some cruel jest, the orchestra was still playing, and notes of a waltz threaded though the scene of horror before me.

The jackal-headed warrior stood heads taller than the crowd, and he battled with a glittering curved sword, his army of the dead falling in behind him.

I glimpsed Anaïs battling her way to Marie Antoinette and the doctor. The doctor was edging them away through a dark archway, stabbing at the onslaught of Guillotin's men with a long barbed cane.

"Anaïs!" I shouted. "The Divah—she's getting away!"

Gaston heard my cry and sent an arrow flying. It lodged deep into the doctor's thigh, where it burned with a cold, blue flame. He fell but for a moment, scrabbling to his feet, hissing.

It was then that I saw it. Trampled in the scholars' advance was a golden oval—my feather still attached, lost in the melee.

I shook Laurent's silly girl, hard. "Wake—you stupid thing!" The queen's mask was being trampled. I raised a hand to slap her. *"Réveille-toi!"*

"Hey—easy on the merchandise!" she spoke, eyes suddenly clear and focused.

"Maurice?" I scowled, my arm still tensed.

"You break it, you buy it," he said, running a delicate hand through his luscious hair.

"What took you so long?" I growled, turning to run.

"I think Laurent put a block on her," he called after me, but the words rocketed off the stone chamber and were lost.

I clubbed several woodwose, sending them flying as I angled for another view of Marie's golden mask. The fighting was thick beneath the archway, and I skidded to a halt, dropping to my knees. I felt around blindly as the battle surged over me. A soiled, cold foot pressed down on my hand as a corpse wrestled with a scholar nearby. I wrenched my hand free and continued searching madly, feeling about the pitted stone floor for any sign of my beloved feather. Something tripped over me, and, cursing, I saw a broad pair of naked, hairy legs before me. I raised my head level to a filthy loincloth.

"Cassedents!" I cried. "Be gone. I have no issue with you, you old fool."

The grave digger raised his shovel, his eye lolling from its socket.

"My *feather*—you're blocking my path, you dumb fool." I drew my arm back and deposited my club into the soft putty of his stomach, and he fell back. "How's that grave the queen promised you? You were right about one thing, Cassedents. The dead do outnumber us."

A sickening squelching noise accompanied my second thrust, and I rolled away. As I did, my hand brushed a smooth leather boot, and scales of a reptile hide rippled beneath my fingers. A flinty spur jutted dangerously from the heel.

I raised my eyes and was greeted by the enormous head of a jackal. The warrior bared his sharp teeth in his long snout, his ears pressed against his skull. A rabid foam slathered his gums. My hands found the folds of my cloak and from it I pulled Marie's dagger, but it was too late. The long, curved sword arced high above his beastly head, and his arm tensed as he lowered it upon me.

A shout rang out over my shoulder. A beam of clear white light caught the warrior's attention, and I rolled away. The jackal's nose sniffed the air.

"Run!" shouted René as a bolt shot from his staff, missing the jackal and hitting the floor. A smoking hole appeared. I belly-crawled to the relative safety of the shadows of a nearby crypt.

Gaston had appeared by René's side, and they hovered, raining blows down upon the creature. The warrior crouched and swung low, his sword a withering blur. René's next shot went wide and it hit a pillar, reverberating up the massive pile of stones. Crouched and snarling, the jackal-headed warrior sprung, snapping at the air, his sword nearly catching René by the cloak.

Gaston fired an arrow at the creature's backside, and when he fell, the ground shook. A dark, frothy scum spilled from his mouth, pooling on the floor.

Gaston and René convened in the air wing to wing, eyes bright. René leaned in, gesturing lewdly, and Gaston tipped his head back and belly-laughed.

They didn't see it coming.

The jackal's eyes wrenched open, his pupils black pinpricks. The warrior's gloved hand closed around the bone handle of my foul dagger beside him. With a dying burst of strength, the creature threw the wicked blade, and it tumbled through the air over the dead and dying, over the damned and fallen. It caught René in the throat. He crashed to the floor, his wings flailing.

There were words on his lips, soft as velvet, but I could not hear them.

"René!" I cried. I looked around desperately. Gaston was hovering, stricken.

I watched as the light of René's staff turned cold, as he flickered and vanished.

An inhuman wail filled the cavernous halls, and I realized it was coming from my throat.

65

I grabbed René's cold staff and swung it around me in an arc, hacking at the jackal and his fancy boots, finishing him.

Gaston pulled me off. The broken pillar was teetering beside us, threatening to fall. A shiver went up it and it wobbled, wavering like a broken spine. I cast about desperately for my feather, for any sign of the Divah.

"Save yourself!" Gaston advised. "Later we mourn."

Others had noticed the column and were scrambling to escape it. Heavy stones from the lower vaulted ceiling of the aisle had already begun to fall. Gaston pointed down the dark cloister to the Lady Chapel, the breeched door. "There—the doors are unlocked. That is your path."

I saw a small animal worrying something in the shadows—gnawing on a ball, or perhaps a bone.

"Mops," I hissed, throwing the icy light on the scene. "Be gone!"

I reached for my flask and the hellhound growled and retreated, and I was left facing an old friend.

"Ah, Nicolas," I said. "No hard feelings?"

I was inspecting the damage Mops had wrought upon the poor head—a better part of an ear was missing and the tip of Nicolas's nose had been gnawed—when the massive stone column indeed failed, falling down upon itself like a giant's toy. In the confusion that followed, there was another rending noise, great stone upon stone, and a dark, dank smell filled my nostrils. I shook, sweating and cursing in the dark, hugging Nicolas. Finally the stone dust settled, and the sagging Gothic ceiling over me scraped and groaned, shedding keystones and long, rib-like shards.

Gaston was gone, off in flight, and I was left alone to peer at what remained. Through the gloom, I forced my eyes to see, raising high René's staff.

"You remember René, don't you?" I asked Nicolas. "He liked you."

The nave between us had vanished into a cavernous hole. My eyes were drawn to a tattered silk banner that fluttered beside the grievous opening. It was burned and battered, and splattered with some sort of gore, but bore the Hermès orange and brown. Where were Guillotin and his scholars now?

A gust of rotted stench filled the air from the dark vault beneath the cathedral. A few creatures, loosed from the crypt below, flitted out, flapping their wings with ghastly squelching noises. In the shadows of the gaping hole, I saw something shift. A terrible talon rose up and crashed down upon the stone, gouging the floor as it pulled itself up. Its thick skin was leather, its claw from stone and coal, and judging by its talon, it was gargantuan.

"What new evil is this?" I asked Nicolas.

We did not stay to find out.

66

I raced with Nicolas down twisting aisles, through evidence of battles won and lost. To my great relief, I spied the Gates, closed and abandoned—no sign of Maurice. The path Gaston had indicated was blocked by the column's wreckage, and, as I skidded to a halt, Nicolas fell from my hands, leaving a large clump of hair in my fist.

"Nicolas!" I shouted as he rolled away into a dark recess. I found him beside a polished wooden confessional, banging against one of the discreet doors. He rolled forward, thumping his forehead against it—the sound of a carcass on a chopping block. Again and again he smacked the door.

"*Qu'est-ce qu'il y a?*" I wondered.

And then I realized, Itzy. Marie Antoinette had called the dead, and Nicolas had answered. He had come to my rescue.

I scooped him up and opened the door in question. Ahead, there was a passage, lit by gleaming tapers. A tattered shred of the costliest silk lay before me—the color of blood.

"Nicolas, I could kiss you!" I said, turning his hideous grimace to me. "At least, when this is done, let me buy you a proper drink."

I snatched up the fabric, feeling it between my fingers. It was soft and scented. It was from Marie Antoinette's dress. She had come this way.

Nicolas rolled on ahead, content to follow the low-slung tunnel on his own volition, and I took up the rear.

"They've not been long this way," I shouted. "The tallows are all fresh, and this foul jelly is from the doctor's wounded leg."

The head bounded along, unconcerned with corners or the few steps we encountered. Soon, we had come to a small iron-hashed door, a little peephole looking out into the night. I yanked it open and we were free.

67

Did I say *free*, Itzy? For I was anything but. There was no sign of Marie, but pikes and iron spikes were every-where, many with human heads atop. The revolution had begun.

"Don't look." I cradled Nicolas.

In the clear dark air, I shuddered. *All this suffering, for naught.*

In my misery, I heard the sound of footfalls coming from the small wooden bridge. Shining René's staff, my heart soared. It was the queen's minion, the doctor, and while I saw no sign of the queen, what I did see quickened my step. Beneath his arm was an unmistakable plume, dancing, teasing the night air.

"My feather!" I cried.

The battle was now pouring from Notre Dame. Shrieks and cries were sounding as panic spread, people trying to escape the monstrous creatures from the vaults, rushing to their freedom only to be met by armed and angry peas-ants at the building's front entrance.

There was traffic in the Seine—no doubt the queen would make for her bateau. But as I rushed to the quay, there was nothing moored beneath me. Brackish water swirled in melancholy whirlpools.

I spied an overloaded hay barge approaching from the west, its load high and heavy. It drew near the Petit Pont, low in the water. Its captain, a man with a nicotine-stained beard and a burlap hat, was shouting something to a few men with long oars and poles who were using them to navigate the approach to the low-slung bridge.

Upon this very bridge the doctor ran, dragging his wounded leg behind him, oblivious to the oncoming barge. He had lost his pitchfork in the fight and was hobbling along angrily without it. On the far side of the old wooden bridge were a set of gates, the very ones I had come through at dusk. But the gendarmes stationed there had abandoned their posts when the cursed bells rang, gathering what weapons they could carry and running home to their families. They had left in fear and locked and barred the doors. The doctor howled at the iron grate, pounding upon it with a clenched fist.

The barge, laden with hay, was swiftly approaching the small wooden bridge, and as it did the shouts increased from the ship's deck. The captain was gesturing wildly at the height of his load, and a few of his men scrambled atop the unsteady pile to let loose armloads so they might pass beneath.

Hay was everywhere, in the air, clogging the narrow section of the Seine, drifting by with the clean pleasant scent of pasture. Nicolas sneezed. "Bless you," I said.

The bridge was all that lay between me and my feather. The doctor was cornered.

"Shall we?" I asked Nicolas, ambling over to the Petit Pont.

A fiery woodwose streaked by us. The queen's wildman was burning, his hunched figure engulfed in oranges and reds, and as I watched languidly, he bounded over the stone wall and made to jump into the cooling river. Flailing through the air to save himself, he succeeded only in landing on the hay barge.

Nicolas didn't say anything—he didn't need to.

"Stupid, foul creatures," I cursed. "*Now* he wants a bath?"

The hay ignited in a *whooshing* gulp.

The captain and his fellow sailors jumped ship, bobbing in the oily water beside the inferno, swearing with raised fists. With no one to man the barge, it sped forward with the current, ambling toward the low bridge, and we had naught to do but watch.

The hay lit up the night sky, raining fiery wisps and black stalks down upon the quay. It was the purest tinder, the driest of kindling, in hindsight—a boat meant for burning. A boat of ash. I could just see the scorched silhouette of the woodwose as he became one with the roaring fireball. With a sickening thud, the barge made its way beneath the bridge, wedging itself aflame beneath its low wooden supports. The doomed bridge caught flame.

I tried to restrain Nicolas. He lurched about in my arms like a greased ostrich egg. Finally, he sunk his teeth into my thumb, and, cursing, I dropped him. The last I saw of him, he was making his way over the Petit Pont, bobbing and bouncing, a silhouette of wispy hair and withered skin, bounding forward gallantly. That was the last, too, I saw of my feather—reds and yellows of the flames reflected in its glossy plumes. The doctor and the feather were gone, seemingly vanished into thin air.

It was a noble gesture, the gesture of a true friend.

I looked on as the scorching flames closed in on Nicolas. I could have saved him—but for one thing.

Itzy, I had no wings.

68

Charred ribs and a few floating, fiery stalks of hay were all that remained of the marriage of the Petit Pont and the barge. It was not a moment for me to appreciate irony, Itzy, yet I do so now. Fire transforms everything.

The captain's burlap hat was floating idly, but I saw no signs of its owner. I stared blankly at the swirling eddies of the Seine and felt a slight wind upon my neck.

"René's gone," I said.

"I know." I felt Maurice's hand on my shoulder. It tingled.

"My feather is, too. All this was for naught."

"We will turn Paris upside down for your feather."

"You won't find it," I said. "She will never let me go."

We heard shouts and the sounds of gunpowder.

"The peasants are coming—best be gone," said Maurice.

"I do not think I care for peasants. For France. For anything."

Maurice took my head in his hands. "We are winning, Luc."

"Is this what winning feels like?"

"Come—" He looked over his shoulder more urgently. "I will carry you home."

And he did, Itzy. He gathered me in his arms like a babe, and cradling me, he rose up, hovering over the smoldering Seine. I saw the streets as I hadn't seen them in years;

I saw them as I was made to see them—from on high. I saw the raucous gathering of revolutionaries storm the cathedral, fearing not the giant's roar that greeted them, nor the flying buttresses snapping like matchsticks in the rear. Their banners waved above them as they piled upon the courtyard, trampling the ring of ash. Some daring ones climbed the very walls of the cathedral, scaling as high as a gargoyle might. They were calling for the queen of France, of course; they were bloodthirsty and tired. Tired and sick of the demon queen from Hell.

I knew just how they felt.

Maurice rose still higher, and I saw the sun readying itself implacably upon the eastern horizon. I kicked off my boots, to better leave behind the torturous earth. They fell, one after the other, down to the tiny city below. The City of Lights, some call it. I might call it something else entirely.

"They won't find her there," I said to Maurice. "She's slunk back to Versailles."

"Perhaps not tonight," he said, a slight smile gracing his sturdy face. "But they'll get her in the end."

69

They did, of course. But you already know that, Itzy.

It was a proud day for Sanson, the executioner, who, by then, had perfected his showmanship.

It was a proud day for Professor Guillotin, too, who I am sad to say would soon follow Her Majesty to the scaffolds and experience his invention firsthand. Being a scholar is dangerous work—and in the end, he succumbed to the dangers of his profession. When his time came with Lady Razor, the blade was so dulled from use that it had to fall twice. By then, though, the guillotine had nearly done its job—16,594 demons had been vanquished in France, sent back to Hell where they belonged, their demon queen along with them. France would remain demon-free for the next several centuries, and demons throughout the Underworld would rue the day they heard the language of love, of all things French.

The guillotine was not to be my salvation, though. On that, Maurice was wrong.

"This is not over," I said, as they brought Marie Antoinette to the scaffolding that day in October 1793.

She was remarkably poised, in that dress, the color of a thundercloud.

Remember that color, I told her wordlessly. *They have no clouds in Hell.*

As the blade fell, Gaston leaned in to me. "Taking out the trash," he said over the exulted crowd.

Her banishment blew the lid off the city's catacombs and sent bone dust thick as ash into the air. It settled all around us—an early snow.

"For René," I smiled at him weakly.

"Well—thank god that's over, lover boy," Laurent announced, dusting the ghostly film from his waistcoat. "I've got a date."

"Over?" I repeated, hollowly. "It's not over. Perhaps for them"—I gestured at the crowd, at those who were destined to die—"it is over."

"They will forget," Maurice sighed. "Humans and history. No matter how much they write it down, they never get it right."

"And Luc's feather?" Gaston asked. My feather had never been found, for all of our searching. Not in Versailles, after the peasants sacked it, not in her palaces in Paris. My feather had simply vanished alongside the doctor.

It was Maurice who realized it first.

"She still has it," he said. "You must call her back. Luc's right. This is not the end."

"Call her back?" I asked, horrified. "I'd rather walk in these shoes for all of eternity."

"You remember the last war."

"*I* wasn't the cause of that one."

"Luc, this is no longer about you. We saw what she's capable of. Besides, Anaïs said."

"Anaïs said what?" I asked.

"To appeal to her vanity. Trick her out of hiding. Bait her. The feather must be retrieved at all costs."

"Bait her with what?" I cried. "It is she with my feather, not the other way around!"

"I dunno," Laurent drawled, appearing to think. "Another soul? Something irresistible. Ah! Don't divahs find fledglings particularly juicy?"

"A fledgling?" Gaston scoffed. "As if."

"But we've just rid ourselves of her!" I gestured to Sanson as he paraded with the queen's head. A puppet theater nearby was reenacting the execution with marionettes and a miniature guillotine.

"*Jamais!*" I wailed. "Never!"

"There's time. Think on it. Laurent's had the marvelous idea of writing her a few letters. Love letters. He's even volunteered to do it himself."

"How terribly gallant." I scowled at him.

"It'll be my pleasure. I'll sign them Lover Boy. She shan't resist them." Laurent grinned wickedly.

"Well then," Maurice said. "It's decided."

I stepped away from my friends and into the rowdy crowd. My eyes, even then, were searching through drifting ash and bone dust for my feather. *Lover boy*, Laurent's taunt echoing through my mind.

They were selling trinkets the day she died.

"How much?" I asked, pointing.

"One livre," the boy said. I tossed him the coin. The boy looked astonished—he had expected to haggle.

I brought the lock of her silver hair close to my face. It smelled of roses and dungeons. I snaked it through my fingers and lifted it to my nose.

What could have possessed me?

PART III

HELL HOTEL

Gates from gristle and hides for hinges
Gates from thew and bones for bolts
Gates from sinew and teeth for keys

70

Itzy gasped awake. She saw blue—blue sky filled her vision. Was she flying? Where, then, were the clouds? *Luc loves clouds,* she thought dreamily. *I love Luc, and Luc loves clouds.* She, too, would love clouds, for Luc. She blinked and the color flattened out, dulling, and she recognized it finally as the blue of the wallpaper and the faded ceiling of her room at the Carlyle. Beside her, there he was. Gorgeous. But dark circles beneath his eyes made him look gaunt and worried.

"They call you lover boy?" she rasped. "That's rich."

A book in his lap clattered to the floor as he looked up at her.

"Itzy?" Luc asked, wide-eyed with relief. "How—how do you feel?"

"Like Hell."

"No wonder. You've been very sick. A bad fever."

Itzy blinked, looking at Luc's chair beside her bed. "You stayed with me." Her insides lit up. She resisted the temptation to touch his messy hair. Several days' stubble made his chin irresistible.

"Yes." His eyes crinkled around the corners when he looked at her.

I can't believe they make them this good, she thought.

"I had the strangest dream." She rubbed her eyes, and the room went dim and wobbly.

"In dreams begin responsibilities."

She stopped rubbing her eyes and the room came back into focus. Itzy sat up, suddenly panicked. "The doctor—" She looked at Luc with wide eyes. "He shot me with something, I remember, before it all went black!"

"It was a cocktail of several antibiotics, I believe."

"You're sure?" She frowned at him skeptically. "Not Botox?"

Luc smiled. "You're a little young, Itzy."

She glared at him.

Luc sighed. "The doctor has a vested interest in seeing you alive, Itzy. You were very sick, remember? Your fever—while necessary—was dangerously high."

"How high?"

"I stopped measuring it at 106. Then the ice baths began."

"Ice baths?" Itzy looked down. She was in an unfamiliar white nightgown, soft as silk. "Who—who gave me these ice baths?" *And this nightgown?*

"I did." Luc looked offended. "Pippa helped."

Itzy was suddenly at a loss for words. The image of perfect Pippa and Luc holding hands over her while she floated naked in a claw-foot tub came to her—little ice cubes clinking against the porcelain, bobbing beneath her chin, her armpits, her legs. The thought was mortifying.

"You were *dressed*," Luc explained, reading her expression correctly.

"Oh."

"The good news is that a high fever like yours is a rite of passage."

"Rite of passage? What sort of passage?"

"You'll soon see." His eyes sparkled and her insides melted.

He looks so damn gorgeou—

Something clicked inside her head.

"I know your voice now, Luc—where I've heard it before."

Luc smiled at her, his eyes softening, the amber color looking so deep it could grab her up like any old insect and trap her alongside the rest of them.

"It was *you*, in Brittany. At the cottage, that awful night. The guest who stayed too long, talked deep into the night." *One of the guests had lingered, and their lilting conversation punctuated her sleep. Her parents had seemed eager for the man to go, but he kept pouring himself wine.*

Luc was silent, but his eyes grew sharp.

"My parents were tired, but too polite to ask you to leave."

"I tried to warn them, Itzy, I tried to warn your parents. Your Aunt Maude was the only one who would listen. There was an attack coming, and I was there to deflect it. I knew the Divah, you see. I knew she would never give up."

Itzy struggled to remember. Her head was still fuzzy and the space behind her eyes ached. There *was* an attack, Itzy thought. Her mother had hidden her in a box for firewood by the old stone hearth and never came back. The smell of ash and sulfur returned to her and she felt a wave of nausea rise.

"Here—" Luc was close, a glass in his hands. She could *smell* him—that old library, deep-knowledge smell. "Drink this."

It was water, a crescent of lemon floating in it. He was closer then, and her heart beat so loudly she wondered if he'd hear it. She struggled to sit up.

"Well, you failed then, Luc. Because that night was the last night I ever saw my mother," Itzy said, her eyes plainly disobeying her and tearing up.

"It's true; no one's seen Anaïs since that night in Brittany." Luc's voice was sad. "She left soon after I arrived, hoping to find help. Your aunt, she stayed up with your father while we waited, keeping vigil. Maude hid you with ashes when I commanded it. Ashes are a shield, Itzy. Maude saw the danger. She knew what you were. She protected you, Itzy. Your whole life she protected you."

"Hardly." Itzy wiped her tears away with a sleeve angrily, and Luc produced a folded silk square, which he handed her.

"Do you know why your mother named you Itzy?"

She shook her head; her neck felt stiff.

"Because you were just a tiny thing—against such great forces." His voice was gentle. "I did not fail that night in Brittany, Itzy."

Itzy snorted. She had meant it to sound more delicate, but she needed to blow her nose.

"I was there that night to save *you*."

71

The window was open against the stuffiness of her sick-room, and this amplified the noise that had begun from outside. It sounded to Itzy as though a bird might be trapped, a pigeon perhaps, for something was making an awful racket against the bricks, and it was coming closer. Something big.

"As I was saying, fever is good. Fever sharpens your ability to see."

"To see what?"

"The truth, Itzy."

To Itzy's great surprise, a man appeared in the window, a young man about Luc's age. First his legs, and then the rest of him, until finally he stepped upon her window ledge, and Itzy saw the young man had a pair of wings upon his back, sturdy and flecked with copper, like those of a large sparrow, and tawny-colored skin. At the joints, the talons sparkled like a new penny.

"*Et bien. Enfin!*" he said, lifting the window higher.

"Gaston, that was quite a racket. Maurice would say you're losing your touch."

"Tell me about it. That was the fifth airshaft I've been down. Oh—the things I've seen here at the Carlyle. My eyes will not soon recover." He grinned mischievously. "*Salut.*"

Gaston nodded at Itzy. She grinned shyly back. He was tall and lanky, quick to smile. His nose appeared to have been broken at one time, and his face was somehow better off for it.

"Where are you staying?" Luc asked.

"The Mark—just up the road." Gaston shrugged.

"Not the Pierre?"

"Nope," said Gaston. "Full up."

"I suppose everyone's in town." Luc sighed. "You'll be happier at the Mark. They're quite discreet."

"It's adequate," Gaston allowed. Gaston stood by the window, arms crossed, leaning casually on the sill. "Luc, we should be going."

"So soon? You've only just arrived." Luc's voice had turned bitter.

"You've kept them waiting long enough."

"They can be so impatient, for immortals."

Gaston's face was implacable. "Don't make this harder than it already is."

Luc glanced at Itzy.

"Going?" she squeaked.

Luc waived her worry away. "A convocation. Nothing more. Gaston's been sent to collect me. Everyone's waiting. Apparently, I'm a little tardy."

"He wouldn't leave your bedside," Gaston explained. Something in his eyes caused Itzy's worry to return tenfold. He turned to Luc. "I can carry you, if need be."

"I can manage myself."

Luc stood, stretching, and Itzy gasped. Emerging from his shoulder blades were a pair of mismatched, bulbous nubs. The odd, stunted feather jutted out here and there. They reminded Itzy of her Aunt Maude's arthritic hands, the knuckles swollen and painful-looking.

Luc turned, and she looked away quickly, her heart in her throat.

"Well, there you have it, Itzy." His voice was sad and low. "The fever has lifted the clouds from your eyes. The truth isn't always pretty."

Luc nodded to Gaston, who threw open the window wide. Luc pushed past him, his feet alighting easily on the stone ledge. He stood, grasping at some unseen hand-hold, and began to climb.

For a moment, Itzy was alone with Gaston. She considered asking the angel one of the million questions on the tip of her tongue, but her determination abandoned her and she merely hugged her knees to her chest.

He gazed at her silently.

"I gather you've been quite ill, Itzy. He sat by your bed-side the entire time, you know. Talking you through it, whispering you his secrets—anything to keep you from slipping away. He refused to leave—even when *commanded*."

Itzy blinked. Her head hurt.

"Tell me something," he said, his copper-colored eyes unblinking. "Are you worth it?"

72

Alone, Itzy swung her legs over the bedside, her head woozy. Flinching, she put weight on her ankle, easing herself up. It was stiff, but the pain was gone. The skin was puckered and pink where Paris had bitten her. When she stood, her head spun. Flashes of black skirted her vision, quick and unexpected, and she sunk into Luc's chair to steady herself. Pulling open the drawer, she saw her clothes had returned from the laundry, pressed and perfectly folded. Little tags had been ironed into the lining discreetly: 1804.

Like camp, she thought.

These were the clothes from her basement adventures, but they bore no evidence of the soot and rips she had endured in the unspeakable pipeworks. Her favorite pair of Levi's were just as they should be, almost as if it had never happened.

She pulled open the next drawer, and the next.

Someone had thought to reorganize.

Blinking, she looked around the Blue Bedroom.

Her camera was nowhere in sight.

Gulping, Itzy opened the closet door. Last she knew, the closet had been host to unthinkable noises—scratching and skitterings that made her skin crawl. But perhaps her

Leica had been stowed in there while she was sick, for safekeeping.

The closet's light blinked on cheerily on its own and shined its golden light down upon the contents. There was the usual rack of Aunt Maude's fur coats—a few of which had fallen and seemed to form a nest on the floor along with her old duffel bag. There was an obvious indent where something had slept. Itzy wrinkled her nose and craned her neck, staring into the darker recesses. The light barely reached the end of the closet, but there appeared to be nothing besides her aunt's collection of steamer trunks.

Frowning, she shut the door.

On top of the dresser was a small vase with an elegant bouquet and a card. The card was embossed with a name—PIPPA BRILL. Itzy ran her fingers along the raised letters. *Get well soon,* it said in perfect, slanted script.

The flowers were brown and wilted. *How long have I been sick?*

Itzy threw on her Levi's and picked a T-shirt at random, messing the neatly ordered stack. She lifted the tarnished hand mirror and instantly regretted it. Dark circles were birds' nests beneath her eyes and her face was gaunt and pale. Her illness had brought out more strands of silver hair, she saw; it was now a pronounced shock at her brow.

Gray hair and a governess, she thought grimly. *That's a first.*

Her teeth would need brushing, and a shower would be dreamy after her long convalescence, and she also felt the faint pangs of hunger beginning to stir. But first, she needed to find her camera.

73

Itzy stood for several moments in what used to be the living room. Aunt Maude's suite had been redecorated. Gone were the toile couches, the thick velvet curtains, the fusty standing lamps.

Here now was Versailles in all its splendor. Gilt mirrors hung from every imaginable space on the walls. Chandeliers dripping with crystal hung from the ceiling, and the ceiling itself was painted with frescoes of dead kings. The floor was magnificently tiled in a checkerboard of black and white marble, and from somewhere Itzy heard the unmistakable sound of a lute.

Yet the room was oppressively dry and hot.

Aunt Maude's fireplace had been revived, but there was no pleasing scent of wood smoke. The ashes had been allowed to accumulate and the fire was acrid and stung her nose. Strange powders and scorched herbs were sprinkled about the carelessly piled embers. These threatened to roll free of the hearth, as they apparently had been allowed to before—the marble floor was singed and pitted with black burns. A large bellows lay off to one side, the shadows from the fire dancing on its pleats making it appear to breathe.

Itzy stared into a mirror. It was old and the reflection distorted; her face was wavy, one arm was longer than the next. The girl who stared back at her was a stranger. Her head felt light, and she debated returning to her sickbed.

Cautiously, Itzy made her way down the hall. Even her aunt's priceless art was gone, the picture of Itzy as a child in Brittany nowhere to be seen, and for a moment—since the memory of that sunny day was not one she could recall anyway—Itzy wondered if she'd ever seen the picture at all. A faint cloying, unpleasant smell was in her nostrils—smoke, she reasoned. From the fire.

Itzy paused.

She heard humming coming from her aunt's rooms, a sort of tuneless waltz.

She could turn around now, she thought. Was she really certain her camera had been moved? Had she, for instance, checked under her bed? *Under is a place, Itzy,* her father's words returned to her. He would say them whenever she was searching for something, and inevitably he'd be right—she'd find her shoe, or her school books, hidden under something else.

The humming grew louder, and she realized her governess must be emerging from the bathroom.

Under is a place, Itzy.

She started backing noiselessly down the hall, one timid foot after the next. Beside the missing photo, her foot touched something small and soft. A cold sinking feeling filled her gut as she prodded the thing, not daring to look down. She didn't have to. She knew just who it was.

Mops let out a throaty growl.

Just then, her governess rounded the corner ahead of her and stopped.

Under is a place called Hell.

"Itzy!" her governess was saying—if indeed this was her governess.

For starters, she looked like a million bucks.

Her voice rang out with a throaty resonance, like a nightclub singer, and her face—her high cheekbones and dewy skin—sparkled with the light of diamond dust. Her lips were puffed and pink, beneath a perfect nose. She wore a sleek and shiny leather catsuit that accentuated her trim waist and bountiful bust and finished in tall black boots. Itzy could see herself reflected once, and then twice, in the patent leather.

Itzy narrowed her eyes. "What *happened* to you?"

"I just needed some time to get back on my feet." She reached for Itzy's shock of white hair and ran her perfectly manicured fingers over it, a lingering touch that sent goose pimples down her neck. Itzy recoiled. "You see, while you rested, I've been gathering my *strength*," the governess whispered, her eyes as dark as ebony.

Itzy wrinkled her nose. The smell had grown worse.

"We have a surprise for you." She smiled. Her teeth, little white Chiclets, chattered in her jaw. "Don't we, Mopsie?"

Itzy had forgotten the dog who now plodded by her slowly, nails scraping on the parquet floor.

"A surprise?" Itzy's stomach clenched. She never did like surprises.

The governess beckoned Itzy, and Itzy found her feet moving down the hall and into her Aunt Maude's bedroom.

The room had been emptied of Aunt Maude's elegant bed, emptied of everything. Ragged strips of wallpaper were all that remained, hanging limply from the wall. Coils of wire for space heaters snaked across the floor. A screen carved the room in two, made from pleated fabric stretched upon metal bars, and from behind that Itzy could make out a cluster of powerful lamps. The only other piece of furniture was a large vanity to one side of the room, its vast mirror enshrined with lit globes.

"In here, dear," she said. The governess was standing beside the door to a closet.

The closet stretched out into the darkness. Itzy hesitated.

"Don't like the dark?" The governess smiled, snapping her fingers. The closet light fluttered on.

Before her, a dress.

But what a dress! Itzy's breath caught in her throat. The garment hung languidly from impossibly thin straps on a wooden Carlyle hanger. Silver silken fibers came together in a plunging neckline and a tailored waist and continued into a puddle of liquid metal upon the floor. Shimmering crystals were scattered everywhere, like an explosion in a diamond mine.

The best kind of dress, Itzy thought, as she drew near. *The kind of dress that leaves nothing to the imagination, while inspiring the minds of everyone around it.*

A small crinkle appeared on her brow. Her eyes darted to the governess and then eagerly back to the hanger. "It's beautiful," Itzy whispered.

"Quite. For the party."

Itzy was only half-listening. Her arm had reached out to touch the glimmering fabric on its own; it was cool to the touch, and heavy.

"Party?" Itzy asked, her voice dreamy and thick.

"Tomorrow, Itzy."

The dress was twinkling, sparkling in the low light, sending barbs of radiance out into the shadowy depths of the closet, which seemed to have no end.

"Tomorrow?" Itzy asked.

"Yes—tomorrow! July fourteenth."

The dress slipped from her fingers and they ached to feel it again. "Bas-Bastille Day?" Itzy blurted.

"Ah, I see you know your French history."

"My father teaches it."

The governess laughed her throaty laugh. "Really? I can't *wait* to meet him, then. I wonder, though—so few people seem to get it right. We'll have lots to talk about!"

"He's in Paris," Itzy squeaked.

The governess nodded solemnly. "And what might he be doing there?"

Itzy lowered her eyes, embarrassed suddenly. "Research," she mumbled.

"Paris is such a *dangerous* city, don't you find? Lawless. Filled with savages. I do hope he'll take precautions."

Itzy blinked. She had never thought of it that way. "I'm sure he will, ma'am."

"Yes, I'm sure he will. Shame he'll miss all the fun."

Itzy admired the woman's smooth, polished skin, her perfect eyelashes. A lock of her platinum hair fell off to one side of her temple in a coy little curl.

"Would you like to try it on?" the governess asked. Her voice was low, conspiring, utterly bewitching.

"M-me?"

"Of course, Itzy. It's *yours*. I had it made for you."

Itzy looked at the dress longingly. It was the most beautiful thing she'd ever seen. The fabric sparkled even in the low light of the closet and seemed to defy logic—being both weightless and woven of silver and thousands of crystals. It was a dress at home in the dark. The flickering lights of a cocktail party would set it aflame. It was a dress for a movie star—

Something clicked.

"I-it looks like Marilyn Monroe's," Itzy squeaked.

Marilyn had worn it in flickering black-and-white footage Itzy had seen. She was performing for a roomful of politicians in a way that made Itzy both uncomfortable and thrilled.

Happy Birthday, Mr. President

It was 1962, the year she died. Itzy thought of that famous clip, the scratchy footage, the overexposed look, as if the very air were on fire.

Ava had told her some of that night, the night Marilyn had sung to the president. It was at Madison Square Garden, late in the evening, and Marilyn almost didn't make it at all. She had been delayed—waylaid, actually—by a raving devhil lurking near the stage entrance. So many devhils surrounded the president, Marilyn had confided to Ava, that she had to be ever-vigilant. They came out of the woodwork when he was around.

When she finally made it up to the mike, shimmering, hair slightly tousled from battle, the host introduced her as "the late Marilyn Monroe." The man must have had a crystal ball, for a short few months later, the demons would get her for good.

The governess was peering intently into Itzy's face. The surface of her eyes were glassine—dark, congealed pits. Familiar pits. It was the blackness of the ash bin, Itzy realized, the darkness from her childhood. It was the darkness that took things. Itzy felt her stomach clench. These were eyes of the wicked, the devious—not at all human. Itzy took a step back, tripping over Mops.

"I'm more of a jeans and T-shirt girl," Itzy whispered.

"A pity. Still, I bet you'll change your mind. I hear you are *particularly* fond of Ms. Monroe." The governess's smile suddenly lacked any humanity.

She knows about the tunnels, Itzy realized. *It's as if she's in my head.*

"My camera seems to have gone missing," Itzy said, jutting out her chin.

"Camera?"

"Yes—it was by my bed before I got sick. You didn't see it, did you?"

"Perhaps you should ask one of your little friends," the governess hissed.

"I'm sure it'll turn up." Itzy's forced herself to smile. "I'm sure I've just misplaced it." *Under is a place, Itzy.*

"Itzy?"

"Yes?"

"You haven't thanked me for the dress."

"Oh. Th-hanks for the dress."

"Itzy, we must work on your manners."

"Yes, ma'am."

"Remember, gratitude is the only appropriate emotion for a child of your circumstances."

The little hairs on the back of Itzy's neck rose. *Her aunt had said the same thing in her letter.*

74

Itzy's heart drummed loudly in her ears as she raced back to her small bedroom.

Itzy hadn't bothered to read her Aunt Maude's letter twice; she had been relieved, in fact, that the tiresome old woman wouldn't be around to grumble about her studies and dole out useless chores to keep her hands from being idle. She had never liked her aunt—and the feeling seemed to have been mutual. Now, however, Itzy found herself wishing something she would never have thought possible—wishing that her Aunt Maude had never left, that her summer at the Carlyle stretched out ahead in tedious, tiresome, and predicable ways, that the woman's toile couches were back where they belonged and her smell—the smell of old newspapers and the twang of her perfume were here, returned, where they belonged. And the truth now, that Aunt Maude had *saved* her that night in Brittany—not her mother at all, as she had always thought—nearly took her breath away. Her mother had not even thought to save her. She had fled to save herself.

The camera wasn't under her bed.

It wasn't anywhere.

Itzy was crying, tearing apart her dresser, upending entire drawers upon the floor. The orange box from Ava containing her Hermès scarf clattered to the floor, the splendid silk spilling out. Itzy bent down and unfurled it. Scarlet and golden feathers floating on a sea of slate gray. She tied it around her neck, rising.

Remember, gratitude is the only appropriate emotion for a child of your circumstances. The words raced through her mind.

Where *was* her aunt? Where had she gone?

She tore the sheets from her bed and even lifted the complaining mattress, heaving it on its side against the wall. Still, there was no sign of her camera. Wheeling about, Itzy scowled at the closet door. There was no place left to look. She threw open the door determinedly and set about ransacking it.

Fur after fur came flying out. The dank nest on the floor held what appeared to be a bone, and she kicked it away, disgusted.

All that remained were her aunt's steamer trunks.

Hadn't Johnny said her aunt always traveled with them?

There were half a dozen of them of various sizes, a matching set, stacked at the far end of the closet. Rich brown leather with golden initials patterned upon their sides. The first was empty; Itzy could tell merely by hoisting it, but all the same she opened the brass latch and peered inside. The second, the same.

But the third—the third was larger than the rest. Itzy could barely maneuver around it to find the side with the clasps and lock, but needn't have bothered. The trunk's lid was open a crack —whatever was inside was too big for the top to close properly.

Got you, Itzy thought.

Sometimes when you look for something, you find something else, her father also said. He was very smart. He was a professor.

Itzy hauled the heavy lid open and found Aunt Maude.

Flies were crawling on what were left of her eyes.

75

"I'd like to report a murder."

Itzy was back in the concierge's private offices, staring at Wold.

Wold blinked at her, but said nothing. Finally, he sighed. "A murder, Miss Nash? Surely not."

"Well—a body then. But I know who did it!"

"Miss Nash, these are serious accusations you are making."

"My aunt is seriously dead."

Wold drummed his gloved fingers on the polished desk before him.

Itzy crossed her arms and waited, her Hermès scarf flattened beneath them. The scarf, for all its expensive silk, felt scratchy and uncomfortable around her neck. As she pulled at it, she examined the concierge's desk. It was neat and tidy, a stack of letters the only thing upon its glassine surface beside the phone.

"Do I have to call police myself?"

"We prefer to handle these things . . . *internally*. Our clientele, you see—" Wold made a showing of lifting the phone and dialing a few numbers. He eyed Itzy. "Dead you say? In a trunk?"

"She didn't get there by herself."

"Security?" he said into the receiver, an air of tired skepticism settling into his voice.

Itzy looked at the phone, urging him to talk. One of the letters caught her eye, peeking out from the tidy row. It was on the cream-colored Carlyle stationery from her aunt's writing desk. On it was the unmistakable scrawl of her own hand.

Wold had never mailed her letter to her father.

Back in the lobby, Itzy tried to remain calm. She felt weak and her breathing was shallow. She looked around unsteadily. The black marble floors were polished to a mirror sheen, a pool of obsidian. The chandelier, an island in its midst, clung to the ceiling. The murmur of conversation threaded across the room from the dining room, where somehow, incredibly, people were eating. Off to the left, the elevators chimed in the small vestibule, the hearth spit. A clerk behind the front desk was helping a guest in quiet tones, and Itzy watched the interaction as if from a dream.

She looked around at the picturesque scene and wanted to scream.

A seated diner eyed her steadily from a table laden with crystal and a deep-red wine. He looked strangely familiar to Itzy—a faint recollection, vague and unreliable. She frowned, trying to place him. His eyes lingered on her as he sipped his wine, his hand wrapped about the glass stem.

A phone buzzed, and Itzy startled. The desk clerk excused himself from the guest, answering it. He listened for a brief moment, and then, turning, he scanned the lobby, locking eyes with Itzy. He said a few deliberate words into the receiver, never taking his eyes off her.

The guest was fumbling in her purse. She was an older lady, her nails like claws. She turned to leer at Itzy. Half of her face hung slack, the skin pulled down by gravity, her one eye bulging and red-rimmed.

Itzy was out the revolving doors in a flash.

76

"Maurice!" Itzy said, relief washing over her. Obscura & Co. was empty; none of the younger photo assistants were in their usual places by the lightbox and file cabinets.

Maurice looked up from a catalog. "Itzy, I've been expecting you."

She saw his wings then, smaller than Gaston's, with tight little silver-flecked feathers built for speed. They flexed and then folded.

"I've been sick."

"I know."

He reached out with his weathered hand and tipped her chin up, inspecting her face. "Nice hair." He brushed a lock of white hair aside.

"Thanks." She smiled. She tried to mean it. "Blondes do have more fun."

"Such a tiny thing," Maurice said.

A single tear ran down her face.

"Hey—what happened to fun?"

"Aunt Maude's dead."

"Your Aunt Maude died in the line of duty, Itzy."

"How?"

"It was a family business. She worked in her own way alongside her brother, your father, keeping the Upper East Side safe. When she went missing, I feared the demons finally got to her. Seems I was right."

"Th-the governess. She's the Divah, isn't she? Her eyes, they're black as pitch—and that dog. She calls it Mops, like Marie Antoinette's."

Maurice removed his magnifying lenses, folding them carefully and placing them on the glass counter. "Yes, Itzy. She is. And that dog is her trusted hellhound."

"Oh."

Maurice's voice softened. "I know this is a lot to handle, Itzy. I'll do my best to explain. While in Hell, demons maintain loyal subjects on the earthly plain and rely upon them for news and gifts—burnt offerings, even letters. And passage back topside, should the opportunity present itself. The doctor has apparently been successful in procuring a body for the Divah and conjured her forth."

"I thought Luc *invited* her," Itzy said.

"Luc may have invited her, Itzy. But you brought her here. In your bag. And from there, the doctor carefully nourished her as she grew in strength."

"So—everything? This is my fault?"

"No, child." Maurice held her gaze.

"What does she want?" Itzy managed.

"The same thing we all do." He pointed at himself, the empty shop.

"Which is?"

Maurice thought this over. "Has anyone ever explained to you about the war?"

She shook her head.

"Angels and demons are more alike than we'd prefer to admit. In the end, we are all just soul stealers. Some work in the dark and some in the light. Those destined to die—as we call humans, Itzy—will depart the earthly plain with either an angel or a demon by their side. Where your soul ends up next depends on your escort, as I'm sure you can imagine. Or so it was for eons. But, well, things have gotten muddled—ever since the last great war. Ah, the good old days, when good and evil were so easy to define! While, classically, angels have fought for good, and demons for evil, these lines started to blur. There are sorcerer angels who battle for evil, and even demonic entities who align with the heavens. And then, there are ones like Luc and myself—ones who owe their alliegiance to no one. For that, we are ostracized or persecuted. We are deemed Fallen. Flies in their ointment. The traditional angels prefer instead to see themselves as on the side of righteousness in some grand battle between good and evil. We are soldiers in a war, it is said, and it would do no good to have no cause to fight for. But the futility of war weighs heavy on us— Luc especially. And Itzy, we've come to believe that the lines between good and evil are murky, and as so, all war is false."

Maurice paused, stretching his wings.

"But while war is a murky affair, one thing is an *absolute*, Itzy. And that is that angels—demons, too—are not whole. We are beings of dark or light. Extremes. Dark or light, but not both—never both. And this, Itzy, is unendurable. All we want—all angels and demons want—is to be whole. So we wait at your bedsides. In the corners of darkened rooms. In hospital wards. And when it's time, we slip your soul out of this realm and into the next. It is the closest we can ever come."

Maurice eyed her critically. "Do you know what a soul is, Itzy?"

Here, words failed her.

"It's quite simple. A wholeness, a union of opposites. It's the part of you that came into this world before you were named. Before you were Itzy."

"So, you want a soul?" Itzy asked.

"I want to be whole. Although I'm old enough to know that this can never be."

"And Luc wants a soul?"

Maurice sighed. "In the sense that a soul is the integration of darkness and light, then yes."

"And what does the Divah want? A soul?"

"Not just a single soul, Itzy. The Divah wants *all* souls—every soul that has ever been, or ever will be. She wants to open the Gates of Hell and rule oblivion."

A silence decended upon Obsura & Co. while Itzy digested this.

"Wow. Luc sure can pick 'em," Itzy finally said.

Maurice smiled. "Something I've been telling him for centuries."

77

"You say a soul is the integration of darkness and light," Itzy said. "That reminds me of something."

Maurice raised an inquisitive brow.

"Photography," Itzy said.

"Well, exactly!" Maurice smiled. "Now you see why we're all drawn to it."

He produced a waxy envelope and slid it forward to her on the counter. The tattoo on his finger was old and timeworn, Itzy saw, the crisp lines fading.

Her last roll of film. Itzy slid the glossy paper out and looked.

Another contact sheet, from her tour of the basement with Johnny. The infrared film was high contrast, ghosty. The film was sensitive to heat and could pick up traces of people even after they've left the room hours later. The body heat from a fingerprint on a window. Bare footprints.

Her eye was drawn to her photograph of Paris in the stairwell when she had surprised Itzy, the animal's demon eyes frighteningly evident. Her eyes scanned the awful pipeworks—and something fierce with matted fur, a blur. It appeared to be holding a wooden club.

Then Itzy came to the image of the coal room with Johnny. She had snapped a picture in the dark of Marilyn Monroe's monogram.

"What does that look like to you?" Itzy passed the loupe to Maurice, who looked down with a wrinkled eye.

"Hard to say. It looks like a woman? In white. There, off to the left."

Could that be Marilyn? These were her tunnels.

Maurice scrutinized her carefully. "Remember, Itzy. Film has the power to capture the unknown."

She flipped off the lightbox.

"And infrared is an honest film. Beautiful. Brutal. But it always reveals the truth. Next time you're down there, take another roll."

"The Divah's taken my camera. There won't be a next time."

"Bah." Maurice shrugged. "Photography is a dying art." His eyes found hers again. "Here—don't say I never gave you anything."

A long silver package was now on the counter between them.

"What's this?" she asked.

The angel shrugged, a little ripple of coarse hawk like feathers. "A little souvenir. From 1793."

Itzy examined the object with growing interest. A row of four fingerholes were punched in one side, a grooved grip for her thumb on top. A thin, elegant chain dangled from either end. Itzy pushed her hand through, gripping the cold steel, and pulled. The room rung with the sound of metal on metal, and Itzy had unsheathed the most unusual blade she had ever seen.

Her breath caught in her throat. "Is this—"

"It is. I had it modified to fit your hand. Cut down to a more manageable size."

"But Ava said it was missing! Destroyed in the Reign of Terror—"

"Hardly! I've just been waiting for the right person to give it to."

Itzy lifted the guillotine blade.

"Itzy, you brought the Divah to the Carlyle. Now's your chance to send her packing."

She hefted it in her hand, curled her fingers tighter through the cold metal holes. She made a fist. The slanted and honed blade that once beheaded Marie Antoinette was now part of her hand.

"How does it fit?"

"Like a glove."

"You'll want to practice, Itzy. That thing's no toy."

"That shouldn't be too hard, Maurice. The hotel's crawling with demons."

As she turned to leave, a question came to her. "Maurice? You're saying it's impossible to be both angel and demon?"

"Did I say that?"

"Well, wouldn't that solve everything? Dark. Light. All in one. Wouldn't that make you whole?"

Maurice thought for a minute, and then sighed. "Now that would be really something. And for an angel, not much is new."

78

"Hold the elevator!" Itzy scrambled across the gleaming black floor. Of the hotel's three elevators, one was open, but the doors were shutting as she ran. The tip of a polished cane emerged from within, and the doors bounced open again. Itzy clattered into the small enclosure and leaned against the back wall, clasping her case from Maurice, chest heaving.

"Thanks," she said to a stoop-shouldered man in a pinstripe suit, leaning on a cane. He wore the thick black glasses of the blind.

Itzy brushed her shock of white hair from her face, considering her options. She had no intention of going home—to 1804—with her aunt's dead body stuffed in a trunk in her room. But Ava would know what to do.

"Eighteen," she said to the operator. But the floor was already illuminated. She glanced again at the blind man. He stared straight ahead through the open doors to the Lobby.

A couple boarded—a businessman and a mousy girl in a pantsuit, his secretary, Itzy thought. Now it was tight in the small enclosure, and the four endured some polite reshuffling, the mousy assistant jostling the operator and apologizing.

As the elevator doors slid closed again one final time, Itzy saw the hellhound. Mops was warming himself beside the blazing fireplace, as still as stone. Their eyes locked, and the dog bared its yellowed teeth.

"Where's Johnny?" Itzy asked the operator, a potbellied man with a preponderance of nose hair. She felt the elevator lift off the ground.

"Gone," he shrugged. There was something between his teeth, Itzy noticed.

"What, on vacation?"

"Something like that."

Maybe Johnny tried to say good-bye when I was sick. Itzy liked that idea. She'd ask Luc, she thought, but remembered the dark look on his face each time Johnny's name came up. Instead, Itzy took in the new arrivals. The businessman wore a charcoal-colored wool suit, and the mousy girl carried a leather attaché case. They, too, seemed to be going to eighteen.

When the elevator stopped at the fourth floor, Itzy grew impatient. A man with a mustache and slick black hair boarded, some sort of crest sewn on his velvet jacket. His hair was in a style that could only be called a pompadour, smooth and velvety, like his attire. He glided in on silent slippers, smiling offhandedly. "Afternoon," he said.

At the sixth floor, the elevator braked yet again and Itzy had had enough.

"You've got to be kid—"

But Itzy never finished her sentence. The elevator doors opened on a woman with long flowing hair, intelligent eyes. The gleam of fame was on her, as distinct as wings.

"Going up?" Julep Joie asked the crowded elevator.

Itzy had seen pictures of Julep Joie, paparazzi shots of the actress as she embarked on some humanitarian trip to Ethiopia, and again on the streets of Paris with her famous husband and gaggle of children. She was a maverick, Julep Joie, which Itzy admired, and the star's secretive lifestyle intrigued her.

Room was somehow found for the superstar, and quickly.

Itzy was now pressed against the back wall, a pin-striped elbow at her neck. She could just make out Julep's distinct profile.

"Floor?" the operator grunted.

Julep turned and caught Itzy's eye. "Eighteen," she said, winking.

The elevator operator pressed a button and the doors closed.

Her stomach heaved as the elevator glided upward. She looked again at Julep, who was staring straight ahead now. Peeking out from beneath her collar was a splash of silk.

Julep Joie, Itzy thought. *I can't believe that's really Julep Joie!*

The elevator was gaining speed, hurtling upward. Itzy's feet seemed heavy, her body slow and clumsy feeling. The elevator, actually, seemed to have a mind of its own. The burst of speed now ended suddenly, and the ride came to a sudden, grinding halt. But before Itzy's stomach could leave her throat, the elevator lurched and jerked—sickening grinding noises rattling her nerves.

Something was troubling Itzy though. There was something about the secretary that she couldn't place. Something about her eyes. While she had her next thought—*they are black pools of tar*—the mousy secretary had already begun moving about the elevator in a blur. With one hand, the woman jammed the controls, and Itzy's feet shuddered as the bank of lights blinked distressingly. With her other, she broke the operator's neck, effortlessly twisting it around to face Itzy.

Spinach. He has spinach between his teeth.

The man's mottled face stared at Itzy, a grimace contorting his features, until his knees buckled out from under him, and he crumpled, sagging to the floor. A grinding and repulsive shudder rattled the elevator, and Itzy found herself thrown to the far side of the small enclosure. The blade from Maurice was now wedged beneath the dead operator's slack jaw. A line of thick spittle joined one to the other.

Julep Joie's beautiful face was so close she could smell her perfume, see the print on her Hermès scarf. "Stay down, kiddo," Julep said.

The lights were flickering, and the floor was swaying beneath Itzy's feet. A voice was in her head—her own, she realized. *Please don't let the lights go out*, it said.

Julep was gone from Itzy's side. Holding the railing, the superstar pushed off the wall, scissor-kicking the businessman. Itzy heard a greasy cracking noise, the crunch of bones as Julep's foot connected with the man's throat, knocking him off balance. Spinning, Julep pounced on him again—a well-placed kick and her heeled boot pierced the side of his neck. One sharp elbow to his temple, and he was down with a guttural snarl. Something flashed silver, and the man's neck opened from ear to ear; dark oily fluid spurting out, the charnel stench of sulfur filling the air. The demon writhed, a horrid gurgling pouring from his torn throat, and then vanished in a puff of heavy brown spores and the smell of decay.

"Jules!" The man in the velvet jacket shouted a warning. The mousy secretary whirled through the air, scratching at the superstar's face with polished red nails. The two went down, thudding hard upon the uniformed body of the elevator operator.

"*Hhhhhhssssssssssss*," the demon growled as she spat out a hunk of Julep's hair.

From the corner, Itzy saw the unmanned elevator panel blinking sedately. She edged her way along the back wall, the small of her back pressed hard against the handrail. *I'll call for help*, she thought. *There's a phone in that panel, and I will call for help.* She thought of Wold, and her Aunt Maude lying dead in a steamer trunk, and knew there as no one to call.

With trembling legs, Itzy forced herself forward, avoiding the beige uniform of the operator, the golden tassels and embellishments on his uniform stained with dark matter.

Luc, she thought. *I'll call Luc.*

Julep Joie was wrapping her Hermès scarf tight around the demon's wrists and ankles. The transformation was instant. The demon ceased her struggling, a limp and vapid secretary once more. The superstar staggered to her feet, wiping something sticky from her boot onto the secretary's pantsuit.

"You're out of practice," Pompadour said, jovially. He had his elegant hands around the neck of the blind man, who struggled with silent strength.

"And your hair's ugly," Julep spat, feeling her scalp.

They looked at the wreckage from the battle in the small elevator as Julep nursed her wounds. "This is nothing," she said. "I just got back from the Congo. You should have seen the mess I made there. They're getting more brazen with the Divah's arrival."

The blind man struggled, guttural words foaming from his mouth.

"And then there was one," Pompadour said, lifting him off his feet with one hand.

The elevator creaked as Itzy inched along the wall. The panel was in reach. A small recess held a familiar beige phone; she could just see its curved handgrip, the tangled coil of cord. As Itzy reached for the phone, though, the elevator gave one final groan and hurtled downward, sending Itzy reeling. The small beige phone jangled loudly in its recess, the noise filing the elevator.

"Shall I finish him off?" Julep was saying, unperturbed by the new developments.

"He's all yours."

"Ever the gentleman, Gaston."

"Wait, I have a better idea—"

Itzy reached for the phone. Her stomach was in her throat as she answered it. "Hello?"

"Miss Nash." It was the familiar, melodious voice of room service.

"Y-yes?"

"What can I do for you this afternoon?"

Itzy looked around at the inconceivable scene before her.

"I—uh. I could use some help."

"No doubt, Miss Nash." The voice was sympathetic. "Do you see the panel before you, Miss Nash?"

Itzy looked at the blinking numbered buttons wildly. "Y-yes."

"There is a red button. Do you see it—in the recess beside the phone?"

"No—I, uh. Yes! There it is."

"Press that button, Miss Nash."

"All right—"

"Oh, and Miss Nash?"

"Yes?"

"Hold on."

Itzy pressed the button and the elevator's descent ended in a screech of metal on metal, and the next thing she knew she was on the floor in a heap, the lifeless face of the operator close enough to kiss. *Nope,* she thought. *Not spinach. Rotting meat.*

Pompadour kicked the operator away, looking down at Itzy. His eyes were unreadable. "You. Luc's girl. You do it."

"Leave her alone," Julep said.

The mustache vanished, the dark hair too, and Pompadour became Gaston. His wings were dappled brown and tan.

"Watch, Itzy, and don't blink," the angel said.

Gaston had a mace suddenly, a long rusty ball full of spikes. His fist was tight and his knuckles white. He swung it underhanded from a chain, and Itzy saw then that it glowed a cold, hard blue. The blind man had lost his glasses in the scuffle, and Itzy saw his pale, unseeing eyes, like the underbelly of a snake. And then the mace caught him beneath the chin and he exploded in a cloud of spores, which sifted down upon her.

Julep brushed brown dust from her hands, shaking a few earwigs from her elegant cuffs. Gaston reached for the secretary, dragging her to her feet by her hair. Her ill-fitting pantsuit clung to her body wretchedly.

"Do it," he commanded Itzy.

Itzy stared at him blankly.

He kicked at the operator, and something slid across the floor, hitting her foot. The blade from Maurice.

"Do it," he said more fiercely. "And be quick about it."

"She's subdued," Julep pointed out. "We want her at the Institute for study."

"No," Gaston said quietly. "I want to see just what folly Luc has begotten us."

Itzy stared at the smallish demon. Her face was blank—gone was the savagery Itzy had just seen. She blinked dumbly, her demon eyes dilating.

"Slay the demon," Gaston was saying. "She would not have spared you."

"Gaston—" Julep began.

"She's unarmed," Itzy protested.

Gaston wrenched the silk binds from the demon, slicing them off with a quick flick of his wrist. The Hermès scarf drifted to the floor in pieces. A shrill, guttural shriek issued from the creature's mouth as she realized she was free.

"Not anymore, she's not."

In an instant, the mousy secretary transformed into a seething fury and launched herself at Itzy. Hot, bitter breath reached her nostrils and a searing pain arced across her face as a red talon nearly missed her eye. She landed on her back with a thud, the air leaving her lungs. As Itzy felt the elevator spin, her hand closed around something cold. Julep was shouting something in French, Itzy heard, but whatever it was sounded miles away. Gaston's eyes watched her, his gaze inscrutable.

The End of Days is nigh.

Somehow, she was on her feet, swinging the blade with a deadly fury.

Maurice was right. The blade was sharp. Itzy made quick work of the demon, slicing it open from ear to ear. Dark, oily blood spurted from the gash, sulfurous bile following in sickening spurts. Itzy's eyes never left Gaston's, save once: to wipe the blade clean on her Levi's.

"Wow, that's some badass blade," Julep whistled.

The last thing Itzy saw before the lights went out were Gaston's glinting copper eyes.

79

The elevator shot upward in the dark. The illuminated panel above the elevator doors ticked off numbers: 28. 29. 30. 31—and then nothing. The little lightbulb sputtered and then expired. *We've run out of floors. Or numbers. Or both.* Still, they sped up.

"I've seen this movie, and I don't like how it ends. Hell—I've been *in* this movie." Julep's voice was calm in the dark. "Gaston—you doing this?"

Gaston was at the panel, pressing numbers to no effect. Something shattered, and glass rained down upon the ceiling, and they stopped—a clatter of heels sounded on top of them now. Itzy felt the elevator sway with the weight of the new arrivals. An access panel wrenched open above them and blue light poured in, a beam landing in a small square on the floor. Luc dropped down within it, crouching by Itzy.

"Are you hurt?" he asked, a dark urgency in his voice.

Itzy shook her head.

His face filled her field of vision. *His perfect face—* there was worry there, causing his eyes to tighten, which, incredibly, made her flush.

Vaguely, she was aware of others, too, entering through the ceiling. Wings flashed. And more jostling above. Luc bent over her, protectively.

"Next time, I'll take the stairs," she said.

Luc slammed his fist into the sputtering control panel and it purred. Itzy felt the elevator descend, slowly, while Luc returned to her side. Itzy couldn't see Gaston, but she could feel him. The memory of his eyes—his deep, piercing stare—was not likely to leave her soon. She could feel anger coursing off Luc. Fury—at Gaston.

The doors opened, and more angels gave way silently as Luc and Itzy stepped out onto the eighteenth floor.

He eyed her critically. "You're injured."

"It's not my blood." Itzy shrugged. She was a sight. Deep, oily splatters smeared her Levi's, and her T-shirt was completely soaked through.

"I was referring to your cheek."

Itzy's hand fluttered to her face where the demon had torn at her.

"And your rash." He pointed to her neck, where her Hermès scarf was tied.

"Seems every time I see you lately, I'm covered in demon gore. I don't normally smell like this, I swear."

"No, you don't."

Something about his tone made her skin prickle as a rush of heat overtook her.

She stood beside several angels she recognized from Maurice's store—the young, hip photo assistants, talking shop over their espressos.

"And how's *your* day going?" Itzy smiled at them. She was feeling giddy and reckless—not quite herself.

"Not as bad as yours," a gray-eyed girl with silver-tipped wings answered. Her hair was long and jet-black with short dark bangs. She appraised Itzy from head to toe, eyes lingering on the blade hanging from her hand. "I'm

Virginie," the angel said, holding out her hand to shake. A black ring was inked on her fourth finger.

Itzy looked down, surprised to see the blade still in her hand, and sheathed it. "Itzy."

"You're the girl with the Leica," the angel said.

"I was. It was stolen."

"Oh, you *are* having a bad day." Virginie's eyes softened. "I saw some of your photos—hope you don't mind. You're good."

"Yeah?" Itzy flushed.

Luc and Gaston were arguing nearby, a few angry words drifting over to the pair.

"Don't let this little bump in the road stop you, okay?"

"You all work in photography?" She examined the host of Maurice's angels behind Virginie with a new eye.

Virginie shrugged. "Angels are drawn to it. We understand the complexities of light. From what I understand, you might know a bit about that, too."

Luc had wrenched his arm away from Gaston and was striding back to Itzy. Gaston fell in step behind him, fuming.

"Boys, boys." Julep stepped between the two angels, keeping them apart. Luc grabbed Itzy by the wrist and brandished her blade-arm. Streaks of gore were smeared along the underside of her sleeve and her knuckles were skinned.

"What is this then?" Luc demanded.

Gaston was silent.

"One kick-ass weapon?" Julep offered. Luc ignored her, thrusting it further into Gaston's unflinching face.

"You should recognize it," Gaston finally said.

Luc glared at him, the bitter words on his lips died. Lowering Itzy's arm, he gently unclasped Itzy's fingers, which were stiff and numb.

"You could have gotten her killed, Gaston, cutting that demon loose."

"We needed to see what she was capable of."

"Satisfied?" Luc growled.

Gaston frowned. "Hardly—Julep helped her. Started in on the French. Had her flask at the ready."

"It was Rimbaud, you savage." Julep brandished a dog-eared book. "They seem to really hate *A Season in Hell*, though there was that one in Nepal who would only go down with Camus." She threw the book at Itzy. "Here, kiddo. Page sixty-one's a real scream. 'Night of Hell.'"

Itzy caught it with her free hand. "Don't you need it?"

"Are you kidding? I keep a stack beside my toilet for times like these. Right under my Oscar." She turned to Luc and Gaston. "I, for one, think the girl did fabulously. You should have seen *my* first slay—nothing scholarly about it. Itzy—great work. Like father, like daughter."

Julep smiled, leaning in, a twinkle in her eye.

"Go get cleaned up. Next time I see you, I owe you a drink," Julep said, making quickly for the stairs. "It's a tradition," she called over her shoulder. "On your first demon slay."

"Something off the children's menu?" Gaston called. The stairwell echoed with a particularly juicy French obscenity.

Luc knocked on Ava's door. The angels were shifting behind them, the dry sound of wings on wings. Their bodies were so close, their wings nearly interlaced, and Itzy felt them brush her skin. The unmarked door swung open, a bright light falling on their faces.

"Itzy!" Pippa shrieked. "Back from the dead!"

80

Pippa pulled Itzy inside, embracing her happily, and Luc followed, leaving Gaston glowering in the hall to guard the door.

"You're better! You had us so worried. *Ava!*" she called over her shoulder. "Ava—you'll never guess who it is!"

"You know Ava?" Itzy found herself asking.

"I know *everybody*." Pippa shrugged, marching Itzy into the open room, the bright white of Ava's suite made her eyes hurt. "I live here! Jeez—what *happened* to you? You're a mess." Pippa crossed her arms. "I'll run a bath"—she marched off—"and send for some of my clothes. These, we can burn."

Itzy heard the water run from down the hall and Pippa soon returned.

"Is that room service?" Ava's voice came floating over to them. "It's about time. Tell them I said to stop burning everything. Tell them I have half a mind to go down there and see what they're getting up to."

"She's a bit tipsy," Pippa stage-whispered. And then louder, "No, Ava, silly. It's not room service. It's *Itzy*! Itzy Nash—Maude's niece."

Itzy heard someone fall off the piano stool, followed by some muffled swearing. Pippa shut her eyes and took a deep breath. "She's been like this all day."

Ava stumbled into view, rounding the white baby grand. She wobbled in her heels, deliberately placing one foot in front of the other like a tightrope walker. Her bangles clinked on her lean arm.

"Itzy!" she slurred. "I knew you would make it through. You're made of tougher stuff, I said."

"Ava was just about to take a nap." Pippa's voice was sing-songy. "Weren't you, Ava?"

"I was not."

"Yes you were. You were going to nap, and I was going to call down to Zitomer's for those pills you asked for."

Ava considered this. She nodded sagely, reaching into her back pocket and producing a flask. She unscrewed it and tipped it into her throat, spilling a clear liquid over her chin.

"I think you've had enough to drink," Pippa said more firmly.

"I drink for a *reason*." Ava's eyes narrowed. "It keeps the demons away."

The aging star muttered something, and Itzy was startled to notice how old she looked. Her eyes darted around the room with exaggerated alarm until they finally settled on Itzy, seeing her as if for the first time.

"Itzy Nash?" Ava squinted. "Is that you?"

"The one and only."

Ava snorted. "You look like her, you know." Ava drew herself up to her full height with the help of the piano, but her elbow sprawled on the polished surface, and she slumped down again.

"I look like who?" Itzy smiled patiently.

"Your mother."

The room went dead silent.

A part of Itzy leapt at this news, somewhere behind her rib cage.

"She does, doesn't she, Luc?" Ava slurred.

Luc cleared his throat. "Your mother was a great beauty, Itzy," he said.

"Bah—more trouble than she was worth, was more like it," Ava scoffed.

"Ava!" Pippa scolded.

Ava waved away the indiscretion. "Please. Anaïs? We *know* Anaïs. *Tie up your men when Anaïs is in town*, we used to say."

Pippa made apologetic sounds and tried to guide Itzy toward the running bath, but Itzy shook free.

"If she set her sights on anyone, she wouldn't stop until she got him. Married or not. It didn't matter to her," Ava spat. "Hard to compete with those angelic charms. I guess when you're an immortal, you learn certain ways to make men—"

"Ava, that's enough." A warning in Luc's voice surprised Itzy.

Ava blinked at Luc, lost in a memory.

"Sounds like you have an ax to grind," Itzy said nervously, looking at Pippa.

"Or maybe someone's just a nasty drunk," Pippa offered.

Something like a *harrumph* escaped Ava's lips and her tone changed. "Your mother stole my husband," Ava said simply, and Itzy felt herself flush. "Frankie. He was the love of my life, but he left me for Anaïs. And then, in some sort of poetic justice, she left him—on the shores of a lake in Italy. I even offered to take him back—but after Anaïs, he looked right through me."

Ava peered again at Itzy, first with one eye, then the other.

"And here you are. Little. Itzy. Nash. With your mother's good bones, her gap in your front teeth. But she left you with something else, too, didn't she? That vague impression of ruin—that feeling that awful things have happened to you at some point in your past, and those things aren't finished yet." Ava turned and plodded away. "Maybe that's what made the men so crazy about Anaïs—they all wanted to save of her."

Out the windows behind the aging star, the hulking guillotine was silhouetted against the backdrop of the city.

"I am not my mother," Itzy said quietly.

"No. You are not." Ava inspected her critically, over her shoulder. "You're half-angel. A fledgling. The rarest of creatures."

"What does that mean?"

"I don't know. So few survive."

81

Awful things.

Awful things had happened to her, she knew. In Brittany, when she was a child. The hearth, the smell of sulfur. But what else?

She thought about her life with her father. It was quiet, but she liked that. Protected. Sheltered, even. She suffered through school, feeling vaguely alone. From her classmates, she got shifty glances, awkward stares. She hid behind her camera, preferring to see the world through its reliable grid, manipulating her surroundings with a click of the aperture dial. Her classmates kept their distance from her, but she learned to like that, too, for she found friends who were older—her father's students.

Suddenly, Itzy felt her father's absence like a punch in the gut. She missed home, too—that rambling old house full of papers and books, the smell of pipe tobacco and the sound of the old typewriter her father still worked on. Her bedroom, the small closet her father had converted into a darkroom, its glowing red light and sharp chemical smell. The university—its ivy-covered buildings and wandering paths.

But her father was in Paris. Wasn't he?

And her mother? Her mother was—what *was* she?

Nothing is as it seems.

Itzy felt herself grow hot, anger seeping in through her pores. It rose from her feet, closing her throat, gripping her mind. Something burned in her heart—a tiny ember ignited that night in Brittany when she was hidden by the hearth. She drew a breath, feeding it. It burned orange and red, her anger. She let it wash over her. Flames were fanned. Her heart, the ember in her chest, glowed.

Her camera had been stolen. Her aunt was dead, stuffed in a trunk. Demons had just tried to kill her.

Ava was prattling on, Itzy noticed, self-pity thickening her voice. "When I die, no one will remember my real, true work."

"Now Ava," Pippa scolded. "You won't die!"

"Stupid girl—we all die. And most of us before our time. Fools rush in where angels fear to tread. Princess Grace. Diana. Marilyn. The list is as sad as it is endless."

"Well, you will hardly be forgotten!"

"Please—I have no illusions. I'm just a washed up pinup girl. A recluse. I can't even bear to leave my own room! They'll show a tidy montage of my films on the news, flash my star on the Walk of Fame. And then, they'll forget me." She laughed bitterly. "I wonder what the world would say if they knew the truth."

Itzy was at the window, neck craning to inspect the hulking guillotine's blade. Even in the low light, its honed edge gleamed.

Itzy turned.

"Really, Ava," she said. "For someone who abandoned the theater, you're awfully dramatic."

Yes, awful things had happened to her. But no more.

Itzy narrowed her eyes and walked to the phone.

It was time to get even.

82

"Room service." The melodious voice was soothing in her ear. Itzy felt her anger abate, a sense of serenity appearing in its place. A buoyancy. "A pot of coffee, please. Strong, and quick."

"Of course, Miss Nash. Will there be anything else?" Itzy turned around, surveying the room.

"Food. Nothing burned. Burgers, maybe. Rare. Whatever else you recommend."

"Glad to see your appetite has returned, Miss Nash."

Itzy thought of the elevator. She turned away from the room and leaned into the phone. "Um, thanks for before," she whispered.

"We aim to please."

"How did you know—"

"Just doing our job. Oh, Itzy?"

"Yes?"

"Might I recommend something?"

"Of course."

"Ask her why she quit acting."

"Ava?"

"Yes, the legendary Ava Quant. Oh, and Miss Nash? It's been a pleasure to serve you."

Itzy turned, looking at Ava sprawled on mounds of white cushions.

"Who are you—?" Itzy asked into the phone, but the line was dead.

Itzy answered the knock on the door when it came. She intercepted the cart, signing for it, and hurried to close the door again. Looking out into the hallway, she paused.

Mops was there.

She slammed the door on him, his snarl cut short.

Curls of steam were coming from the silver spout of the coffee urn, and Itzy poured Ava a large cup. The coffee had dripped in a few places on the pristine white tablecloth, and Itzy watched as the brown blots spread. Turning, she plunked it down before the couch on the low, glass-topped table.

"Drink," Itzy commanded.

Ava sat up, bleary-eyed.

She held the coffee, sniffing. "Smells okay. Not burned. How'd you manage this?"

"Friends in high places. Do you want milk or sugar?"

"Vodka."

"Ava—"

"Kidding."

Itzy smiled thinly. "Ava. We don't have a lot of time."

"Ah—on that we both agree."

Ava took a gulp of coffee and then another.

"They killed Aunt Maude."

Ava was silent for some time. Finally, she turned her bloodshot eyes to Itzy, her face grave and grim. "She wouldn't listen, your aunt," she said. "I tried to warn her."

On the wall behind the couch was a black-and-white image. A pair of girls walking arm in arm, seen from some distance behind. A boardwalk, a Ferris wheel in the distance. One, a blonde, is blurred. Her head has turned, she's seen something off-frame. From her posture, Itzy can tell she is startled. The other girl hasn't seen it and is chatting, laughing, pulling her companion away.

"Coney Island," Ava said, her voice flat. "My first demon slay."

Itzy's eyes grew wide, and she rose to get a better look.

"I didn't see it, of course. It was Marilyn—it was *always* Marilyn. Her instincts were impeccable. Beneath that coat there, she's got her claw hammer tucked into her girdle—her weapon of choice. I wasn't even armed. It was our day off. Who takes a weapon to an amusement park?"

Itzy thought of Julep in the elevator, the flash of silver.

"That's Marilyn? The blonde beside you?" Itzy asked, peering closer. Ava nodded.

"Marilyn saved me. Afterward, laughing, she grabbed my hands. 'Ava,' she said in that breathless way of hers. 'You're a natural!' I never left home again without this." Ava's wrist flashed as she slipped off her armload of bangles. They clattered upon the table, each bracelet linked to the next, an intact and heavy chain. A deadly weapon. "Until finally, I just never left home."

"Ava—" Itzy suddenly felt cold, shivery. "Why did you quit acting?"

Ava looked at Itzy for a long time. "There are enough monsters in real life, Itzy," she said, softly. "Who needs the Hollywood kind?"

Itzy was feeling really peculiar, a throbbing at her temples. Her hands fluttered to her throat, where her Hermès scarf felt like a necklace of thorns. Black swaths like giant shadow-wings shuddered in her peripheral vision, beating a slow, menacing rhythm. Itzy tried to concentrate. "What is that *smell*?"

Luc was at her side as the room started to spin.

"My head—" Itzy clutched her temples. Ava's voice was scratchy, far away.

"Itzy?" Pippa's voice wavered. Luc was carrying her to the white couch. "Itzy, what's wrong? Luc? Call someone. My god, she's gone so pale—"

83

For the second time in recent memory, Itzy awoke to a field of blue, but this time there were clouds—beautiful clouds. Clouds of opals and yellows and ochres. Clouds of spun cotton, clouds that billowed and roiled as with a giant's breath. They leveled out into a flat plane, and Itzy realized she was staring at a painting. A painting on a ceiling.

And then someone leaned over her, and the clouds vanished.

A penlight was being waved at her, her eyelids were brusquely pulled back and, as the light passed over each pupil, it seared the inside of her brain like a white-hot poker.

She groaned, turning her head.

A skull—a human skull—was staring at her, its cavernous eyes deep pits. A tiny crack ran the length of a cheek bone. The bones were brown with age and polished to a patina from handling, charred at the temples as if burned. It appeared to be grinning.

Someone else bent over her and turned her face this way and that, looking for something, releasing her chin roughly. She recognized Ava from her fire-engine red hair and propped herself up on her elbows, squinting. Words floated past her, but she hardly cared.

"Memory lapses," Ava was saying. "Whitening hair—"

Other whispers, like the buzz of insects.

Luc was all that mattered. And he was sitting right there.

His perfect eyes, she thought. *His perfect face*. She felt herself flushing. A great shivery sensation in her chest, like jumping off a cliff. *Lover boy*, she thought—or had she spoken it? She hardly cared.

"—*and a lack of impulse control*. These are all definitive signs." Ava brandished her bangled arm, clinking loudly as she pointed at Itzy.

Luc chuckled. "Itzy—how do you feel?" he asked.

"Never better," she said, regarding the ceiling of clouds. Time and gravity released their hold on her, and she seemed to soar. "I feel like I'm flying. Am I flying?" she asked, sitting up.

"No, Itzy." Luc's amber eyes stared deep into her. "Someday, I'll show you flying."

She was in an unfamiliar room, vast and airy. There was a balcony off in the distance, a dock floating on a sea of night air. It was filled with angels. Some perched fearlessly on the railing, the city open and infinite behind them. They were modern and chic, torn from pages of a magazine. Itzy recognized a few—Virginie, the silver-winged boys, and some of the others—from Obscura, but many more were new to her. Wings of all shapes and sizes—colored feathers sprouting from their backs. Pippa was there, too, gesturing grandly, recounting some story with practiced confidence. Gaston watched her closely, laughing. A waif-like angel walked by, her wings bound behind her back with golden cord. She passed out drinks from a silver tray, weaving in and out of powdered wings.

"Sorry. I don't know what's gotten into me." Itzy cleared her throat, hardly recognizing her voice.

"I've got an idea," Ava said. From her tone, Itzy knew she wouldn't like the answer.

Itzy looked again to Luc, this time for an explanation, but the impulse was so strong to touch him that she had to look away. She sat on her hands, feeling them sandwiched between the denim of her jeans and silky sheets. Someone laughed.

"This is no laughing matter," Ava scolded. "This is very serious, very serious indeed. Luc—a word?"

Luc shut his eyes, his own inner battle raging, and pulled away. "You heard the girl." Luc looked at Ava sharply. "Everything's fine."

"What we have here is a classic example of possession-by-inches. The girl's bedeviled—and it's worse than I thought," Ava said.

"Possession-by-inches is the rarest of all afflictions. It's impossible. Nicolas was the only known case—" Luc glowered.

"It is slow, insidious. By the looks of things, it's my guess she's been compromised for some time, and her angel blood is fighting it off. How else to explain the Hermès scarf? I had to *peel* it off her neck—just look at those blisters." When Ava next spoke, her voice was low, desperate. "When the Gates open, all is done, Luc! The Divah will have all the power she needs to complete the possession."

"You've got your head in too many of those old pamphlets, Ava."

"And you've got your head up your—"

"Easy now." Maurice scowled. "We're all on the same side."

"This is your doing." Ava pointed at Luc. "It was you who led the Divah to this hellhole. You who doomed Itzy."

From somewhere across the room, a voice spoke.

"She was doomed from the start."

No one was laughing anymore. It was Gaston who had spoken, and something about what he said must have been true, for the room was awash in shifty glances; an awkward silence descended.

"What do you mean *doomed*?" Itzy blinked.

"Oh tell her and be done with it," Ava growled.

Gaston glared at Luc. "The Divah's preening you," Gaston explained. "When the Gates of Hell open, she'll have all she needs."

Itzy looked around wildly. "To do what?"

"When the Gates open, she will take possession of your body, Itzy. Your power as a fledgling will join with hers. With your mouth, she will call forth the damned and visit ruin upon all that is good on this green earth until there is nothing but a scorched wasteland. With your feet, she will walk her kingdom of ash and ember and turn finally to the sky. The clouds will heave with thunder. And then, when there is nothing left, she—no *you*, Itzy—will conquer them, too."

"She needs a body," Ava said matter-of-factly. "And she wants yours."

Itzy was silent for some time.

"Why me?"

"Ask him," Ava said finally.

"Luc?" Itzy turned to him, wide-eyed.

Luc looked miserable, his jaw tensed and eyes flinty where the light abandoned them. "To be with me," he said. "She thinks we are meant to be together. Her eternal lover. The body she has now—your governess. That is a temporary body, a hasty choice arranged by the doctor to accommodate her arrival. It is failing her. Itzy—"

"She sees the way he looks at you, Itzy." Gaston interrupted. Luc whirled about, bristling, but Gaston continued. "And she wants that. And then, with Luc by her side, she will rule over the wasteland."

"How very reassuring." A grim smile crawled across Itzy's face and she looked around the room, catching Pippa's eye. "I thought the Gates were in Paris."

My father went to Paris to find the Gates of Hell.

"Change of plans." Gaston scowled.

"She tried Paris once. It cost her her head," Maurice explained.

Itzy's eyes fell on the skull. "What makes her think the Carlyle will be any more welcoming?" Itzy asked, grabbing it from its perch on the nightstand.

"Itzy, this is the *Carlyle* we're talking about." Ava smirked. "White-glove service and a reputation for excellence. What better place to raise Hell?"

84

"I wonder if that's what she plans for the party tomorrow night."

"What did you say?" Luc demanded.

"The party," Itzy replied.

The chatter ceased.

"Ooo. Did someone say party?" Pippa clapped her hands.

"Yes, tomorrow. The Divah's having a party at Bemelmans Bar."

Luc turned to Maurice, his words rushed, urgent. "Maurice—*tomorrow*. What is the date tomorrow?"

Maurice looked stricken. "July fourteenth."

"July fourteenth," Pippa said. "That's—"

"Bastille Day," everyone spoke at once.

"Here we go again." Gaston grinned.

Luc's suite was open and airy, and the sounds drifted down on her. A cool breeze raised the little hairs on her arms. The party had broken up quickly at the mention of Bastille Day, a selection of thoughtful, exuberant, and worried expressions on the angels' faces as they said their good-byes. In the air, the soft fine powder from their wings twinkled, catching the golden light of the candles. Luc locked the balcony door with a soft click.

Itzy turned to the charred skull by her side.

"You must be Nicholas," she said, examining him. "I've heard so much about you."

She held him close. His eyes—or the holes they once nested in—were dark caverns, and his teeth, what few he had in life, were yellowed and loose. French dentistry did not leave many teeth in Nicolas's mouth at the time of his beheading. She saw the cracks running haphazardly along the skull's ridge, splintery little lines that crept along the surface following their own mysterious design.

Itzy smiled to herself, a laugh bubbled up from deep inside her, and she giggled into the feathery pillow. The place inside her that always felt alone and small—that place had disappeared. She felt full and complete—as if every inch of her body, from her skin to her marrow, was bursting with vitality—with new life. There wasn't a part of her body that didn't feel flushed, like a newborn babe, scrubbed pink.

She had never felt better.

The problem was she had never felt less like herself.

85

Luc was lying beside Itzy on the sprawling bed in the quiet penthouse. The wispy sheets were tucked under her chin, and she was curled up like a baby beside him, shivering. The skull was between them, a candle jutting from the polished dome of his head.

"Nicolas, meet Itzy. Itzy, Nicolas."

Itzy giggled. "Hello, Nicolas."

"He only speaks French," Luc said, a smile beginning in the corners of his mouth.

"*Ah, excusez-moi. Bonsoir, Nicolas,*" Itzy said to the skull. "Not very talkative, is he?" she asked Luc.

"He's had a hard life."

"You don't say."

Luc smiled, touching her cheek. "A good friend is hard to find."

"I've met Maurice, and Gaston, and now Nicolas. Everyone except Laurent, it seems. Where is he?"

Luc's face hardened. "I wouldn't know. I'm not his keeper."

"I didn't mean—"

Luc had gone silent, staring at the ceiling, brooding. Sighing, Itzy leaned back on her pillow; between them, the candle flickered atop Nicolas. The ceiling was even more spectacular in the low light.

When Luc finally spoke, his voice was gentler. "I had the clouds painted by Ludwig Bemelmans when he did the bar downstairs. He lived at the Carlyle for some time while he painted, until his family went missing and he went mad. He was a scholar, you know. Like your father."

"Who knew being a scholar was so dangerous?"

The clouds on the ceiling were still tantalizingly out of reach. *So real I could touch them.*

"Why do you like clouds so much?" Itzy asked.

He lifted a glass. "They remind me of home."

Itzy smiled, stealing a glance at his profile.

"Why don't you paint anymore?" Itzy asked.

Luc was silent. When he spoke, she could barely hear him. "Because after Marie, I burned down my atelier."

She reached for his hand, and his tattoo caught her eye. It was made of ink of the blackest black, as if a crack in the world of light were etched upon his fourth finger.

"What is this?" she asked, tracing the circle.

"My halo."

"Your halo." His face was deadly serious. "Do all angels have them?"

"Just us. The Fallen."

Itzy peered at it closer. The band encircled his finger where it met his hand.

"It's a ring," she said.

"It's a reminder."

"Of what?"

"It's complicated."

"Try me."

He sighed. "It's a brand, of sorts. It marks me. As a dark angel."

"Maurice says things are muddled. Good and evil are blurring. That you owe your allegiance to no one."

"This is true."

"Is that what that ring reminds you of?"

"No. It is a reminder, but not for me. For others. To remind them to keep away."

Them? Itzy wondered. *Or me?*

Itzy stared at Nicolas, the charred bones—scars from the Petit Pont—avoiding Luc's eyes. Luc turned to her, a great sadness on his face. He stared at her for some time, her stomach flipping over.

"You don't look like an angel," Itzy blurted.

This was met with some amount of amusement. "What does an angel look like, Itzy?"

"Oh, you know. Flowing white robes, for one. Brooding, another. A tendency to be lurking in a corner of a room, brandishing a harp."

"Lurking?" Luc smirked.

"I'll take you to the Met sometime," Itzy said.

"Oh, you needn't bother. I've seen them all. Many even as they were being painted. But, Itzy, I promise I've yet to meet an angel like those floating wastrels with harps in their hands. That was a result of too much opium in the pipes of the Renaissance masters. In fact, it is *demons* who love harps. Marie, in particular. I can't stand the sound of them. And while we're at it, demons are hardly red with pointed serpent tails and ears. But that, you already know." Luc raised a glass. "Here, drink this. It'll help you sleep." The crystal goblet was filled with a thick, deep amber fluid. She sat up and sipped from it—it tasted complex on her tongue, warm and soothing. Liquid gold, like his eyes.

"*Porto*," he said, examining the glass. The crystal looked like it was melting, the wine clinging to the inside of the goblet like tears. "1811. From a cave in Cima Corgo."

"1811," Itzy said thoughtfully. "I don't suppose you remember what you were doing then?"

"In fact, I do."

"Tell me."

"Feels like yesterday."

"I bet."

"Time is different, Itzy, for me."

"1811?" she reminded him.

"That's too easy." He took a sip, placing the goblet beside Nicolas thoughtfully. "I already said I was buying this port."

"Well, how about 1799 then? Harder?"

"Nope."

"1897?"

"I was at the Ritz, in Paris. But you're just throwing out random dates now."

"Luc, you can remember what you were doing at all of those times?"

"Yes, Itzy."

"That's nice." She yawned. "Tell me."

"It's very simple. I was waiting for you."

Itzy kissed him now—a kiss quite unlike their first, with the rickety horse and carriage approaching. This kiss was long and dark, full of shadows that mixed in the back of her mind, sensations on her skin like sparks, the smell of the hearth from her childhood. A kiss that stretched out over time, tasting like the year 1811, when, although Itzy could not have known it, the summer's cool temperatures combined with an early frost to produce the sweetest,

most sought-after vintage in the history of tawny ports.
High on a windy bluff, a young angel waited. The angel,
in his dark greatcoat and white billowing silk scarf, stood
on a rocky cliff against a gray sky, negotiating with a stout
vintner. He produced a bursting billfold, purchasing the
entire vintage and loading the wooden crates onto small
ships in the nearby harbor. The ships, built for smuggling,
would carry the thick green bottles to a cave in Corsica, to
be stored for nearly two centuries.

Her hands ached as they brushed his jaw—the faint-
est stubble there against his smooth skin—and snaked
their way into his dark curls. She opened her mouth and
felt his smooth line of white teeth, tasted his faintly cinna-
mony tongue, as he pulled her closer. His lip—his perfect
lower lip—was between her teeth and she bit down on it
lightly. She felt herself tremble—the tremble of a slow,
earth-moving machine, with a low rumble and infinite
power. As if someone else had crawled into her skin.

The kiss did finally end, and Itzy held her head to his
chest, feeling the rich Sea Island cotton against her cheek,
waiting for the thudding of her heart to subside.

> *Elle est retrouvée!*
> *—Quoi?—l'Eternité.*
> *C'est la mere mêlée*
> *Au soleil.*
>
> —*Arthur Rimbaud*

Here was her life, her short life flashing before her.
The seventeen years notched in her belt, each a battle-won
victory. But there was something else, she was realizing.
Something very different, a newness—a glimmer of

something bigger, something vast. Bigger than she—bigger than Luc and the Carlyle, and his angels even. Something *eternal within her*. A door had opened in her very core and through it was her mother's everlasting legacy. She need only to walk through.

"I've been waiting for you, too," Itzy whispered. The stranger in the cottage in Brittany, the one who stayed too long and drank their wine. The one who saved her.

Luc studied her face.

"I tried to warn them, Itzy. I tried to warn your family."

"I know," Itzy said.

"I knew Marie, you see. I knew she would never give up. I told them to go into hiding, but it was too late. They came that very night. They took your mother, Itzy. But they wanted you."

86

It was dark. She must have fallen asleep again. The sweet taste of Luc's port had soured in her mouth, which was dry. She swallowed, feeling her throat rebel.

She had lain next to him, watching the Bemelmans clouds. Luc's body. The memory of it beside her. Shyly, she had touched his ruined wings. They were warm, surprisingly so. Little patches of eiderdown had grown over the gnarled joints and sinew like moss. Here and there was a stunted, broken quill—a small calcification at the tip, sharp and curved. The talons were ruined, cracked and blackened like Nicolas's skull.

On his face while she touched them:

Sorrow.

Loss.

"Do you trust me, Itzy?" he had whispered.

She nodded.

"*No matter what?*"

"No matter what."

"Listen carefully—we have little time left. Itzy—you need to save me from myself."

She squinted at the dim ceiling. Blue. Sighing, she tried to turn, to find Luc beside her on the bed, to feel him again.

She couldn't move. Breathing, in fact, was difficult. Eyes wide this time, she stared at the ceiling, concentrating.

Not a cloud in the sky.

Her mind went numb. How had she gotten back here, to the Blue Bedroom? She must have fallen asleep. Where was Luc? Fragments of her conversation with Luc returned to her, but it was a blur. She squeezed her eyes shut, listening. Horrible screeching noises, some sort of hissing from somewhere further in the suite. And breathing—someone's raspy breathing was closer. Much closer.

The itzy bitzy spider, crawled up the water spout.

A voice was in her head, and it was not her own. It was singing, garbling the words with a swollen tongue. After several attempts, Itzy managed to lift her head. Her body felt distant, shaky. Like the worst case of pins and needles. Little shooting stars popped across her vision. Someone had dressed her. She had been *sewn* into the silver dress, which bound her tightly and made even breathing difficult.

Down came the rain and knocked the spider out.

She felt a cruel shove, and all the air left her. Her head fell back on her small iron bed. She felt her back arch and contort as her body writhed.

Itzy heard a voice then, a real voice, from the head of the bed.

"Miss Nash," came the sinister, velvety-thick voice of Dr. Jenkins, "so good of you to join us."

The appalling shrieking had quieted, and there was nothing to hear but the thudding of her heart.

And then the footsteps. A click of a high heel. A thud, something dragging. A pause.

Knock, knock.

87

"Ged ub," the Divah said. And then again, more spitefully, "I said, ged ub."

Itzy was blinking up at the Divah. Her skin felt hot and prickly and the smell was back—overwhelming her lungs with the bitter tang of sulfur. The demon leaned forward, bending over her, sniffing, scanning the bed. Wads of gauze protruded from her nostrils, making her nose bulbous and misshapen. Her skin puckered and sagged from this angle, Itzy saw, all the newness seemingly gone. Around her shoulders was her Aunt Maude's fox fur.

Itzy stole a look around the room.

"Your freds hab lept you."

"Sorry?"

The Divah pulled the gauze from her nose.

"*Friends*. They're gone—abandoned you. They always do. They scattered into the nearest cracks in the wall like the roaches they are."

Itzy was hauled to her feet by some hot force.

"That's right. What we do for beauty, yes?"

There were shoes, apparently, which Itzy's feet had been wrenched into while she was asleep, and she wobbled on these unsteadily, the heel a solid spike of glittering steel.

"You'll get the hang of it. Although it hardly matters. Soon enough *you* won't be needing those shoes. Soon enough *you* won't be needing those feet!"

The Divah's nose leaked, and she wiped it angrily with the back of her hand.

"Come now—follow me. Time to do your face."

To Itzy's great horror, her feet moved on their own.

The Versailles living room had been ransacked, as though by angry peasants. The Divah led the way through the incomprehensible mess. Gilt mirrors were cracked, shards lying dagger-like on the marble floor. Itzy picked her way across the rubble—broken ashtrays, plates of putrid food, parchment scrolls torn and discarded, befouled with scarlet paint. Something black and unsettling oozed across the low hearth, pooling upon the floor.

"Nearly there." The Divah smiled. With each step, her knee bones ground together.

Soft cartilage is the first to decay, Itzy. A body is such a fickle thing.

Cold fingers crept down Itzy's spine.

Itzy's feet were moving of their own accord. Passing the sooty mirror above the hearth, she saw herself as if in a dream, pale and shimmering. Her reflection peered back out at her, and where the glass had cracked, a jagged line distorted her left cheek. Her hair, cloud-white at the brow, fell in a shock about her face. On her forehead was an unimaginable symbol, painted in blood.

She felt a shiver of annihilation.

She had skin, which was plainly her own. And beneath that, nerve endings, she supposed. And it was as if those synapses had been hijacked, like the electric feeling from the doctor's mallet when he had tested her reflexes. Her hips swayed, and she sashayed—entirely against her will, her long silver dress dragging out behind her over the chaos of the room, the debris catching in its hem.

I cannot escape myself, Itzy realized with a jolt. *How can I run from the terror when it's inside me?*

Aunt Maude's bedroom had not been spared the ransacking.

An operating theater of some sort was arranged in the room, a long metal table and rolling carts with hooked blades and scissor-like clamps, beakers of amber fluid. Bright spotlights hung over the platform, their unforgiving light pooling on a wrinkled and stained sheet.

"This way, poppet," the Divah was saying. One wall was devoted to a huge mirror, framed with glowing bulbs, the narrow table beneath it littered with pots of makeup, tubs of sparkles, sharp little brushes like fans. Blank, faceless heads wore wigs of various styles, whispers of the French Revolution. Flesh-colored powder had spilled and was streaked across the entire work surface. Pencils with coal liner were blunted; lipsticks broken and smeared from their casings.

Throughout this mass of refuse, thin, gleaming ampoules were everywhere, some bearing teeth marks, other cracked open like peapods, their contents long gone. Bent and fouled syringes were scattered like pine needles on a forest floor. Itzy recognized them from the doctor's office. From his bag. They bore some sort of medical label.

BOTOX.

A shower was running from somewhere back in Aunt Maude's bathroom, and the air was warm and misty.

Itzy sat—or rather, her body folded itself back upon the stool of its own accord.

"Yessssss," the Divah hissed, taking Itzy's chin in her hand. She leaned in, inspecting. Itzy could smell her putrid breath.

The Divah grabbed a brush, and licked it, then plunged it into a cake of black paint.

"Still now," she said, applying a black line above her eyelid.

Itzy felt her stomach recoil. Her face was smeared with something cool; her cheeks were brushed with shimmery powder from a cracked tub—and then her shoulders as well. A small comb was run through her eyebrows, and Itzy felt the pinch of the tweezers as the Divah pulled at them. Long, black, spidery things were glued atop her own eyelashes, a mole worked onto her cheek.

Itzy watched the Divah's eyes with a morbid fascination. They were just inches from her own, black and dead. When she turned, the light caught them, and they flashed with a deep, fathomless depth—portals to a corrupt and tormented place. A dark place. A place beside a hearth.

Fear of the dark coursed through Itzy's body like a current.

Here was the very darkness she feared—here was its source, the place of torment. She understood now why she hated the dark. The Divah *was* the dark.

The Divah caught her own reflection in the mirror and turned to it. The skin of her neck was uneven, and a waddle jiggled beneath her chin. Her cheekbones and jowls were puffy with excess fluid. Pulling at her neck, she tightened the skin against her windpipe and a mass of tendons, inspecting herself from all angles. Her hands moved to her face, pulling, prodding. Her fingers played over the crowded countertop, finally alighting upon an unopened ampoule. The Divah cracked it with her teeth and sniffed at the contents.

"Ever think of getting work done, Itzy?" She readied a syringe, tipping the bottle to meet the needle. "Don't bother. It's a slippery slope. I wouldn't recommend it."

The Divah pulled the skin beneath her eyes taut, and stabbed it with the needle. "What we have here is an inferior body." She gestured to herself, to what lay beneath Aunt Maude's fox fur coat. She pulled at the other eye, pushing at the sagging skin. "Not like my last one, mind you." She straightened, examining her face anew.

A small drop remained at the tip of the needle, and the Divah collected it on the tip of her finger, dabbing it behind each ear.

"Humans—there's a lot of mediocrity out there."

The shower had been turned off, Itzy realized with some surprise.

A drip sounded, *plink*, and then another, as the showerhead emptied onto the marble tiles. From the corner of her eye, she could see someone moving about in there. A shadow on the wall, the mundane sound of water running in the sink, mirrored cabinets opening and closing.

"Darling, come see," the Divah called over her shoulder, razor-sharp nails running through Itzy's hair.

Itzy saw a flash reflected in the bathroom mirror, as an immense ivory wing unfolded, the talon on its tip gleaming gold. An angel rounded the corner, an angel of such incredible beauty but wearing nothing but a hard, foul malevolence upon his proud face. He was unabashedly naked, save for his astoundingly beautiful wings that draped all the way to the floor, and he moved with transfixing power and grace. Itzy flushed and tried to look away from him, straining impossibly to move on her own accord.

"Laurent," the Divah said—only it was Itzy's mouth that moved, Itzy's voice that spoke. Her body coursed with fear. "What do you think of my handiwork?"

88

The door to Bemelmans Bar was of curtained-glass, accessed by both the street on Madison Avenue and to the residents of the Carlyle through a small, low hall that bespoke of speakeasies, of rare secrets. Itzy stood before it, hesitating. She wore an oval mask the color of opals.

Mustn't keep our guests waiting, the Divah had said in Suite 1804. And then, as if the puppet master abruptly left the stage, Itzy felt control return to her body; she felt the exquisiteness of the control of her own movements, and she promised herself that she would never take that for granted again. As the Divah turned her attention to her own ravaged face, Itzy found she could take small steps on her own—away from the horrible scene of the Divah preparing for the party.

Itzy heard a piano inside Bemelmans Bar.

She paused before the curtained-glass threshold, gathering her strength. In his bed, beside Nicolas and beneath the ceiling of clouds, Luc had told her his plan. Only with her help could he get his feather.

Damned if I do, damned if I don't.

A laugh—sharp and shrill—of some nearby guest ended abruptly as Itzy threw open the heavy door. The room reeked of the twang of flint and musk.

Bemelmans Bar was a low-ceilinged affair, the walls and ceilings the color of custard. Immediately before her

stood a polished baby grand played by someone in a tuxedo. A coat check was in a corner where pitchforks and
furs were gathered. Dark leather banquettes lined the
walls, and at the far side of the room was a small, gleaming bar. Miniature lights dotted the corners here and
there, and the tables held lamps—their sulfurous pools
of yellow providing little illumination. But the defining
feature of the room was the eerie paintings upon the
yellowed walls, the low light rendering them like cave
paintings.

Just as Johnny had said, Ludwig Bemelmans had chosen rabbits for his subject matter. Not as much painted
as *smeared* upon the walls, the rabbits stared out at her,
frozen. Scratches from an unsteady hand—a frightened
hand. Rabbits in human dress, busy at human pastimes,
visiting a zoo, roaming among caged humans. On another
wall—a guillotine. A marauding band of bunnies, heads
on spears.

Bemelmans was a scholar like my father, Itzy remembered Luc telling her. *He went mad after his family
disappeared.*

All conversation ceased, as masked revelers inspected her.
Itzy stood in a pool of yellowed light. Her dress danced
and spun, reflecting against the jet-black piano and onto
the many eyes of the crowd. From the bar, the distant
clinking of glasses and a slash of amber light and polished
glass.

Music, which had been halted, began anew.

Off somewhere in a darkened corner came a harsh
whisper followed by a brittle laugh. And with that, a collective chatter returned. A girl-child in a glistening doll

mask greeted Itzy with an orchid, and Itzy thanked her with a grateful smile. There was no sign of Luc.

Itzy walked though a suffocating sea of tuxedos and ravishing gowns. People jostled her, closing in on her. There were whispers, pale shoulders beneath indelicate glares. From behind their masks, people leered, their eyes dark and empty. Breath fell upon her, hot and arid. Someone brushed past her and she felt cold fingers on her shoulder. She passed a tower of champagne coupes, their cool effervescent bubbles fading in the heat of the gathering.

Shreds of conversation wafted over her.

"A scholar? You don't say . . . their clothes are so *worn*—"

"They say it's from rubbing shoulders with demons—"

A hand closed around her elbow and she found herself waylaid by Mrs. Brill.

"Darling." She took Itzy's hand in hers, her eyes dreamy. "You look wonderful. Who knew you had it in you?"

"Mrs. Brill?" Itzy asked, unsure. Pippa's mother had undergone yet another transformation, her cheekbones seemed somehow enlarged, her brow impossibly smoothed, her face strangely catlike. "Is Pippa here?" Itzy looked around, but saw only unfriendly eyes in the process of turning away from her own.

"Isn't it wonderful?" Mrs. Brill said, laying a bejeweled hand on Itzy's arm, squeezing it too tightly. "Do you even know how fortunate you are to be *chosen*? How very *blessed*?" Her voice wavered with emotion.

"Chosen?" Itzy asked, heart racing. She tried unsuccessfully to reclaim her arm.

"Little Itzy Nash." Mrs. Brill smiled. "You're in the big leagues now." Mrs. Brill's eyes wandered to the corner. "Oh look, there's Dr. Jenkins. Yoo-hoo! Doctor!" Itzy looked, her stomach sinking at the sight of the doctor at a corner table. He was watching her intently from the shadows.

There was a hand on her elbow. Itzy turned and found herself for the second time in recent memory staring into the flawless face of the international superstar.

"J-Julep!"

"Let me buy you that drink," Julep said firmly.

"Are . . . aren't they *free*?" Itzy looked around at the waitstaff and their trays of champagne, the tower of over-flowing coupes.

"It's an *expression*, Itzy."

Julep turned and delivered a million-dollar smile to Mrs. Brill. "Excuse us," she said, and led Itzy through the remainder of the crowd to the bar.

"Wait!" the older woman called, eyes brimming with emotion. "You must tell me what it's *like*—"

Julep expertly steered Itzy away.

"You could throw a drink on anyone in here and see someone sizzle," Julep muttered. "The place is filthy."

At the bar, Itzy had heard a familiar voice.

"Pippa!" Itzy cried, relief washing over her. Pippa and Gaston were leaning against the polished counter, bodies drawn together in conversation. Gaston's smile was easy with Pippa, his copper wings laced with scented laurel leaves.

"Oh my god, Itzy!" Pippa held Itzy at arm's length, whistling. "That is *you* under that mask, isn't it? That dress—it's—it's—words fail me!"

"That's a first." Itzy smiled.

"You look stunning," Gaston said, his voice holding none of the ridicule Itzy expected.

"Thanks, Gaston." She turned to Pippa, who was in black silk, tall and elegant, a ribbon of sheer black lace tied over her eyes. "Pippa, you look beautiful!"

"Tommy." Julep smiled at the bartender, a man with a history nearly as long as the hotel's.

"Evening, Ms. Joie." He polished a thick-cut glass with a white towel. "Tough crowd tonight." He winked. "What'll it be?"

Julep turned to Itzy, deferring.

Itzy scanned the room. The piano player was eyeing her, moving his hands like a puppeteer behind the black casket of a piano. A small spotlight caught his eyes. They were dark as death.

"Evian," Itzy said.

"Good girl. Make that a double," Julep ordered.

89

"Julep, this is Pippa. Pippa, Julep Joie. And you know Gaston already, I believe."

"Ah! Your hair is much improved," Julep said to the angel. "Careful. I hear if you make a face long enough, it'll stick." Gaston and Julep grinned at each other, and Itzy found herself happy to see Gaston's crooked smile.

"Jules!" Pippa exchanged a series of kisses with the star. "It's been forever! How are the kids?"

"Is there anyone you don't know?" Itzy asked.

"No," Pippa said simply.

"I guess Ava's not coming," Itzy said.

"By definition, recluses never go out."

Pippa pulled Jules aside, and they began catching up like old friends. Itzy found herself beside Gaston and the famed murals by the bar. Ludwig Bemelmans had painted a warren of rabbits here. It was a shadowy gathering, and the animals were dressed in costume, parading about an enormous crypt inside a vast cathedral.

"I met a friend of yours," Itzy said.

"Who?"

Itzy thought of Laurent as she had seen him in Aunt Maude's room. His broad, impossibly perfect shoulders, a living sculpture, without the fig leaf. His wings—immense things, ivory iridescent feathers, powdered and glittering as the air moved through them, as he breathed. The shivery feeling as she was made to move, to talk, to obey—the Divah's words flowing from her mouth.

"Laurent."

Gaston's face betrayed nothing, but his voice turned bitter. "Laurent is friend to no one."

"But I thought you and Luc—" She paused. "You and Maurice—" Itzy's voice drifted off.

"Laurent is an angel disgusted with humanity. It is an unfortunate combination. He is power-hungry and devious. Maurice feels that his talents come in handy, but we are not as sure. And, Itzy, he is not our friend." He shrugged. "But we all have our parts to play."

Itzy looked again at the mural beside her.

And I'm doing mine right now.

The smell of rotten eggs reached her nose like an abrupt assault. "Do you smell that?" Itzy turned to Pippa.

"Smell what?"

The smell was all-encompassing and growing stronger. The curtained door to the bar opened.

"Divah at one o'clock," Julep hissed.

Itzy didn't need the warning. She smelled her. She *felt* her. Her insides were jerked forward as if by an invisible string toward the entrance. A wave of nausea overtook her and her skin prickled uncomfortably, like a bad sunburn. Itzy fought against the magnetic pull, closing her eyes and concentrating. The back of her throat heaved as her stomach turned over.

The room grew hushed as a pair of silhouettes filled the entrance.

Pippa squeezed Itzy's hand encouragingly.

"Whoa," Julep whispered. "What the hell is that?"

Itzy's mind raced. *The miracle of Botox.*

The Divah stood on the threshold in a brilliant deep-red dress. It clutched at her body, her wasp-like waist, and fell toward the floor in a cascade of waves. The fox coat had been ripped into a stole, the fox hide wrapped around her neck. She wore a lacquered mask over her human skin and borrowed skull, upon which she'd placed an elaborate white wig with a froth of curls.

On her arm was her escort. He was tall and poised— regal, even.

Laurent, Itzy thought, as her stomach dropped. *At least he put some clothes on.*

The Divah had advanced into a pool of light, her face pulled tight behind her mask—eyes deep pools of tar. Her mask, a golden oval, had an exquisite black feather. Her escort emerged from the shadows on her arm wearing a simple, unadorned mask. She smiled and pulled him close, whispering something in his ear.

Not Laurent—a sudden realization shook Itzy.

It was Luc.

90

"Eww. She's all over him like static cling," Pippa said. She gripped Itzy's hand tightly as Itzy steadied herself against the bar. It felt solid and smooth behind her, whereas the room—the view—was unreal. Her dress was tightening around her ribs. A blackout threatened; the sides of the room wavered uncomfortably.

Luc said to trust him. No matter what.

Itzy's head was spinning and each gulp of breath was foul-tasting. With the Divah's arrival, her body was once again not her own. She shut her eyes, fighting to retain control.

"They make a lovely couple, don't they?"

It was the cadaverous voice of the doctor—and it was close.

"A love affair for the ages. Dark angel and demon queen, the ultimate power couple. They do this, you know. He searches out girls to fall in love with, and she, in turn, joins him, possesses them. Marie Antoinette was not the first. You will not be the last. Theirs is an eternal love. The stuff of dreams."

"Or nightmares," said Pippa.

Itzy watched from across the room as Luc and the Divah made their way slowly through the throngs of adoring acolytes. His amber eyes now struck her. Amber caught insects, and they reminded her suddenly of flypaper.

"Oh, child. Did you really think he loved you?" the doctor sneered.

"Well look what the devil dragged in." Julep was by Itzy's side. The doctor ignored her, his eyes glittering in the low light.

"Let's get you some air," Pippa said at her other elbow. "Excuse us."

The doctor made no move to let them pass. "Shame about your father." His smile was a jagged slash across his face.

Itzy froze. "What do you mean?"

Pippa had heard enough. She grabbed Itzy's hand. "This way."

But the doctor was again in front of them.

"Oh, hadn't you heard? He never got off the plane in Paris."

The room wavered and threatened to collapse entirely before Itzy's eyes. *My father?* she thought. Dark things skittered in the corners of the room, at her feet. *My father went in search of the Gates of Hell, but I found them instead.*

"Pick on someone your own size." Jules snarled from somewhere oddly far away.

Itzy's brain burned with fever. She thought she saw a flash of crystal, the low light catching the cut glass of the tumbler, sparkles burning her retinas. Imported French water arced through the air from Julep's glass and splashed squarely upon the face of Dr. Jenkins. Sound itself slowed to a standstill, and for a moment there was nothing but her beating heart. Then, a low, awful rumble.

The Evian, where it landed, was burning his flesh. His mouth and neck had erupted in shiny, putrid sores and steam rose from a misty puddle that had formed on the floor. But Julep was not finished.

As he sizzled before them, she swung about, pivoting, catching her foot squarely in the doctor's gut. The impact sent him sailing across the room, arms clawing at his face, where the famed Carlyle piano caught his fall. The piano played its last horrible symphony to the sound of splintering wood and demon wreckage. A final note sounded, and then deathly quiet.

Itzy opened her mouth, but the words died on her lips. The room had filled with a low, inhuman growl. A concussive round of pops rattled as a row of champagne bottles exploded along the bar, and a crystal ashtray sailed by, leaving a trail of ash in its wake. It shattered on the floor, followed by a muffled swear, and then the famed Bemelmans Bar erupted into chaos.

Itzy and Pippa found themselves in the relative calm beneath a small circular table beside the sparkling tower of champagne coupes.

"We've got to get out of here." Pippa's red lips were set in determination. "I've got a date."

Polished shoes, ladies' spiked heels, scrabbled about them as guests joined the fray.

This was news. "With *who*?" Itzy shouted.

Pippa turned, eyes ablaze. "Oh, Itzy. I've been meaning to tell you but, well—he's so secretive."

"Who is it?"

"The most amazing angel. He's a loner, keeps to himself. But so *incredibly* handsome. Our little secret, okay?"

A devhil in a tuxedo fell face-first before them, and Pippa kicked at him. He rolled farther away, his face pulled back in a grimace of missing flesh.

"An *angel*?" Itzy shouted, but the question was lost to the chaos. She heard Julep off somewhere taunting a demon.

"Back door!" Pippa shouted, indicating the discreet exit by the bar that led through the Café Carlyle to the hotel's lobby. She uncapped a bottle of Evian and raised an eyebrow. "One for the road."

"You bet," Itzy said.

They crouched, Pippa leading the way from one table to the next, as the tower of champagne coupes shattered behind them, raining down bubbles and crystal shards on their overturned table. Something black with too many legs dropped to the floor, skittering away in the dark. Jules shouted loud, gutteral French from somewhere behind Itzy, and she felt something light and ghostly touch her cheek. Through the chaos, she saw Luc, standing completely still as the battle crashed down around him. His face was calm, unworried. Slowly, he raised a hand, pointing. Itzy turned her head. There, in the middle of a steaming puddle, Itzy saw it. A golden eye mask, two empty black holes. And a feather.

Luc's feather.

Her fist closed around it.

The air had taken on a deep-red glow, casting the bar in an eerie dimness. Soot and ash floated lazily by when, suddenly, the room descended into pitch black.

"Wh-where are the lights?" Itzy stammered.

The eerie red glow of the EXIT sign above the door was all that remained—and then, with one final *pop*, it too was extinguished.

"Come *on!*" Pippa urged.

Itzy half-walked, half-stumbled, her hands outstretched, her heart pounding with pure fear. And then she could go no farther.

"The dark—" Itzy whimpered. *The dark is where every-thing falls apart.*

"Itzy—"

But Itzy was a little girl again, by the fireside. In the ash bin. The smell of burned cinders flooded her nostrils.

A hunched figure shrouded in shadow stood framed in the open door, and Itzy felt a chill trying to crawl into her skull. Her head was buzzing, a humming noise, over and over.

Pretend you're loading film in the dark. You do it all the time.

Itzy closed her eyes. She thought of her Leica, loading film into its chamber in the musty workshop with Johnny in the pitch black. She struggled to find the image of her father's house in Brittany, of the pale yellow sunshine. Of Marilyn prowling her tunnels.

Pippa yanked her hard. She pushed Itzy and sent her staggering toward the doorway.

"Pippa!" Itzy turned, stumbling on her heels. A horrible thought had just occurred to her. "Pippa—what's the angel's *name?*"

But there was no reply.

Dr. Jenkins, burned skin pulled back over bare gums, was holding Pippa by the throat. A scattering of jewels rained down from her hair.

"Itzy—go!" she rasped, eyes wide with terror.

Itzy pushed through the door. There was a sucking sound—as if the room itself contained a vacuum—and then nothing.

From somewhere deep within the lobby, the phone was ringing.

91

Itzy was alone. She stumbled into the lobby, which was empty, abandoned. With each step, her head was clearing as she distanced herself from the Divah, but her heart ached at leaving Pippa behind in the doctor's clutches.

Now what? Itzy's mind raced. Luc's plan to retrieve his feather did not involve a barroom brawl. Or being the Divah's armpiece. Still, here it was, in her hand. *What had he said?*

Itzy examined Luc's feather, its pitch-black plumes catching the smallest of breezes in their curlicues, on the Divah's gore-stained mask. She held it to her face, trying it on.

He said he'd meet me here.

But the sight of Luc and the demon queen together was burned into her memory.

I think I'm going to be si—Itzy retched, her body wracked with chills, the sound echoing wetly across the bare floor.

From the corner of her eye, Itzy saw movement. Several small, hunched men covered in matted hair darted into the shadows. She squinted for a better view, pushing her hair back from her face, and wiped her mouth. One carried a knotted club. Above her, the Carlyle's crystal chandelier flickered—once, twice, and then died.

The fireplace was blazing, bigger than Itzy remembered it being, crackling like a medieval hearth. The painted cherubim stared down at her, eyes flickering.

The discordant phone sat on the counter and Itzy headed for it. Candles fizzled and popped, dripping wax in pools upon the marble.

Itzy lifted the phone from its cradle, bringing it to her ear. A silence descended upon the room, but then, from the earpiece, a far-off scratching began.

"*Itzy . . .*" the scratching called out. "*Itzy, it's me.*"

The voice—she knew it.

"*It's your aunt. Your beloved Aunt Maude.*"

"No! You're *dead.*" Itzy whispered into the receiver. "I saw you in the closet."

"*Itzy, listen closely. You needn't fear anymore. We are Nashes, you and I. Aunt Maudey is here. We always liked one another, did we not? I always kept a special place in my heart for you, and now it's time to repay the favor. It's really ever so simple. Come to the basement. We're all here, my dear. Your father, too. It's a regular family reunion. You know the way don't you? Under is a place, Itzy.*"

Those last words sent a shiver down Itzy's spine, and she slammed the phone down.

The phone ripped through the silence, commencing its clamorous ringing again, and Itzy jumped.

One ring.

Two rings.

By the third ring, she was upon the wretched thing and, grasping the snaking cord, she yanked it from the wall.

In the silence that followed, she heard a gentle *ping* of the elevator alighting, doors sliding open.

"Miss Nash!"

Itzy had long given up examining the operators in their monkey suits, concluding that Johnny was a lost cause. She turned.

"Johnny?"

Itzy crossed the lobby in a flash, hearing her heels click against the slick black floor like rapid gunfire.

Itzy threw her arms around the boy, relief washing over her. She hugged him tight, until her heart stopped thundering in her chest, and then she hugged him more. She pulled back to take him in. "Where have you been?"

"My father was sick." He shrugged, embarrassed.

"Oh, sorry—"

"Nah, it was nothing. He's feeling better every day." Johnny's eyes twinkled and Itzy felt herself flush. "Wow, you're dressed to kill. You going to the big party?"

"No, actually. I think it's breaking up early." She smiled at him. "It's good to see you, Johnny."

"You too, Itzy." Johnny smiled back, and Itzy was again reminded of the whiteness of his teeth. "Hey, I heard you were sick, too," he said.

"I was."

"Feeling better?"

"Better every day."

"Say, I've got something for you," he said, a note of pride creeping into his voice.

"You shouldn't have."

"No, really. It's in my locker."

Itzy shuddered, remembering being trapped inside it while Johnny distracted Wold from some errand.

"Thanks, but I've seen enough of your locker for one lifetime."

"Aw, don't be like that. You're really gonna be surprised."

"I don't like surprises."

Wounded, he fretted with his lips, chewing on the lower one. "Jeez—I thought you'd be excited to get your camera back."

My Leica.

"What? Where did you find it?"

Johnny flushed with pride. "In the basement."

"The *basement*?" Her excitement curdled.

"Come down and get it?" His thumb was poised above a glowing button.

Aunt Maude's voice came back to her, scratchy from the phone line. *Under is a place, Itzy. We're all down here. You know the way, don't you?*

Itzy peered behind him, into the elevator. Splatters and stains were sprayed across the walls and ceiling, and the floor had a wide bloody trail where something had been dragged across it.

"S-sure Johnny. Maybe later."

"Nice feather." He reached for the mask on her head, and her hand fluttered up defensively. "A girl can get into a lot of trouble with a feather like that."

"Do you hear that?" Itzy asked, her throat suddenly dry.

Impossibly, the phone was ringing again. She was sure she had pulled the phone cord from the wall.

92

Itzy backed away from Johnny. A pair of small, furred men darted by the fireside, their hides covered in ashes.

A burst of noise echoed through the lobby, and for a moment Itzy could hear the crashing of glass and an otherworldly, high-pitched scream from Bemelmans Bar—and then nothing.

Luc? She hoped, desperately.

But the hairs on her arms stood on end.

The unmistakable sound of heavy footfalls. The sound of something dragging, metal on stone.

Tap. Tap. Drag.

Tap. Tap. Drag.

I know that sound.

It was the sharp-tipped edge of the doctor's cane as he labored across the polished black marble floor, dragging a useless leg behind him.

Johnny. The doctor. The whole hotel. Everyone. They were out to get me from the start. I never had a chance.

Itzy backed away, until suddenly—horribly—she couldn't anymore.

"Miss Nash."

She found herself staring at the barrel chest of the hotel's concierge.

"Mr. Wold?"

"Allow me to assist you."

"Oh, I've had enough of your help, Mr. Wold."

The concierge was holding her wrist.

"Please, Miss Nash," he said, indicating the feather.

Itzy scowled and opened her mouth to protest. Wold's fingers were elegantly cared for, as befitted his position at the hotel. They were scrubbed and manicured, the nails buffed to a near-mirror shine. He had neglected his gloves this evening. He never neglected his gloves. Encircling its fourth finger was a tattoo of a ring.

Itzy felt the doctor closing in.

Itzy, eyes wild, looked up at Wold, realization dawning. *He has a halo, like Luc.*

His face was unreadable, an amalgam of professionalism and decorum—calm in the face of the coming storm. But for a moment the curtains parted, his reserve cracked, and, ever-so-quickly, his eyes urged her to the doors. Itzy ripped the Divah's mask from her head, handed Luc's feather to the angel Wold, and then sprinted for the doors.

93

Outside, the streets of the Upper East Side were dark, and a stale wind blew in a pungent smell of musty stables. The streets were strewn with the sweepings of a barnyard. Itzy found her feet moving before she knew it. Some deep part of her told her to run, and run she did.

Run, Itzy, when you cannot fly.

From somewhere behind her, Itzy heard the sound of an engine gunning, and a black town car roared to a halt, one wheel mounting the curb and sending a hubcap rolling.

"Get in!" A darkened window sailed down smoothly from the backseat.

Itzy had come to like town cars, their sleek black presence a constant in the city streets, the ferries of the rich and powerful along the rivers of cobbles and potholes. Pippa and Mrs. Brill kept one idling at all hours, should the impulse overcome them to shop or to lunch. Aunt Maude had slipped around town in one as well, like a dark shadow. This town car was like all the others; in particular, it had the advantage of *not* being a funeral carriage.

"I said get in, Itzy! The traffic's hellish."

"*Ava?*"

The door swung open, and Itzy jumped in.

The engine revved and the car shot off down the side street before Itzy could close her door. It slammed on its own as the driver took another screeching turn down Fifth

Avenue, and they headed downtown by the park. The noises of the city streets immediately dulled and the sedate leather interior of the town car took over. Itzy caught a profile of the driver, a man in a visored cap, staring straight ahead. One of his eyes was clouded over, blind.

"Ava—what are you doing out? I thought you never left the hotel!"

Ava's eyes were sharp, and her bangles clinked as she gripped the armrest.

"You asked me why I quit acting."

"Too many monsters in Hollywood," Itzy remembered.

"Something like that." Ava smiled a sad, soft smile, and then was silent for some time. When she finally spoke, her voice was flat, and Itzy had to strain to hear. "The truth is much harder to bear. We lost a bright light when Marilyn died. And I could have saved her. I let down a friend, Itzy. I wasn't there when the demons came for her. I vowed never to let that happen again."

Outside, the Upper East Side was sailing by, smudges of lights against the darkened windows. Cars were burning, abandoned, and hunched figures darted in and out of shadowy doorways. Itzy stared blankly out the car's dimmed window as they sped down Fifth Avenue.

"You left this in my room." Ava handed Itzy the sheathed guillotine blade. Itzy pulled it from its casing, hearing its pleasurable metallic call, feeling its weight.

"I cleaned it for you."

"Thank you, Ava." Itzy slid the weapon back into its case and slung the thin chain over her shoulder.

"Sometime we'll train together."

Itzy's heart leapt. "That would be great. Ava? Can I ask you something?"

"Why stop now?"

Itzy smiled. "You said once, 'Angels are selfish things.'"

"Did I? Probably had too much to drink."

"What did you mean?"

Itzy was silent while Ava considered the question.

"Imagine a life, chasing a feeling that you're missing something. Forever lacking. Born without a limb—or worse. Born without a soul. And then imagine that you can never, ever, feel whole. Because what you lack you simply cannot have. Then walk this world with those who have it all—with those who have the soul you lack—*and don't even know how lucky they are.* I imagine you would become a bit disillusioned with humanity. Bitter, even. Yes, angels exist for themselves alone. Look what your mother's capable of. But surely you realize that now?"

Itzy's stomach lurched, thinking of Luc. Did she really *know* him? The ring on his finger, she thought. It was there as a reminder. To keep people away, he had said.

"Ava—" Itzy began. "Do you think Luc used me? You know, to lure the Divah out of her lair?"

"You mean, are you demon bait?"

Itzy wasn't sure she wanted to hear the answer, but Ava just shrugged.

"Angels are selfish and capricious beings. But never forget, Itzy, you have angel blood, too. Maybe it's time you stop being the victim and start knocking some heads together instead."

The town car had stopped.

"Where are we going?" Itzy asked. There was a knot in her gut. They were idling beside a large corner building, a discreet orange and brown sign above her read HERMÈS.

"To see your father."

94

Piles of silk and fine leather disguised the flagship store's true identity: Hermès was an ancient order of demon hunters—a covert and impenetrable society. Ava and Itzy were admitted immediately by a uniformed guard with a walkie-talkie who muttered something in French into the mouthpiece.

"Hermès was named for the ancient Greek god, the guide to the Underworld. You see, we were fighting even then. Since the beginning of time, there was evil, and there were those of us who fought it. You know Hermès as an exclusive company, Itzy," Ava explained. "Timeless fashion for the eons of demon-fighting."

They stopped beside a wall of leather purses with gleaming hardware. "That's the Kelly." Ava pointed to a classic purse. "Named for the scholar Grace Kelly. And there's the famed Birken bag—Jane Birken was legendary for her demon-hunting prowess. They say there's a three-year waiting list for those. Who knows? Someday we might be waiting for an Itzy."

The retail space was open and airy, but Ava marched Itzy through it without a second glance. At the rear of the shop was a lounge—a sort of area to rest while the pressures of shopping dissipate with an espresso, a flute of champagne, or a glass of Evian. Another guard was stationed there, but Ava paid him no mind. A row of leather-padded doors lined one wall—all of them, save one, opened to dressing rooms with long oval chevalier mirrors. The last was closed.

"Go back a thousand years—then go back further. Then a thousand more," Ava was saying. They entered the last of the padded doors, which opened to a rambling set of wooden stairs. Pictures lined the walls—many of familiar faces, actors and filmmakers, singers and artists. All scholars. Little spotlights threw soft amber light upon each of the portraits, which were entirely of notable celebrities sitting in quiet alertness. They all wore the same intent gaze, a striking contrast to their public personas. And then there was Julep Joie, sitting in a great and open library, light streaming in. Her face resonated a calm confidence that was at once arresting and haunting.

"One of our most promising hunters," Ava said. "It is difficult to have a successful career in the public eye while ridding the world of demons, but somehow Julep does it effortlessly. I hear you've made her aquaintance."

Itzy nodded, and they kept on. The framed photographs faded to black-and-white, then to lithographs, and then more classic oil paintings as they marched up the stairs. *They have one thing in common*, Itzy thought. *They all have the same watchful look upon their faces. The look of a hunter.*

They had come to a glass-enclosed atrium, a clean, open floor above the store. With no curtains to keep the city lights at bay, the streets and towering buildings became a kind of light—not moonlight, nor starlight, as Itzy was used to from home, but citylight. Ghostly rectangles of it stretched across the room.

A figure leaned against a far window. Even though his back was to them, Itzy knew her father at once.

"Jack," Ava called. "I've brought Itzy. She seems in one piece."

Jack Nash hesitated, breathing deeply before turning to the room. He was tall and lanky, and, like the best of teachers, entirely captivating.

"Little one," he said.

A rush of relief swept over her, soft as velvet.

"Dad." She ran and hugged him, feeling his comforting arms around her finally. "Where have you been?"

She looked up at his face, which was worn and tired-looking.

"Putting out fires, little one."

They sat in leather armchairs, a pool of stained glass from a small lamp illuminating the space between them.

"How are you?" he asked carefully.

"Having one hell of a summer vacation."

He smiled, reaching for her hand. "Well, I'm here now."

"Aunt Maude—"

"I know." Looking out the window, lost in thought, her father suddenly looked quite old. His chin was lost in days of stubble, and there were dark circles around his eyes.

"She was right, your aunt. She wanted you to be trained, but I thought to do so would expose you—and risk everything. It was safe, I thought, at the university. And quiet. And my students looked out for you, the few who I trusted. But I was wrong. I was wrong to keep you in the dark."

"I was wrong about Aunt Maude, too," Itzy realized. "But, she wanted you to give me up for adoption!"

"She had a way with words, my sister." He smiled. "That was her way of saying she wanted you placed with a scholar who would train you—if I wouldn't. It was our biggest disagreement. And now my biggest regret.

"I sent you to the Carlyle for the summer because I thought it was the safest option. We had it on good authority that the Gates would rise again soon—and again in Paris, where our organization is based."

"Dad, why didn't you *tell* me?" Itzy gestured to the room, to him. "About this? You? Anything?"

"As hard as it may be to understand, Itzy, I did it to keep you safe."

"How's that working out for you?" Itzy felt tears well up, and she angrily stabbed at her eyes with the back of her wrist.

He looked hard into her eyes, nodding finally.

"They hunt fledglings down, you know, Itzy. They come for them in the night. There are consequences when an angel lies with man. When they came for you all those years ago in Brittany, I took you away. Hid you. Kept you safe from anything with wings—both feathered and scaled. It was my only choice. You are half angel, half human. The rarest of rare. The Divah's wanted you since you were born, and that time in Brittany she almost got you. You have a corporeal body and angel blood. And with that, she will be unstoppable. But she underestimated you, didn't she, Itzy? Such a tiny thing against such great forces."

"Who hunts down fledglings, Dad? Demons?"

"Demons, yes." Her father's voice was sad. "But the real danger is our own kind. Scholars, Itzy. It is the scholars who fear you the most."

"Scholars!"

"Yes. Fledglings are killed because they attract powerful divahs. Holy wars are won and lost over them."

He examined her eyes with a penlight.

"Plato, the ancient Greek philosopher, suggested that a soul was a carriage drawn by two horses, one white, one black. One good and one evil. The dark and the light are at constant odds within us. We all have our own demons to slay, little one. Yours just happens to be the queen of the damned."

"That's some beginner's luck."

Her father kissed her forehead and pulled her close. For a moment she was safe, back in his arms in their rambling house on the university grounds. The stacks of dusty books. The sun through the window where it warmed the table in the morning. Her quiet and boring life.

Pulling away, her father began pacing, fists jammed into the pockets of his worn blazer. His eyes were alight with grim determination.

"Itzy, this is my life's work! You understand that the Divah must not be allowed to open the Gates under any circumstances. They lock away all that is truly evil. If they were to open, Itzy . . . it would be the End of Days. But she is weakened now, as she tries to inhabit you, to possess you. She has made a strategic error: she has spread herself too thin. Your angel blood is fighting her off.

"Two battles rage, Itzy. The first, between us—the scholars, and the Divah and her legions. For thousands upon thousands of years. The dark and the light. And the second? The second is *inside* you. *Within your skin, a war rages.* The Divah against your angel blood, as she slowly tries to possess you. As the possession progresses, she becomes more and more entrenched inside you. Imprisoned, like a genie trapped in a bottle. Conquer her within you, and she is defeated on this mortal plane, as well. She cannot open the Gates when you have already banished her to Hell." He stopped his pacing; his voice had reached a crescendo. And then, more quietly, "Itzy, you are our salvation."

Our salvation. Or our ruin.

"For the first time ever, we have the advantage. She is *here*, in the room with us. Inside you. Come, little one. We're going to fight fire with fire."

He removed his tweed blazer and donned a worn leather apron, muttering to himself. He upended his Hermès attaché case, littering the table with a disorganized heap of ancient leather-bound books, stacks of paper wrapped in old twine, glinting charms, pockmarked coins, packets of dried herbs, bulging velvet satchels, charred wood, vials of potions and oils, and a lone broken mirror. Finally, he produced a bottle of Evian and some crumpled silks. He loosened his Hermès tie around his neck. "This might sting a bit."

"But what if the Divah wins?" Itzy's voice cracked. "What happens if your exorcisme doesn't work?"

"Well, my dear," Ava called from the shadows, "we have a machine for that."

"That's what I was worried about." Itzy looked to her father, who was lost in thought. "Dad? What happens if my angel blood isn't powerful enough to keep her out?"

"Itzy, you have everything you need right here, inside of you." He lifted her chin, and his hand, the long elegant fingers, remained there.

"Dad, why did you protect me?"

Silence.

"You're a scholar. If the scholars hunt down fledglings, why did you protect me?"

His eyes had gone unseeing, vacant, staring somewhere off above her head. Itzy watched as a tremor passed through him, a roiling energy that began at his feet and left him stiffened in its wake. His jaw was slack and his head lolled to one side.

"Dad?" She touched his broad shoulder, which was hard and unyielding. "Ava!" Itzy shouted. "Something's wrong with my father!"

"Itzy Nash," her father said in a voice from the grave.

Itzy stumbled backward.

"*You. Are. Summoned.*"

Cold fingers played about her skull. She did not hesitate. Itzy turned and sprinted with all her might.

Run, Itzy, when you cannot fly.

95

Outside on Sixty-Second Street, the air was scorching, even for the night, and smelled of foul smoke.

"My car is around the corner." Ava stabbed at the air, an orangey light playing about her face through her red hair. After a few short steps, she stopped short.

The town car was there, along with several others. All were on fire, burning placidly as ash and embers rained down on them. Ava was scanning the deserted street, alert, her sinewy muscles taut and ready. Soundlessly, she slipped the long row of bangles from her wrist, letting the chain fall at the ready. But Itzy's eyes were drawn to the blaze. Through the angry flames, a visored profile could just be seen.

"Your driver—he's still inside!" Itzy shouted.

Running, Itzy shattered the window with the butt of her blade and fell back as the inferno leapt out at her. The man's silhouette was warped by the flickering flames, but she watched with relief as he turned to unclip his seatbelt and throw open the door, stepping out languidly from the burning limousine. He wore a suit of fire.

Ava was shouting something urgently from somewhere behind her, but Itzy was transfixed. The man's mouth had fallen open, a dark hole within the daggers of flame.

"*Itzy Nash,*" he said.

One by one, the other car doors opened, and from each emerged a burning driver. The nearest one looked up at the night sky, as if to check the stars, his hair flaming like a large candle. And then they were coming, crackling on burning legs, walking toward her up Madison Avenue.

"Demons!" Ava screeched, and then she was gone, kicking and shouting in guttural French. The chain of bangles whipped around her head, cracking like a whip.

Itzy was backing away quickly now.

The drivers moved forward in leisurely horror, men on fire.

The second driver called to her.

You.

And then the third.

Are.

The fourth neared, opening his scorching mouth.

Summoned.

But there was a new horror to contend with. Something was rumbling, something familiar, a resonance that caught her deep in the gut, that shook the pavement beneath her feet.

Ava had fallen upon the drivers, her chain whipping about her head at lightning speed and finding its mark around a burning neck. The driver staggered, but came at her again, his neck a gruesome gash of flames. She was surrounded. Her chain streaked through the fire, alight. Crouching low, Ava spun, knocking the knees out from the nearest demon, and he fell like a towering inferno, his body crackling like a bonfire.

Itzy smelled it before it arrived, galloping though the wall of smoke from the burning automobiles. The horses, small tornadoes of steam gusting from flared nostrils, their eyes wide with terror. The black funeral carriage pulled up beside her, and from somewhere—from everywhere—came that unspeakable voice.

Your chariot awaits.

Fear coursed through Itzy's body at the sound of the Divah's voice in her head.

The delights of damnation. You didn't think I'd let a little thing like your father come between us, did you?

Her stomach curdled.

The horses were spooking, rearing in the complex rigging, hopelessly tangling it. A lash from a whip snaked down their backs, spreading fear like the flames behind them.

Ava was a whirlwind of red hair amidst the scorched men, her chain lost in the fury of the flames.

Get in now and I will spare your friend.

The door to the black carriage swung open and a few iron steps led up. Ashes swirled out from the inside like a filthy snow globe, settling in her hair, on her lashes. Itzy saw that Ava could not last long. Indeed, as Itzy watched, Ava suddenly stiffened, arms falling to her sides. She turned to stare at Itzy, a shudder overtaking her petite features. She opened her mouth to speak, and Itzy's stomach sank.

"You. Are. Summoned."

The rusty steps creaked as Itzy scrambled up them, plunging into the darkness of the stagecoach, breathing fast and hard. The interior of the carriage was bleak and musty, moldering cloth pulling away from the sideboards in shreds; the bench was made of crumbling leather. *Like the inside of a coffin.*

There was a small oval-shaped window to which Itzy pressed her face—it was soot-covered and barely transparent. But she saw all she needed to see. Streaks of fire arced from the blows of the demons over the fallen figure of Ava, landing cruelly on her small, still body.

"You said you would spare her!" Itzy cried.

The voice in her head laughed. Itzy bent over, wracked with sobs.

I lied.

The carriage jerked forward as the horses struggled to move in unison. Their iron shoes mauled the pavement. What was left of the town cars was still burning, but the flames had died down, leaving blackened frames upon the street, the tires having long ago burned away. The bright figures of the drivers were huddled in a seething mass, Ava somewhere in their midst. Itzy could not bring herself to look.

A lantern hung from a hook beside the door and clattered noisily against the carriage's wall as they made their way north. She could hear shouts now, in the distance, as the guards poured from Hermès.

Itzy took a shuddering breath. She hugged her blade to her chest and felt its cold comfort.

Two wars were waging, her father had said. Itzy shut her eyes, feeling the rattle of her bones as the carriage lumbered uptown. Both were orchestrated by the Divah. The eternal one, between light and dark, good and evil— the battle to open the Gates. And the other one. The war inside herself. The darkness was there, inside her, taking hold, digging in—inch by inch. She could *feel* it. For her whole life she had feared the dark. Well, here it was.

She knew what to do. Itzy would meet the Divah on her own turf: inside her own body where the Divah was slowly possessing her. She would let the Divah in.

Two wars were waging—win one, and win it all.

Alert and focused, Itzy calmly explored her mind. She reached into the dark ether, that place of all possibilities. She let the darkness engulf her. *I am coming for you*, she thought. That place, she now saw, was like an antechamber. A waiting room. Something big, something hideous, was waiting for her on the other side. She spoke to it.

I am not afraid of the dark.

96

At Seventy-Sixth Street, the carriage, with Itzy seated calmly inside, pulled up to the curb. A deep, ghostly tolling of bells marked her homecoming to the Carlyle. They boomed and resonated eerily off the city's tall buildings, along the streets and avenues alike, impossible to ignore. Those who heard them shuddered, their children clinging to their night robes, their servants dispatched to bar the doors. In the gutters of Central Park, rats scrabbled and gathered, chittering in large armies, writhing in a sea of greasy fur.

The bells called the darkness out, for they were forged in the bowels of the earth, and nothing living should be made to hear them. A molten surge of dark joy swept through Itzy at their sound. They were hers alone. They heralded her return.

At the doors to the hotel, Itzy scanned the skies, her neck swiveling.

Things were flying in the slash of night between buildings—things on wings of flesh, of scales. She opened her mouth and called a greeting, thrilled when she heard their wordless answers.

The Carlyle's intricate awning was now a row of curved meathooks, slabs of carrion glistening from where they hung. She surveyed these offerings with a deep pleasure.

This was Itzy—and this was not. The possession was taking hold. Itzy was no longer the same person who left the Carlyle. She stepped over a ribbon of ash and entered the demon-haunted ruin.

"It's good to be home." She sighed.

The lobby was lifeless and dark. The heavy smell of rotten eggs was familiar, comforting. The sleek black marble floor was littered with discarded luggage, overturned and shredded by sharpened talons and left in disturbing piles in the corners. Soil had been tracked everywhere, dirty footprints wandered haphazardly in all directions, and something large had been dragged through them, leaving behind a dark smear. Candles were now burning in the chandelier, but except for a few sputtering stragglers, most had guttered. A haze of acrid smoke drifted about the room. Wax congealed beneath it in the center of the smooth floor, opaque pools, like tentacles, oozing slowly across the marble. The Carlyle Restaurant had been transformed into a long banquet hall, with rough tables and remnants of a bloody feast. From around the corner, Itzy could see the flickering of the fireplace, the flames casting snaky shadows along the far wall.

Itzy let her fingers trail down the brass railing as she descended the few stairs to the lobby floor. A shiver of excitement rose up through her.

Behind, there was a grinding noise, something heavy and metallic slithering into place. The revolving doors creaked and spun crazily—then jammed. Bars settled over hotel windows, swinging down over doors, sparking metal against stone. The hotel was embracing her, sealing her in.

There was no sign of Wold. The concierge's counter
had vanished along with him, plastered over, and a wet
bloom of damp rose up from beneath the newly applied
paint. Beside it, a lone figure stood at the front desk. As
Itzy stepped around an overturned room service cart, she
saw that it was one of the tiresome clerks from earlier. The
clerk followed Itzy's progress mutely, her head pivoting
on her neck as Itzy inched forward.

"Welcome to the Carlyle," she said, her voice pert and
soulless. "We hope you will enjoy your stay."

"Oh, don't worry." Itzy's voice was deep, raspy. "I will."

The broken phone was ringing beside the woman, its
jangling echoing along the empty room. The clerk had
lost interest in Itzy, her head wandering slowly off to
stare into a darkened corner. Reaching for the handset,
Itzy listened. It was airy, crackling like a fire. A few words
threaded through the distance.

"You. Are—"

Itzy let the phone drop from her hand. She scanned
the wasted lobby.

The shadows were elongated, no longer pools of darkness, but possessing depth and personality. She could
read them, a translation of shadows. How trite and impossible was her fear of the dark! For the first time ever, the
shadows were her friends.

She walked toward the Carlyle's towering mirrors. The
soles of her feet felt hot. The mirrors were dark with age and
corrosion—angels' breath, she had called it so long ago.

She examined her reflection. She liked what she saw.
Her face—so young. This was good—youth was power.
Her hair was now completely platinum white, and it
framed her face. Her party dress, the many jewels, shim-

mered in the low light. The chain of her blade's sheath pressed comfortingly across her chest. She leaned in further to examine her eyes. Her eyes were dark and infinite. They glinted like a beast's.

She licked her lips.

To her right, the elevator bank displayed a sign.

OUT OF ORDER

She took the sign and threw it over her shoulder, pressing the golden button. A whirring noise followed. The door slid open, and the operator stepped out.

"Johnny."

"Evening, Miss Nash." He doffed his hat. "Where to tonight?"

Itzy walked toward him, her heels sinking into the black marble, like walking on licorice. The fireplace was roaring, the paintings to either side had taken on a sheen, melting in the heat. The still life had rotted, and the cherubim were missing entirely.

Itzy thought of that time—so long ago, it felt—when they had explored the tunnels beneath the Carlyle together. *Buried secrets. The perfect place to hide something.*

"The basement, Johnny," she said.

"Atta girl." He winked. "I knew you'd come around."

As she boarded the elevator, a loud *whoosh* followed her in, the sound of combustion. Turning, she stared across the dingy lobby.

The desk clerk was on fire.

97

Itzy felt the elevator lurch as it slid downward. The heat was thick, each breath like sucking gasoline. Johnny's skin was dewy with perspiration. Itzy drummed her fingers on the handrail, her nails tapping an impatient *clickity-clack.*

Johnny stole a sidelong look at Itzy.

Everything was new in her body, Itzy was finding. Great waves of excitement coursed through her veins, filling her up with a supreme sense of satisfaction. The elevator boy was talking, a slight smirk upon his lips, but his words were the buzz of insects' wings.

"I was just remembering the day I met you." Johnny smiled.

Itzy's head swiveled, finding Johnny's.

"All fresh from the country, wide-eyed and innocent. You were just a scared little girl with a camera."

"I'm not scared now."

"I could tell you liked me. Go on, admit it."

Itzy considered Johnny, his toffee-colored skin, the dark lashes.

"You think?" she said.

A polite chime announced the end of the ride. The elevator doors slid open to a small gloomy service area with low ceilings. The staff room, with Johnny's locker, lay to one side. The kitchen, Itzy saw, was straight ahead. But it was the passage to the far side that called to her. A vast stone archway straddled old crumbling bricks. A hole had been punched through these, wide enough for several men abreast—if such men could be found to walk down such a passageway. There were flickering torches along with a pressing, urgent feeling. It spoke to her in this new language of shadow.

"Itzy, how do you like me now?"

She turned her head, but Johnny was gone. In his place stood an immense angel, with glittering opalescent wings falling from his shoulders to the floor below.

Itzy sighed, an indescribable feeling of excitement washing over her.

A flood of memories came rushing back at her: Luc's dark moods whenever Johnny's name came up, his anger at the young elevator operator as Itzy was preparing to tour Marilyn's tunnels with him.

"Evening, Miss Nash," Laurent said, a wicked smile spreading across his face. It was Johnny's voice he used now—his young, polite voice. The one that came with the slight fuzz upon his upper lip.

The angel drew himself up, a shiver passing down the feathers of his wings, the golden talons protruding in sleek ridges from their nesting places, glittering in the torchlight.

98

Laurent pinned her with his powerful arms. A flash of a golden wing, and a razor-sharp talon was now at her cheek. Itzy felt her spine scrape against the rough stone wall as she stared up at him. His eyes were metallic, quicksilver. His face was alabaster—sleek, creaseless, somehow lit from within. It was a wickedly beautiful face. Irresistible, fierce, and proud. His smell—so different than Luc's— was of stone. An abandoned castle, dark with siege and secrets, covered in fierce thorns.

"Laurent—" she heard herself say, but the thought was lost. Warmth spread across her chest where his skin touched hers, and she felt a surge of dark glee. *This is not me*, she heard a distant protest. And then that part was gone, sealed off in an airless vault deep inside her.

"Where's your boyfriend now?"

She felt his voice, thick, all-powerful, throughout her entire body. Itzy could feel the long, curved talon scraping her skin, a sharp slow dragging, the beading of blood in its wake. She held the powerful angel's gaze, unflinching.

"He's so tedious, your Luc. All those years without wings made him grow a human heart."

Itzy thought of Luc's sun-drenched eyes. And then the terrible truth buried in his look at the Shadowsill, arm in arm with the Divah. Luc had betrayed her for the Divah, she was sure of that now. He had procured Itzy as an offering to her. Nothing was as it seemed.

Over Laurent's shoulder, Marilyn's tunnels were calling her. Waves of urgency surged through her body—nothing else mattered.

"Angels," Itzy said. "You're *all* so tedious."

Itzy touched Laurent, and he was shot back, thrown on a hot wind, his powerful body smashing against the far wall.

"It's about time we finish the tour, Laurent."

She entered the yawning passage. Behind her, Itzy heard the sound of Laurent's wings as they scratched like dry bristle against the walls while he scrambled to catch up. In the distance there was chanting. The floor dropped down severely, burrowing beneath the hotel, wide stairs marching them deep into the earth. When the ground finally leveled out, they were before an immense pair of brass doors, carved with twisted figures and ancient writings.

At her touch, they swung open and she stood before a marvel, a wonder of creations.

"One of the Seven Wonders of the Underworld," Laurent said.

They were in a subterranean cathedral of smooth, black marble, carved from the living rock beneath the hotel. Soaring obsidian arches were held aloft by impossibly thin spindles of polished black stone. The floor was slick and black and disappeared into darkness, and before her was a single inlaid golden letter C. Far above, the ceiling was indiscernible, the realm of dark, shifty things.

The air smelled crisp, acrid—on fire.

Laurent was whispering to her now, reverent. "You see, the Carlyle hotel was *built* for this," he said. "Tonight will see the realization of Moses Ginsberg's lofty dreams. A world of fire, and flesh, and scales—in the gilded Upper East Side. Itzy, welcome to the Cathedral of the Damned."

A knot of woodwose appeared, their fur mangy and singed, their faces slavering, eyes bright with anticipation. A wave of stench accompanied them, the smell of the grave.

"Come. It's time for the hell-raising."

Above them was the choir balcony, a gallery of sorts, where party-goers and masked Bemelmans revelers now gathered. Those she spied were sweating, their makeup running in streaks, wigs and masks askew. A few held opera glasses perched on the bridges of their noses, their polished ends like wide, unblinking eyes. A group of masked musicians was seated to her side, their withering music echoing off the walls. Demon flags and swallowtail banners were draped above them like snakes' tongues.

In the center of the chamber was a throne of black and gold.

In the throne sat a figure.

Itzy. So good of you to join us.

The Divah stood, her body wracked with a ripple of spasms.

My body. It's betraying me.

A red ring of coals encircled the Divah, flaring angrily. Approving murmurs came from the viewing audience in the balconies above her. Itzy stepped forward, toward the ribbon of embers, the marble hot and slick beneath her shoes.

Itzy's head swiveled, her glinting eyes taking in the full specter of the underground cathedral, its bleak statuary, the choir balcony. Finally, they alighted again on its queen.

The Divah's teeth were loose, and her face bloomed with rotting, weeping sores. She swung a stringy arm, securing Aunt Maude's fox stole around her neck. Her delicate boot seemed to be collecting some sort of fluid, which sloshed as she paced the confines of the circle of embers.

"Wow. You've really let yourself go."

The coals flared into angry flames, and Itzy saw insects crawling in the Divah's elaborate wig.

"Botulism." The Divah spoke aloud. "In small doses Botox can be relied upon to stave off age, the ruins of time. But taken more liberally, it only hastens putrification. The *Clostridium botulinum* bacterium is toxic to the human form. Yet—what wonders it is capable of! So intriguing. So—delicious."

The Divah snapped her finger and an entire fingernail went flying, arcing off into the shadow. "But no matter. For I am about to shed this mantle. Great things are in store for us together, Itzy. The realization of Hell on earth. Such a shame you'll miss it."

With a clap of her pincer-hands, the music ceased. A lone violin exhaled its last harrowing note, which echoed throughout the chamber. The silence was filled with whispers and sighs, and the noises of things skittering in the corners.

And then came the bells.

They were so close, they rung Itzy's bones. They rung like bells that had been wronged, of bells buried alive. Sand and mortar sifted down on the cathedral until the very stone walls of the vast chamber were shaking.

Itzy counted the bells as they reverberated within her.

Midnight had arrived.

99

There was some new commotion off to the side. Laurent was bringing someone forward. As the pair came into the light of the torches, Itzy recognized Pippa. She was dressed in white, her bare shoulders dappled in the flickering firelight. She was tottering on her bare feet, swaying to music only she could hear.

Pippa's mystery angel.

Suddenly, Pippa's eyes brightened. "Mother?" she said, looking off into the dark.

Itzy looked around for Mrs. Brill, and at first saw nothing.

Then, from the darkened halls of the vast chamber, they came. The dead stepped forward from the shadows. Some were newly dead; they bore an expression of confusion, and shambled forward on stiffened legs wearing their funeral finery. And there were those whose eternal sleep had been interrupted much later—shreds of their burial shrouds clinging to them. Stacked bones, skeletons yellowed and gnawed on by mice, clattered forward to their queen.

They love the Carlyle so much they never left.

Itzy recognized the elevator operator, his head twisted at an awful angle, his brownish teeth still carrying the remnants of his last meal. A doorman. A maid. These were the Carlyle's dead, dressed in the uniform of the hotel, splattered with grave soil, worm-eaten and defiled. Dead chauffeurs, telephone operators, and uniformed bellboys from the ages. Waiters shambled with their trays of spoiled food, titans of industry beside their skeletal wives. The happy couple Itzy had seen in the restaurant. Former guests, their corrupt clothing rotting from their forms, their fine timepieces and jewels dulled with dust. Kings and queens, and—

Mrs. Brill.

What was left of Mrs. Brill, Itzy saw, stood on her bird-like legs, her face missing.

They ate her face right off, Itzy thought wildly. *The Botox. They can't resist it.*

"Mother!" Pippa waved happily, her voice a breathless sing-song.

Beside Mrs. Brill, a shriveled figure stepped forward. The figure's jaw fell open and something wordless emerged, a wave of comprehension hitting Itzy in the gut. It was Aunt Maude.

A jagged crack appeared in the black marble floor between Itzy's legs. It zigzagged along the polished surface, splintering the black rock, a red glow oozing from the void, stopping only at the cathedral's center, the golden C. The stench of sulfur, thick and pungent, filled the air, as a sickly yellow smoke poured from the gap. Huge slabs of marble heaved and groaned as something vast, something evil, began to rise.

The Gothic archway shot up savagely through the floor like an enormous, jagged fang, sending broken rock and burning stones scattershot across the room. A roiling cloud of stone dust and ash filled the air, raining down on the Shadowsill guests. The heat from Hell blazed upon them all, like hot breath from fetid bellows. The few wood-wose that dared approach burst into flame, their shrieks echoing through the long halls.

A deathly quiet followed.

Itzy watched the Gates; their iron-studded portals seemed to breathe. They appeared alive, striated with scar tissue and shiny from old wounds. *Gates of sinew*, Itzy saw. *Gates of gristle. Gates of bones.*

The Divah's fleshless joints ground bone-against-bone as she prowled the edge of her burning circle of embers, her breath ragged and quick. Her arms were black, shiny, skin falling from them in tatters. She raised them, recit-ing an ancient incantation.

Beside Laurent, Pippa's face had taken on a look of rapture. All around them, the dead pressed forward. Something was stirring in the void beyond the Gates, something wasted and damned.

Mops trundled over, sniffing at a few foul, protruding spikes that dotted the Gates of Hell. He approached the foul doors, bristling with rusted iron nails, and stopped, circling. He lifted his leg. A hissing stream of steam rose from the heaving archway and up into the shadows of the ceiling.

100

Light burned her retinas. An arc of blue shot past, leaving a ghost-trail for Itzy's eyes. Another followed from somewhere above on the balcony. The bolt clattered to the floor beside a woodwose, who turned to club it, grunting. Another arrow shot past, this one finding its mark deep within the creature's greasy hide, inflating the hairy woodman like a bloated wineskin until it burst in a drifting cloud of spores and earwigs.

The room erupted in streaks of icy blue. Itzy crouched down. From the ceiling, a dark shadow was upon her, its wings outstretched—a wide curtain of darkness. She ducked, throwing her arms over her head, her blade dangling uselessly from its chain. The world had gone black, and she was gathered up, as if caught in a net. A sharp snarl escaped her lips.

Soft breath filled her ear, the familiar smell of *him*, mixing with something deeper, something new and different—a startling rustling sound, like dry leaves. Or feathers.

"It's not a party until someone calls the cavalry," the angel whispered.

"Luc?" Itzy asked, and somehow her heart spilled out upon the floor.

She stood back, and the angel drew up his wings beside her. He was bigger, a force even beside the Gates. His wings were thick, dark, ravishing things, a blue-black and the largest Itzy had ever seen. They stretched from his broad back into a wide and sturdy arc. The darkest angel of all.

"Nice wings," she said. "Now I see what all the fuss was about."

"Itzy, it's midnight." He looked into her eyes and a deep crease appeared upon his brow. A ripple of alarm swept down his feathers. "Your eyes—"

"Isn't this what you wanted all along—to be with *her*?" Itzy accused.

"No! Itzy—what have you done?"

"You brought her here, Luc. *You* brought her here to *be* with her! And then you brought me as an offering. Demon bait."

"There were letters, yes, invitations. But not from me."

"Who then?"

"Laurent. It was all Laurent, Itzy. Maurice ordered him. To prevent a war." His voice turned soft, his magnificent black wings ruffling. "For my wings."

"You can thank me later."

The room had erupted in battle as the host of angels swept down from above the balcony and the statuary, shedding their disguises. Vaporous blue arrows shot through the air, finding their marks on the grunting woodwose and party revelers.

One arrow went wide.

It sped across the sleek black marble, the polished stone like black ice. It shot through the gnarled, calloused feet of wildmen, its silver tip racing between Mops's legs.

Laurent was holding Pippa by the waist. Something wasn't right about her posture, Itzy noticed. She was swaying and unsteady. Glowing a fierce blue, an arrow raced between Laurent and Pippa and pierced the sinewy Gates of Hell.

A rumbling, undulating quake, and a lone curl of heavy black smoke belched forth.

And then all Hell broke loose.

101

There were searing-hot whites. Brutal bright light held writhing, twisted forms. This overexposed world, a world of light, a population of shadow and gray. *Was this Hell?* Itzy wondered. But when the answer came, it was little comfort.

This wasn't Hell. This was the Carlyle hotel.

The Divah's roar ripped through the confusion.

Where are you, you little savage?

Itzy was on her belly, and some part of Itzy's mind knew to keep crawling. The battle raged around her while her insides were at war. She clawed her way forward, but with each hard-won inch, she felt a sickening tug deep inside. She needed to reach the crumbling hot stone of the stairs of the exit, to leave oblivion to the damned.

"Going so soon?" Before her, magnificent in ivory and gold, was Laurent. "We were only just getting to know each other."

Itzy staggered to her feet, steadying herself. Possession rolled over her like waves of nausea.

"Laurent." The angel moved so quickly she barely had time to blink. "Thanks so much for the tour. Too bad I've got to cut it short." Itzy threw open her arms, the guillotine blade flashing.

Suddenly, the air crackled, electrified.

Laurent had retreated just above her, to the overhang of the balcony, where he hung bat-like upside down from his legs.

"Oo. It has a bite. I'm beginning to see what Luc liked about you."

Itzy stepped back, searching for any way up.

"You know something? I liked you better as Johnny."

Again the air crackled, this time more heavily, and Itzy was left with the bitter taste of ozone in her mouth. Laurent was gone from his ledge. Looking desperately around, she leveled the blade, slicing in a wide horizontal circle. She came up empty.

"After I kill your boyfriend, I will teach you some manners."

Itzy dropped, rolling along the ash-covered floor, just in time. A wide flash of white swooped down where she was standing, and uncoiling, it became Laurent—his face white with fury. His statuesque arm brandished a sword, dull blue flames burning from the blade.

He spun around, leveling the blazing sword at her. Itzy scrambled to her feet, but her heel caught in the hem of her dress, and she fell sprawling to the floor.

The world erupted in sparks, and they rained down on Itzy. The tang of electricity stiffened the air, and shock-waves washed over her.

Luc stood before her, dwarfing Laurent, holding an immense blue-black staff. A noise—a *shriek* unlike any other—perforated her eardrums, slamming her head back onto the ground. The cathedral spun. The two angels fell upon each other, talons streaking in the low light. A vortex of blue-black and creamy gold reeled first before her, then above her, vanishing in a cloud of vapor only to appear on her other side.

Luc and Laurent were locked in battle midair. A large smoking hole had opened up where Luc's staff had sent a smoldering ball of blue flames, and Itzy watched as a woodwose teetered on the edge. Luc had Laurent cornered against a pillar, and Itzy saw her chance.

She slashed at Laurent—but there was only empty air, a few sheered feathers floating lazily in the wake. The feathers were caught in an updraft, bobbing—taunting her—in the empty space where Laurent had just stood. She grabbed them.

Again, the angel's unearthly shriek filled her ears but Itzy turned away. Behind her, in the center of the Cathedral of the Damned, were the Gates. The sinew and slick tissue of the closed doors heaved—as if breathing. Pippa was dwarfed before them, swaying slightly on bare feet. Above her, Gaston and Maurice were a whirlwind of flashing wings and flying arrows. Itzy could just make out a little shadow, a skulking worm-of-a-thing, pulling on the hem of Pippa's white dress. It was Mops. He was pulling Pippa closer to the doors. Itzy watched as Pippa reached out a langid hand and pulled on a twisted, bony handle, and to Itzy's horror, the door began to open.

Itzy crawled across the floor slick with ashes.

A wave of flames rushed past Itzy, searing her eyebrows. Sulfur and burning hair stung her nostrils. The ceiling was a plane of fire, and the walls were burning, controlled, as if made of flame. She heard the tinkling of breaking glass, the polished stone cracking in the heat. Blindly, she clawed her way forward, through coals and fire. Within her ring of embers, the Divah was bent, the borrowed body of the governess weak and failing as the Divah pushed her way inside Itzy's skull.

Fire transforms everything, Luc had once said.

My wise, wise Luc, Itzy smiled wickedly.

My *Luc,* said the Divah inside her head.

Itzy stood, throwing her arms open.

The fire—it was so close. *Just like in Brittany.* Her mother left her in the dark, by the ash, by the embers. She had wanted to see, she remembered. Just a peek. The flames were calling her then. She could answer now.

At last—at last. It was time to run in the fire.

The Gates to Hell stood open and she teetered on the threshold. There was no sign of Pippa. Behind her, there was the crisp crinkling sound of burning feathers. She hoped it was Laurent, but soon that somehow seemed distant, unimportant. Someone else's war.

It was just her and the Gates.

A burning curiosity filled her and she sunk to her knees, her blade clattering on the stone.

She slithered forward on her belly.

She felt the demon inside her, and she wanted her dark world.

This is mine, she thought. *I'm your Divah now.*

Beyond the Gates, stretching out for all eternity, was a never-ending black sea, a slick of boiling oil, smelted iron, bubbling tar. It lapped the shores of the stone floor of the cathedral. A coagulated mass of the darkest, most vicious stew.

Her stomach lurched, dizzy with vertigo, at the infinite size of it all. She heard a low, desperate call over the ocean,

at first one reedy voice, but then a chorus, a cascade—
finally a tidal wave of voices that swept up off the black
sea and blew upon her with the force of a gale—calling for
her. Calling her name.

Hell is a cauldron of souls. A stew of the damned.

The hot wind blew her white hair crazily about her
face. She reached out a trembling finger. The surface
looked sticky, treacly. She felt a great longing, an irresistible urge. Itzy touched it.

The ensuing shock was wordless. No—it was as
though every dark and dreary word she'd ever known
were spoken at once, a sea of sound.

Hopelessness—
    Agony—
        Broken dreams—
            Regret—
                Betrayal—

Her mind whirled forward at lightning speed, and she
saw the world overrun. The Carlyle, the Upper East Side,
New York City—all of humanity fell before her. She saw
her father's university, a ruined wasteland, Paris crumbling. Ruin rained upon the green earth, until there was
nothing but a scorched inferno. Itzy walked her kingdom
of ash and ember, finally turning to the sky. The clouds
heaved with thunder. There was nothing left but to conquer them, too.

The souls of the damned called to her. They wanted
her. They *thrilled* her.

And then, an inexplicable vision of white. Searing,
drifting, pure light arranged itself before her in the shape

of Marilyn Monroe. A ghosty carnival behind her, a vacant Ferris wheel spinning soundlessly. Marilyn's head was tipped back and she was laughing a throaty laugh, talking to someone, some shadow. A world of black-and-white film. She held in her hand a twinkling claw hammer and turned to Itzy and winked.

"*Here's to all those stars that burned so hot, died so young,*" Marilyn said to Itzy, in her breathless way.

And then, as sometimes happens in dreams, Itzy felt Marilyn's touch, light and cool on her hand. And what was left behind was Itzy's blade, her fingers threaded through the holes, the chain slung around her chest.

In dreams begin responsibilities, Marilyn smiled.

Itzy was staring at the endless span of the molten damned.

No, Itzy thought. *No. Hell is not my domain.*

Itzy yanked her hand with all her might, and it came away with a sickly gluey thread.

She skittered away from the horrendous pit on all fours.

Already the surface of the sea was studded with debris, spent arrows, embers bobbing on the sticky waves. A careless woodwose tumbled in, his hair caught on the gluey surface, like flypaper. More followed, drawn by the shrieks of their comrade, and a few of the dead shambled in and began to slowly sink.

Itzy raced through a high vaulted aisle beneath the choir. Near a crypt, she stopped. Behind it was a scratching, pitiful sound. It was worrying something in the shadows—gnawing on a bone.

"Mops!" Itzy hissed. "Begone!"

The animal had hold of something between his teeth and was growling, pulling at it, shaking his head trying to tear it free.

That's no bone, Itzy saw.

Itzy peered around the corner of the crypt. "Ava?" Itzy's voice was scorched.

Ava turned then, and Itzy recoiled at her gruesome features. "Hello, Itzy," she said, her voice like a rusty old can.

Itzy sunk to her knees.

I am finally going crazy, Itzy decided. *This is more than I can bear.*

Itzy felt the world grow dim. A hand closed around her elbow and Itzy turned, disoriented, her blade-arm hanging limply by her side.

"Miss Nash?"

She blinked.

I am crazy, she confirmed. A wild laughter bubbled up from her belly.

Wold stood before her, bowing slightly, clean and crisp in his morning jacket, as the battle raged behind him. A slight bluish aura surrounded him. "If I may be of some assistance, Miss Nash?"

Itzy glanced madly at Ava and Mops, and Wold followed her gaze. The concierge slipped something from his vest pocket—a glittering dagger, encrusted with rubies, the handle carved from bone. With an expert flip of the wrist, Wold sent the weapon flying and it lodged in the haunches of the small hound. A thunderous noise followed, and Mops lifted his head in astonishment. Turning in circles, he snapped with fury at the dagger, which was now glowing blue, roaring at his backside.

And then, quite simply, he was gone. A small pile of brown spores rose like an anthill where he had been standing.

"If you would follow me, Miss Nash. I have it on good authority that things are about to heat up in here. The scholars are storming the lobby as we speak."

A fireball exploded somewhere nearby, but the concierge did not flinch.

"On whose authority?"

"My master's."

"Your—who is your master?"

"Mr. Beauvais, Miss Nash. I am his manservant. If you would be so kind—" He gestured with his manicured hand, his left one that was inked with a black tattoo. All argument left Itzy and she followed the concierge up the winding stairs of the tunnel, letting the pleasant tones of his occasional "Watch your step," and "Yes, very good of you to keep up such a fine pace," and, finally, "Mind your blade, Miss Nash. I've already shaved this morning," wash over her like earthly delights.

102

They arrived in the hotel's industrial laundry room, beside a set of plain metal doors.

"The cargo elevator?" Itzy asked as the doors folded open.

"Indeed. You'll recall that Miss Monroe would on occasion find them useful, when discretion was called for."

They stepped inside, and the doors clanged shut. The interior was wide and unadorned. Wold pressed the button for the Tower Suite and the elevator shot up.

"The Tower Suite?" Itzy asked.

"Indeed. Although Mr. Beauvais was quite recently"—Wold cleared his throat delicately—"*displaced.*"

"Displaced? What does that mean?"

"He vacated his quarters. For someone more senior."

Itzy contemplated this until another thought occurred to her.

"Wold, you never mailed the letter to my father."

"Ah, well. Your father never got off the plane in Paris."

The elevator doors opened upon a small butler's pantry, lined with cabinets and shelves and a small service sink. Wold held the doors open for her while flicking a lever, locking the elevator in place. Through a set of swinging doors, Itzy saw she was in Luc's airy suite, the blues and whites and golds of Bemelmans's heavenly cloudscape upon the ceiling.

Itzy felt her before she saw her.

"How's your father?" a voice said.

Somewhere, some part of Itzy at her deepest, knew the voice.

Itzy turned.

Anaïs was beside a long, ornate bar. In her hand, she held a small, delicate drink with something bright and red floating inside it. Anaïs had delicate wings of the lightest blue; they fluttered in the breeze with plumes of down. Itzy scrutinized the room more carefully. One corner held a pile of luxurious luggage, carelessly stacked and obviously rifled through.

"Mom?" Itzy asked, inanely.

Anaïs raised her glass. "In the flesh. Well—sort of. If I were made of flesh, that is."

"*You* displaced Luc?" Itzy asked.

"I do so love the Carlyle. Don't you?" When Itzy didn't answer, Anaïs continued in a different tone. "Oh, don't worry. He's a big boy. He can take care of himself. Actually, come to think of it"—she twitched her mouth in annoyance—"maybe he can't."

Anaïs peered at Itzy and sighed.

"Oh, don't be like that. I'm not here for long. Just long enough to clean up the mess you made. And I understand they've found him quite a suitable set of rooms on one of the lower floors. Is that not so, Wold?"

Wold stepped forward, nodding curtly. "Quite satisfactory, madame. If I understand my master correctly, he considers it a privilege to vacate the Tower Suite for you and yours, as he has been forced to demonstrate so many times in the past."

"See?" Anaïs said to Itzy brightly. "Now. Can I get you something to drink before we begin? You look parched. It's too bad we don't have time for a little *toilette*—it would make what comes next ever much more agreeable." Anaïs fixed Itzy a small drink with a bright red cherry floating in it and glided over to her daughter. "Here. *Salut!*" She clinked glasses and tipped hers back in one gulp.

"Mom." Itzy took a small sip. It was sweet and cloying. "Where have you been?"

"Whatever do you mean? I got here as soon as I could. How funny of you, child. In one breath you chastise me for displacing your beloved Luc, and in the other for being delayed at doing so."

"Where have you been *my entire life*?" Itzy clarified.

"How old are you?" Her voice softened. Anaïs reached forward, curling a stray lock of Itzy's white hair behind her ear. "Twelve? Thirteen?"

"I'm seventeen, Mom. Nearly eighteen."

"My sweet. That is but an intake of breath for someone like me. That is but the moment between dawn and the time I slip from my sheets with dreams still clinging to my nightclothes. That is—"

"I get it." Itzy threw back the rest of her drink, which somehow tasted much better the second time around. "Who are they?" Itzy nodded at a pair of angels who flanked the doors to the balcony like statues. They were tall, severe female angels, with light emanating from their haughty faces.

"Colette and Sabine."

Itzy eyed them critically.

"What are they doing here?"

Anaïs looked taken aback. "They are my *entourage*. They go wherever I go, Itzy. Oh! It's nearly time. Sweetie, are you ready?"

Anaïs walked to a large rolling cart from room service. A tray was set atop, with the biggest silver dome Itzy had ever seen. Anaïs gestured. "Go on, then. I took the liberty of ordering something. The convenience of room service cannot be overstated."

After a quick glare at Sabine and Colette, Itzy lifted the lid. Inside, a folded card.

Compliments of the Carlyle

She turned the card over thoughtfully. On the reverse side, in smaller script, was another message.

Demon Bait

Itzy inspected the silver tray.
It was loaded with orderly vials glittering in the light.

103

Itzy was aware of the familiar sound of the elevator approaching—Johnny's elevator.

Johnny's gone. He never existed. Nothing is as it seems.

"Hear that, girls?" Anaïs chirped. "Lovely sound. Reminds me of the rattle of the guillotine."

Itzy was prepared, blade in hand. Her dress, once an enviable collection of organized jewels, was now torn and defiled and her face and hair were streaked with biohazard.

"If I can leave you with one important lesson, Itzy, it's the importance of looking one's best in battle."

"What do you mean, *leave you?*"

"Ah, well." Anaïs hemmed and hawed. "When I'm gone."

"You're not staying?" Itzy's voice squeaked.

"Well, Luc will be wanting his room back—"

"I mean for *me.*"

"Ah—"

Itzy thought of Ava. *I know a thing or two about angels.*

"Mom, did you ever know someone named Ava?"

"Who, darling?"

"Ava Quant. Or maybe you'd remember someone named Frankie."

"Frankie? Frankie. Seems I remember a man called Frank—something about a weekend by Lake Garda, or was it Como? He had the cutest baby blues. Oh, but that was a lifetime ago. And when I say *lifetime*, I do mean that in your terms, dear."

Itzy eyed the elevator nervously. The whirring ceased and the elevator made its usual clicks and adjustments as the doors readied to open.

"Why do you ask?"

"Ava was a friend of mine, Mother. Seems you stole her husband."

"I see you have a flair for the dramatic, Itzy." Anaïs sniffed. "You must get that from your father." Anaïs surveyed the room quickly. "I do hope I ordered enough of that stuff."

Anaïs cracked a vial and doused Itzy's hair with it.

"Ever think of getting work done?"

"Mom—I'm seventeen."

"Going on eighteen, as you yourself reminded me. I'm just saying, you're looking a bit peaked."

The remainder of the Botox was unceremoniously poured on Itzy's face, her shoulders, behind her ears. It ran in streams down her spine.

Anaïs made for the balcony. Sabine and Colette closed in behind her, longbows at the ready. "I am sorry about this, Itzy. But you know you have to fight your own demons. I'm sealing the room now, sweetheart."

"You're what?"

"Sealing the room! The Divah cannot be allowed to escape. We're all counting on you!"

"That's your plan?"

"Just cleaning up your mess, my dear. Don't take it personally. It's what I do."

And then, with an efficient chime, the elevator doors slid open.

The creature advanced into the suite in two great strides, head turning on an articulated neck. Itzy felt the nauseating yank of her insides as they were stretched forward invisibly like elastic. The Divah was more insect than human, a horrifying apparition in a dress and a huge powdered wig. She had thin shining joints where the flesh had fallen away, and her legs were punctuated with little dartlike hairs. Aunt Maude's fox pelt hung at an unnatural angle from her shoulders, its small beady eyes a matching pair to the Divah's—black, dark pits into a dreadful place.

These eyes found Itzy immediately.

It's like looking in the mirror, isn't it? the Divah said, picking her way onto the foyer, knees bent in a half crouch. Huge, leathery wings jackknifed open, the scaly skin nearly transparent and torn in places. They hung like fire-ravaged curtains. They beat a foul air Itzy's way, and she staggered backward. And then they were gone, folded up from where they came. Nearly. Itzy saw one was broken, twisted, dragging on the floor. Horribly, Itzy heard the Divah begin to hum.

The itzy bitzy spider crawled up the water spout.

Out the windows, the angels congregated. Sabine and Colette had their longbows drawn, guarding the glass doors, the outlines of which were bleeding with a bright blue light. The Divah cocked her head, sniffing.

Breakfast of champions.

The Divah squatted down beside a puddle of Botox and recommenced her humming. Itzy saw her chance. The sprint across Luc's floor took forever. Her body felt as if it were moving through molasses, like dreams of running but getting nowhere. Each step brought on more pins and needles, and as Itzy neared the Divah, her limbs were numb, her body barely responding to her commands. Somehow she leveled her blade, aiming for the Divah's unnaturally long neck. A war cry escaped her lips as she raised the blade high, bringing it down in a deadly vector.

The Divah raised a hand, her scaly back still to Itzy, and a ball of flames exploded, shooting lights off in her skull. Itzy was propelled on hot winds across the room, landing in a bone-crunching pile against the wall, shattering Luc's expensive sound system.

Anaïs's voice came from the balcony. "Oh, oh—that one looked like it hurt."

Itzy rose to her feet unsteadily, her blade-hand clattering on the room service cart as she pulled herself up. She coughed once and spat out something black and charred, wiping her mouth on her shoulder.

The Divah's voice ripped through Itzy's head, reverberating around her brain, bashing her eardrums and needling her eyeballs.

Didn't your mother teach you any manners?

The wig, its coils of silver curls, fell from the Divah's head as she turned, rearing on Itzy. Her bald head was like a winter field of wheat—dead stalks of hair in patches of flaky white skin. Two scaly horns sprouted above her hairline like the pincers of a stag beetle. She leveled her dead eyes at Itzy.

Wait—I forgot. She left you, didn't she? That mother of yours. She abandoned you in the ash bin. Her own child! Left you there to save herself. Just like she's doing now.

The Divah surveyed the room, then staggered once, loping on a trick knee. Itzy came at her again—by sheer force of will—with a series of unsteady uppercuts aimed at the demon queen's head. She heard the sound of the Divah's breathing, gurgling and hissing, and then her foot connected with the Divah's throat in a wet, sickening crunch.

Again, some gargantuan force shot her backward into the wall—and this time through the wall.

The itzy bitzy spider—

Electrical wires snaked though the gaping hole, sparking. Itzy staggered to her feet in a white marbled bathroom and made her way back through the hole in the plaster. Dusting herself off, she found she was again by the room service cart, which she began to consider more seriously.

She saw her own freakish reflection in the silver domes and the balcony beyond. Luc had arrived, his magnificent wings tensed. Gaston and Maurice were there, too—their faces sharp and serious, their weapons drawn.

"The restoration of your powers, Luc," her mother's chirpy voice continued, "are you enjoying them? I must say, it's quite a relief to us all. After we get this little matter fixed, we're ready for a month at the spa." She nodded at Sabine and Colette. "Have you stayed at the Waldorf?" Anaïs was asking. "Would you recommend it?"

"Try the Sherry-Netherland," Luc growled.

"Really? The Sherry-Netherland? I do hear it's nice this time of year."

A bubbling noise was coming from the Divah as she struggled to clear her windpipe.

I am in no hurry, poppet, the voice gurgled. *It is nearly done.*

A scorching wind picked up, dimming the light. Itzy's hair whipped about her face.

It *was* nearly done, Itzy realized. The possession was nearly complete. This slow, stalking, incidious possession had nearly run its course. She felt the last torrent of herself leaking away; she felt her heart burning and her hands icy at once.

I am not afrai—Itzy said, but the words seemed indistinct, meaningless. Jumbled together. *I am*—

Her blade was glowing blue, she noticed. But her hand seemed so far away. Was this her hand? Seeing was difficult, too, she realized. As if everything were a double exposure. That happened sometimes with her Leica. Her Leica.

She swiveled her head. Here was the dim balcony, Luc's anguished look as he pressed against the glass. But superimposed over him Itzy saw her own self—but through the eyes of the Divah. Her own eyes were dark and hollow pits. The stench of sulfur and brimstone overpowered her.

She fumbled for the last silver dome from room service with her numb fingers. Beneath it was a glistening bottle of water. Itzy seized the Evian and turned again to the window. With some difficulty, Itzy found Luc's eyes. She let herself get lost in them, the deep amber, the golden flecks. He nodded, once.

She readied the Evian.

All the air, as if by vacuum, left Itzy's lungs. Her heart thumped loudly as she tried to breathe. Something was burning, Itzy saw from the corner of her eye. She looked around desperately—off in the distance, through the glass doors, was her mother, her manicured wings catching the night breeze. She had her hand on Luc's elbow, restraining him, and a deep-blue light was seeping from her grip. Her mouth was moving in causal conversation, her lips glazed with gloss.

Her mother's angels glared at Itzy from across the room, their eyes icy and indifferent. Their longbows were glowing blue, and they were pointed at Itzy's head.

Thanks for the vote of confidence, Mom.

Itzy's stomach was churning, her temples constricted with the pounding of her pulse. The Divah's dank breath was congealing on her cheek. She leaned in, sniffing, and from her mouth came a long, telescoping tongue—more of a proboscis. It flickered, and then slowly, sickeningly, it touched her face, licking the Botox from Itzy's cheek.

I don't know what he sees in you. Such a scrawny thing, no? It's me he loves.

Itzy's body was trembling as the tongue retraced its path, leaving a slick of yellow behind.

"Go. To. *Hell*."

Itzy emptied the bottle of Evian over her own head. The searing pain was blinding. Itzy was on her knees, the agony crippling. Her skin was on fire, the nerve endings refusing to burn away. There was nothing but the world of pain—that, and the howling. At first she thought it was her own, but her voice had died in her throat. The howling, shrieking, withering screams were from the Divah.

Itzy felt a loud *whomp* as though her face had been slapped.

Fiery creatures were everywhere, like a switch had flipped on a gas main. They danced as the flames licked at them, a brutal vision of combustion, figures wrapped in shrouds of flame. Another *whomp*, and Itzy's body was propelled into the air with such force that when she hit the window, she stuck there, her body pressed to the glass. A storm was brewing; the clouds were dark and injured. A single flash of lightning curdled the sky, and Itzy saw

Luc unfold his magnificent wings. His majestic outline was all crisp edges, the arch of his tensed wings looming above him, his face in shadow. His hand shot out to touch the glass, and they faced each other now, so close, separated by the translucent window.

A deep weariness overtook her now, as she pressed against the glass. Her small hand was there against Luc's—so close, but she could not feel it. She felt only numbness and exhaustion—and something new: defeat. Luc was saying something; the words scattered and rolled away, lost through the glass.

I was the last queen of France, Itzy. You are nothing but a little girl.

Glasses were flying, shattering against walls, and one of Anaïs's little red cherries slid down Itzy's cheek. Anaïs's extensive luggage, stacked in the corner, flew open, and its contents disgorged in a large belch. Things flew by—blouses, ribbons and jewels, lacy underthings. The room was awash in color and silk. A scarf snagged on Nicolas, fluttering like a dying bird.

Nicolas, she thought wildly. *I will end up just like him. A candle jutting from my skull.*

With my mouth, she will call forth the damned, and visit ruin upon all that is good on this green earth until there is nothing but a scorched wasteland. With my feet, she will walk her kingdom of ash and ember, and turn finally to the sky. The clouds will heave with thunder. And then, when there is nothing left, she—no, I—will conquer them, too.

Itzy stared into Luc's amber eyes through the thick glass and tried to stand, but her knees buckled. She felt herself slipping away, dark waves lapping at her shore.

Luc, she thought. Or had she spoken it? It hardly mattered. Nothing mattered. *I'm sorry I doubted you.*

She looked at him again with all her will, locking eyes with him.

The amber of his eyes held her, and she felt as if she were falling down a deep well. Only his eyes were no longer amber. And she wasn't falling—rather, she was floating, buoyant. And then, as his eyes glowed a fierce, heavenly blue, she felt as if her body were singing, as if every nerve was alive with sublime energy, rousing her soul. Waves of ecstasy rolled through her body, she felt shivery and flushed, and what she realized next thrilled her more. Luc was there, with her, *inside* of her body.

The demonic possessions always want closure. The angelic ones never want it to end.

Welcome air filled Itzy's lungs.

In her trembling hand, Itzy saw her blade flash—a second jagged line of lightning reflected in it. The Divah was staggering, fumbling blindly, as Itzy's arm swung the guillotine blade.

I am unsssssstoppab—

104

Luc was squeezing her hand.

"You did it." He breathed. Luc's arms were around her, pulling her away. Anaïs was picking her way over daintily, kicking away broken glass, stomping on earwigs. Maurice was beside the Divah's severed head. Old and dead languages bubbled from its lips.

"*Adieu.*" Maurice spat.

Itzy turned to Luc. "Did I?" she asked.

"Itzy . . ."

"Didn't you—you know? *Help* me."

"What do you think?"

Itzy looked at Luc, his eyes, their tawny amber pools like molten gold. Her stomach lurched as she felt him looking back at her—deep within her, a place that Itzy didn't know could be *seen* with eyes, a place that might not even be called Itzy, but rather the part of her that came into this world before names. Her soul. She did not blink.

Finally, she tore her eyes away.

"What do I think?" she asked. She looked at her party dress, splattered with black oily blood. "I think I need a bath."

She buried her head in his warm chest.

"Such a tiny thing," he whispered, his voice soft and sweet in her ear. "Against such great forces."

From the corner of her eye, she saw something shadowy skittering across the floor from the Divah's decaying body. It moved with a horrible *click-clack* as it darted across the room, heading for the corner. It was black and shadowy, and slithering beneath Aunt Maude's fox fur pelt.

Itzy stiffened, watching it.

It slinked toward Anaïs's leather trunks and various sturdy and enduring suitcases, where, quite quickly, it disappeared into an open valise.

"I do believe there is a demon in my mother's bag," Itzy smiled.

"Shh. It's our little secret," he said.

105

Itzy stepped out of the shower into the steaming bathroom. Marble counters and a pair of matching sinks emerged from the white fog. Grabbing a plush terry robe, she groaned as she wrapped herself in its folds. A voice spoke to her from within the steam.

"You'll be sore for a while."

It was Pippa, standing in the large bathroom with an armload of clothing. She was still in her white dress, somehow impossibly pristine. Gaston had helped her escape the Cathedral of the Damned, flying her to safety when the scholars stormed in.

"No kidding."

"I can call down to Zitomer's for something. Take the edge off."

Itzy flashed her a grim look.

"How about some breakfast then?"

Itzy leaned forward and rubbed a small circle free of moisture on the mirror, but it clouded over again just as quickly.

"Just as well," Pippa said. "You're quite a sight."

"Is she gone?"

"If you mean your mother, yes."

"Sabine, Colette?"

"Gone. Gone. You know her plan B was to burn down the Carlyle if you didn't succeed?"

Itzy sighed and began the painful process of dressing.
"She said to tell you something."

"Of course she did."

"She said, and I quote, 'Don't take it all so personally.
You're not a person.'"

Itzy sighed. "Anything else?"

"And if you want her, she's at the Plaza."

Itzy tried the mirror again, swiping it with a thick towel
this time. She was rewarded with her gauzy reflection. Her
white hair remained, but there was a fistful of raw scalp
where the Divah had torn some free. Her eyebrows were
burned clean away. A large, raised welt was purpling on one
cheekbone and a deep scrape from Laurent was on the other.
And her eyes—Itzy leaned in for a better look. They were
startlingly bloodshot and painfully sensitive to the light.

"Oh, I forgot." Pippa handed Itzy a pair of Hermès
sunglasses. "There you go."

Itzy finished dressing and ran a quick hand through
her wet hair.

"Ready?" Pippa asked.

The suite was quiet as the pair emerged. Itzy saw
Maurice and smiled. Gaston and a few of the younger
angels were gathered in a small knot and they eyed her
curiously. Order was slowly returning to the Tower Suite:
Luc's possessions were being rolled in on polished luggage
carts, and his presence restored to his rooms. Wold was
beginning the laborious process of inspecting the luggage
for demons. A long table had been erected, and on it were
vases of spectacular flowers, boxes of bonbons, pyramids of
marzipan fruit, and other offerings for Itzy. In the center,
a brand new camera, a spectacular one of Swedish design.
A Hasselblad.

"Isn't it divine?" Pippa whispered.

Dawn was breathing its own colors into the room through the open windows. The room quieted as everyone turned to her, and a reverent silence descended.

Wold cleared his throat finally. "Miss Nash," he said.

"Wold," Itzy smiled. She hadn't thanked him properly and was about to do so when an angel stepped forward by the concierge's side.

"Allow me to introduce you to Ms. Bellerose," Wold gestured. "She will be taking over duties for the late Dr. Jenkins. She is the new hotel doctor."

Itzy examined the angel, who wore a simple black dress, her wings flecked with gold. In her hand was a silver penlight. "I see things are looking up around here." Itzy smiled.

"May I?" the doctor asked, gesturing at the light.

Itzy nodded, removing her sunglasses.

The penlight swept across Itzy's tired face, finding her eyes. The doctor leaned in, eagerly examining her. The angel clicked the light off and carefully put her hands on Itzy's shoulders. "If you don't mind," she said, indicating Itzy should turn around.

Itzy pivoted on her heel.

There, upon her shoulders, were an unmistakable set of wings. They sprouted from Itzy's shoulder blades, the feathers in gold and rich, deep reds. Here and there, interlaced with the plumes, were scales the color of dark, burned paprika.

"Where are your manners?" Pippa scolded the stunned room. "Haven't you ever seen a fledgling before?"

Wold—bless his heart—clicked his heels together and performed a slight bow. "Miss Nash. Since all seems to be in order here, allow me to tell you that your aunt's rooms are being readied for you as we speak. They are to be yours now." He turned to the doctor. "If you don't mind, Itzy has a very impatient visitor."

Itzy turned to the balcony where a dark figure stood waiting. Her heart quickened.

"Oh, and Miss Nash?" Wold called. "Welcome to the Carlyle."

Luc stepped forward, opening the door, as the early morning breeze stirred his wings. She joined him on the balcony.

Luc held her close. "It's over."

Itzy suddenly felt incredibly weary. "I don't think I care for scholars. Or demons. For the Carlyle. For anything."

He stared deep into her eyes. The morning sunlight was burning them, but she held his gaze. He was looking at her intently, searching her face.

"Has anyone ever told you how beautiful your eyes are?"

Itzy felt herself flush.

"For angels, eternal beings, not much is new. That's why Laurent loves war. Eternity is boring. You, Itzy, are something new. I think I shall begin painting again," Luc announced. "Beginning with you."

"Luc—"

"The Divah was too entrenched," he said softly, examining her wings. "A part remains. The angel blood will keep it in check."

"So I am both angel and demon?" Itzy asked.

"And *human*," he said. "You are the new, new thing. Dark. Light. All in one."

She smiled.

They were quiet, Itzy feeling his sturdiness beside her.

"The scholars stormed the basement, with your father's help. They opened up the pipeworks and are drowning the Gates as we speak."

"What will they do?" she asked eventually.

He looked out over the city.

"They will fight, I suppose. But it doesn't matter. They will fight nonetheless. It is what *you* do that matters. Part demon, part angel. You straddle both worlds. I suppose you can do anything you want."

"Laurent? Did he—" Itzy asked.

Luc's face turned cold with fury. "Laurent got away. Nursing his wounds."

"Well, he can't get far." She reached into the pocket of her jeans, pulling out something small and glittering. Luc stared at her outstretched hands. They fluttered within her caged fingers like moths, a few angel feathers, white as ivory, dusted in gold. She cupped her hands, smiling.

"Laurent's feathers." On his face, a flash of sorrow and loss. "A girl can get into a lot of trouble with feathers like that."

"Do you trust me, Luc?" she whispered.

He nodded. "Come. I have a promise to keep."

"The others—they're waiting inside."

"Let them wait."

He rose up, hovering over the smoldering hotel, reaching his hand down to her from above. The air from his great raven wings fanned her white hair. Perched atop the Carlyle's jade roof were hundreds—maybe thousands—of angels, all watching her silently. The towering scarlet guillotine rose from Ava's balcony, its blade winking in the morning sun, casting a beam of light down upon Madison Avenue.

Itzy stepped upon the balcony wall, as she had seen so many angels do before. She took his hand and stepped into thin air.

They soared above the city streets, Itzy and Luc, the morning clouds kissed with yellows and ochres, purples and dusky red. There were new colors, hidden colors. A constellation was on the horizon—she saw its faint outline as it sank into the western sky. It reminded her of Grand Central, the twinkling ceiling, of first meeting Luc.

Luc rose still higher, and Itzy saw the sun readying itself implacably upon the eastern horizon. She kicked off her shoes to rid herself of the torturous earth. They fell, one after the other, down to the tiny city below.

There, her father and a raucous gathering of scholars were storming the hotel, their banners waving above them as they piled into the lobby and over the ring of ash. Some daring ones climbed the golden awning, scaling the art deco walls. They were calling for the Queen of the Damned, of course; they were bloodthirsty and jubilant.

Itzy knew just how they felt.

Acknowledgments

The author is indebted to the following people, for inspiration (spanning history, languages, and two continents), encouragement, and guidance:

Virginie Elston; Ann Malavet; Jana Potashnik; Karmen Ross; Kate Klimo; Emma Parry; Grant Manheim; William Charnock, Daniel Flebut, and the Dejoux House; Gregory Ortiz; David Hershkovitz; my wonderful and creative students at SUNY New Paltz; Moshe Seigel; Mark Shaw; Heather Jones; Josh Molay; Maggie Brimijoin; Mike, Helen, and Sophie Nist; Nicola Tyson; Lisa Jack; Steve Warner; Steph Whitehouse; Nancy Bowles; Stephen Ellcock; Adrienne Szpyrka, Julie Matysik, Jay Cassell, and the entire Sky Pony team; Deidra Altman; Noelle Damon; Sol Melamed; Rhett Weires; Cynthia Lisort; Robin Jacobowitz; Marissa Rothkopf Bates; Judy Elliot; Dr. Brian Campolattaro; Dr. Michael Sinkin; Wendy Monk; Harvey Marshak; Michael Reynolds; Lisa Metz and Studio Stu; Veronika Jachimek; Nan Satter and her creative-writing group where *Divah* was first workshopped; Katy Bray; David Appelbaum; Joshua Appelbaum; and my two beautiful children, Harper and Henry.

And with much love to Kevin Zraly.

About the Author

Like every child, Susannah Appelbaum realized at an early age that the world contains both good and evil—and she wanted nothing more than to write about it. By day, she does so. The night is reserved for keeping the world safe from shadows and demons. She has lived both in Paris and at the Carlyle hotel, where the service is exquisite and the food is never burnt.

Susannah resides in New York's Hudson Valley and is the critically acclaimed author of the Poisons of Caux series.